PENGUIN BOOKS

HEAVEN AND HELL

Frederic Raphael was born in 1931. He was educated at Charterhouse and St John's College, Cambridge. His first novel, *Obbligato* was published in 1956 and this was followed by *The Earlsdon Way* (1958), *The Limits of Love* (1960), *A Wild Surmise* (1961), *The Graduate Wife* (1962), *The Trouble With England* (1962), *Lindmann* (1963), *Orchestra and Beginners* (1967), *Like Men Betrayed* (1970), *Who Were You With Last Night?* (1971), *April, June and November* (1972), *Richard's Things* (1973), *California Time* (1975), *The Glittering Prizes* (Penguin, 1976), *Sleeps Six* (1979), *Oxbridge Blues* (1980) and *Think of England* (1986).

He has also written two biographies, *Somerset Maugham and his World* (1976) and *Byron* (1982), translations (with Kenneth McLeish) of *The Poems of Catullus* (1976) and of *The Oresteia* (1978, televised as *The Serpent's Son*), and plays for radio and television. His screenplays include *Nothing But the Best* (1964), *Darling* (1965), *Far from the Madding Crowd* (1967), *Two for the Road* (1968), *Daisy Miller* (1974), *Rogue Male* (1976), *The Best of Friends* (1979), *Richard's Things* (1981) and *Oxbridge Blues* (1984). For his highly acclaimed sequence of television plays, *The Glittering Prizes* (1976), Frederic Raphael won the Royal Television Society's Writer of the Year Award. He is married and has three children.

Frederic Raphael

HEAVEN AND EARTH

PENGUIN BOOKS

PENGUIN BOOKS

Published by the Penguin Group
27 Wrights Lane, London W8 5TZ, England
Viking Penguin Inc., 40 West 23rd Street, New York, New York 10010, USA
Penguin Books Australia Ltd, Ringwood, Victoria, Australia
Penguin Books Canada Ltd, 2801 John Street, Markham, Ontario, Canada L3R 1B4
Penguin Books (NZ) Ltd, 182–190 Wairau Road, Auckland 10, New Zealand

Penguin Books Ltd, Registered Offices: Harmondsworth, Middlesex, England

First published by Jonathan Cape 1985
Published in Penguin Books 1987
3 5 7 9 10 8 6 4

Made and printed in Great Britain by
Richard Clay Ltd, Bungay, Suffolk
Typeset in Trump Mediaeval

FOR BEETLE

'Au bout de longues années ce ne sont que les anciens ennemis qui s'embrassent.' – Michel Pic

'There is no contrast here between the perfection of *heaven* and the imperfection of *earth*, between eternity and time, between good and evil. *Heaven* and *earth* belong inseparably together . . .' – G.B. Caird, commentary on *Paul's Letters from Prison*

1

'WE SHALL have to move,' Gideon said.

'We'll talk about it later,' Pamela said, 'shall we?'

'It's all right,' Tom said. 'Don't worry about it.'

'But I do worry about it, old son, and it's very far from all right. That's really a very nasty eye you've got there this time, isn't it, nurse?'

'Don't, Gideon. He's been attacked enough for one day.' Pamela nagged sticking-plaster from the narrow reel. Anchoring the loose end to the Formica, she frowned for the kitchen scissors. 'Won't be long now, love.'

'Who's attacking anyone?' Gideon offered her the handle of the scissors, the point pinched in his fingers. 'Not that I wouldn't like to, if only someone smaller than I am would oblige by coming into my sights. Woof!' He began to dry a dry saucepan from the plastic rack. There was a recipe for *ratatouille* on the tea-cloth. 'I'll go up and see Monahan as soon as he gets home from work, or whatever it is that he gets home from.'

'I tried to use my karate,' Tom said, 'but it was all four of them. And Sean Simmonds.'

'No one's blaming you,' Pamela whispered.

'Oh, do I sound as if I am?' Gideon said. 'A fine new friend he's turned out to be, I must say.'

'Can I go now?' the boy said.

'I want you resting on your bed, Tom,' Pamela said, 'for at least ten minutes now. You've had a real shock.'

'Can't I work on my W.W. II Spitfire? I'm just getting to the undercarriage mechanism.'

'Yes, why is that always the best part for some reason, I wonder?'

'Mum, we don't really have to move, do we?'

'Nothing binds us to Chaworth for ever, you know, Tom,' Gideon said. 'It's not as if generations of Shands have dwelt at 17, Beacon Terrace, the Middle-of-Nowhere LI23 4DS.'

'Chaworth used to be quite an important place,' Tom said.

'So did England, but all good things come to an end, and so do some bad ones. We must cling to that. Maybe the gods are telling us something in their own cryptic fashion, and we ought to heed their signals. And now you'd better go and have that rest. On your undercarriage, go on.'

Repaired, the boy fitted his glasses back over his freckles. He looked at his parents as if they were a simple sum that did not quite add up: there was a puzzle there, and reason to dawdle over it. He gave a sort of yawn that stretched only one side of his mouth and winked an eye. 'Mum, what's for supper?'

'I thought fish fingers,' Pamela said, 'and I'll put some sprouts through the what's-it, the way you liked them that time, what do you say?'

'Scrumpsherama! Any sauté potatoes at all?'

'You're a terrific chap, Tom,' Gideon said. 'Don't think I don't think so.'

Tom smiled at his mother. Their complicity made Gideon read the *ratatouille* recipe with particular attention. 'Coriander seeds,' he said. 'That's a new one!'

'I'll call you when it's ready,' Pamela said.

Tom went out of the kitchen, taller than the small boy who had come in, bleeding. Gideon pushed the tea-cloth into the rubber boss whose lips pinched and held it. 'How many more times is it going to have to happen,' he said, 'before we decide to do something?'

10

'Oh Gideon,' she said, 'not now, shall we?'

'When?' he said. 'And after when, where? Because what is actually keeping us here? What vital interest?'

'However are we going to move?'

'I'll talk to my mother,' he said.

'And you know what she'll say.'

'This place must be worth a bob or two. The mortgage is almost ... We don't have to go anywhere *fancy*, but I'm damned if I can see why we have to go on ... You don't agree?'

'If I had a magic wand, of course.' She groped for a net of sprouts in the one-hinged cupboard under the sink. 'But I haven't.'

'Maybe I have,' he said, desire and resentment so close that he could not distinguish them. 'You're too patient, too generous, too – '

'Don't forget "too busy", will you?'

'Look,' he said, 'I know you're bloody good at what you do, but your patients could always find another physio-therapist, if that's – '

'I wasn't meaning them,' she said. 'I only meant that I couldn't cook *and* – '

'You could if you wanted to,' he said. 'You could anything if you wanted to.' He bounced the palm of his right hand on the copper springs of her hair. 'You do dye it, Oxford, don't you?'

'Trade secrets,' she said, the back of her hand to her nose, for a sniff.

'What bullying bastards those Monahans are! Kevin must be nearly fifteen, and built like a Saracen tank. And hairy to boot, and how I should like to boot him!'

'I thought Saracens were armoured cars,' Pamela said. 'Tom's got one in a cupboard somewhere, hasn't he?'

'I didn't know military equipment was your special subject, Oxford. In that case, I wish he'd drive to school in the damned thing. I've offered to go with him in the mornings. And I'll gladly meet him out as well.'

'You know he'd hate it. If only this freezer compart-ment didn't get quite so enthusiastic! Don't start blam-ing Tom, will you, for what happened? Look at all this ice.'

11

'If the polar cap fits,' he said, 'wear it. Console yourself that it might come in useful, should Kevin and Co. start using napalm, and we need an ice-pack in a hurry. I don't blame Tom in the least. I wish . . . '

'The door's dropped,' Pamela said, 'that's the main problem.'

'Would that it were! It's time we made a clean break, Pam, and you know it is: new neighbours, new problems, new doors! I won't take it down and use it as evidence against you, but tell me the truth: doesn't it sound attractive?'

'It sounds expensive,' she said. 'Apologies for the bump, but we have to come back to earth some time.'

'Someone else can bring the feeling back to old Fagin's knees,' Gideon said, 'if you're not around to do it. And equally the Open University will find someone else to be their local nark, if I'm no longer available for the onerous responsibility. It's all bits and pieces, Pam, what we do here, joined together with miracle glue to look like the great Portland vase of a full and useful life.'

'Where's Miranda going to find another Peppino Rizzi?'

'Another ritzy Peppino? Oh I know he's irreplaceable, but that said, he can be replaced. Flute-teachers may be rare, but they're not unique or they wouldn't come in the plural, would they? Logic.'

'There's no arguing with it, is there?' she said. 'Or so you were always telling me. You wouldn't eat fish fingers tonight too, would you? That way we can have the gammon tomorrow.'

'Anything you care to put in front of me, with or without coriander seeds, I'm your hungry man! Oh listen, I too shall be sorry to bid *addio* to the colourful little *professore* who's 'a dunna so much for our daughter, but the Girls' High School scarcely promises the kind of results that bring the quality flocking, or the quantity staying, if they can find alternative accommodation.'

'She's in her last year, Gideon,' Pamela said.

'And so may Tom be, if we stay here. I mean it, Pam.'

'You're so *quick*,' she said.

'You mean flippant, don't you? Well, I'm not being flippant. I'm simply being rather more practical than is

12

comfortable for once. The world is our oyster, Pam. Well, O.K., our fish finger, if you insist.'

She worked on the ginger-leaved sprouts with a broken-tipped knife, hands silvered by the falling water. A husk flipped from the blade to the floor and Gideon bent to collect it from where rust-pimpled plumbing went into the bowels of the house. The tendons in Pamela's feet flexed and slackened as she worked. Frog-legged, he gaitered an ankle with one hand to make her look down at him. Copper curls lolled on her frown. She put the back of her hand to them. 'They'll find someone else to pick on soon,' she said.

' "Mum, what's for supper?" Didn't you love the way he said that? I wish I could be as optimistic. Listen, I'm going to wander down to the post, all right?'

'She doesn't need you to.' Pamela winced as she shut the squeaky tap. 'The Monahans don't bother her.'

'I wasn't thinking of Mandy. I've got a big wodge of stuff to go off to hello-it's-Jack, among other worthy destinations. To time and tide, add East Midlands Educational Television when it comes to great forces that wait for no man! Shan't be long.'

'It'll be ready when you are,' she said.

'But I'm ready now, missus!' He took his black donkey-jacket from the hook. 'Some people call it love, you know, but let it pass.'

The red brick and pigeon-grey slates of Victorian Chaworth rose in alternate layers towards the bluff where the sidelong Minster capped the city. The faces of the terrace houses had that rouged rawness of litmus smacked by acid. As Gideon walked down to the Nottingham Road, the October evening bit his nose. Tracy, the Monahans' seven-year-old, was bobbing up towards him, one foot up, one foot down along the kerb. 'Hello Tracy!' The pretty little face, with orchard-shiny cheeks and puffed lips that could not answer because they were counting, tilted and went straight again, carrying a gleam of mockery past Gideon and up towards the child's home, number seven. Her sister, Sharon, was a statistic in Ulster: she had been run over by an army Land Rover and lay in a coma for three weeks before she died. Compensation had supplied

13

the metallic-bronze Toyota, nearside tyres snubbed against the pavement, outside the Monahans' house.

Gideon was almost at the corner of the Nottingham Road when Miranda came free-wheeling round it, bump-bumping over the ill-set drain. She rode the same high Raleigh which Pamela had used when she worked at Addenbrooke's hospital. Its nylon skirt-guard blurred yellow where the spokes creamed it. 'Hi, dad!' Miranda stood into the pedals, calves flexed, as the gradient made her heavier. New breasts thinned the ribbing of her purple sweater. Sleeves rucked to the elbows, she was brilliant with energy. Her feet mounted the slope of Beacon Terrace as if they were running up easy stairs, with good news.

The pillar box was beyond the entrance to the Fredk. Steggles works. The evening wind gorged orange and blue anoraks as workers cycled past the monogrammed gates or halted, one-legged for a moment, while a lorry boomed by. Gideon fed the metal mouth a mongrel sandwich of buff and white envelopes, business and personal, his eyes on a board wired to the railings of Fredk. Steggles. Slots were available for various categories of workers whose services might be required. All were blank. Gideon was reminded of the rack in school chapel where hymns were advertised.

Grey clouds hurdled the Minster and raced towards the derelict stand of the Chaworth Racecourse as Gideon barged the hard air on the way back to Beacon Terrace. He was almost level with the Simmonds' house, number twenty, on the other side of the street, when Athol came out. He was wearing a mustard-coloured, many-pocketed corduroy safari suit and an American-style red golfing cap, with an elasticated gap at the back. 'Hello there, Shandy! Trouble in paradise again, do I hear? Sean tells me they've been getting at your lad again.'

'Well,' Gideon said, 'he certainly ought to know.' He stepped between Sid Minches' green Volvo taxi (a white plastic tiara carried Sid's twenty-four-hour number) and his own beige Renault 5, a slump of library books on the chapped back seat, and crossed to where Athol Simmonds was building a chin-high stack of cardboard boxes

14

on the tail-gate of his white Taunus estate. 'Can I give you a hand?'

'Better than a foot any day,' Athol said. 'I'd give the law a bell, if I was you.'

'We tried that,' Gideon said, following Athol into the house with not quite as many boxes as the other man. 'Either you bring charges or you're wasting their time. T' Chief Inspector doesn't rate that.'

'Bring charges,' Athol said. 'Show them the big stick.'

'And where do I find the big wallet, not to mention the little witnesses? It's no use going to law. All it does is create ill-feeling.'

'In that case, mate, come in and have a sherry. No harm in that, is there?'

'I ought to be getting back,' Gideon said.

'One sherry won't stop you getting back, will it, Shandy, big strong lad like yourself?'

The Simmonds' front door was luminous with cerise paint; the window-frames were puttied with what looked like fresh toothpaste. In the front room, a glass-topped chromium table carried magazines from several countries: there were quite a lot of German breasts. A three-seater woollen settee carried chocolate-covered cushions in transparent plastic. The overflow from silver and maroon curtains drooped in swags over its Swiss-roll arms. Athol switched on a chandelier, all milky glass varicose with red veins, from Venice. Alpine landscapes, of sugar mountains and blue treacle lakes, in gun-metal frames, hung against the flocked Prince of Wales wallpaper. Athol pulled down the chromium-handled front of a pickled walnut cabinet and a quiver of bottles tottered out. 'You could always try facing them with it at the next parent-teacher shindig,' he said. 'Sweet or dry, what's your pleasure?'

'Dry would be perfect,' Gideon said. 'They don't go to them. Come on, Athol, that's much too much.'

'Use what you want, man; the rest I'll pour back into the bottle as soon as you've gone, so's you won't ever know that a man in my position needs to do that sort of a thing. Tommy wants to give one of those young bandits a black eye. That's what I told our Sean to do, the first time

15

he had any trouble. They never come back for seconds, in my experience.'

'Yes, well, even young Darren's a year older than Tom is, not to mention a ton heavier.'

'Feed him up, Gideon. What do you give that girl of yours? She'd knock anybody's eye out – doesn't even have to touch 'em if I'm any judge, or any jury, if it comes to that. Try him with a dose of the same, morning and night.'

'We shall have to sell up and clear out,' Gideon said. 'I don't see any other way to it.'

'Careful. By the time you've exchanged contracts, Tommy and the dreaded Monahans'll probably be such close mates your lad'll be in tears at having to be parted from them. I used to be a lawyer, you know, in Cape Town, in another life, this was, and I dealt with no end of divorce. You'd get these people, didn't have a civil word to say to one another and then the damnedest things'd start happening, just when you had the final papers typed out. I had one couple met by chance in the waiting room, my secretary found them having a trial reconciliation under her bloody desk, ballock naked and at it like jack-rabbits. Babs and Charlie Dirk-Geyl. Respected citizens, grandparents by now, I shouldn't wonder.'

'Is that where you met your wife?' Gideon said.

'Under the desk? No place like it for romance.'

'Cape Town.'

'Cora? You're joking, with a ho and a ho and a ho-ho-ho. Cora comes from Jamaica by way of Finsbury Park, can't you tell? If I'da laid a finger on her in S.A., let alone any more pleasurable instrument, I'da been straight in the clink. Matter of fact, I *was* in the clink, but you probably know that.'

'I gathered you had a distinguished past,' Gideon said.

'Lurid, I can tell you, and may very well do so, unless you drink up. No, when I was in the white man's paradise, I was married to a proper Afrikaner, if you must know, Petula Raysmaker. You'll never guess what everyone called my little Petula. Yes, you will too: Pet. Don't look for wit in sunny climes colonised by bloody Hollanders, will you? You'll find diamonds first. She was a real

16

looker, sometime beauty queen, Miss Transvaal, no less. Statistics can look good on some people, believe you me, Gideon. I was quite a dashing fellow when I was younger and, make no mistake, I was once a hell of a sight younger. How old are you, chiefy? Forty-two?'

'Not quite,' Gideon said.

'But it's the end of a long day, right? You musta started early then, judging from that girl of yours. She has to be nineteen.'

'Eighteen actually.'

'If I'm not there, I'm thereabouts, aren't I?' Athol said. 'No, listen, you look good: you've got your hair, you've got your teeth. You can read the bottom line at twenty paces. Too many spuds under that jumper, but what's a hungry man to do? I lived a pretty full life down there: worked hard, played harder. I had the town flat, the lakeside cottage, the Porsche, the power-boat, what else would you like? The dolly on the water-skis? I had her too. Those were the days; and the nights didn't noticeably cool off either. I had one of those eight-by-eight Japanese beds, and the population to fill it. They nipped in, they nipped out: well, they wouldn't have been Japs if they hadn't, would they? I once had four little sweethearts in one night, loveliest sight I ever saw, Gideon, like a parcel of kittens. The way women smile at each other, you never saw anything like it! The way they know each other, tongues, fingers, toes! How's your drink?'

'It's a year's supply, frankly.'

'I lost the whole shoot in the end, but I lived to tell the tale, didn't I, so it can't really have been the end, can it? No regrets, or at least that's the story I'm telling. And I *am* telling it too. Have you ever come across a cove called Graham Noble on your travels at all?'

'I'm not that much of a traveller.'

'London publicity character, lots of contacts; lots of con, lots of tact, you're absolutely right probably. Anyway, he said to ram it all down on paper and he'll give it serious consideration. I'd sooner have the money, but what can you do? I've knocked out about forty thousand words of my life-story so far. Pretty soon, I'll be out of

17

that damned pram and taking my first faltering steps. What do you think of the new furniture?'

'Well,' Gideon said, 'it's very – it's very new, isn't it?'

Athol stropped the back of his hand on his leather throat. 'Every stick of it! Cora likes it that way, so why not? How do I do it? I'm into franchises; it's a new sideline, inferior decorating by mail order, female order, I'm not fussy as long as the cash flows. So I thought why not have a showroom where I can put it to practical use? Like in my own front parlour. You know what puzzles me, Shandy, as a disinterested student of human nature and other thoroughly disgusting phenomena, and that is what you're doing in Beacon bleddy Terrace in the first place.'

'Mightn't I ask much the same of you?'

'Except I'd tell you,' Athol said. 'I was stuck for somewhere to expand my operation and I came across this clapped-out factory at Blackley Cross, didn't I? They were lashing out development grants, so I stuck my hand out and, lo and behold, some much-needed cash, with compliments. I kept the cash, cashed the compliments and here I am. Your turn.'

'I've got this loose but useful connection with East Midlands T.V.,' Gideon said. 'And I've got this Open University job, and I've got my classes; and Pam has her patients. And, and, and the kids are in school and we could afford the house, just, when we just couldn't afford anything else. It's not Araldite exactly, but it keeps us sticking around. Or has. We had some good friends here when we first came, but they moved away. The Stoics used to say that one ought to be able to be happy anywhere. I'm not sure they'd ever taken a close look at Chaworth, but there it is. There must be worse places. And pretty soon, if I have my way, we'll be looking at one or two of them.'

'Comedy?' Athol Simmonds said.

'I beg your pardon.'

'This work you do for the T.V. people. Do you do the funnies?'

'I'm doing the background for a series on battles for the schools' service,' Gideon said. 'If I did funnies, I'd be

18

living in a middle-class ghetto, and the kids'd be in private schools. I'm basically a historian, or at least that's what I wanted to be.'

'You know what I do basically, don't you? I'm in the micro-biz: not micro-chip, micro-shit. That's what you've been humping in for me, although you didn't know it; ignorance is no excuse, though it's certainly pretty widespread, isn't it? Know what's special about these?' He opened the flap of one of the boxes and brought out a fistful of small, flat envelopes. 'Look like condom packets, don't they? Not though. I'll tell you what's special: they're none of 'em more than a tenth of an inch thick. Three millimetres, tops!' He opened a copy of *Der Stern* and put one of the envelopes inside. 'See the point? Of course you don't; and that *is* the point: no bump, no visible protuberance whatsoever. Get it?'

'In a word, no.'

'No distortion, no packing problems. The well-endowed Rhine maiden on the front still doesn't have one melon noticeably bigger than t'other; or if she does, it's not down to me. Talk to her *mutti* about it. I'm in the novelteaneous novelty game, Gideon, fodder for the freebie trade. Dead giveaways are my bread and butter; I'm looking to the chairs and tables to put some jam on it. I couldn't practise law in the U.K., once I got here, so I had to come up with something else, or stay down without it. Novelties for mugs wasn't quite what my mother had in mind, but what can you do when you can't do nuffin much? Only one way to get rich and that's create a need for something nobody ever much needed. You wouldn't do me a favour, would you, and take a squint at this life-story of mine? All you ever needed to know about Athol Simmonds, his rise, fall and subsequent resurrection, not to mention a thousand other intimate details calculated to set the blood a-tingling. I'd appreciate a professional opinion.'

'Failing which, you'll take mine, right? Provided it's double-spaced, I'll read it with pleasure.'

'And if without, then say without. Don't spare my feelings.'

'I'll sharpen the red end of my pencil,' Gideon said.

19

'Thanks for the sherry, but I've done all I can, I'm afraid. You're altogether too generous.'

'Something eating you, Shandy, is there? I get this impression you're a trifle miffed somewhere along the line. Am I right or am I right? I've got a nose for when people are hedging. Relic of my court-room days. Got an ear as well. This one, and. it's burning. So out with it: what's your gripe?'

'I thought Tom and Sean were developing into rather good friends,' Gideon said. 'Until today.'

'On to your Tom too was he, the beggar?' Athol threw open the two-tone (apricot and orange) door of the front room and called up the flowering Axminster stairs. 'Seany, will you come down here a minute, please? I believe in having things out, Gideon.'

Sean's face was the colour of peanut butter. His pale scalp showed through lustreless tan curls. He looked like a Polaroid that had not fully developed. A vermilion track-suit (with flashes on the shoulders) and Puma leisure shoes, with Velcro latches, made him big in the doorway. 'What's the matter then?' he said.

'Say hello to Mr Shand.'

'Hello, Mr Shand.'

'How are you, Sean? Look – '

'Now let's have it straight, man,' Athol said. 'Did you have anything to do with what happened to young Shandy this afternoon?'

'No.'

'You saw what happened, though, did you?'

'I saw. I told you. But I wasn't involved.'

'The boy is clearly guilty,' Athol said. 'See how it's done, Gideon? Candy from kids. Ask an innocent quezzy in an innocent voice, they'll always put their lollapaloozas in it. You damned well *should* have been involved. What else do we toss you bones for, tiger, eh? Tommy has a bit of bother, why not try and level things up a bit?'

'I didn't see nothing till it was over pretty well. Is he O.K.?'

'No permanent damage,' Gideon said. 'But . . . '

'I'm going up the club, bish, all right?'

'Drawn your rations?' Athol said.

20

'I'll get a burger at Moffatt's.' The leisure shoes squelched on the waxed boards. 'Want me to take Tom along, Mr Shand? No bother.'

'Another time he might like that, Sean, thank you.'

'He goes to see this brass he's got to know, works in the town hall: makes out he's going for the ping-pong, but I reckon he's got more than his forehand going these days. Life's an in-and-out business, if you're lucky, isn't that what they say? Talking of which, how are you for money just now?'

'Money?'

'Stuff comes in notes of varying denominations; and goes likewise. Only I'm planning to recruit some élite blokes – highly educated types for whom the present economic climate has proved a little too shady – to go out into the highways and byways and flog this furniture scheme of mine. Don't worry, you won't have to hump anything heavier than a three-colour brochure and a pen that says "yes, please" as soon as it's shown a dotted line.'

'I don't really have the time, frankly, Athol.'

'One day a week, the odd evening or two, it'd put a new silencer on your banger, whatever else it did. Not offended, are you?'

'Supper's waiting,' Gideon said. 'Offended?'

'I've already had mine. I'll go rout out that manuscript for you. Cora goes to her Sisterhood on Wednesdays; that's when I get my Golfball out of the rough – the old I.B.M. – and start Proosting away in the back room. Here we are.' The manuscript was in two Cambridge blue folders, belted with pink laces. 'Another time, don't wait till your kid stops one, O.K.? It's nice to have some company that can sign its name without having to think about the spelling.'

'I didn't know I'd signed anything,' Gideon said.

'The book finds a publisher, I'll cut you in, promise!'

Athol Simmonds gave him one on the shoulder, old pal, as Gideon went out of the cerise door. He walked on past his own front door (should he repaint it before they tried to sell the house?) and up to the Monahans'. Athol's folders under his arm, the hand in the pocket, made him

21

seem less belligerent; a modest master coming away from a class. When the green door opened, throwing applause from the T.V. and the Police from the record-player over him like swill, he was able to play the diplomat. 'Hello, Darren, is your dad there by any chance?'

The youngest of the Monahan brothers was blue-eyed, straw-haired and muscular. He had a baby-face with old creases at the corners of mouth and eyes. 'I'll see if he's in,' he said, in a hoarse voice.

Gideon stood by an oleograph of a blond Jesus with Irish eyes, sweating wine-gums under a chaplet of thorns. The kitchen door opened (Radio Two was playing in there) and Aileen Monahan was crossing a gold and black stole across her breasts. The smell of supper, or laundry, came with her to the door. 'Oh Mr Shand,' she said, 'what can I do for you?'

'I was hoping to have a word with Gavin,' Gideon said.

'And he's not here,' she said. 'The supper's on the table, but he's not back. Is there nothing I can do?' She offered more sympathy than the case deserved, even though she did not appear to know what it was. She had the unfair wisdom of the victim, the driven dignity of the slave. What could have happened to him that she would not find enviably mild? The visitor wanted a mere word with Gavin; and here she was obliged to a life with him. Gideon shifted the pale blue folders and backed from the noise and the smell. 'Shall I be telling him you called?' she said. 'It's not about the voting, is it?'

'No,' Gideon said, 'it's not about that.'

As he reached the pavement, the margin of the darkness was bleached by a gush of brilliance. Chaworth City had a Milk Cup re-play; the ground staff had kindled the lights. Another fatuous allegiance came alive: they would listen anxiously to hear whether the eleven local louts had been hailed as giant-killers or gallant minnows who had all but held their first-division opponents. There was a big drama at the moment over whether local lad Bryan Grant, an England B prospect, would stay with the club. If he did well against tonight's class opposition, his price would probably become irresistibly high and

City would have to sell. Only failure would keep him faithful.

Gideon threw his donkey-jacket over the saddle of Pamela's bicycle behind the front door and turned his face aside, a mere flinch, from the silence. 'Is something wrong?'

'Mum's cut her finger,' Miranda said.

Pamela was sitting at the plank table, shoulders down, low. The freckles on her nose were like bran on milk. 'That wretched knife,' she said. 'It's so damned sharp.'

'Should we get you to casualty? How bad is it? What were you cutting?'

'I'm all right now,' she said. 'What does it matter what I was cutting? I was cutting the bread.'

'How about a cup of strong tea?'

'We've got soup,' she said.

'Anyway, tea's a stimulant,' Miranda said. 'It's not generally recommended these days.'

'Thank you, Mandy, for your professional – '

'You're so welcome, dad. You would've been even more welcome about ten minutes ago. Where have you been?'

'Bearding assorted lions, and lionesses; much good may it do us. How's Tom?'

'D.F.C. and bar,' Pamela said. 'He's got his undercarriage working and he's been passed fit to fly.'

'Poor Pam,' Gideon said. 'You've really had a day, haven't you?' The telephone was ringing in the front room. 'Oh, who the hell can that be?'

'There's this subtle way of finding out, popsicle: you lift the black detachable bit and it'll tell you, if you ask it nicely.'

'You deserve your own series these days, Mandy, you really do.'

'Get them to call back, Gids, whoever it is. Supper's been ready for ages.' Pamela stood up as Gideon went along to answer the telephone. Miranda put an arm round her mother's green and black waist (she was wearing an old rugger shirt of Gideon's) and a nipple quivered under the cotton. 'It's not really a knife at all, that thing,' Pamela said. 'It's a weapon.'

23

'It's Steve,' Gideon was calling from the front of the house. 'I shan't be a tick.'

'No,' Miranda said, 'he'll be two.'

'Don't make trouble tonight, Mandy, would you mind?'

'Trouble, *maman*? *Moi*? Oh, just to cover this awkward hiatus, have I told you that Peps thinks your daughter may be ready for grade eight, no less, come Christmas?'

'That's very good news,' Pamela said, putting out Gideon's supper with an oven-gloved left hand, all scorched marigolds.

'I say, dad's having a merry chortle, is he not? Our famous friend certainly knows the way to his funny bone and other anatomical rarities.'

'He's probably telling him a bridge hand.'

'They can be riotous, can't they? *Can* they? Do you like him? Sir Stephen?'

'It's getting cold,' Pamela called. 'He's daddy's friend, not mine. I can't honestly remember when I last saw him even.'

'They keep asking you to go and stay. Why don't you?'

'Could it be that I have these two children who don't care to spend hours and hours in the car for the sake of a spoonful of caviare?'

'I don't seem to puke in motors as much as I used to,' Miranda said.

'Oh well, off we go then!'

Gideon's soup was creased with a cooling skin before he returned to the kitchen. 'Sorry about that.' He left his smile at the door. 'This is the stuff to give the troops.'

'But failing them, you'll have to drink it yourself. What was the joke?'

'Or jokes indeed,' Miranda said. 'Someone underlead his ace?'

'That's no laughing matter,' Gideon said. 'No, he was just telling me that they've had to re-jig the dates for this Gold Cup match against the Proctors on the seventh.'

'No wonder you couldn't contain your guffaws, papa.'

'One of the twins has got shingles, Steve was telling

24

me, and they're having difficulty deciding which one it is. Appparently he looks frightful and they've had to postpone the match on aesthetic grounds. The way Steve told it, it was rather amusing.'

' "I say, dad," she said casually, "are you coming to his recital after dins?" '

'Recital? Tonight? Whose? Not yours?'

'Piers's's's. He's pedalling a proggie of boy Bach and Captain Scarlatti. Piers told Peps it was open Minster for the privileged few, if that's all he can muster. The privileged many would, of course, be greatly preferred.'

'What do you say, Pammy? It'd make a change from that god-awful series on the box.'

'I can't leave Tom, you know that,' Pamela said. 'He's had a horrid shock and I want him in bed and settled down early.'

'You're right, Pam. One hundred per cent.'

'You sound dubious, papa.'

'Miranda, if you look up, you will see a sharp sword suspended by a fraying thread – or is it a fraying nerve? – directly above your pretty head.'

'Reminds me: it needs washing. The head; the raven tresses thereon. May I have outline planning permission to use some of the hot water, despite the sobering implications of the latest spending cuts?'

'Don't invent new grievances,' Gideon said. 'Use some of the ones we have already. Aileen Monahan thought I was trying to recruit them for the Alliance; she was all set to sell her vote dearly, dear. Are you sure you won't catch cold, if you're going to this recital affair?'

'Borrow my dryer,' Pamela said.

'And I was just going to ask if I could borrow your dryer, *chère maman*!'

'This isn't the French oral, Mandy. And if it is, you've passed; you've passed. Stopped bleeding has it, Pam? They're hell those things, aren't they?'

'Go with Mandy, if you feel like it,' Pamela said. 'I rather fancy that bloody awful series. He's rather super, I think, the lover.'

'I suppose he is, in a way.'

'Papa's patent method of saying "balls"; right, papa?'

'Hello, miss, you still here? I could've sworn you'd gone upstairs.'

'I say, if she suddenly went suspiciously affectionate and nicely spoken, you wouldn't consider running your talented daughter to the scene of tonight's cultural highlight in your defective but none the less serviceable motor, would you?'

'Talented?' Gideon said. 'Which daughter is that?'

'Secret life then, have you, dad?' Miranda said. 'Local Intellectual's Second Family Sensation, is it, then? O.K., so I'll walk by myself along the lawless roads. Only you know what that unfortunate movement can lead to: Teen-Age Pregnancies, The Modern Scourge, among other nasty topics for later in the programme.'

'Of course I'll take you,' Gideon said. 'Just call me dog's-body.'

'Oh, dad,' she said, 'may I?'

'And how are you planning to get back? City've got a home match. By the time you're out of effective range of the cathedral organ, the pubs'll be brimming with Brummies and other choice examples of what seriously concerns Chief Constables and other bucklers of our state.'

'Someone'll run me home with a good grace,' Miranda said. 'Someone beginning with R, if I know anything about it, and I must say, under the influence of a vigilant press and a full-frontal parental environment, I am beginning to.'

'If you're not going to miss the opening toccata, you'd best fugue off and do your hair.'

She ran up the stairs and the pipes began their noises. Pamela's white bandage lay on the table in front of her as if the finger it sheathed did not belong to her; tied with a bow, it could have been a delicacy waiting for him after his fish fingers. A touch of strawberry bled through it. Pamela had chewed the lipstick from her slightly chapped lips and the little gap in her front teeth was there between them. It was as if she drew all her breath through it. 'Every single one of us seems to have eaten at a different time this evening,' she said.

'I am sorry, but Steve was being so funny, and you know what he's like when he gets going. A torrent is a gently running stream. He sent you his love. I saw Athol Simmonds earlier. He thinks we should put one of the Monahans in the hospital, *pour encourager les autres*, which is exactly what I think it would do. How can one possibly agree that violence is the only answer to violence, especially when one is pretty certain that it is? I then went and had a word with Aileen, Beacon Terrace's own Niobe, but I couldn't bring myself to persecute her with the news that her male offspring had passed into the Waffen S.S. without having to take the written exam, so what do I come home to? A wife who's had a quarrel with a cleaver. I'd like to take that damned thing and chuck it in the river. In fact, I might just do it when I've run Mandy to the Minster. Alternatively, I could give it to my mother for Christmas.'

'We have to have something to cut the bread with,' Pamela said.

'Why do you think the Simmondses called that boy Sean? It gives him a sort of spurious affinity with the Monahans, rather like putting the Gurkhas in kilts, I suppose. After all, neither Athol or Cora is markedly Irish, or should it be Celtic, are they? Is he or she? Presumably, they elected to slop a pail of local colour over the kid, on the principle that anything is better than *café au lait* in a society bursting with inter-racial harmony and other forms of grievous bodily harm.'

'Where did the name Gideon come from, for that matter?'

'The land of Canaan, didn't it, like so many funny ideas? I rather think my parents had Wingate in mind, as a matter of dated fact. Names are strange. According to certain pundits God is pure silence. Don't call Him and He certainly won't be calling you. Names are to the pristine purity of the Creator as the colours of the spectrum are to pure, white light. Whirl the dictionary around fast enough and on a clear day you'll see God himself, the unnameable Name of all names, the totality of true facts, in person. Call a thing by its real name and you're messing about with the ingredients of the ineffable. The first time I ever saw you, Oxford, was after Stephen cut his finger in my old digs in Portugal Place and had to go to Addenbrooke's for some qualified needle and thread.'

'I always thought Wingate's name was Orde. Orde Wingate?'

'He also called himself Gideon. He fancied himself an ancient Israelite, or a modern one. It takes all kinds. My father met him in India.'

'What did he cut himself on, Stephen, that time exactly?'

'A tin of ravioli, ma'am, an innocent tin of ravioli, or so it claimed. The action replay would tell all, but our outside cameras were otherwise engaged. Actually, we'd been playing in a team of four match and he was talking about a hand – *with* his hands, of course, what else? – and opening the aforesaid tin at the same time – '

'What a lot of trouble you do take!' Pamela said. 'I'm never quite sure whether it's pride or despair.'

'Ask not for whom the beau toils,' Gideon said. 'Anyway, he opened his hand as well. Blood everywhere. Stretcher-bearers called for, but otherwise engaged, so off he dripped to Addenbrooke's, driving himself with one hand in his Renault Dauphine. I only had a provisional licence and he preferred the frying pan to the fire. Do you remember those Renaults?'

'I remember that one,' Pamela said.

'Welcome to the club. No subscription; no facilities either, but you can't have everything. And about an hour later, back he came with you. In white stockings.'

'And that's how it all began.'

'Why he needed the services of a fledgling physiotherapist for a cut finger careful analysis has yet to reveal.'

'I held the other hand,' she said. 'He was very persuasive. He always could talk, couldn't he?'

Gideon put up a hand to catch her as she sidled past him to go out of the kitchen. 'Listen,' he said, 'if you seriously don't want to move, we won't.'

'When did I say that I didn't?'

'Listen again,' he said. 'The dog not barking in the night.'

'Poor Gideon,' she said.

'But honest,' he said.

'Are you?' she said. 'Can anyone be as nice as you are and still be honest?'

2

Miranda was at the bathroom basin, her almost dry hair glistening from the shampoo, loose-buttoned Indian shirt hanging, empty-armed, over jeaned hips. Pamela's little plastic dryer was a fat gun in her hand. 'Hullo, pops,' she said. 'Do you too find me particularly gorgeous?'

'Yes, and so modest with it,' he said. 'Are topless shammies the latest style advocated by the *Church Times*?'

'In a typically forthright editorial? Bound to be. Do my tits bother you then, dad?'

'They age me rather,' Gideon said.

The first cheer of the evening sounded like anger from the City ground; it was hard to tell whether the crowd was happy or enraged. Miranda was watching him in the steamy mirror as he reached across her for the soap. (He had ketchup on his fingers.) 'Don't worry about Tom too much, will you? He's not half as bothered as you seem to be.'

'How genial of you to be so unselfish in your estimate of your brother's sentiments, fair daughter!'

'And yes, the knives are out here tonight, ladies and gentlemen!' The creased shirt came up with an arm in each sleeve. 'And so am I, luckily.'

Gideon looked in to smile at Tom. He was reading his

subscription copy of a magazine devoted to military tactics in the Second World War. Above his head, on the canted ceiling, luminous stars spangled his private universe. He kept his eyes steadfastly on the tanks manoeuvring outside Kiev, in perhaps the biggest set-piece battle of all time. Gideon recognised the docile resolution of his son; it was almost a joke against him. Once again, the distant football crowd rumbled like weather.

'Are you ever going to have this thing fixed, dad?' asked Miranda, as the Renault made its usual bronchial boom.

'I'm waiting till my ship comes in,' he said. 'Then I'll put this shambles on board, sail into uncharted seas and dump the damned thing over the side. It's all right once it gets going.'

'You ought to come and hear Piers,' she said, a purple angora scarf across her nose, Pamela's eyes bright above it. 'What will you do if you don't?'

'I have a rich range of alternatives, even though strictly speaking there can be but two. I could get on with this translation I'm due to deliver at the end of last month. I.e., I could make a start on it. Or, or, I might join your convalescent mother in watching that seductive, if flawed, classic serial in which the windows open the wrong way, but otherwise we are in nineteenth-century France. To the purist, all things are impure.'

'She's only suffering from shock, you know. You'd much better leave her to get over it on her own.'

'Mandy, I realise that you have now attained your majority, but could you conspire to give it another month or two before being wise beyond your years?'

'Sorry, dad. Not to say sorry, *sir*. But only just. You really are handsome in profile, you know.'

'I know,' he said.

He held the car steady on the steep cobbles as they reached the blind corner leading into the Close. The machicolations of the castle, over to the left, took regular bites from the sky. The Minster commanded the crest of the hill; a rumour of light showed from the organ loft and kindled soft flames in the gleaming forecourt. Gideon's tyres made a sound like peeling adhesive as he rolled the

Renault up to the shuttered souvenir kiosk. Miranda ducked to look through the window, mouthed 'Bye!', and ran into the Minster. The racket of Peppino Rizzi's Honda swarmed up Magnus Hill ahead of him with a promise of virility hardly kept by the actual appearance of the music teacher. Wearing a black cloak and a sacerdotal hat, he disembarked at the back of his motor bike, like a monk quitting a donkey, before taking a flute-case from the copious saddle-box. Since he had turned out the lights of the Renault and Rizzi was not conscious of his presence, Gideon was a petty god for a moment. Close to the unsuspecting maestro, he was startled by a brief sense that violence and benevolence could clown so easily together. He was grateful for the pains the music teacher had taken over Miranda and, so far as he was aware, he felt nothing for him but a kind of patronising deference. Yet now, casually, he could play at frightening, even killing, him merely because he was at a silly advantage. He switched the car lights on and they flared against the rust-brown wall of the Minster, welcome vulgarity. Rizzi turned and frowned into the glare and saw a couple coming, on foot, from the darkness behind the car.

Gideon released the handbrake and the Renault rolled away down the rake of the Close. The cobbles had been relaid, to the annoyance of some rate-payers, and the precinct had the complacent cosiness of a Cambridge courtyard. Gideon took pleasure in what he could not wholly approve. The Alliance, in which he had for a time taken a practical interest, had been uncertain whether to second the expenditure or whether it was too élitist for an élite to support. That had been before Bill and Paula Sadleir moved on to pastures greener. Bill's defeat at the general election, by that cruelly narrow majority, had put an end to Gideon's involvement, even though, when he saw Bill being bravely philosophical on the box, the shade of the Duc de La Rochefoucauld reminded him that the misfortunes of one's friends are not wholly unpalatable.

He rolled down Parvus Hill and into Jackson Avenue before engaging the gear and allowing the engine to lurch to loud life. The one-way system took him into Hankin Street and down to the Regency roundabout development. Rows of trolleys gleamed behind the long glass of the new supermarket. Tasteful lettering pointed out the multi-storey car park behind its collegiate façade. Toilets were available. The wide road, luminous with accurate embellishments, crossed the river before a sign, RAMP, warned where the money had run out. The bookshop had closed on the corner of Cheapside. Kinsey's Auction Mart (Sale This Day) had nothing but an old stove and a tuba to show in its half-cardboard Gothic window. Gideon wound down the car window and the noise of the football crowd crashed and ebbed like breakers. The empty streets smelled of the zoo.

He had to stop at the level crossing by Stonewall. The main line stayed east of the city and seemed hardly to serve it; there was a different town down here, warehouses and a station hotel with several bars, to which no one whom Gideon knew ever admitted paying a visit. There were even said to be whores. There were certainly funny clubs. The road to Blackley Cross went off to the left directly after the level crossing. Gideon sat in the softly humming strangeness and was in no hurry for the train. Who would he have been, he wondered, if he had quit the car and walked along the blackened arches below the goods yard and into the Black George? What would he have wanted to drink and whom did he fancy meeting? How nearly one was someone entirely different! The French novel was waiting for him. Being a translator added one more patch to his coat of many colours.

A weighty, jeans-hobbled figure, in a pale blue anorak, tried the pedestrian gate on the far side of the line. When it did not give, he flung himself on it, like an enemy, and almost fell to the ground on the dangerous side. Gideon flashed his lights, but without clear purpose: it could have been warning or encouragement. The stranger wore a black and red scarf and seemed to shake off an invisible assailant as he paraded across the wooden planking between the rails. He kicked and flung his arms and looked back towards the football ground, yelling silence. It was as though he was being harried by an invisible

32

mob. Gideon, sitting low in the little car, was not big enough, it seemed, to deserve his hostility. The stranger looked at him mildly for a moment, like a soloist briefly excused from duty, before going into another routine of rage. He made his sole spectator into a critic for whom the performance was mounted but who was spared its full, confused impact. Unthreatened, Gideon could almost resent his exemption. 'Well,' he called out, 'what's the score?'

The menace was merely a fat boy now. Two straggles of blood from his nostrils gave him a wet moustache. Had he lost his glasses? He narrowed his eyes, without offensiveness, as if asked a difficult question in class. 'Nothing-nothing,' he said.

The furious flesh stood adjacent to Gideon. Was there anything else he wanted to know? A train racketed delicately past, more surprising in its height than its sound. Pink people were having dinner in the light of shaded lamps. The wheels te-tocked over the wooden ramp that covered the track. If flesh had been under them, would anyone have eaten any differently?

Gideon expected to see the electronic stammer of the television in the front room, but the ground floor of 17, Beacon Terrace was in darkness. He stood for a moment at the bottom of the stairs and heard the donk of the hot water pipes: Pam must be having a bath. First shifting the volume control as low as possible, he turned on the television. Brightness flopped on to the screen. The episode had been running for twenty minutes, but he soon recognised where he was. Ready to extinguish the picture, should he hear Pamela open the bathroom door, he listened to the soundlessness, dubbing the silent activity of the characters with his own version of the dialogue. The notorious scene in the lawyer's office – once deemed an insult to the public morals of the Third Empire – was truncated by the credits; modern dreams were received on licence, but they suffered teasing abbreviations. He would have to wait until the following week before he could see exactly how Mathilde offered herself to Maître Vigier. So did one know and not know what was coming next. His naked wife was upstairs. He could

33

guess more clearly than she would show him the shape of her body, that tuck below her terse buttocks which proved how neatly she was made.

He carried his desire, like a dangerous weapon, past the bottom of the steep stairs and along the narrow passage – sideways past the damp-fattened paperbacks in his nursery shelves – to his small back room. Tilted in his captain's chair (Kinsey's lot number chalked under the wicker seat), he put his feet on the busy desk and opened Athol Simmonds' typescript.

Sheila was a brunette and gorgeous; Rosemary was honey-blonde and gorgeous. Beth-Anne was a looker, everyone agreed, and Janice's legs were parallel lines that met at something that beat infinity. Young Athol was a high-flyer all right and nothing but the best was ever good enough for him. He kept the finest cellar in Cape Town and upstairs had something to be said for it too. He loved them and he left them, but rarely empty-handed. He liked variety, but he hated the idea of unpopularity. He didn't want to boast, but he never made a girl do anything she didn't want to do. The big seducer, he never undid a button against its owner's will; promise you. Beth-Anne was the most gorgeous physical specimen he could ever remember and when they went skinny-dipping up at the lake, he had problems getting out of the water without drawing attention to his measure of admiration for her considerable assets. Rosemary was mild and bashful when you were playing tennis with her at the club, but she was a little firebrand once she got out of her whites. Janice could put those legs around you like an erotic python and squeeze you to a death worth having. Sheila was a naughty girl when you got the Porsche revving at anything over 4,000 a minute; it seemed to turn her on to be belting down the highway and what she liked to do wasn't suitable for a family audience, but Athol was willing to bet that no red-blooded male would be likely to cancel his subscription. Janice was a funny one, but she knew exactly what she wanted, and how!

In the end, though, Petula was incomparable. There were lookers and lookers, my friends, but Petula Raysmaker was *sans pareille*: you could see her in a swim-suit and not turn a hair, but you'd have to be bald as a coot to do it. Athol had a hard time wrestling her from the handsome attentions of Piet Hokluyt, a rugger international from an old Cape family that was used to playing hard and playing to win. With a little luck and some tight cornering, Athol managed to get her up to his lakeside pad and into that Japanese bed and after that, there was no holding her, if you'll forgive the wholly inappropriate expression. This time it was love; the girl was a stunner, but she also had character. She wanted something more than Piet's fifteen and a half stone of flesh and Afrikaner blood, even if it did come in the handily packed form of a prime athlete. She told Athol's mother that she had never met anyone as intelligent as her son, and never expected to. The Porsche and the beautifully chosen wines (and the useful backhand) had their charms, like those clever brown eyes of his, but what counted was the sheer get-up-and-go of the fellow.

Athol could not pretend that he was anything but the best bloody lawyer on the Cape. His clients were rich and they were, of course, all white. He spent one evening a week at a 'clinic' for coloureds and blacks and he hinted, with unusual discretion, that he sometimes took payment in kind. He did this, he said at the bottom of a page, more for the thrill of the forbidden than from any particular greed. The next page had been re-typed, evidence of second thoughts. A left-over sentence was inked out at the top of the following page and Gideon spent a minute or two deciphering the words 'her sister too'. Athol admitted that he never questioned the political structure which made him a favourite of fortune. If he excused his privileges, it was by being a generous tipper; he liked to be liked, and he could afford to be. Pet's parents flattered him with suspicions that he was a liberal, by which they meant a Jew, and Pet was excited by the challenge of a relationship with a dangerous man. The Raysmakers treated him with cold politeness, but he was used to hostility and neat with ingratiating insolence: he could make the women smile, and sometimes laugh. Old man Raysmaker resisted longest, because resistance was his pleasure, but his daughter was in love and the marriage took place. Athol recalled the kiss that Pet gave her father after the ceremony: 'I thought for a moment that maybe the whole thing had happened just so she would win that one battle against the old brute.' But when they got to the Japanese bed, up at the lakeside, Pet proved she had other pressing motives, bless her heart.

Athol's practice was mostly to do with tax and property. He was a leading authority on company law. His partner, Bram Pollock, took care of the bread-and-butter criminal stuff. One weekend, when he and Pet were driving up for a few days on water-skis, they were flagged down by the cops. He assumed that some bigshot was in trouble and had got the police to trace him: would it mean one more bloody first-class trip to London or Zürich or New York? You never knew, or cared. As for himself, he had never done anything more illegal than test the old Porsche to something near destruction. (Payments in kind were not mentioned again.) It turned out that Bram Pollock had landed him in it. His partner had been arrested at a country house conference of some banned organisation. The colonel in charge of the case could not believe that, with his brains, Athol was not behind the whole conspiracy. Then why was he not at the conference? The colonel smiled at that: 'You're too damned tricky to be that obvious, man, aren't you?'

At first, prison seemed so unreal that he worried more about what Pet might do to his Lamborghini (you had to change with the times) than about his own fate. At every stage of the proceedings, he waited for an admission that the whole thing had been a joke, which he had taken in bloody good part, man. Expectation of the colonel's congratulations made him ironically subservient. The hardest thing to bear was the unsmiling suspicion of the other detainees. He had never been of their party and his innocence, of which they alone were certain, convinced them that he had been the agent of their arrest. Having done nothing wrong, he had no friends at all. The colonel was more concerned with Matthew Kayser, the leader of the banned black union, than with a marginal playboy who demanded more of his time than made any sort of practical sense. The colonel's name was Hensch and he was suspected of being partly Jewish. Athol had the uneasy feeling that he was waiting for some appeal to a solidarity which would be repudiated with scorn. Athol himself could not resist a measure of secret snobbery towards the hard man who carried that hidden taint. Pet's sources of inside information had armed him with a weapon that cut both ways.

Inconvenience lengthened into tedium. Never doubting Athol's innocence, Petula came constantly to the gaol. There was something heroic in her loyalty and, though he scarcely liked to admit it, something demeaning. She lacked the imagination to distrust him; the support of her family was a crutch he could have been spared. Her visits commanded the respect of Pretoria, just as they excited the envy of his gaolers. Her prize-winning charms convinced them that he must be quite some bloke, little Athol. Even the suspicions of the other prisoners were mitigated by jeering amazement. Only Matthew Kayser remained aloof from their vulgar solidarity. Athol's own resentment was concentrated on Bram Pollock: his partner had not only torpedoed his easy life, he had also slighted Athol by never once attempting to recruit him into the conspiracy. A man he had always patronised had judged him unworthy of confidence and incapable of altruism. He had, after all, been punished for those slices of dark meat. Petula's fidelity was hardly less shameful; it promised that although she was a beauty, she was a simple soul for whom the way things seemed must be exactly how they were. In the visiting cubicle one day, she undid her buttons and showed him her boobs to cheer him up.

Gideon put the second folder into his desk drawer for another time and went upstairs. Tom was asleep under the glowing astronomy of his private universe, spectacles folded on the chair next to his glass of water. He lay like a baby, guilelessly open, and did not stir at Gideon's creaking weight. Such trust seemed a kind of foolishness, almost an enticement, something sly. How could one think such things? Gideon touched his son's wrist and went across the short landing to where light showed under the warped door of his and Pamela's bedroom.

'Mandy home?' she said.

'Not yet.' He stood by the bed so that he could prove why he had come up. 'J.S.B. goes on for ever, doesn't he?'

She was wearing her glasses, black shell frames, and put aside her book to look politely at him. The complicity between her and the female novelist ennobled on the back flap made his arrival an intrusion. 'Are you going to get her, or what?'

'The latter.' He shucked his desert boots and undid his belt. 'Tom's asleep all right.'

Pamela looked at her watch. She was wearing her Laura Ashley and the bed was neat around her, as if she had been told to rest quietly. 'Are you coming to bed then?'

'Then what?' he said. 'Mandy'll be fine.'

She drew her knees to her chin and clasped her shins, arms outside the old Lanaircel blanket, and looked at him with an uncritical frown. 'You seem odd,' she said.

'Imagine I was a patient. Wouldn't you have some idea which limb was bothering me?'

She put warm fingers, casually, to where he wanted them. She had to turn her body slightly, creasing her breasts, in order to reach him with her unbandaged hand. 'I'd much sooner wait,' she said. 'She'll only come home in the middle.'

'I expect you're right,' he said, 'but . . .'

'It's been a strange kind of a day.'

'And it's not over yet.' He hauled his tartan shirt over his head and had trouble unbuttoning in the darkness he had foisted on himself. He took his time on purpose, blinded to his own flesh, pleased to leave it for her to see. Under the checkered hood, his face was relieved of genial duties; it was no closer to him than his foot. Fingers sized and then left him alone.

'You're getting a tum,' she said.

'Athol said the same. That must constitute a quorum. I shall have to give up fish fingers.'

'Give up ketchup,' she said.

'Why are you so sane?' he said. 'I've been reading his

38

book. He gave me his life-story, in manuscript, and I've been dipping into it. Quite fascinating. One doesn't know whether to believe it or not. Actually, I believe it. I think I believe almost anything. Man's fate. What's woman's?'

'Man, isn't it?'

'He was quite a Casanova, if his confessions have any truth in them.' Gideon drew the bedclothes down and sat into his half of the bed. Flowers were printed about Pamela's thighs. Her slim legs were golden from the warmth of the sheets. She fretted one knee against the other and opened her eyes a little wider, as if asking whether she had passed. He smiled, with affection, and bitterness. He had written a different scene. 'This house is too small,' he said. 'I don't know why you want to stay in it.'

'I don't want to stay in it,' she said, 'but it is useful having a roof over our heads.'

'I could easily write one of those serials, you know. If we were nearer London and I could get some connections. Hello-it's-Jack could give me an in. Mortgages aren't that difficult at the moment. Why stick in the mud when we could stick in the clay?'

'I'll go anywhere you say,' she said, and her fingers were apologising, too generous for pleasure.

'Let's not now,' he said. 'I don't think you really want to.'

She slid her legs flat and was full length, looking up at him, drawing breath, so it seemed, through that little crack between her front teeth. She had first been called Oxford because of the marmalade colour of her curls. They were bunched over her forehead and gave her a little face that fitted into the bent pillow, neat as a divot. 'Come on,' she said, 'don't be a spoil-sport.'

He took her hand and kissed the fingers, sipping the bones. His hand went the length of her arm, under the cotton to the stubble, and his thumb jogged her nipple. 'I could kill you sometimes,' he said.

'You could kill me any time.'

'I love you, Oxford.' He leaned his mouth against hers. She had to take her breath through him. He stayed there till she gasped and shifted. One leg pushed the covers back and, with a gesture he liked, she pulled the nightie up and showed rusty curls. He sat up and considered her until she moved, to prompt him. She turned and was on her back, face enlarged again; she seemed to be asking him to say that there was nothing wrong with her, between vanity and apprehension. 'And twenty years are but as yesterday,' he said.

The whooping sirens could have been receding until, suddenly, they were in the street. Pamela said, 'Mandy!' and was in her dressing gown, a hand making sense of her hair. They got in each other's way across the landing to Miranda's room and looked down into Beacon Terrace where blue light fanned the bricks. Two badged Fords, a Granada and an Escort, had stopped in the middle of the street, two or three houses further up from number seventeen.

'Can't be anything to do with us,' Gideon said. 'They're probably raiding old Mrs Stinson, well-attested East Midlands pusher and god-fearing mafiosa.'

Pamela looked down at the invasion and put a hand across to each of her own shoulders and seemed to despise his quick confidence. 'Something's happened,' she said.

'A baby is born every split second,' he said. 'And another conceived. Something is always happening, but not always to us, for which relief brief thanks, no?'

She leaned against the window pane, pressing for more from the show. There were peaked caps and two helmets down there, and a mackintosh. They were up at the Monahans', weren't they? 'You didn't call them, did you?'

'I don't command that kind of muscle,' he said. 'About Tom you mean? Of course not. And if I had, they'd scarcely have thrown a girdle around the world.' He stood against her, snug in the cleft of her firm behind. He lifted the folds and found flesh and wanted her there, with her head against the glass, eyes on the street. Hands on her slim hips, he liked it in the blued darkness, with Miranda's mural at his shoulder, the Tuscan village, the donkey, the drying pimentos. He went home, not quite sure which tight darkness he was living in. He held her, forced almost to stay where she was, between him and the business below. One hand at her breast promised tenderness, an afterthought. Did she have to cough? She coughed again and he sprang from her. She turned and coughed and smiled and said, 'Sorry, must have been the angle!'

'I suppose I'd better go down,' he said, 'and see if they need any boy scouts.'

Sid Minches, in a sleeveless nylon parka and a tweed cap with a large boss on the top (he took his holidays in Brittany), was leaning in at the window of the leading police car. 'Hear what's up, Mr Shand? Young Tracy's gone missing. Gavin sent her down the Paki shop for some fags and she's not been back since. They've only just twigged she wasn't home. Looks nasty, doesn't it? Two hours, all but.'

Aileen Monahan was in the doorway of her house. The police lights bruised her face again and again. She had the black shawl about her shoulders and her black hair completed a frame around all her gallant sufferance. She was blessed with anguish. 'Oh Gideon,' she said, 'oh Gideon, Gideon, what are we to do?'

'They'll find her, Aileen,' he said, 'never fear.'

'He's a good man,' she said, and he could feel the warmth of her breath, 'he's a good man, believe me, and never unkind.'

Her lies touched him like a caress. The hope of tragedy hooped her with a tracery of thorns. Gideon almost wished it for her, to complete something the blue eyes already looked for; vindictiveness and sympathy were in the same plot. Her hand on his sleeve and the tearful steadiness of her gaze had a dumb wisdom that mothered him, even in her distress. She made him a man, with all her nonsense.

Monahan came out of the front room with Inspector Telfer. He was in shirt sleeves, with a Fair Isle sweater under his braces. It seemed that he had dressed in a hurry; he looked a joke which his muscles dared anyone to find funny. Telfer's stoop had worn his mackintosh shiny. He was pulling wool-lined leather gloves over raw fingers. 'She'd no call to do this,' Gavin Monahan was

41

saying, 'no call whatsoever from my point of view.'

'Them Pakis,' Aileen said, seeing the inspector. 'If they've done anything to her – '

'I'll kill them,' Gavin said. 'I swear to God.'

'I've never known them use violence to anybody,' Gideon said. 'They seem markedly peaceful. So do their children.'

'I thought we was finally safe,' Monahan said, 'I shoulda known better, should I not? They'll have me to reckon with, that I promise you.'

'Where are the boys just now?' Gideon asked the question for Telfer, who was making an exercise of thrusting each finger to the limit of its leather stall.

'They went over the club, Mr Shand,' Aileen said. 'I thought little Tracy was with her dad. He thought she was with me. Just like before: with our Sharon. Do you think they've come after us? I think they've come after us.'

'She'll turn up,' Telfer said, as if he had worked something out on his fingers. 'They nearly always do.' He looked at Gideon as though he had not seen him before. 'You're a friend?'

'A neighbour,' Gideon said. 'Gideon Shand.'

'Oh yes,' Telfer said.

Gideon wished subtleties on the inspector, and was ready with answers to them, but the snort of a mauve Mini, measly with rust, drew his attention to the street. Miranda was clearing clean hair from her forehead as she made a grateful face at Piers Rougier. In his khaki sweater, the young clergyman could have been an open-necked cadet who had yet to put up his pips. He had a lot of red hair and wire-rimmed glasses. His face was handsome enough to suggest that he did not really need the glasses; there was a sort of tact in their owlishness.

'Well, well,' Miranda said, 'excitements! What's it all about then?'

'Young Tracy Monahan, she seems to have disappeared. I'm glad you're all right.'

'Isn't that amazing, Piers, after what we were just talking about? My father in God has been telling me about little Geoffrey and now here we are with . . . Oh

42

sorry, is it heavy then? Bet she turns up; she's no one's helpless little victim, that one. Shall I whisper it, and not necessarily in Gath? She sometimes looks to me as if she was on the game already.'

Piers had walked over to the panda car where busy-eyed Telfer was talking into a hand-set. Police light sparked in Miranda's eyes like the snap of a flint repeatedly struck. 'You might tell Pam what's going on,' Gideon said, 'when you go in, because . . .'

'You're not going to deprive me of the chance to search heathland and canal bank for a trace of little Trace, are you, dad? Not to mention fame and fortune. I might get on T.V. and be discovered as a potential star of regional news even. Imagine, I could gain an audition for the latest local lovely to be able to mispronounce the title of the next programme.'

'Miranda, that coach is turning into a pumpkin, if you look closely.'

'Night, dad; night, Rev. Night, all.'

'Miranda is indeed meet to be admired,' Piers said. 'She puts one in the gerundive mood.'

'Who was little Geoffrey?' Gideon said.

'You remember the Chaworth martyr, surely.'

'*That* Geoffrey! I don't actually go back quite that far. I thought it was one of your parishioners, assuming you have them in your position.'

Piers looked at Gideon. There were times when you could see a man thinking, and Piers was a thinking man. He had published articles on local curiosities and, having read philosophy at Cambridge, he was working on a study of ethics and perception. In spite of his battle-dress, there was something of the dandy about him: he had decided how he was to look. He was ten years younger than Gideon, but he managed to be his examiner, for all that. At once intense and impersonal, his present appearance made him the superior even of Telfer. He seemed to belong to a secret and privileged rank. Modesty was his transparent incognito.

When the Monahan boys trooped home just before midnight and said that they had not seen their sister all evening, Telfer decided to organise a quick search. 'So

that we know where we are.' The police had already
knocked on most local doors, but it was worth a cull
down the Nottingham Road and across the racecourse.
Gideon went into number seventeen and collected the
commando torch which Tom had given him for his
birthday. It had a supplementary switch to make it blink.
('Especially for flashers,' Miranda had said. 'Predictable,'
Tom said, 'that.')

Darren Monahan approached Gideon as he came
through the gate into the street again. 'Do you mind if I
come with you, sir?' the boy said, in his hoarse voice. It
lent him a tone of intimacy. 'Me mother says I can.' The
blue eyes looked out from their puckered shells. 'You can
ask her if you like.'

'Tell me, Darren, what happened tonight?'

'Sir?'

They were passing Steggles' gate. Gideon wondered
whether his letters were still in the box. There had used
to be a numbered tag which promised that the previous
collection had gone, but now there were no such guaran-
tees. 'At the football.'

'They won, sir, in the end, we did, three-one.'

'Who scored the goals?'

'Bryan got one. Maybe two.'

'Good news and bad news,' Gideon said.

'Sir?'

He took the boy's hard hand to cross the road. The
corrugated fence around the derelict grandstand bellied
and rumbled, thunder without lightning. The wind was
driving hard down the Nottingham Road. Rust had
nibbled scabby hoops in the noisy metal; Gideon ducked
through, followed by Darren and Sid Minches, his
cigarette and his wheezy breath. 'Why don't you nip and
check among the seats, Sid? Darren and I'll have a look in
the cellars.'

'Smells of wee,' Darren said, as they went down the
passage to the tote room. The sellers' booths rustled with
an old autumn of fallen bets. Gideon divided the darkness with his torch. Somehow the boy was always in its
light. He seemed to dart about the room like a moth.

'Tell me, Darren, do you ever come round here at all?'

'Not really, sir.'

'Meaning you do?'

The boy's mouth was moist with words it did not utter.

'Did your sister ever come with you? Tracy? Because if you have any idea where she might be, now's the time to say. I won't tell anyone.'

'Why tell then?'

'That it came from you. Did she ever say anything to you about running away?'

'I want to go home now,' the boy said. 'I want to do a wee.'

Speeches chattered in Gideon's head. He took the boy by the collar and led him out of the tote room, along the yellow smells and out on to the grass. The fence swayed as if an army were storming it. Darren reached under his shorts and looked serious. Gideon switched his torch's blade towards the grandstand. 'Anything, Sid?'

'A few losing tickets is all, Mr Shand. Somebody's horse is still running then.'

'No shortage of those. Perhaps we should try shouting. She's not all that bright, little Tracy. She may not even realise that anyone is out looking for her. A whole troop of people're more likely to make her hide than anything else. Let's give her a shout. Tracy! Oh Tracy? TRAY-AY-ACY!'

Other searchers relayed the cry. The night rang with the girl's name. It seemed to reach the horizon and then fade as Darren rejoined Gideon, lifting one leg to the side. 'She's never here, sir, is she?' The boy rubbed a used hand down his jeans. 'I reckon someone knows where she is.'

'None too warm, is it?' Sid Minches said. 'I'm off home for a muffler.'

'Take Darren with you, Sid, would you? He needs his mum.' Gideon shivered and ambled to the fence and undid his buttons and watered a bald patch of ground. Why did he keep the torch on?

'Case of plan P, sir, is it?'

'No law against it, is there, inspector?'

'I'll have to check the book. I gather that you and the Monahans aren't exactly good neighbours, Mr Shand.'

'Oh? I think *we*'re quite good, actually, in the circumstances.'

'There's a history, I believe.'

'And more to the point, if you must make one, there's a geography. My son has to pass their house on his way to and from school every day unfortunately, which is roughly equivalent to a rabbit having to pass a fox's burrow equally often. Which would you say was the bad neighbour?' Gideon extinguished the torch.

'Little Tracy,' Telfer said, 'when did you last see her yourself?'

'I saw her this evening. About six o'clock. On the way home from school. She was doing one foot up and one foot down along the kerb.'

'Has she ever been in your house at all, sir?'

'None of the Monahans has ever been in our house. We take a good deal from them, but I should certainly feel entitled to repel boarders.'

'You sound rather aggrieved, if I may say so, Mr Shand.'

'Having one's children assaulted does have its unpleasant side.'

'You didn't see any strange motors in the street?'

'Had I seen anything,' Gideon said, 'I should not have failed to tell you.'

'We keep our eyes open,' Telfer said, 'but we can't see everything.'

'That's rather a comfort,' Gideon said. 'Do you think it might have been revenge?'

'For what, Mr Shand?'

'They did come from Derry,' Gideon said. 'There must be some crackpots about who think they shouldn't be here, or shouldn't be there, or whatever people think who can't think at all.'

A policeman and three civilians, among them Piers Rougier, ducked through the yawning fence. The leading torch haloed Telfer's head with a beading of mist. 'I think we'd best resume in the morning,' the inspector said. 'We can be more methodical in the light. And, of course, she may come home in the meanwhile.'

'Little Geoffrey did, after all,' Piers said.

'Though not before there had been a certain amount of

46

damage to people and property, so the legend promises.'

Telfer frowned on the parade of banter between Piers and Gideon. The two of them walked back towards Beacon Terrace with the straight faces of scholars rebuked by the sports master. 'I've been doing a little digging, as I was telling your daughter. The odd thing isn't so much that he disappeared as what happened to him afterwards. Even the local guidebook acknowledges that the mob burned down the ghetto – '

'It was more or less where the football ground is, wasn't it? I like to show a little knowledge.'

'There's a cul-de-sac called Snog Court, near the slaughter-house, which I take to be a corruption of Synagogue Court, though I don't want to get too Proustian about it. Anyway, wee Geoff was never kidnapped at all, of course. He may have been kidding, he may have been napping, but he was certainly never baked in any Passover pasty. The only people who suffered that particular fate were the kosher baker and his twelve-year-old son.'

'It is not only under Pontius Pilate that men have been known to suffer,' Gideon said.

'Several other persons of an immigrant cast were chucked in the river, but the fate of little Geoff has never clearly been established, until now. I believe I can show that he was the only participant in the drama – if indeed he can be said to have participated – who came to an undoubtedly *bad* end. If I've identified him correctly, he was hanged at Lincoln when he was twenty-four years old, for blasphemy and robbing churches.'

'Hanged for a sheep, after being spared as a lamb? God moves in a mysterious, not to say downright perverse way, doesn't He rather?'

'Can the ubiquitous be said to move at all?' Piers said. 'The ghost of Parmenides walks and talks, with our heads tucked underneath his arches.'

'God never ceases to puzzle me,' Gideon said.

'Then He renders you a service perhaps.' Piers borrowed adenoids from a stage curate. 'Miranda is a very extraordinary girl. Am I allowed to say that?'

'I know no interdiction.'

47

'You must let her go wherever she wants to go. There's something – what? – limitless about her possibilities.'

'I hardly see myself in the role of a barrier to her progress.'

'You've given something up, haven't you?' Piers said. 'You'll think me impertinent to have said so, but you – you're a clever man, who for some reason – '

'Are you reading my palm, Piers, by any chance, without holding my hand?'

'I've said the wrong thing. I'm sorry, formally, but I mean no harm. You're still a young man, aren't you?'

'Perhaps I should be allowed to go where I want to go, which is bed, just at the moment. The self-employed also carry their crosses, indeed that is their main employment, I sometimes think.'

'I should like to be your friend,' Piers said.

'I appreciate – '

'Dammit,' Piers said, 'can't you bloody well take me seriously? Do you think so little of me? You tell me something's wrong and when I try to answer your call, you adopt this tone of – of – dated courtesy. Courtesy is the devil sometimes.'

'You strike me as quite grammatical yourself at times. Your articles in the specialised press positively brag of their erudition.'

'That's all irony,' Piers said. 'I didn't know you read them.'

'The *St James's Review*? Doesn't everyone?' Gideon said. 'I'm not sure what you mean by friendship.'

'A friend is someone who can be honest with you; nothing more, nothing less.'

'How does one distinguish him from an enemy then?' Gideon said. They were whispering now. Beacon Terrace had turned out most of its lights. Rags of cloud were polishing the stars. 'I sometimes think that God is just another name for death.'

'And where does that leave a man of God? I think He may be another name for life. At least that's the best answer I can offer in the way of a late equaliser. Heads or tails? We shall see, or not see. City won three-one, I hear.'

'They'll never keep Bryan Grant now, will they?'

'Leave her her pride, Gideon,' Piers said. 'Leave her malice. Don't civilise her before she's had her days in the wilderness.'

'Hanged at Lincoln, was he?' Gideon pressed the dented door of the Mini shut behind Piers who sat there, like a sedate sentry refusing a photogenic smile, making a decision to be direct and a little dangerous. Then he started the car and reversed between the parked cars, one arm along the seat where Miranda had sat.

'Dragged to eternity by the heels,' Gideon quoted to the sky. He stood near his own house, but then set off, as if a shop might still be open, on an errand he could not name, fuelled by a mood that carried no ticket. He knew he would come back and he had no purpose in walking up past the Monahans, for all his purposeful style. He went like a spy, the night-prowler whose wakefulness alone was a questionable crime.

Strang's Steps came steeply down from the Close to join Beacon Terrace after cutting under the castle walls. Over four hundred prisoners were still kept in the hard old building. Gideon gave fortnightly lectures to the inmates, on Our Century. At first, he had gone there eager to redeem and instruct. He liked to think that he could win the interest of the prisoners by the directness and energy of his manner. He was disappointed when the numbers soon diminished. A local psychoanalyst who also lectured in the prison gave him the Freudian answer: he was failing to satisfy the inmates' craving for orality.

'What do you mean?' Gideon would not forget having asked. 'I don't allow them sufficient time for their own opinions?'

'I mean, my old son, that you don't dish out enough fags.'

'I don't believe in smoking,' Gideon said.

'It's not a matter of faith, old lad. Just take a few packs of slow death with you and leave them lying about, *and* forget to collect them at the end. You'll find Jack's appetite for the subtleties of the democratic process and his understanding of the scandal of totalitarianism in our time will both sky-rocket.'

Gideon had been a popular lecturer ever since. There

49

was no greater disgrace in thus easing the prisoners' condition than in sugaring any other kind of pill, but he had become their dupe in becoming their stooge: he could not be one of them if he had to be nice to be so. Such understanding was a kind of fall.

He climbed Strang's Steps, sometimes pressing a knee with his palm on an abrupt stretch, until he came to the landing that made a break in the ascent. In gardens adjacent to the prison, the taller trees had been cut back lest they prove accomplices to an escape. Freshly severed limbs were stacked against the bossy wall. A single lamp laid a drugget of shadow on the steps. Buttons of moss seemed to hold it to the greening stone. Gideon spotted eyes under the lopped bough. Could it be little Tracy, sly as the baby bear in one of Miranda's first books, who was as obvious as anything, in an oak tree, if you looked carefully, but who, if you looked again, seemed to have vanished into the foliage? Did not Piers still see God in England in much the same tricky way?

Old Mrs Stinson's Tom slid from the logs, shrugged a back leg and spilled up the wall. There was a flutter of spent leaves and then, as if the cat had turned into something heavy-footed, Gideon heard the rap of heels. He was a criminal without a crime: what excuse did he have for being in that place at that time? Strang's Steps joined the landing at an angle, so that Gideon was able to back away and be out of sight, hurrying down to Beacon Terrace. Panic kicked him left instead of right, up towards the turning into Jackson Avenue, a bulging street of Victorian mansions, with a vet's on the corner and solicitors and estate agents on the way up to the Close. Cars had to be parked with their wheels turned in to the kerb in case their brakes sprang free and they hurtled into Beacon Terrace. Pamela's patient Mr Fagin (Tuesdays and Fridays) lived next to J. Syme, vet.

Cora Simmonds, carrying a cretonne-lined basket and a transparent plastic umbrella, her head luminous in a white, black and scarlet scarf, emerged from the bottom of Strang's Steps, shoes tapping and clicking as her loose heels hit the pavement and then snapped against the bottoms of her feet. The black moon of her face drew darkness out of the night and became the essence of it. A queen in jet nylon fur and silver-clocked stockings, Gideon watched her all the way to her house. When she turned the lights on, knives flashed back and forth in the front room, from landscape to landscape. She moved through the blades in uncurtained show.

Gideon climbed his own stairs in darkness. The bedroom was downy with sleeping breath. He left his clothes on the floor and felt for the bed. Why was Pamela on his side? He touched the sleeping shoulder, the uncurled hair, the cheek, the lips, and realised that it was Miranda. He stood above the two women, naked, and as he made sense of them, cupped his balls in his hand and drew them forward, like someone checking the change in his pocket. Then he went across the landing and into Miranda's room and lay down on the narrow, unused bed, under the glassy eiderdown. He had many dreams.

3

Pamela was in white stockings and shallow shoes, the
green skirt belted slim with a professional buckle,
when she came in to say, sorry, but Athol Simmonds was
on the doorstep. Gideon was slow to move from under
the covers. His nakedness was a kind of confession and,
like all confessions, it carried accusation with it. He was
not ready for the part he had to play and frowned at
Athol, imperial in dressing gown and slippers. Simmonds
wore a green tweed suit, with a half-belted jacket, and a
red roll-necked sweater. He smelt of advertised products
Gideon was in no mood to buy.

'I apologise for the ungodly,' Athol said, 'but I know
you're an early riser and I'd appreciate your opinion on
something.'

'Come on in,' Gideon said. 'My opinions are all under
wraps in the back.'

'If it's all the same to you, would you mind stepping
over to ours? Cora would like to speak to you.'

Gideon went upstairs and pulled his clothes on, the
belt at its tightest notch, instead of a diet. It was not yet
the time when he usually went to work (after the
eight-thirty news and the first exchange of double-act
facetiae that followed it) but Athol's arrival came like an
interruption. What could Cora Simmonds want and what
could he want listening to her?

Cinder-black chairs surrounded a pedestalled, all-in-one-piece white composition table in the Simmonds' showy kitchen. An orange coffee-machine hissed on the laminated work-surface by the flush hob. An extractor fan conjured fumes into the garden. Cora was wearing a Mao-collared housecoat. A hot-tongued dragon lounged across its glossy scarlet lapels. 'You was *late* last night,' Cora said, her hair all beaded snakes today. '*Real* late. You want some coffee?'

'Thanks, but I'll have my tea when I get back to t'mill. Is something wrong?'

'Maybe right, maybe wrong,' Cora said. 'You was out looking for the Monahan kid, right?'

'The entire street was,' Athol said, cutting the bread with an electric knife. Sometimes the whole world was made of weapons and every sentence declared war. 'Except for me,' Athol added, having used the silence to be careful with the crust. 'How about some toast? Believe it or not, Shandy, I worked right through the whole to-do. I was hibernating like a hedgehog by the time Cora came stumbling home.'

'I'm surprised you didn't have the S.A.S. in here,' Gideon said. 'The police stopped at everything, which is the usual prelude for stopping at nothing. You had no idea little Tracy – ?'

'First I knew about it was on the local news when the alarm came on and poured our early cuppa. Cora was just telling me what happened last night and there it was, on the airwaves.'

'I do believe I saw little Tracy Monahan,' Cora said.

'Saw her? Where? When?'

'And *how*,' Athol said. 'That's the interesting part.'

'On a railway train.'

'You were on a train?'

'No, no, no,' Athol said, not sparing the Oxford marmalade.

'I was at my Sisterhood. And I saw this little girl, such a pretty thing, sitting on a train; she had something around her, a sash maybe, red and black. Burgundy shade.'

'She had this vision, Shandy.'

'Wearing the visiting side's colours. Got it! Well, I suppose she could have gone off with some of their supporters, or they could have gone off with her. Does this often happen: you going into trances?'

'I see you last night as well, Gideon. I see you flying all round the town. I see you flying round the Minster like a bat out of hell. I see you then and I see you later, with a young girl. You was in her bed.'

'A flight of imagination, Mrs Simmonds.'

'You've met Cora, haven't you?' Athol said.

'You was in her bed,' Cora said. 'A young girl. Small bed. Not a small girl, but a small bed.'

'Good heavens,' Gideon said, 'it so happens I did sleep in my daughter's bed last night. She wasn't in it, of course. She was in mine. With my wife. You *saw* me? How?'

Cora closed her eyes and pointed to the pinkish lids meshed with black. 'Real dark girl,' she said, 'not your colouring, not your wife's.'

'You've seen Miranda up and down the street,' Gideon said. 'Do you do a lot of this?'

'I have the gift,' Cora said. 'You have it, you use it.'

'Or it drops off,' Athol said. 'That's what they taught me in the gutter. No school like it.'

'Well,' Gideon said, 'that's all very interesting. I don't know what it proves, but it's certainly . . .'

A panel of Cora's housecoat fell open and he saw meat. 'You tell them about that train, Mr Shand, will you do that for me?'

'Cora doesn't want them to know it comes from her.'

'Call them from a call box.' Gideon felt that he had been passed the parcel. 'On your way to Blackley Cross, Athol. Even on your own phone, no one's going to trace it, for God's sake.'

'We felt we had to tell someone,' Athol said. 'You seemed the most sane person in the street. Someone we could trust.'

'Don't you want the credit,' Gideon said, 'if they find her on the London express?'

'All we want is she goes home safe to her mum and dad,' Cora said.

54

Pamela was strapping her equipment to the Raleigh. Tom had already left for school. In the kitchen, Miranda was leaning away from some Raisin Bran to blow her mouthpiece clean. 'I'm just on my way to Jenkins' knee,' Pamela said. 'Tea's on the table; sausage is in the pan; Mandy, you'll be late; see you at lunch-time.'

She rolled the bike into the street and stood into the pedals.

'Do you want me to run you?' Gideon said, frowning at the tepid tea.

'Mrs Yuck-Glendinning is always late,' Miranda said. 'I think she gets laid on the way to school on Thursdays. She does something crafty, anyway. Did you sleep all right?'

'I slept all wrong: dreams the whole night through. A retrospective of all my best nightmares, from Eden Grove School on up, and down. The arrangement is not going to be a permanent one.'

'Talking of permanent arrangements, what would you say if I told you I was going to marry a handsome clergyman who was rather hot in the organ department? Would you greet the revelation with stark incredulity?'

'I would greet it with the reminder that Mrs Glendinning need not always be late merely because she is sometimes late. Bertie Russell had something to say on the subject.'

'He had something to say on almost every subject, didn't he?'

'It's a little soon to talk about marriage, isn't it? How about doing it tonight? Has he proposed?'

'Do you know that if you pulled the stops out, really pulled the stops out, and played the thing at absolutely full volume, super extra plus, old Hope-Jonesy would literally explode the Minster, burst the walls and cover the whole town with ancient monument to an undisclosed depth? Chaworth could make the national news, dad! *On pourrait revivre ses moments de gloire!*'

'You'll what?' Gideon said. 'I'll tell you what you'll do: you'll get your skates on.'

'If we're leaving town, fond father, why the manic rush? Nothing will *happen* to me, you know, if I swan in half an hour late and take my place with silent dignity. You're such a slave to routine.'

'I've got work to do,' Gideon said, 'if you know what that is.' He waited for the postman, though, after making a new cup of tea. There were three bills and a letter from a B.B.C. producer, suggesting a 'possible talk' on the French *nouveaux philosophes*, about whom he had written an article in Flo Cameron's *New Edinburgh Review*. There was also a postcard from 'Yours-truly-Glenys-Harrington'. She wrote to him regularly, though they had never met, about his bridge 'causerie' in the *Sarocco Monthly*. Stephen Hellman had represented the company in a big case and, during a grateful dinner, he had steered one of the directors into appointing Gideon as the house magazine's Bridge Correspondent. Sarocco was a rich multi-national and had been made richer by Stephen's adroit advocacy, with the result that Gideon was generously rewarded for his seven hundred words and a clutch of interesting hands.

'Yours-truly-Glenys-Harrington' wrote in a fine and regular script; it was amazing how much she could put on one half of a postcard which almost always displayed a tourist attraction in or around London. Gideon fancied that she stole them. She began with a little flattery ('your usual high standards') and then 'dared to wonder' whether he had missed the possibility of a 'squeeze without the count' in his last column. The only incautious touch was that she filled in the symbols for hearts and diamonds with red Pentel in her tiny diagram. She was quite right about the squeeze. He was at once irked and grateful; he had not denied that there might be another way of playing the hand, but he had not seen her solution, which embarrassed him, even though it afforded him an easy subject for next month's piece. Pamela did not play bridge and never read his articles, but he was in two minds about whether he should mention his loyal reader by name. Would she like it and would people make more of it than was warranted?

Gideon was standing in the front room, near the telephone, conscious that he was precisely in a *mental* state: he was hesitating. He did not know what he was

56

going to do next, whether he would telephone the police and convey to them the unreliable information that they might find little Tracy on a train, with a burgundy and black scarf around her, or whether he would leave it to rational forces to conclude the search. There was something commanding about the implausible; what one did not believe in demanded to be honoured, as one's beliefs did not. The Simmonds had wished the dubious knowledge on him. Why should they pay him such a mocking compliment? Did they regard him as the easiest representative of order? He had canvassed for the Alliance in the election and they had seen him at his most reasonable and suppliant. He had not wanted Bill and Paula to move away; all his support for reason served a hidden desire, an allegiance less passionate than he might have liked but which worked on him as if it mattered intensely. Bryan Grant's transfer to a first-division club, again mooted in the press after his 'class display' of the previous night, seemed hardly less threatening, though Gideon rarely went to the City Ground and was not greatly concerned with the club's 'parlous position'. As he read Glenys's card again, to make sure that her analysis was compelling, he saw the postman returning to his gate. Backward sloping handwriting had pecked freckles from the brown envelope which he watched fall to the lino. It came from a certain Cyril 'You won't remember me' Lack who asked, on lined paper, for the title of a book about 'disappearing empires, I think it was, you once talked about'. Like the Sadleirs, Gideon's Open University pupils often moved out of his parish and sometimes they got in touch, though rarely more than once.

He should have started on the translation of *L'Inconnu*, but it promised to be so easy that he found it tempting to postpone. Hello-it's-Jack Knightley would probably have the *Meaning Of War* outline on his desk by now; could he possibly respond to it on the same day? It was difficult to start something new until one had had a reaction to the last tranche of work. How many small argosies did he have at sea? Articles, reviews, outlines for educational books or programmes, he could not send enough of them. In order to be dependent on nothing in particular, he had become dependent on everything in general; he could scarcely distinguish the ivy from the tree. Opening his drawer, he took out Athol Simmonds' manuscript, neglecting one call by answering another. He would have to do one of his long hauls at the translation; he could work right through the night, monastic penance for the secret scandal of procrastination.

Between the Athol of the previous night and the Athol whom he now rejoined in prison there was a lurch, of light and of character. Thinned and dignified by the black and white world in which he was clamped, the prisoner was translated into a bracket of the past where everything looked and felt different. Rejuvenation lifted the wattles from his throat and thickened the black curls. His concrete cell was smarter than the beach house. Gideon could envy his fear and his significance, and at the same time generously wish him ill, for Athol's own sake. Otherwise, the book would have to explain, in the end, why the survivor was living in Chaworth and how he came to be so accessible and so cheap. Gideon read the old map of his neighbour's life in the vain hope that somehow one road would not join with another, forking him into the mundane present. Might an impossible twist yet grace the story with tragic dignity?

The prisoner had several meetings with the prosecutor, Moses Freeman, known as little Mo. Freeman had had no very distinguished career at the bar and it was difficult for Athol not to become the accomplice, in some patronising spirit, of a man whom it had been so easy to outwit on other occasions. The banality of little Mo's tactics appalled the defendant who expected them to destroy him. Yet Athol had to respect his pomposity for the sake of his fellow-defendants. Innocence placed a lonely strain on him: charges which seemed a caprice of chance, in his own case, were matters of life and death for Matthew Kayser and the other blacks. Bram Pollock made no attempt to disclaim guilt; his energies were devoted to preparing the defence – and seconding the accusation – of the others. Athol did his best (it had always been better than Bram's) to support his partner's efforts, but the impending trial gave Pollock his one chance to be the leader; he did not advertise any gratitude for Athol's superior shrewdness.

When it came to court, little Mo conducted his rigged case with conspicuous punctilio. After the months of confinement, surrounded by a brutality which was never quite visited upon Athol, almost out of spite, it seemed, the courtesies of the air-conditioned trial were surprising and unconsoling: decorum, in such a place, had a counterfeit ring. Yet the judge's British tones and little Mo's sweaty rhetoric almost persuaded Athol that the defendants might yet be acquitted.

His dreams, at least for himself, seemed more and more to be justified. He could not resist a hopeful respect for the society of whose perniciousness he was more and more persuaded: it was hard not to connive at what looked likely to be his salvation. He had imagined such horrors, prompted by the cries of pain that splashed against his cell, that he too seemed to be fighting for his life, though it was never in danger. Now he was shocked by the realisation that he was in the dock not to be condemned, but to be acquitted. He was there to be the conspicuous proof that an unjust society is capable of justice. He dreamed of making a great speech in which he denounced the iniquity of men who could sentence Matthew Kayser to die but who found no fault in Athol Olivier Simmonds. In fact, of course, a man found 'Not guilty' had no right to be heard. Little Mo was the first to offer his hand when Athol was declared a free man.

He was not happy to leave his cell. Freedom lamed him. He excused himself at first to Pet because it had been so long. The truth was that he was not alone with her; her nakedness broke some rule she could never suspect. He wanted to want her, but the Japanese bed no longer worked its trick. She had missed him and she had missed it and she thought she knew what was needed. Her willingness was a kind of greed, as generosity sometimes could be. She was not impatient or unkind: she knew her Athol, he'd come good sooner or later. Meanwhile they went out to candle-lit dinners with their soft secret, a couple with nothing to hide, and their *tête-à-*

59

tête blown up in the papers to prove it. He was a despised hero, congratulated not for his innocence but for allowing the state to find him innocent, the brainy fool whose usefulness did not prevent his practice being ruined. Pet's family smiled at him for the first time: his humiliation made them clever for a change.

Because he had nothing to do, Athol decided to give more of his time to 'clinics' in neighbourhoods where sewage dribbled down the middle of dirt streets. He welcomed the change in official attitude: he liked to see them frown. He was followed and photographed by B.O.S.S. Their persecutions were a comfort; Pet's confusion was the gilt on his gingerbread. He offered her a divorce, but she insisted that she loved him. Vanity could not admit that she had made a mistake.

When Matthew Kayser's death sentence was commuted and he was sent to an island, for life, Athol was relieved, and – he had to admit it to himself, if to no one else – he was also disappointed. He would not have wished it otherwise, but he could imagine it so: there was slyness in the authorities' vicious leniency. There would be long cruelty out there, beyond the beaches, but no martyr, no tragedy, nothing final. Little Mo himself was the first to call with the news of the reprieve. Offended by the charmless reaction, he said, 'I'm not basically political any more than you are, Athol. I do a job.'

Had Kayser been hanged, would Athol have stayed in South Africa? Kayser had to live in chains and the free man could not endure it. Once again, Pet was offered a divorce and would not have it; she was determined to come with him to England. Reading the double-spaced pages, Gideon expected a last minute hitch, a change of heart, family pressure, something to throw Athol alone into the rampant liberality of Sixties London. But Pet was with him on the plane, to which her unsmiling parents did not accompany her: they sent a message that there was money for her in London to pay for a single fare home, as soon as she wanted it.

The immigrant couple lived in a one-room flatlet in Camden Town. Pet read all the banned books she had missed over the years. Athol abandoned learning as his wife began to discover it. He had to make a living and proved a shamelessly convincing salesman; his tongue at least could still work. She went to museums and used the public libraries; poverty made her energetic and resourceful. She found Athol a psychiatrist called Emanuel Davies, who advised him to tell her the truth, because what else could he tell her?

His love for Matthew Kayser was not easy to explain. It was a love which had nothing to do with sex or desire or possession, yet if it did not, why had it crippled him with her? How could something so pure, so right, something that could not be accurately qualified but was at the heart of what had happened, have cut him as it had? His gentlest blow blackened his wife's eye. She hit back with manifest loyalty.

His only remaining contact with the legal profession in London was when he gave advice to a 'liberation' organisation in Bermondsey. That was where he met Cora Briffault. She had a way of laughing till she sneezed and sneezed and 'Bless you' made her laugh again. As Athol's poster business expanded, Cora became his part-time secretary; Petula could not cope with the paper work and the telephone by herself. The two women liked each other; they would sometimes leg it out of the office for coffee and a sandwich. Athol enjoyed seeing them together; that laugh of Cora's was infectious. Pet almost caught happiness from her.

One night, after they had landed a big order from a chain of stationers, he took Pet to the Trattoria Terrazza and she was embarrassed because she had asked for the Parmesan with *spaghetti alle vongole*. She actually cried for shame. He hid her tears with a hug and, miracles, he was cured. They went home to bed and he proved it. Pretty soon, Pet's beauty was restored; he took her out to buy clothes, because things were improving on all fronts. They got upwardly mobile and rented a nicer flat, behind the Army and Navy stores. She became his lovely once more and he liked to have people in to admire her; they had a Sixties dining table, suspended on chains to leave leg-room, and he found interesting people to put their knees under it. He invested some money in a disco, and got more out, which made him a smart fellow. When they were alone, the two of them fell on each other as if the flat was not their own and each was deceiving someone else. He was rougher with her than he had been on the Japanese bed. She looked good in minis, and out of them, tights stretched between her parted knees, taken by surprise. She would pull them up again and go on putting a record on the turn-table or getting this recipe right.

The 'liberation' organisation was more garrulous than effective. At meetings of the council he drew girlie graffiti and could not wait to get home. Pet would sometimes be sitting there, one leg up on the Heal's triple-seater. They fucked before they said hello. When he told her that he was giving up black politics, she gave him a smile she had borrowed from Cora.

A few weeks later, she told him that she was pregnant. He arranged for the baby to be born in a private ward. On the big day, he drove her to the hospital in the Jag and did his togetherness stuff on her back when the pains began. He had never felt closer to her. And so it came about that at one moment there were four people in the room and, at the next, five.

The baby glistened in its white make-up and Athol caught a brief sight of its soft tool-bag. 'It's a boy, lovely.' The midwife turned away, with the child in her rubber hands, to wash it, efficient starch between her and the mother. 'Come on, lady,' Athol said, 'let's have him for his mum, shall we? After all, who's done all this work?' When she turned, he saw confusion in the midwife's calm. Looking at Athol and then at the blonde mother, she held out a black infant.

Pet smiled at him for the last time. 'Now you've got what you bloody well wanted, haven't you?' she said.

As soon as she was ready to travel, she went back to South Africa, where she married Piet Hokluyt. Cora Briffault turned out to be wonderful with Sean. She and Athol married as soon as he was free. He was sure that she knew who the father was, but he never asked her and she never told him.

Gideon decided to walk down to the Paki shop. When Pamela was working, he took care of lunch. It pleased him to make his business subordinate to hers. He would do nothing elaborate, a pie with leeks and a white sauce perhaps, some cheese with pickles, fruit. The formality of his preparations was a reproachful compliment. He laid a secret on the table and she seemed never to realise it. Sometimes, as he stirred, he would think of her with the Wing-Commander or with Mr Fagin.

A badged police car was coming up Beacon Terrace. Telfer was eating a sausage roll as he got out at the Monahans' house. It was still last night as far as he was concerned. Gideon hesitated and then went to hear the news. Telfer had no need to ring the bell for Aileen: she was out already. 'And isn't it the best news you've ever heard, Gideon?'

'She's all right, is she?' Gideon said.

'Gavin's all in,' Aileen said. 'He never slept a wink all night. Neither did I, but . . .'

'Where did she turn up?' Gideon said.

Telfer turned away to brush Moffatt's crumbs from gloves and moustache. The blackness of his upper lip was a kind of nocturnal medal, the mark of serious service. 'Some cleaners found her, so we're told. In a railway siding. They were going through the football special from last night. She was asleep on one of the luggage racks.'

'Everyone's been so kind.' Aileen's breath was close to Gideon. 'You'll never say anything, will you, Gideon? Gavin's never been the same since what happened; the shock of it changed him, changed all of us. We'll make it up to her. How are your two? The daughter'll be married before we know it, to look at her. He's a good man, he'll make it up to her.'

Telfer was using the hand-set, watched by his driver. When he was impatient he spoke slowly and was very articulate, but the restive moustache had a lot of exercise. Gideon was at his own front gate when he saw Cora Simmonds in her bay window. She sneezed two or three times before he turned his back on her.

By the time Pamela pedalled into the street, there was a camera car from E.M.T.V. at the Monahans' door.

Money had been offered for little Tracy's story, provided it was a good one, and a journalist was there to help her write it. While Pamela and Gideon were eating their pie, and tepid leeks, Gavin Monahan knocked at the front door. Throned in her father's arms, little Tracy had white ribbons in her hair and was wearing a new pink coat. 'We've come to thank you for your help, haven't we, Trace?' Monahan said. The sound man was inside the gate, with a boom. The cameraman zoomed in from the pavement.

'Thank you, Mr Shand,' Tracy said.

Gideon flicked a ribbon. 'Don't do it again, all right?'

'There'll be no more trouble, Mr Shand,' Monahan said. 'You have my word on that.'

Tracy's legs were wool to the knee in blue stockings, but a large silvery-blue bruise franked the flesh bunched against her father's tartan sleeve. Gavin Monahan looked back towards the director and then, on a signal, nodded to Gideon and went back through the gate into the street. Tracy waved, one thumb latched over a little plastic compact that was certainly not more than three millimetres thick.

4

L'INCONNU was written in the historic present. It took place in a hill town in the Périgord and its main character was a young man who had finally decided to renounce all hope of passing the *baccalauréat* and go into the army. He is waiting to be called up when one of the *profs* from the *lycée* which he has just left is said to have disappeared from his home. He is seen driving away in his car one afternoon and the next day he has failed to return. There is no specific moment when anything dramatic occurs. His absence seems perfectly explicable, in a number of ways, until, slowly, the time comes when there is no explanation for it. The mere stretch of hours turns a vague mystery into a drama. It is neither comedy nor tragedy; nothing has happened, but something has happened.

Daniel, the young man, is living a life of undramatic suspense, during the hot summer weeks, playing tennis at the hill-top club, where the shadows never seem quite to touch the red and green courts, and riding his *moto* to surrounding villages where dances are held. He is a person for whom this narrow mobility is a kind of imagination: there is nothing purposeful in his wanderings, but they fill him with the sense of possibilities which life itself seems on the point of denying him. He watches girls, but he rarely approaches one. His body is golden and brown and he is torn between laziness and the wish to do something testingly strenuous.

The man who has disappeared taught him for a few *trimestres*, Monsieur Carpentier, but he has no particular feelings about him. The teacher has come from a larger town and his wife has no local family, none of those myriad cousins who come to the aid of the lonely or the bereaved in rural France. It is a casual amusement to make a summer's gossip out of a couple who previously never excited interest. Marie-Christine teaches English and is obliged to go daily to the glass and concrete *lycée* whose modernity is a kind of imposition, standing adjacent, on a separate spur, to the tiled disorder of the old town. Daniel has been particularly inept at languages; in all the years of supposed study he can say nothing more than 'Good morning' in Marie-Christine's special tongue. And when he does this first, astride his Peugeot, the bulbous orange crash-helmet like a fat *brassard* on his elbow, it is without warmth or even malice. It is as if he was saying something to no one. The disappearance of her husband has made the woman a solid ghost. There is nothing one cannot imagine saying or doing to her.

Daniel is neither soft nor vicious. He is one of the *jeunes gens*, an unprotesting generality, reliant on the indulgence of his mother, who works as a *femme de ménage* at the local doctor's surgery, to sustain his pride. He attaches his attention to Marie-Christine for the sake, it seems, of example: he wants to know what someone else is like and this woman, forsaken and yet obliged to live on, is as good a target as any. During that hot summer, so the television tells them, in its Parisian accent, there is an epidemic of a particularly haphazard malice. The heat has driven the children of the tower blocks in the suburbs of big cities to play in the gullies between the concrete cliffs where the subsidised tenants, too poor to join the rush to the country or the sea, are marooned during their holidays. The noise of the children infuriates men who, normally, are not obliged to pass their daylight hours in their flats. They yell for silence and the children either pay no heed or make a game of denying it. The first child is killed in mid-July, a little Algerian who bleeds to death in a vandalised lift. The scandal of the shooting – his chest has been broken by an air-gun pellet – is widely reported. Nothing is so quickly imitated as the unthinkable and quite soon a number of children have been wounded and another killed. The deadly game becomes a scourge and a sport. Children deliberately provoke the danger which graces their days with significance and makes every excursion a form of daring. The victims are so urgent for victimisation that nothing can be done to divert them. They do not want portable *discothèques* or the '*animateurs*' who come to organise their leisure. The threat of death or injury puts a spring in their steps. They are anonymous celebrities, tracked by television crews and quizzed by ministers who have interrupted their rural retreats.

The heat in the Périgord is unprecedented. The rivers grow shallow, but their dangers are increased: one of Daniel's *copains* is drowned among the reeds, while friends laugh from the bridge. Daniel is bewildered by his own indifference to Jean-Bastien's death. He goes to the funeral, in a suit and tie, and he watches the tears of the bereaved mother, who says again and again, '*C'est pas possible, c'est pas possible*,' until Daniel feels a smile nagging his lips, like a stranger tickling him. After the funeral, he gets on his *moto* and rides up and down the twisting road between the village and the green valley where Jean-Bastien was snagged by the reeds. His *moto* makes a loud noise, but no one comes to object. He rides up and down until he runs out of fuel. Luckily, he is on his way down and is able to roll through the ghost of the noise he has been making as far as Paoli's garage. He is still wearing his suit and tie. Sweat oils his face and trickles under the tight shirt.

The new tank of *deux temps* fails to revive his provocative mood. He goes gently up the hill and drives, as if he had an appointment, to the small house, where a doctor used to live, in which he knows he will find Marie-Christine.

'You were not at the funeral,' he says.

The heat has swollen his lips and makes his eyebrows glisten. She makes no spoken reply to his accusation, which is conveyed with forced vehemence. She is sitting at the table in the kitchen reading a book. A bowl of white beans is in the centre of the flowery plastic cloth. Their skins pucker before they swell. She wears a yellow overall and her hair is up over her ears; strands fall and need to be pushed back.

'He was in your husband's class,' Daniel says. 'He was his *prof principal*.'

She goes to the basin and takes a cloth, damps it, twists it and brings it to where Daniel is watching her, frowning. She squeezes the cloth again; drops fall on the tiles between them; then she wipes his brow, his cheeks, his lips. The tie is biting his throat. He can hardly breathe. She raises a hand and simply touches him on the elbow in dismissive invitation. He feels that he is bursting out of his clothes; her grave humour seems to connive at his drowning in the dry air. His hands go towards his tie, but the knot is too complicated, the gesture too degrading. He unzips his hot trousers and brings out his penis, stiffly roped with veins. He wants her to see his balls too. Her lips make a quirky move to one side, as if a new task has been added to her curriculum. She fetches a strand of hair from her ear and replaces it under the amber slide and then she sits down (a little shriek comes from the chair as she moves closer), and with an unkind look at his anger she touches first the hairs sprouting beneath his offered balls. She undoes the latch of his trousers and helps them over his hips. He stands with his arms folded as her thumb sizes his prick and fits a ring for it with her forefinger. She flicks gently at his balls, with her little finger, a smile of the hand, it seems, as she reaches the bottom of her slow stroke. The skin draws back as she quickens her movement; his nostrils gasp for air. His mouth hurts with its braced rigidity. She stops. He cannot believe it, but she stops and stands up. Pride forbids him to speak. Every emotion is in his head: he is passion. She goes over to the cooker and he sees that the oven is on; a red light glows against the sun. She takes a thick glove and opens the door of the oven and removes a casserole which she places on the stone windowsill. The smell of rosemary primes his senses as she walks back to her chair and sits down to him again. She uses one finger, from balls to tip. He is dry now. She looks away to frown at the buzzing of a fly, a big one. Violence and fear are together in him. That one finger is stronger than he is. Her hand comes away from him and fumbles her ear. Love makes him want to brain her for that. But then she returns to him, quickens her pace, sitting a little more attentively to him now, but at an angle. When he spurts, he cries out, as if ready to confess, but she continues to work him, steadily, without haste, until the white slaps the floor, arching over her braced feet in a stabbing leap. A last drop she takes on her palm. He looks at the table and sees that she has been reading *Le Grand Meaulnes*, a schoolboy on the cover.

Daniel leaves the house without either of them saying another word. He feels something, he cannot say what it is, even to himself. He cannot distinguish now (any more than he could when she withdrew her hand and went, with that matter-of-fact walk of hers, to the oven) what it is that her action means to him. He cannot even boast of what she did to his friends; in theory, there is something demeaning in not having tailed her. He has not even had his hand on her slit.

He goes down to the river and stares at the reeds that latched Jean-Bastien while the killing water gorged his lungs. The *lycée* glints on the crest of the hill. He scans it with choking uncertainty: if he had worked harder, if he had learnt the vocabulary of his teachers, might he now know what to do or what to feel? He shuns the company of the *copains* whose derision has made him renounce his redoubled efforts to pass the *bac*. He cannot quite tell himself why Marie-Christine's lack of shame seems so shameful, nor why her indulgent response to his insolence should make him wish that he was something different from what he cannot avoid being. He cannot see his reflection in the shallow river, however hard he stares; his image is carried away downstream before it can develop. How long did she wait before she wiped the white trace of him from the kitchen floor?

Daniel has not been particularly interested in Marie-Christine or in the mystery of her husband's disappearance. He cannot say why he went so demandingly to her house and he is, if anything, more impatient than before when his mother, who loves to gossip, comes home with the latest rumour. There is nothing protective in his wish for the subject to be dropped; on the contrary, he dreads it not least because he now has an irrational hope that he is somehow the object of suspicion. He dreams of disposing of the absentee's body. The corpse changes its size with furtive rapidity; he never knows when he will inadvertently produce it instead of small change from his pocket. If he uses his *moto*, on a dream errand, he fears that the schoolmaster will fall from the saddle-bag when the machine tilts against the kerb. He spends one hot night looking for the body among the market stalls and thinks that he sees Madame Parodi's mongrel with the remains of it between his wet jaws.

When he sees Marie-Christine in the village (she has to go to the shops), he turns his back in accusing disgust. He likes to think of her being prosecuted for murder. He wants to see her taken away. He fancies her bewilderment at the abuse of the crowd, in which he himself figures, alongside the drunken peasants, the one-legged veteran and the *ancien collabo* making common cause, the ugly women and the knock-kneed girls. Their malice is contemptible, but he cannot resist letting her see him among the vicious crowd. He conceives of a special intimacy between them, sparked by his open refusal to help her. Dream and reality are confused: Daniel would be done with the uncertainty, even at the price of injustice. Injustice indeed becomes delicious to him. Although there is no practical chance of it happening, he can see Marie-Christine being led to the guillotine. She raises the hair from her neck and tucks it under her amber slide. He wants the head.

During the summer, several unidentified bodies are found in various parts of the country: 'C'est normal,' the local *gendarme* tells Daniel's mother. Pictures of the dead men are brought to Madame Carpentier in case she can identify any of them as her husband. The process is bureaucratic routine, but there is an absurd link between the regularity with which the *gendarme* performs this official activity and the volume of gossip in the village. It appears that every corpse in France is pointing its finger at Madame Carpentier. The frequency of these random deaths seems to amount to an indictment. She neither laughs nor cries at the fatuous rumours. Daniel watches her secretly. His day has a purpose. He seems bored by the whole issue and never ventures an opinion when the subject is discussed. 'I don't know what I think,' is all he will ever say.

He cannot believe, in his ordinary moments, that she has disposed of her husband. Where is the body and where is the car? The likeliest thing is that Marie-Christine has simply been deserted. Yet he resists this conclusion. It would entail the end of his adventure. His desire requires her complicity in some dark purpose. Perhaps espionage is involved, or drugs. One day she takes the bus to the big town some thirty kilometres away. He follows on his *moto*. The bus arrives long before he does and he has the panicky pleasure of trying to find her in unfamiliar streets. Had he passed his *bac*, this is the place where he would have come to begin his university studies. He would have known all the streets which now present themselves to him as a maze. He is almost persuaded that she has gone elsewhere, perhaps having lost patience with her show of resignation, and that he is indeed on the trail, however cold for the moment, of a dramatic plot. Perhaps she has a lover; perhaps she has received a secret call or perhaps – could it be? – she wants to see him somewhere unobserved by local eyes. The more frantically he looks for her, the greater his desire and the greater his hope that her evasion is some sort of challenge to him. He begins to think that his show of indifference has maddened her into coming to the big town in order to find a stranger to whom to offer herself. He remembers visiting the place on a hot morning, in order to see a dentist, and a woman getting off a bus, carrying a green umbrella although there was no sign of rain. He read the brittle article as a futile weapon and also as a trademark. He was quite sure that she was a prostitute, though there was no reason why a tart should tout for business on a Tuesday morning in a provincial town. His suspicions made all her movements delicious. She wore a slim green skirt and matching jacket, with a lacy white blouse and high-heeled shoes. He did not think that he wanted to go with her, but he wanted to possess her. He followed her to a café and watched her drink a cup of coffee as if it were an exciting act of intimacy. When a man came and sat at her table, carrying a flat briefcase, he wanted to believe that they had never met before, that the hurried arrival, the frowning look round the other tables, the brevity of their greeting, proved that they were strangers and that money would pass. After a few moments, the two of them had got up and left the café and walked through back streets until they came to a hotel, the Grand Hôtel de Pau.

He sees her coming out of a shop, Marie-Christine, carrying a new umbrella. Has she had her hair done? It is very neat and her eyes are bold and alive. As if he were a detective, Daniel pursues her with a sort of commissioned impertinence. Having followed her for several blocks, he follows her into a *pâtisserie* where she is buying a *pain au chocolat*.

'Madame,' he says.

'Daniel!'

'Will you come with me, please?'

She frowns and takes her change and, of course, goes out of the shop on his heels. He turns and stands close to her. 'What're you doing here?' she asks, as one might any young person.

'Will you come with me, please?'

'How did you get here?'

'That is of no importance.'

'Are you all right, Daniel?'

'I want you to come with me.'

'I don't know what you mean.'

'It won't take long,' he says.

She laughs and looks at her watch. 'I hope not. I have to catch the bus.'

'There's plenty of time for that,' he says.

'How did you get here?'

'That is of no importance.'

The repetition of the stiff phrase almost makes her

72

smile. Instead she touches his elbow, as if to reassure him. 'Where do you want to go?' she says.

'I know somewhere,' he says.

She follows him to the Grand Hôtel de Pau, which he cannot find without asking in a warehouse full of beer. She waits outside with her umbrella. He sees her, moving a step here and a step there, through the mottled glass of the warehouse door. She seems to swell and shrivel in the grey frame.

'*Daniel!*' she says, with her head on one side, when she sees the Grand Hôtel de Pau. 'Daniel, really!'

'Please,' he says. 'Please.'

The man at the desk asks for money in advance and she allows Daniel to offer it. They are given a key and go upstairs. It is unlikely that the sheets on the bed are clean. 'Daniel,' she says, 'what do you hope for from me?'

'Where is he?'

'Who is that?'

'Your husband. I think you know.'

'I don't have any idea.'

'Why do you stay? Don't you know they hate you?'

'I don't think they hate me,' she says. She sits on the bed, with her new umbrella leaning against the brass end. 'Why should they?'

'Because you endure it,' he says. 'Because you're so arrogant. You should go home, to your own *pays*.'

'I have a job,' she says.

'Why do you not apply for a transfer? Has he got another woman?'

'It's possible.'

'Take your clothes off.'

'Daniel, you're a nice boy.'

'I think you know where he is. I think you perhaps arranged for something to happen to him.'

'I'm a provincial schoolteacher,' she says. 'How could I arrange any such thing?'

'You humiliated me,' he says.

'I don't think so.'

'I've told no one of it,' he says.

She seems to understand that. She sighs and stands up. 'How do you know this place?'

73

'Do you know it too then?'

'Never. You've been here before?'

'Of course not,' he says. 'I know people who come here. It's the place to come if you want to fuck.'

'I'm too old for you,' she says. 'You don't care for me, why do you come back to me?'

'We have to finish something.'

'He probably works for the police,' Marie-Christine says, 'the man at the desk. In places like this, they always do.'

'You think I'm going to harm you? I'm not going to harm you, if – '

'Ah if! If what?'

'Take your clothes off.'

'This is already a crime, you know, Daniel. What you are saying to me is a crime.'

'Men say it to women all the time. You like it. They've said it to you. He's said it to you. Deny it.'

'You want it to be a crime,' she says, 'and you wouldn't be saying it unless – '

'After the war,' he says, 'they shaved women's heads, didn't they? They paraded them through the streets. That's what they would like to do to you. I've heard them say so.'

'You want me to do what I did before?'

'No,' he says, looking at the stained carpet on the sagging floor, 'I don't want you to do that. I want you to take your clothes off and then I want to fuck you. Properly.'

'Like a man,' she says. She sighs again and glances at her watch. 'Don't you have a sister, Daniel?'

'No one,' he says. 'Do as I say. You know you want to.'

'You're a clever boy,' she says. 'Oh, not because you think you know what a woman wants but because you know that I have no rights. I too have disappeared, isn't that it?'

'I don't know,' he says, and makes a peremptory gesture with his hand.

'Perhaps I am not doing right,' she says, 'for you. Perhaps I should not let you do this.'

'It's your decision, madame.'

'We are both victims,' she says, 'though I don't suppose you can see that.'

She seems to hesitate as she begins to take off her clothes. It might be an unfamiliar act; she looks to him for confirmation that she is doing it right. Power distresses him a little, though he tries not to show it. She takes off her skirt before her shoes, then her blouse. She wears a tight white bra. She draws the slip up over hips and her head and he stares at the black bloom she shows him for a faceless time. Her legs are slim and rather muscular, braced above those high heels. She shrugs through the straps of the slip; her hair is shaggy from it. She removes the amber slide and her face changes. '*Et toi?*'

He flushes at the premature intimacy. The second person singular, before he has had her, keeps him a child. He would like her more frightened than that. He puts his hand on her cunt and sinks his thumb in the hair, to puncture her. She looks weary at that and sits on the bed and takes off her bra, head forward, and then her shoes. She has the style of someone going to work. He is boxed in his clothes and feels the choking pressure of a drowning man at whom, from a distance, someone is smiling. He has no secret to offer her and turns away from her to take off his trousers and pants. Her body, when he catches a glimpse of it in the mirror of the *armoire*, is as white and tasteless as those soaking beans, but when he faces her again, there has been a change: he sees the tenderness of her flesh where her blouse has covered it, the shading under her arms, where she has shaved like a foreigner. His own body lacks hair, except in the groin and under his arms. He sees himself fat and without menace, a big baby, and has to twist away from her, to hide the horror of tears. He swallows salt like medicine and has to think hard thoughts before going towards the bed. The shag of the carpet nips the soles of his feet. She is reaching to pull back the tufted counterpane; diagonal creases rumple her back. Her buttocks are proud towards him and he sees the tuck between her legs, scribbled black with hairs, like the kind of art the groups of pupils scan, in smirking reverence, on worthy trips. She brings the cover under her body and her behind lifts to let it

75

pass. He puts his hands on her hips to keep her there and her face is lower than he expects as she looks up and back at him, to make sure, it seems, who it is. The prong of his penis bobs heavy before him. He brings her hips back to him and stands by the bed, as he stood before, and fits the notch of it under her buttocks. She reaches languidly between her legs and makes him more comfortable and rides back to trick him into her. He stands there, branding her with it, not bothering to move, taking slow inventory of the room in the Grand Hôtel de Pau.

She shifts her knees and works backwards slightly, biting again at him, and he sees the ripple of her back before he feels its pinch. He has his hands to spare. He does not want to reach her breasts and parts her buttocks, thumbs down. The little hole is puckered like the white flesh of the soaking beans. He puts a thumb on to it and her shoulders come up as she straightens her arms, sprinter at the start. He likes the little gasp she gives, as if she had no idea how late it was. One buttock in each hand, he presses them apart. She cries out, but does not slacken her urgency. His thumbs are together there, nail to nail. He bends his neck to her, but his tongue cannot reach. Saliva and sweat run from his mouth and he sweeps them into the cleft to soften her. He is looking up at the ceiling now. There is a race between them. He takes her unguarded cries as cunning and is set to thwart her. Her promise that she is happy is enough to curdle his pleasure. What he longs for he soon procures, a glance over her shoulder of a face yawning with shock and desire as he takes his glistening thickness from her cunt, like something newly born.

Her face in the pillow, hiding from decision, she leaves it all to him. He stands alone in the room and then, bowing his knees slightly, he leans against the coolness, slices her flesh with his, presses himself with his hand and feels the clinch of her around him. He leans forward and has his hands again on her hip bones, pulling her towards him, as a client in a shoe shop tests a fit. He slides into the brown, face up, and comes out, flinging a stutter of white on to smooth behind and arched vertebrae. He has his fingers around her neck in a moment and she is agile to duck away from him and look at her killer. He raises empty hands: only me.

It glistens on her flesh. Smelling, she walks it to the screened basin. There are towels and a bidet. He goes behind the screen after her and she is drying herself, reaching the places with nursing casualness. He puts a hand on her shoulder. 'Not finished,' he says.

'I have a bus to catch,' she says.

'Can't you afford a taxi?'

'No.'

'I'll give you money,' he says.

'And how do you have money, Daniel?'

'I should prefer', he says, 'that you not call me by a name.'

'I shall still know it,' she says.

'That is of no importance.'

'I must go,' she says, and walks to the bed and shakes her clothes into shape.

'Not finished,' he says.

'That's enough,' she says. 'More than enough.'

'I'll tell them,' he says, 'I'll tell them everything you made me do.'

'Made you do!'

'You're older than I,' he says, 'and more experienced. Those are things experienced people know how to do. I'll tell them you made me do them to you.'

'My husband will come back one day,' she says, 'and when he does I shall tell him what you did.'

'It will make no difference,' Daniel says. 'And I don't believe that he will return. I want you to stay here with me.'

'No, Daniel.'

'You are not to call me by that name.'

'I've given you what you wanted,' she says, 'and now I am going home.'

'You'll have to do what I say or else you'll have to leave the district.'

'I thought you were a nice boy.'

'There are no nice boys.'

'There is no question', she says, as she dresses, 'of your seeing me again.'

He puts his hands to her throat and smiles. She looks him full in the face. To be helpless gives her liberty. He moves his hands to her cheeks and kisses her on the lips. Their faces are so close that the tears seem to flow from her as well as from him. He does not sob; he is not unhappy. He simply cries. 'I love you. I love you.'

'My poor friend,' Marie-Christine says.

They hear the rhythm of a bed upstairs. He is embarrassed. The idea of the Grand Hôtel de Pau has brought him to it; he has imagined such things often enough, but unoiled reality affronts him. He becomes polite again. She puts one arm around his neck, at the door of the room, and kisses him on the cheek. He looks at her with the resentment of the lover whose own violence has made him captive.

Between the hour in the Grand Hôtel de Pau and their next meeting, Daniel behaves badly. He has always been a good son, a smiling neighbour, a laughing companion. Now he becomes sulky and gruff. He goes with an air-gun into the woods and shoots pigeons and doves. One flutters slowly to his feet, the deadly pearl in its breast, and settles, as if to hatch an egg, folding its whiteness around its death, head sunk on high shoulders. He picks it up in both hands and lifts it to his ear, like a grandparent's watch, and listens to its last beats. When it is dead, he holds it for a moment and then, abruptly, flings it upwards with both hands, a child with a model. It falls at his feet like a wet bag. He does not know what to do with it. The ground is hard and he cannot want to cover those white feathers with soil. He walks through the wood with the bird until he comes to a large oak into which he climbs, awkwardly, the dove in one hand. Finding a forked branch with a hollow at the shoulder, he nests the dead bird and covers it with leaves and flowers he takes from the floor of the wood. The next day he comes back, but he does not climb the tree and cannot see the whiteness under its shroud of leaves. He likes to think that the bird may have recovered and flown away.

He knows that it is dead, but he chooses to imagine it alive. Belief avoids decision and postpones truth. Freedom is the refusal to recognise necessities. Daniel's sullenness deserts him and he again becomes the amiable young person who can be relied on to lend a hand when it is wanted. He goes to see Marie-Christine and asks her if she wants any shopping. Would she like him to clean her windows?

Her new umbrella is in the stand in the hall. It has not rained since she bought it. 'Why did you buy this?' he asks her.

'Oh,' she says, 'no reason. Impulse. It will rain one day, won't it?'

'No one questions a person's right to buy an umbrella, do they?'

'No one except you,' she says.

'Did he hate you, madame?'

'He never said so,' she says.

'Do you miss him?'

'Yes.'

'I should like to be your husband,' he says.

'Oh Daniel,' she says, 'I don't think so.'

'I should like to be your husband,' he insists.

She touches his elbow. She has listened to his precision and sees the point of his odd confession. The boy does not wish to marry her, as she first assumed, but quite literally to be her husband, Pierre-Henri Carpentier, the absentee whose fate remains unknown, the thing she thinks of, the man who has possessed and then, apparently, abandoned her, the person, as Daniel likes to think, whose disappearance she may have plotted, the definition of her existence. No lover can be what her missing husband now is, the essence of her character. She can escape, this woman in her mid-thirties, only by becoming one of the women who go regularly to the Grand Hôtel de Pau. The umbrella is there for the bad weather in which she will have to walk, and stand. But then he looks at her again, this scarcely beautiful professional person, a member of the F.E.N. specialising in English, and he perceives her reality. She is the sort of woman for whom one runs errands; she cannot escape from the web of kindness and malice in which she consents to live. Suddenly, it is impossible to sustain the fantasy of her guilt, of her subtlety. He remembers the brown smell of her and she seems an everyday kind of lie, with her smile and her clean floor. She has bought the umbrella because it is the only kind of treat which a woman between widowhood and a garish trial can afford to give herself. Had she come home in new shoes or in a new dress, it would have proved that she was enjoying the fruit of the insurance for which she had disposed of her husband, or for which they had conspired to report his death. An umbrella is a pretty need and can be acquired without scandal.

When they have talked for a while, as he cleans her windows, she makes some coffee and he tells her of his regret that he is not clever. She offers the usual consolations, but she fidgets and looks at her watch. He asks her whether she does much reading and she is polite in indicating her literary preferences. At last, when he is still reluctant to go, she touches his thigh with her warm hand and then puts her palm on the soft mound. There is impatience in her generosity: she flicks at the button of his jeans. It is too much trouble to make an elaborate seduction. He feels sick, shakes his head and walks out of the house. Through the clean window, he sees her taking the coffee cups from the table. Her legs are like those of a retired cyclist.

The summer draws to an end. Soon Daniel will be in the barracks. He has a lucky escape on his *moto* when he narrowly misses a party of Dutch tourists in a narrow lane (two green Volvos one after the other) and is forced to cross the verge and ride into a field of deep tobacco plants. The heavy stems and lolling leaves slap him to a halt. The peasants dock the flowers from the plants where they can, but some always escape them. Breathing the sweet evening scent of the field, Daniel pinches a few flowers from the crests of the plants amongst which he has ridden, wheels his machine back to the road and returns to his home. He finds the envelope with his call-up date waiting for him.

The day Daniel is due to leave, the *gendarme* comes to Marie-Christine's door with yet another photograph. A man has been found high in the Pyrenees, dying of exposure. When the mountaineers ask him for his name, he simply smiles and replies: '*Je suis un inconnu.*'

Marie-Christine looks at the photograph and says that she is certain that it is her husband. The police come for her in a car in order to begin her journey to the mortuary for formal identification. Daniel sees her head in the frame of the car window as she is politely escorted to her painful duty. The rumour is, of course, that she has been arrested. They stand on opposite platforms at the local railway station, waiting to travel in different directions. She is carrying her new umbrella. The summer is about to be fractured by cracking storms.

5

Gideon finished the translation on an afternoon when
Pamela was at Mr Fagin's, her arthritic patient who
lived on Jackson Avenue. His family business was church
furnishing; the large house, with its Victorian turrets and
wrought-iron latches, was solemn with pews and altar
tables adapted to domestic use. He lived alone; daily
servants came to clean and cook. There was a single-
seater electric lift, running alongside the staircase, which
enabled him to reach his bedroom without assistance.
Pamela thought it unwise of him to be alone in the house
as much as he was. His wealth was not famous, but it
was enough to attract burglars and, perhaps, the kind of
sadist who was capable of torturing an old man in the
hope of further loot, or for the pleasure of it. Mr Fagin
was small and bent and he wore thick spectacles, but he
shook his head at her warnings. 'Let them come, my
dear,' he said.

Once Gideon had shut the text, he felt that the
translation was his own. He went through it with a green
Pentel, polishing the rough surface and excising, so far as
he could, any Gallicisms which the first draft could not
avoid. Into what language then did he hope to put it? The
tone had to remain French or the particularity was lost,
yet it could not sound French, except in the trivial
touches supplied by the names and the use of Monsieur

and Madame. He was commissioned to appropriate the text, but translation remained a kind of colonisation, a suave brutality that flattered the mastering tongue. He himself had no need of the version he had done; it was rougher than the original and something was certainly lost in it. It was an old charge, that the translation was a traitor, but its antiquity did not render it false. The original text accused him and he was glad to shut its face. He had committed a licensed violence, as a surgeon does to his patient, and he threw aside his mask with relief, washing his hands of the thing.

Sitting alone, job done, he took out the postcard from 'Yours-truly-Glenys-Harrington' and started to outline his new causerie for the *Sarocco Magazine*. Then he began to hear an odd sound, a rasping wheeze which began and then stopped and then began again. It was as if some furtive animal was working in the corridor outside his room. He thought of death-watch beetle, serving inhuman notice that his lease on 17, Beacon Terrace was coming to an end. The sound seemed louder when he edged past the paperbacks in his nursery shelves and then he saw the enlarged shadow of a man in a brown hat and mackintosh diffracted by the glass panels adjacent to the front door.

'I'm terribly sorry,' Gideon said, 'but you're wasting your time there. That bell thing hasn't worked as long as we've been here.'

There was a rusty rosette with a bell-push in the middle, set in the brickwork next to the front door. The stranger had pumped at it so determinedly that a pollen of orange cinders gloved his right hand and wrist. He brushed them politely in the direction of Sid Minches' house. 'Cyril Lack,' he said. 'You were kind enough to write to me.'

He had large hands with moony nails, very clean and rather long, as if they belonged to a foot. Gideon was six feet tall, but he was diminished by the size of the man who removed his mackintosh, on invitation, and walked delicately down the passage to the kitchen. Someone might have been building a cardhouse which he was anxious not to disturb.

'*Vanished Supremacies*,' Gideon said, as he plugged in the kettle, 'did you manage to get a copy?'

'Disappointing,' Cyril Lack said, 'truth to tell.'

'Well, of course, it is rather a specialised topic. The academic mind flinches from largeness; it prefers accuracy to conclusions, you might say. Do you know, I'm terribly sorry, but I don't have any smokes in the house.'

'I don't do it,' Cyril Lack said. 'I got out of the habit in there.'

'And how are things?'

'You gave me a lot to think about, Mr Shand. I used them for money, if you know what I mean, in there, and now I don't have no wish for them. The wife wouldn't have me back. I wasn't surprised. Modern man, I never thought about him before, but you're right, of course, aren't you? He's in a strange predicament, neither tragic nor comic, I think you said.'

'One is capable of it. Biscuit?'

'A biscuit I'll not say no to. I've been thinking principally about violence, in the light of your remarks. And I've come up with a bit of a theory, if you've got a moment.' Cyril Lack wore a sports jacket with stretched pockets, as if they had once been filled with stones. His poplin shirt was someone's kindness. The olive-green sweater looked as though it had been knitted by a learner: it had knots in it, like cheap planking. 'Do you remember something you used to ask us? "Anything you want to say?" Do you remember that?'

'It's a lecturer's stock question, I'm afraid, when he runs out of puff.'

'I never liked it,' Lack said. 'It did something to me, that question. I wanted to go and hide my head. You're not the only one used it, you know.'

'"Anything you want to *ask*?" surely,' Gideon said.

'Say. Say. That's why I didn't like it. It's what they used to say when they were sending you down. I'd never say anything. I didn't want to give them the satisfaction. I had things I could've said, but I wouldn't; I kept my freedom that way. I remember something else you used to say to us, "You haven't got women, but you do have books."'

'That I do remember,' Gideon said.

'I came out, I went to her house, she wouldn't even let me in. I remember that woman when she'd wake me up in the morning for it. "Won't hurt you, will it?" she'd say. "You don't want to take it to work with you, do you?" She thought I was carrying on with a young woman in the canteen. I probably was. She wanted to take it off me before I was even awake properly. Yes, I went to the house and she wouldn't let me in. I said to her, "It wouldn't hurt you, would it?" Because I'd not had a woman for four and a half years. I had this cell-mate, a nance he was, not a bad bloke, but it's not the same: you don't get the same feeling, because women, they're another species, aren't they? She wouldn't let me in the door, called me proper disgusting and I don't know what. I was lucky, mind, with this nance, because *he* liked it. He liked me, never mind how I thought of him. Unselfish. I don't look at them now. It wouldn't have hurt her, would it? Books. I still read a lot of books, after what you said. You know what I'm seriously considering, Mr Shand, and that's going into a monastery? A place where they don't do no talking at all. There's one over Southwell way, they tell me. Because I'll tell you my theory, in a nutshell, and that is, violence and talk are the same thing. Violence and talk are one and the same.'

'But are they, Cyril?'

'Predominately, yes,' Cyril Lack said. 'In my theory. Because all talk corrupts truth. Violence is like static electricity. It's what's left over. And sooner or later it comes out: you get a storm, you get violence. I could repair that bell for you, if you wanted me to.'

'It'll only ring if you do, Cyril.'

'What I liked about you, Mr Shand, was that you wanted something from us. That was what I call generous, wanting something from people who didn't know they had anything to give. You have to be what they call an aussiliary when you start.'

'In the monastery? Auxiliary, do you?'

'In the monastery, yes. Only I shall have time to work on my book, you see, get my thinking organised. May I wash my hands, Mr Shand?'

85

'There's one under the stairs,' Gideon said.

He took Cyril Lack's plate and cup to the sink and washed them thoroughly; they might have been evidence. The tolling of the lavatory and the opening of the door, the footsteps of the returning visitor came like an assault, though there was no smell. When Lack had gone, with a soft, large handshake, Gideon opened windows and sat there for ten minutes, perhaps longer, waiting for what had neither sound nor sensible dimension of any kind to be gone from the house. Then he locked up and went out, in his donkey-jacket, striding across the racecourse towards the Roman camp where a corrugated plastic roof marked some abandoned excavations. The archaeologists' grant had been withdrawn; the dig would soon be covered by a new supermarket and housing estate. Blown rain had first smudged, then obliterated the chinagraphed writing from the markers which stippled the side of the main trench.

Gideon jumped over the plastic chain into the pit of the dig. The floor was slick with unbroached mud. He squatted to inspect the caked sides of the trench and played like a cunning child in a treasure hunt, picking at the damp crust till he came to dryness. He knew little of ancient Britain, but he had a suspicion that the English exaggerated their connection with Rome, seeking to prolong their pedigree and make themselves closer to great events. If he were to find coins, he would not have the will or the nerve to offer them for sale. It was a sand-pit, this bed of abandoned scholarship; the discovery of a provincial brooch or even of a pouch of gold could never rehabilitate him with Cambridge or make his name as a researcher. The dig was a place where angst and puerility could both be served. Working his fingers deep into the softness, he came out with a clutch of round stones which might have been used as marbles. Putting them in his pocket, small change from a silly hobby, he walked on towards the Annesley Road, brushing evidence from his sleeve.

The Minster pivoted on the forehead of the red and grey city, as he climbed West Hill towards the wall of the prison. There were boxed geraniums outside the unbar-

86

red windows of the governor's house. Opposite it were the old judge's lodgings, now a local museum appealing for funds; there were no longer assizes in Chaworth. The garden had been covered with Portland slabs and a chain, slung between posts, made shallow swoops along the front. There were parking places for local government officers.

Gideon heard running yells as the judge's high clock rapped the end of the afternoon. Boys in maroon and yellow blazers were soon mixing with girls in purple hats as they came up the small lane from the comprehensive and the high school. Gideon would have promised that his stroll had no purpose, yet here he was as the schools emptied, patrolling with policeman's feet among his son's friends, and enemies. He was not looking for Tom, and at the last moment he positively hoped not to see him, but there he was, flushed at the sight of his father.

'Dad, must you?'

'I was hoping to get to the library before it closed,' Gideon said.

'This isn't even the *way* to the library.'

'Not from us, I grant you, but I haven't come from home. I went for a walk and came up West Hill.'

'Hullo, Mr Shand.'

'Hullo, Darren. I'm just on my way to the library.'

'He doesn't even know what the library *is*,' Tom said.

'There's nothing to worry yourself about, Mr Shand,' the boy said. 'Tommo and I was just going for some sherbets, wasn't we, Tommo?'

The Monahan boy cleared his rough throat, but said nothing more. He ran off towards the Close where Brendan and Patrick were waiting for him. Gideon wanted to touch his son. 'Since when does he call you Tommo?'

'Since he saw you coming.'

Sean Simmonds was sauntering up the little lane with his arm round the tightened waist of a girl who had secrets she had to keep leaning to tell him, while her eyes dared the world. 'Daniel!' Gideon said.

'Who are you talking to, dad?'

'*Sean*,' Gideon said, and tried to be greeting someone else.

'Are you going to the library now then?'

'I don't seem to have timed things very well, do I? I shall probably forget my own name in a minute. Gerald? Jeremy? How was your day? All right until I turned up?'

'You won't make things any better,' Tom said.

'I had not the smallest intention of interfering with your internal affairs, Tom. I hope you believe me. On the other hand, I'm not walking past my own son without saying hello. Life's not worth living if one does so entirely on other people's terms. I shan't make the mistake again. Now please cease treating me as a delinquent parent, O.K.?'

'No need to freak,' Tom said.

They walked in odd step to the edge of the Close. Something was going on in the Minster which required a lot of women in hats to go in and out, some of them with chairs. A secondhand bookshop, run by two ex-S.A.S. men, occupied a wedge-shaped building at the corner of Magnus Hill. You went in on the ground floor, took a few steps and were in an attic from which you descended, between tight shelves, to the floors below and found yourself again at ground level, further down the hill. Bill and Tosher specialised in Warfare and Ecology/Nature. 'We could pop in and see what they've got that's new,' Gideon said.

'I'd sooner get home.'

'Do you want to go on with this school, really, or would you fancy a change? Tell me the truth. No one thinks you're running away if you absent yourself from infelicity, you know.'

'Why do you have to complicate everything so much?' Tom said, and started down Strang's Steps with a spurt of nimbleness, suddenly a sharp animal that knew a trick or two. Gideon tried to keep up with him, but skidded on a green stair, snatched at the rail and had to stop.

Narrow gateways were cut in the wall of the defile. Steps went up to the back gardens of the houses that faced Jackson Avenue. It was rare to see anyone using them; the gardens were long and often overgrown and the gates offered short cuts to nowhere in particular. But now, as Tom reached the landing and disappeared from view, a set of hinges snarled and Gideon, under the cliff of the prison wall, saw a woman back into the gully, closing a gate behind her. Her legs were flexed in white stockings as she leaned back to settle the latch. Hips thrust out, skirt nicely flared over the whiteness, heels up from the flattish shoes, there was something at once tense and relaxed in her casual activity. Gideon was excited by her unawareness of his presence; it blessed her with innocence. What a fool Cyril Lack was, and how patronising it was to have treated his theory with such solemnity! For the talking man, silence was the violent medium. The simplicity of Pamela's movements, the way she gathered herself before starting down the steps ahead of him, this ordinary evidence of her separateness, primed him with the desire to rob her of it. Decency was always the quality of the victim. He watched her slim back, the sweet shift of legs and the drop of the right shoulder as her hand confirmed the railing it scarcely touched. Would Tom turn at the bottom of the steps and see that his father had been translated into the other parent and would he smile and run to her? Gideon was divorced from his son by the guileless intrusion of his wife.

He had to hope that Tom would not say that they had been together. Standing by the gate through which Pamela had come, he looked up the leaf-felted steps leading to Mr Fagin's privacy. The back windows of his house had buff blinds which left only a wink of dark glass beneath them. Gideon's stare was accusing and officious, as if some obscure duty kept him from running down to join the others and making light of the triple coincidence. Each second that passed had to be repaid with a minute of further delay; he would have to tell a lie now in order to explain what had become of him. He decided that he had cut back to see Bill and Tosher about a book they had been trying to get for him, realised that the shop would be closed and then, almost angrily, concocted a meeting in Magnus Hill, during which they offered to re-open the shop. Every false move in life demanded a marvellous ingenuity.

Pamela was filling the kettle. Tom was sitting at the kitchen table, the Falaise Pocket three-colour-printed before him; his failure to look up made him the foreman of an unfavourable jury. 'I went for a walk,' Gideon said, 'and bumped into Tom by mistake. You certainly can take those steps at a lick, old son, can't you?' Tom turned a page and made sure that it would stay turned by running his palm the length of the binding. 'That wasn't you I saw in the distance, was it, Pam?'

There was a bent bundle of five-pound notes on the draining board, next to her keys and a slowly uncrumpling tissue with lipstick on its edge.

'How was your patient?'

'He's not very well,' Pamela said.

'Would he be your patient otherwise?'

'This one is rather outside my province.' She turned to make the tea he wished he had had ready for her. When Tom took his magazine to the loo under the stairs, Gideon waited anxiously for his return. The ex-convict might have left a puddle on the plastic which would prompt a question. Tom came back only to say that he was going down to the Paki shop for some glue and then he would be working on his model. Did Pamela need anything?

'If you want fish fingers, bring some fish fingers.' She took a fiver from the bundle and sat down at the table with Gideon, the rest of the money between them. 'He seems to have cancer,' she said.

'I'll do Tom's supper,' Gideon said. 'Poor old bastard. Is he taking it badly?'

'In some ways he seems almost to be relieved. At least it's something new. He told me all sorts of things he never mentioned before. It makes him rather gay.'

'*Gay*?'

'He can see how it will end. Carefree. It makes you realise how different life could be, just one inch further over.'

'Fancy being called Mr Fagin all your life. It seems a particularly capricious tax, doesn't it? Why didn't he change his name, one wonders?'

'He's very short,' Pamela said. 'He says if he couldn't

change being short, there wasn't much point in changing anything else.'

'You've actually asked, have you?'

'I can ask him anything,' she said. 'You know when he was happiest? In the war. He was a wireless operator in occupied France. A place called Tourcoign.'

'He must be one of a very small group of people who have ever been happy in Tourcoign. I once drove through it, when I went on that tour with Stephen, one long vac. There was a superb railway station, all red brick and elaborate cast-iron, but the rest was suburban Manchester on a bad day. Tourcoign! S.O.E., was he? Did he get caught?'

'Unlike most of them,' Pamela said, 'he did everything he'd been trained to do. He never took taxis, never even took trams or buses if he could avoid it, and he never got involved with women or spent too much money on drink. He's a Catholic, you know.'

'I can't say I did.'

'He supplies furniture to all kinds of churches, but personally he's Catholic. He was in Tourcoign for eight or nine months and then he volunteered to go to Dijon.'

'Keen as mustard!' Gideon said. 'I suppose death in your bed comes as quite a pleasant option after an experience like that.'

'He liked it,' Pamela said.

'No one called him Fagin,' Gideon said. 'He was Monsieur Inconnu, I suppose. Nice to know what names he actually travelled under. What a strange pleasure there must be in having a cover story, something false to which it becomes a duty to remain true! Every action must be satisfying at that point; nothing you do must be sincere, everything is a fake for a genuine purpose. Was he ever married?'

'Just a few months before he went overseas. To the daughter of his partner. They were roofing people. On their honeymoon she had an epileptic fit. She said she had never had one before. Imagine what that meant to a Catholic.'

'Did he go back to her afterwards?'

'Where else was he going to go? He told me that the

strangest thing about not being caught – and a lot of people were, in that area – was this incredible temptation he felt to do something foolish, just once, this itch to make himself noticeable, even if it meant . . . well, hell. He knew what they did to people. One of his friends got out; he saw the burns. He thinks perhaps sinners are like that with God. The man who was caught, he was a fool; spent time in brothels and bars and talked too much as well. But Paul felt that that other man was the hero; he certainly got all the attention when they got back, and the gong.'

'The rejoicing is not limited to heaven,' Gideon said, 'when a sinner is redeemed. You get the George Medal as well. Whereas virtue . . . '

'I don't know if I should tell you this,' she said, 'but he loves me.'

'I don't know why you shouldn't,' Gideon said. 'He can't be the first, can he?'

'He feels that I can help him,' she said, 'even when it isn't my . . . well, field. He thinks if I'm there, he'll manage . . . the last bit all right.'

'What does he mean by loving you exactly?'

'I haven't asked for exactitude,' she said.

'And you? What do you feel?'

'It's a strange thing,' Pamela said, 'taking money from people for being kind to them. Of course, it's the treatment they pay for, but it's the kindness they want. And the regularity.'

'He must be quite a rich man.'

'He's got enough to last him out,' Pamela said.

'Do you love me, Pammy?' Gideon said.

'I'm your wife.'

'That's why I thought I'd ask.'

'Is something wrong?'

'I saw you this afternoon,' he said, 'as you were shutting his gate. I was on the steps and I saw you go down ahead of me. Did Tom not tell you – ?'

'He mentioned you were trailing along somewhere.'

'I finished my translation,' he said.

'I'd like to see it.'

'Rather an ordinary froggy novel: a few fine phrases, a

fair ration of sex and very wide margins.'

'I never said I loved him. There's a peculiar kind of pleasure though in being intimate with people for whom you don't feel anything personal. There's almost nothing you can't do for them. It's feeling things that makes it difficult.'

Gideon's hand played with the money on the table. 'Does he ask you to do things?'

'Why do you ask?'

'You were kind to me, weren't you? In Cambridge. I thought you were the nicest woman I'd ever known. Not that I'd known many. There didn't seem to have to be any preamble between us; I thought that was marvellously mature. It seemed to allow me to escape from the sense of being examined all the time. The body never bothered you, did it?'

'Little you know,' she said. 'I did physio because I hated blood. I couldn't bear the idea of cutting. Even injections made me feel funny.'

'You're very natural,' he said.

'Oh Gideon!' she said.

'When he says he loves you, what do you say?'

'He's seventy-three, Gideon, and he has a prostate condition. He doesn't want to have it treated. It gives them breasts, you know, the treatment. He dreads that. He says he'd sooner have a short time than a long.'

'Can one even be jealous of a wizened little old man of seventy-three with cancer of the prostate? His wife is dead, I presume?'

'In childbirth. The child died too.'

'No wonder he looks back to Tourcoign as his *très riches heures*.'

'I shouldn't have told you,' she said. 'I don't know what it means myself, love, when he . . . Perhaps it's because he's afraid that if he's really ill, I'll find a reason for not coming.' She had the money in her fingers now. 'He doesn't want to believe that this is the reason I do it.'

'Do you feel differently about penises?' Gideon said. 'I mean, a limb is a limb, but what's a penis? Is that a limb?'

'I don't have anything to do with his penis, if that's what's bothering you.'

'Nothing's bothering me, except a stack of mature students' essays on the causes of friction between the British and the Americans in the Pacific theatre of operations. The only really interesting wars seem to be the unspoken ones between allies, don't they?'

He worked on the essays with merciless tact, filling the margins, and the spaces at the top and bottom of the pages, with suggestions and rebukes. How close were indifference and punctiliousness! It was almost a vice with him to give better measure than the occasion merited. He had become the kind of scoundrel who never broke a rule.

When Pamela started to go more often to Mr Fagin's house, Gideon found painful relief in her absence. The pain was not jealousy; it came from the feeling that he had no right to complain. Precisely nothing was being done to him. Pamela brought more money home and the family fattened from the new income, as if Gideon's contribution had been insufficient. Mr Fagin told Pamela not to declare more than her usual fees to the revenue; there was no way anyone could know of the extra notes which sweetened her bundle. It was the mildest possible corruption, but Gideon was driven to something like prudishness by her easy acquiescence. He had the impression that his long habit of responsible industry was being mocked. He had been robbed of his command and there was a complicity between Pamela, Tom and Miranda, or so he could imagine, which made him their fool. The attentiveness of his comments on his pupils' essays could be read as a call for help; perhaps one of them would love him as Mr Fagin loved his wife.

One lonely afternoon, as he was finishing the second draft of his latest bridge causerie, the telephone rang. He did not have an extension in his little room; he liked to be quarantined against temptation. There was a nice luxury in having a call when the house was empty: no one could call him to table or ironise about his garrulity. Yet he answered the phone with asperity: 'Yes?'

'Hello, it's Jack.'

'Jack! What's new in the exciting and glamorous world of East Midlands showbiz?'

'Is this a bad moment?'

'You're not ringing to ask me that? Here in Chaworth the day is grey and colourless, but I have my chalks to hand: shall it be blue, red or indigo?'

'Not celebrating, are you, Gideon?'

'Not yet, but the corks are ready to pop. You got the stuff?'

'Indeed, and I've authorised payment, if that's what's –'

'That's not what,' Gideon said. 'I'm more interested in the aesthetic dimension. The subtle mixture of library footage and original animation which may well make this series a breakthrough in the realms of tea-time self-improvement for the late developer.'

'I'll tell you where the main problems seem to lie, from where I'm sitting.'

'You're sitting, they're lying; that still means that you're head and shoulders above them, doesn't it? The topography favours our cause.'

'Budget,' Jack Knightley said. 'Do you know what our contribution was to this wretched Fourth Channel this past financial year? Diabolical.'

'They're not bleeding you white, are they, Jack? Because I'm sure that's in contravention of the Race Relations Act. God knows, I thought I'd been pretty damned modest, given the brief I had from your people in the first instance. Let loose the dogs of war and other slogans of a rich originality, that's what I was handed when we beered and sandwiched with your boss that time.'

'Perhaps too modest,' Jack Knightley said, 'because here's what I have in mind, and that's for you to front the whole series. Frankly, my budget has been slashed to ribbons – '

'And you want me to wear them in my hair? I've never done any of this presenter stuff. And, although I hate to mention it in the chaste context of a penny-pinching programme, I can't be expected to do it for nothing, can I?'

'Nobody's asking that. But I always had a secret hunch that you could make quite a go of doing the whole shooting match on your own. Obviously we can insert archive material as and when, but basically, it'd be you eyeball to eyeball with the audience. It couldn't originate from me, quite candidly, Gideon, but my Head of Programmes came up with it at our weekly meeting, quite spontaneously.'

'Careful, Jack, or may I call you Mr Knightley? That sort of thing can lead to quite a nasty mess on the carpet if it becomes a habit.'

'Are you sure you're not celebrating or something?'

'One second, Jack, while I breathe into this little plastic bag. No, I'm not celebrating; just something. It means a hell of a lot of re-writing.'

'All you have to do is make a go of it and you'll be deluged with further offers. It could lead to a quantum leap, even within our organisation.'

'When I do quantum leaps,' Gideon said, 'I tend to strain my back.'

'Christ, man, you've been hinting ever since I've known you. I don't mean to be impolite, but I get the impression you're chickening out because, come crunch-time, you don't have the nerve to give it a go.'

'What I'm actually afraid of, to be honest, if that's not too suspect a thing to be, is that I shall rejig the whole bloody shoot and then it'll be cancelled after all, with nothing to show for my efforts but this little pile of sawdust and a very reasonable letter in the circumstances from yours-sincerely-Head-of-Proggies E.M.T.V., esquire, C.B.E.'

'I think we'd better have a meeting,' Jack Knightley said. 'You have my absolute assurance that this series is something that is going to happen.'

'On that basis, Caesar will go to the senate-house,' Gideon said. 'Pompey's statue at ten o'clock as usual? Ides, Nones, Kalends. Name the day.'

'I was thinking of Wednesday the ninth. Hugo says he'll give us lunch. What I'd ideally like to do is shape out our plan of campaign before we see him. He has the attention span of the cuckoo in a Swiss clock.'

'I'll remember to tell him you said that,' Gideon said, 'if there's any trouble over my expenses.'

'You should think about comedy,' Jack Knightley said. 'I'm serious.'

Gideon seemed to be smiling as he went to his room. He was excited enough to take the fat package containing the corrected text of *L'Inconnu*, which had been lying on his desk, strapped in with heavy-duty tape, for several days, and throw it in the air. How was it that being used gave one this feeling of liberation, of unlimited possibility? He walked out of the house with a petty prize, potential celebrity that would allow him to look down on the programmed multitude. Such eminence might even secure him the approval of his mother.

He realised that he had come out without anything to read, a breach of custom that turned him round twice in its honour, before he decided that he might as well go to the post office by way of Bill and Tosher's shop and so avoid the horror of standing in the queue for stamps without the consolation of print.

Tosher was fat and very red and his eyes were as jaundiced as old billiard balls. He breathed in a series of stepped sighs, like a mourning woman who is beginning to regain control of herself. 'Just the man,' he said, when he saw Gideon, 'the very person.' He sidled between close shelves, the boards of the old cottage creaking under his boots, and came back, book first, a slip-fielder, it might have been, claiming a square catch. 'Wasn't this the one you were talking about?'

'*The Future of Violence?* Was I?'

'I thought it was you,' Tosher said. 'We were talking in the Black George, weren't we?'

'I don't think I've ever been to the Black George,' Gideon said.

'Surely. Donne, Sorel, Arendt, Sartre, we were talking about continuities. No society without violence can hope to be secure, or even happy; no man who's never engaged in violence is capable of final gentleness, wasn't that what you said?'

'I'm capable of it,' Gideon said, 'after a few Black Velvets. Why Donne?'

'Rape and love, the proximities,' Tosher said. 'Power as God's overwhelming characteristic and from that, the human desire to be commanded, to be taken, to be beyond civilised compromise.'

'I sound to have been in good form,' Gideon said, 'except that I'm sure it wasn't me. You haven't come across a chap called Cyril Lack, have you? An ex-con from the castle? He was by my place the other day telling me this theory he's got that language is the cause of it all. Not that his thesis was backed by an impressive bibliography exactly.'

'You know what we liked? Not having names. As far as the public was concerned, we never gave our names. We came and we went. See the connection? Bang! In and out and never left a forwarding address. The law beyond the law. You got that with the Spartans, didn't you? The Night Squad. You know who liked us? The Labour people; they always wanted to know exactly what we could do, what the limits were. All over us, they were, couldn't do enough: women, anything to keep us happy. No questions, they liked that. Of course, we never talked about violence; we talked about force, minimum necessary use of. That was one of our stock jokes. In aid of the civil power. You were never in the forces, I suppose?'

'Too young,' Gideon said. 'My father was. He loved it. In the war.'

'Of course you know my theory: they're all against the H-bomb, against the nuclear thing not because they love peace but because they want war. Oh, I don't say every one of them, the women not necessarily, though I don't trust *them*, ever, but a lot of these people, they're frustrated; they want the danger back, not the big danger, but the shit-yourself panic that makes life worth living. Decline of war, decline of politics, decline of hope, it's all one; that's my line of thinking. You have a society that's got damned near everything and you've never seen such long faces. No one believes in anything, that's what they all say, but they're really talking about war. Heraclitus wasn't it, said war was the father of all things?'

'Tosher,' Gideon said, 'you should have a lectureship.'

'I shot three blokes in one afternoon,' Tosher said, 'and went back and read Kierkegaard till three in the morning; I never had a clearer head. Belief, it's based on violence, the hope of it, the chances of something changing utterly, even for the worse, the break-out, the big chance, and the bigger chance to go for it. I've retired; I'm happy; I did it and I'm clean. I'm a contented man; got my books, got my pint; Bill and I are good mates. I've seen life. It's not the violence they want to get rid of, it's what keeps them from it. You ever see what a bow and arrow does to a man at fifteen paces? I have. You want an easy way out, go for the nuclear, believe me. They want to see people die without dying themselves; they can't live without it. Nobody ever tells the truth about these things, except your old soldier, and like as not he'll be patting some kiddie's head, all passion spent, but a little of memory's small change rattling in his pocket. You reckon that Monahan kid was getting it from her dad? That's how I read it. I reckon his old woman gave her a right whacking and she legged it. Jealous!'

'I'm going to miss the bloody post,' Gideon said.

'You want to come back to the Black George one of these evenings. It's marked three quid, give me two fifty and I'll buy you a drink next time I see you.'

It was quite dark when Gideon returned to Beacon Terrace. He hoped for lights in the house, but there were none. He put the kettle on and cut bread for toast; the props of normality were hurried into place. Miranda was at her lesson with Rizzi; Pamela had her warm hands on Fagin's knotty joints; but where was Tom? Gideon waited, not looking up at the ghost of his fears which he knew to be sitting in the kitchen with him. He was a peasant of fortune, at the mercy of events he could not control, lent dignity by helplessness. He stood up at last, when Tom was a full hour later than usual, and walked through the ghost and out into the yellowed street. Certainty marched him like a sergeant, up to the Monahans.

'Oh Gideon, is something the matter?'

'Hello, Aileen. Is Darren here, or Brendan or Patrick?'

'We're all here,' she said, 'just sitting down to our tea. They get so hungry these evenings.'

'May I talk to one of them, please?'

Darren was chewing a stump of sausage bandaged in a fold of white bread. 'Hello there then, Mr Shand.'

'Have you seen Tom this evening, Darren, by any

chance? Tommo, have you seen him? He hasn't come home. I want to know where he is, and what happened to him.'

'I want the truth now, Darren,' Aileen said. 'Oh Gideon, have you thought about the traffic? It's getting worse and worse.'

'I never did a thing,' Darren said. 'I wasn't even there.'

'There? Where?' Gideon's anger seemed to pop the sausage from its sheath. He fielded the hairy thing from the carpet and held it out to the boy who, all of a sudden, had the expression of a canny winner. 'I want to know what happened and I want to know now.'

Darren looked at his mother. 'Have you any evidence then?' Aileen said. The boy was standing under the oleograph of Jesus. Good heavens, he had a fork in his spare hand! 'What are you accusing him of exactly? Is this never going to come to an end? Wait till I tell Gavin about this, because I shall, believe me.'

'Tell him about it,' Gideon said, 'and I hope he's sober enough to take it in. Your boys are a mortal menace, Aileen, and it's about time you realised it.'

'I know what you wanted to see him for,' she said, 'the boy. He told me all about it. You go back in there and finish your food.' Darren backed away and then turned and went into the noise of the kitchen. Aileen gave Gideon a one-sided smile, gathering hair from her ears with both hands and pushing it behind her. 'Oh, Gideon, Gideon, the world, the world!'

He saw the nakedness of her face, the hair held back like clothing, the smoothness of the uncreased forehead like the sheen of an unnippled bosom. The woman had a dangerous presence for him, a candour that promised nothing for the future, either of memory or understanding. At the same time, there was in that handsome head the suggestion that she could have been cleverer: a poetess, or the wife of a poet, could have been fashioned out of the same stuff. Yet she was cunning and she was ready to be savage. She would confess nothing, except through the licensed trap which translated her secrets into complicity with God. Above all, she was a receptacle, bound to accept the spit of Monahan's loins. She suffered his abuse of their daughter as if it were some family treasure that should be buried in conniving silence. Motherhood was her alternative to maturity. She would never be anything but the witness of familiar woes. Wild with docility, she endured, platitudes of comfort bubbling from her lips like a clear and poisoned stream. How could Tosher's brutal training give him an insight which Gideon's fancy education could never supply? Tosher had seen little Tracy's 'own story' in the local prints and had read between the large lines, just as he had when an order winked at what was not contained in it, and three men had to be shot before you could go back to Kierkegaard. Those who said that Hitler had not known of the final solution knew very well that orders are coded in badges and boots, in the machinery of the killing business. Only academics insisted that history was something that could be proved to have happened.

Gideon trotted towards Strang's Steps, turning every now and again to look back at number seventeen, in case Tom was coming up the other way. He continued trotting, backwards, a referee in training. Having taken the steps in one long, loping exercise, he found the Close molten with light borrowed from the last of the solicitors' offices. Two boys in the blazers of Tom's school stood together under the dark brim of the Minster. As they talked, they shifted their feet, never quite still; the earth could have been bucking beneath them. The sound of the Minster organ made a deserted fairground of the Close. One of the boys switched his eyes to Gideon, a tease of intimacy in his glance. Lanced by the false warmth, Gideon stumbled and looked back, seeking a flaw in the regular cobbles. The boy leaned a hand on his friend's shoulder, a little goal for Gideon to attack.

'Excuse me, but do either of you happen to know Tom Shand?'

'Do you happen to know Tom Shand?' said the boy whose glance had tripped Gideon. The other made the face of someone whose prep did not include that question.

'Look, forgive me,' Gideon said, 'but he comes home this way every night. He's at your school. He's twelve years old, about this tall; he wears spectacles, he's fair and he has freckles.'

'Negative, I'm afraid.'

'Sorry if I seem insistent, but you didn't see anyone being ragged, by any chance, by a bunch of kids this evening?'

'*Ragged*?' Both heads denied having witnessed anything so outlandish. Gideon knew that if he had been nameless, properly booted, properly winked at, he would have lit into them both, kicked them against the wall, searched them and found something. He was stronger than they, for a little while longer. As if he had a purpose, as if his conversation with them had been a luxury, he stepped through the half-door into the Minster. Bach pulsed like a heart-beat under the noble ribs that caged the brown nave. An arrowed sign on a wooden stalk indicated the way to 'The Temple of Fortune (Roman)'.

He stood in the heat of the music, head rowdy with jubilation he could not shape into sense. To reach the organ loft, he had to go through a door behind the famous pulpit, with its pelmet of smiling skulls. The credulous grins, work of the fourteenth-century local wood-carver Joshua Smith, were primed by the prospect of resurrection. Above the unfleshed heads, Lazarus rotated in his bandages, tossed in the blanket of eternal life. Did anyone who climbed the Sunday steps to deliver his sermon ever allude, these days, to that single great hope that banished the pagan gods and put Christianity beyond doubt, the magic fuse of immortality that broached the spring of European civilisation? Such a speaker would embarrass a modern congregation; it was better to talk of social problems, race and poverty, the scourge of unemployment and the plight of the aged.

The staircase to the loft was an unfolding fan of Cheddar-yellow stones, ripe with light from above. Bach twisted past Gideon and billowed into the nave to join the congregation of sound singing there in the darkness. He stopped under the panelled hood of the loft, the pipes of the organ stiff above his head, God's artillery, and he could hear the snap of the keys and the pump of feet on the pedals. He was on the point of retreating, but then, one hand leaning on the wall by a panel of switches, he looked round the buttress. Piers had his back to Gideon, but his anatomy made no sense. He was a monster, legs under his arms, toes bent together towards his spine. He was playing, with both hands, but there were hands around his neck, crossed but not latched, the fingers a vee which worked against his gleaming hair. The organist was wearing his khaki sweater, but his legs were bare and golden-fleeced. He rode back and forth as he played, and the girl rocked with him. On the bench at his side, like the airy garment that chaste painters sailed across a Venus, was a purple angora scarf.

Gideon stood, boneless as water, and the music swam through him. It was harder than he, more palpable, more confident and it pulsed through him while the couple in front of him, playing the great joke, rode its strong back, oblivious of the ghost at their loud feast. He could have shouted and not been heard; there was no outrage in him, only horrible lameness, the tax the vision levied. He actually limped down the stairs, the burn of his injury high in his groin, at the peak of the arch.

The ghost of the schoolboys' intimacy was leaning on the buttress where he had left them. He put his fingers against the deep pain and reasoned that it must have happened when he tripped. He took a hop and a step and then he saw Pamela's Raleigh canted against the souvenir kiosk; little bezique clocks gave the times of opening. Gideon stepped into the high frame and pushed off. He rolled down Parvus Hill and into Jackson Avenue where fluorescence faked daylight in the window of Fenn, Bristow, Estate Agents. Coasting down the side of the world, he arrived at his own front gate, without having to press a pedal.

'Where on earth have you been?' Pamela had an alibi of pots on the stove and was peeling potatoes at the sink. 'Is Tom not with you?'

'No, he's not. Tom's not been home, if he's not home now. This time I have the feeling that something's really happened. I've been looking all over the place. You're sure he hasn't been back?'

'He might have gone to visit someone. You can't

expect him to start being independent if he has to account for every move he makes.'

'I've already been to the Monahans',' Gideon said, 'who of course plead innocence, and now I'm going to see Athol.'

The woollen settee had been replaced by a purple velvet trampoline with large white cushions, all zippered. The latest magazines were now on a lacquered orange table, with a golden geisha lotus-positioned in the centre. The cocktail cabinet came rattling out as before, but Gideon was not having any hospitality, thanks.

'He's probably chatting up some bird.' Athol was wearing a caramel-brown mock-vicuna suit, darker brown shirt and white tie. 'Young men's fancy, it hits them harder and younger, my friend. They'll be being born with fur on 'em pretty soon now. Seany's got this Sandra, sixteen years old, she's out here already; they need two hands.'

'He's not in, by any chance?'

'Not yet, but he's getting close by all accounts.'

'A joke's a joke, Athol.'

'And not to be sneezed at on the current rates of exchange. Cora always sneezes when she laughs.'

'I know. I read all about it. I shall have to call the police.'

'You did a great job on the book, Shandy. I much appreciate your comments. Spot on. I burnt the midnight oil crossing the i's and dotting the t's, pony-expressed it to this Noble character and he's promised me a speedy response.'

'If Sean knows anything,' Gideon said, 'and you can get it out of him, I promise you I won't – I'll keep his name – '

'Isn't that your lad now?' Athol Simmonds said.

Gideon turned and saw Tom through the gap in the Regency-striped drapes. He was under a street light, outside Sid Minches' house, reading a magazine.

'Where the hell have you been?' Gideon said.

'Oh hello!' The boy's voice was deeper, the hair thicker over his temples and growing further down his cheekbones. Gideon might not have seen him for several months. 'I went with Clarky to see his stamps. He collects mags as well.'

'Couldn't you have – ? Who's Clarky?'

'My friend,' Tom said. 'My friend Clarky.' He actually turned a page, running his hand down the spine of the magazine. 'He specialises in French and British.'

Gideon took Tom's arm with a grip he needed to exert in order to control himself. Love and close arrest went in steady step.

6

H E WAS TYPING, and had been typing for more than an
hour, when Miranda knocked on the door of his little
room. 'Yes?' The keys continued their nattering. His
mind was sharp and full of energy. Cleverness and
embarrassment burned the same fuel. At the present rate,
he would finish the whole rewriting chore in one mam-
moth session.

'Am I allowed to say goodnight,' Miranda said, 'or is
this a total exclusion zone?'

'I am working,' Gideon said, 'but when did that ever
keep anyone out of here?'

She was wearing pre-shrunk jeans and a T-shirt that
tongued her breasts. Her hair was in a yellow turban and
she looked short-sighted from her shampoo. 'As a late-
comer to my seat in the stalls, forgive me asking, but do I
fully understand what this evening's drama presentation
is actually about?'

'No drama,' Gideon said. 'I wasn't hungry, so I thought
I'd resume my place upon the treadmill with a view to
getting ahead of the game, or at least abreast of it.'

'If there is no drama, why is the curtain up and why are
the chips down and why is there a silence in the house
which would make a peak in Darien sound positively
noisome?'

'Did Pam ask you to come in here and – ?'

'It was all my idea. I'm just your average harmless civilian who doesn't fancy sleeping in an atmosphere thick with undispersed C.S. gas. Fusspot, aren't I?'

'It'll disperse, Mandy. It's the explanations that burn the eyes and can cause prolonged vomiting in some cases. I had every reason to think that Tom was being brutalised again. I've never heard of this Clarky, have you? I'm still not convinced that he isn't hiding something – '

'It's sometimes a good sign, isn't it, when people start hiding things?'

'How was Peppino this evening?'

'He was *un po'* poorly, as a matter – oh, I get it! You mean what was I doing at the Minster without a pass, right? Is that why you nabbed the bike? I had a lesson with Piers, unpremeditated, but none the less enjoyable for that, as they say in the parish mag. Apart from you, he's the cleverest person I've ever come across.'

'He's probably cleverer,' Gideon said. 'I wonder what possessed him to be a parson.'

'He loves England,' Miranda said. 'He wants to be at the heart of it. He doesn't like the way it's going; he's a forward-looking reactionary, he says. He has this fantasy of the clocks going backwards, only so steadily no one ever notices. Orderly progress in the opposite direction! He wants everything to be grand and significant again. He things of England as a real thing, a *person* practically. Those articles of his are love-letters really. He half wishes that Canterbury had never split from Rome, but then again he sees the schism as evidence of England's election. He's completely untrivial, dad, that's what makes him so different. It all matters to him.'

'Shall we see you in church?' Gideon said.

'It's a kind of music,' Miranda said. 'I don't believe in *it*, but I do believe in *him*, very nearly. It's not a question of being persuaded, it's a matter of being able to hear. When he talks, when I'm with him, I almost feel that I do. I suppose I want to, but I'm afraid. I'm afraid of losing what I've learnt from you!'

'You don't have to be polite,' Gideon said.

'I don't love him, but I want him in every possible way. Perhaps he's too clever to be lovable. He's like some kind of white flame, full of heat, wonderful to see and approach, but he doesn't need me, even though . . . you know. He does it for me, not for him.'

'Does what?'

'Come on, dad,' she said.

'He *is* clever,' Gideon said, 'if he's convinced you of that.'

'He has not said a word, my lord, to that effect. Funny, isn't it? Mum's papa being a vicar and now here's Piers. Not that I think the two fellow-clerics would have a great deal to say to each other, with the possible exception of yah and boo respectively. Did you like him at all, grandpapa?'

'Do you know, I hardly ever spoke to him? My own father was so much – what? – on top of me that I suspect I welcomed, well, the chance to be rather grand. It was a bit of a sham, because when I first met him, I'd just not been appointed to my famous fellowship. I took it out on the old boy, I suppose.'

'Those Cambridge shites!' Miranda said. 'I'd love you to do something really earth-shattering, just so they could realise what fools they were. Couldn't you come up with a manifest masterpiece, papa, in between slugging out the educational videos and winning the Gold Cup? It wouldn't take that much out of you, would it?'

'In principle, daughter, a good plan, but I shall never finish rolling this log up hell's hill, shall I, at this rate?'

'It's an excuse, isn't it, all this?'

'And a very good one too. Excuse for what?'

'All these jobs you do, all these bits and bobs, all these duties of yours. I wish you'd cut loose one day and really go for the big one. There must be something in life apart from *happiness*, mustn't there?'

'People aren't very keen on your thinking so,' Gideon said.

'Piers is. Piers thinks it absolutely vital.'

'That's usually a man's excuse for not bothering to give a woman what she wants. All selfishness sails under absolute colours. I sometimes think Christianity is the most selfish religion ever invented.'

'And would you believe it? He's come to life here!'

'That's why it didn't ever really suit the Jews or the Greeks and that's why the Jews and the Greeks were really the great enemies of Paul, in particular. They had an answer he could never tolerate, that life was worth living here on earth. The vanity of the man meant that he had to find a way of being Caesar; the only post available was king of kingdom come.'

'Why don't you blast Christianity, dad? Put the big boot in. Piers could review it and I'd be in the centre of a sentimental drama that would draw world-wide attention to this shy but comely young woman from one of Britain's oldest and least-known cities.'

'I should never be able to compose a credible bibliography. Besides, Christianity — like the myth of human goodness — is now in the glorious position of having been so regularly exploded that nothing can be done to challenge it.'

'Piers wants to get God off the fence, he says. He wants to see Him embarking on a much more *involved* form of presidency. Seriously — I *think* it's seriously — he wants to will God to be active.'

'You should go to university, Miranda.'

'As opposed to a slow cruise around the world with a lady companion of proven character? Are you afraid, pater, that I'll do something rash? I might well, but I doubt if the Reverend Rougier is about to whisk me to the altar. It so happens, if you must know, that I have competition.'

'Have you indeed? And who might she be?'

'*He* be, as in jeebie. The name is Harold.'

'For a reactionary with stern principles, he seems remarkably versatile, your friend.'

'He doesn't just do the library and the organ, you know. He's two-fisted too: he can duck and he can weave. He's not in the least bit ashamed, of anything. He's sort of like a surgeon: there's no part of the world's body that disgusts him. He sees it all as one, body and spirit, head and tail, top and bottom; you separate them, he puts them together again. The desire and pursuit of the whole.'

'Harold,' Gideon said.

'Piers met him when he was combining pastoral duties with instructing under-privileged yobbos in the noble art of inflicting brain damage on their fellow detainees in the Blackley Cross Borstalero. Little Piers, can you imagine? I call him Rocky Four. Our Harold, *his* Harold, blast him, got into the finals of the ape-man division and his opponent decided that he was feeling a bit poorly, not to say shit-scared. So you'll never guess what Rockman did. Oh yes you will! As I heard it from my very own special correspondent, the whole thing might have passed off noisily had it not been for A Funny Thing. They got to the last round when, believe it or believe it not, the timekeeper's watch got jammed, marmaladed or otherwise arrested. The round went on and on. Oh, it can't really have lasted much longer than an hour or two, but it was long enough for Harold and Rocky to realise that they were still at it, if I may be permitted that expression, my lord, long after peace should have broken out. The two of them began to see the joke at the same time, and when they did, still thumping away, they all of a sudden saw each other in their true colours. Harold, I should perhaps have indicated, was not a young person for whom the spiritual side of life has ever held much allure. He thought that clergypersons, and Piers not least, were a right load of rubbish. Then this thing happened and from that moment onwards, there was a bond between them. Not a premium bond but something, so we are assured, more valuable even than that. Imagine! Boggle, if you will, but having boggled . . . what then indeed? So now you have virtually the full story of your little girl's *leçon d'amour*. Boohoo and comparable adult sounds.'

'Is Harold still enjoying Her Majesty's hospitality and similar forms of fat-free diet?'

'What actually happened when Jacob wrestled with the angel, papa?'

'Jake went lame, didn't he? The angel's injuries are not recorded. One suspects that the heavenly creature learnt something from the encounter, however.'

'He's out,' Miranda said, 'and about. Harold.'

'We have to get away from this bloody town.'

'City. Don't worry: he doesn't haunt the neighbourhood. And he's not jealous. I mean, even if he knew about Rocks and me, which he doesn't.'

'It's none of my business,' Gideon said, 'and it's certainly none of my pleasure, and I don't know quite what that leaves, but I do wish you'd be careful, and I doubt if you will be. I'm only thinking of you, Mandy, and that's rather a terrifying thing to be doing.'

'Such is the kinkdom of God,' she said. 'I really do wish you'd do something.'

'Perhaps I'm happier than you think, Mandy.'

'And perhaps you're happy to think so. Piers says that only people who aren't Christians are as Christian as you are.'

'Oh, I furnish one of your topics of conversation, do I?'

'I love you,' Miranda said. 'I love you more than him, but I can't do anything about it, can I? He doesn't want to protect me, you know. He wants to expose me to something.'

'And you want him to?'

'Pity me a little bit,' she said, 'won't you, dad? But only a little bit. If I don't go through this now, whatever it is, I shall go lame. You wouldn't want a daughter called Jacob, would you?'

She sat there, hands thrust between her thighs, looking keenly on Gideon. He read the words in the typewriter: 'Well-meaning people often seek to discover the causes of conflict. Might they be better advised to ask for the cause of peace? What makes men abandon battle as a way of getting the things they want? And can they ever get it, if battle is one of the things? Peace requires ingenuity and imagination on a scale which makes war more accessible and more authentic. God Himself is more convincing as an eagle than as a dove.'

'I'd like to kill them,' Miranda said.

'We want to kill any witnesses of our folly more than we ever want to kill those who've hurt us. The witnesses are always in the greatest danger.'

'Don't go blaming Tom for still being in one piece, will you?'

He held Miranda against him, as if they had called his flight.

111

7

'I HAVE TO get them out of Chaworth,' Gideon said. 'A very dear friend of my sister Rosalie – I think you met Rosalie, didn't you? – was attacked only last week in Roehampton by two nicely turned out young men who said they were gas company officials. Appalling injuries. Poor Rosalie's exhausted ministering to her. There's very little safety anywhere, I fear.'

'Look here, Mr Woodward, I'm over forty. How can it seriously be alleged that I'm insufficiently mature to handle my own money?'

'No one has quite said that, you know. The money in the trust is not, technically speaking, yours. *Hinc illae lacrimae.*'

'The old quotes may well be the best,' Gideon said, 'but I can't believe that you couldn't prevail on my mother if you really had a mind to. You are the protector of the trust, after all.'

'You flatter me, Gideon.'

'Not intentionally.'

'I appreciate your irritation, and personally I'm only too willing to ignore its manifestations, but to put it practically, your mother – much as I value her friendship – can't live for ever. Why not possess yourself in patience?'

'Presumably,' Gideon said, 'you helped my father draft

the terms of the document in the first place.'

'He told me what he wanted to have it say; I saw to it that it did. That's how I pay the rent and avoid being accused of malpractice. It's neither glamorous nor heroic, but there it is.' Barry Woodward used his metal hand to pour more tea into Gideon's Minton cup. The claw was articulated below a Huntsman's four-buttoned cuff. 'You mustn't curse me . . . with more powers than I actually dispose of.'

'It's not for my sake that I want the money.' Gideon shook his head at the sugar bowl. 'Thank you. If I only had myself to think about, I should spare myself this kind of suppliant mission, I can promise you that.'

'Wedlock's the devil,' Barry Woodward said.

'Did you like my father?'

'He was extraordinarily good to me when I was . . . a young officer. I didn't stand back to consider my feelings, I merely . . . had them.' There was an oddness in the speed with which Woodward delivered his words. He might have been watching the hand of a judge as he logged them. 'You married very young, didn't you?'

'What do you think he really wanted me to be?'

'Ray's ambitions for you were probably not of a very arcane order; you shouldn't regard his will as too much more . . . than a caprice. He may have designed its terms in order . . . to give your mother something to amuse her, rather than to keep the cash out of your immature . . . hands. She seems to be prospering, doesn't she?'

'I rarely see her,' Gideon said. 'Graveley isn't too adjacent to Chaworth. He never wanted me to be an academic, as far as I could tell, so it can't have been the Cambridge episode that made me into a pariah.'

'Don't dramatise and don't look for dark. . . . motives, let alone serious moral misgivings. Men like to stay alive; perverse stipulations in their wills give them some ghostly . . . tenancy on earth and more than a few avail . . . themselves of the opportunity. If it's a personal matter, Gideon, it's more probably personal for him than for you. Fatherhood is not an exclusive office by any means.'

'He's not really relevant any more, is he? It's my mother. How would you recommend persuading her to abandon this grotesque pretence that I am still not a responsible adult?'

'The best thing would be to put the whole lamentable . . . joke out of your mind until, in the foulness of time, as Stephen Hellman would say, the inheritance falls into your lap. Your misfortune, if I may say so, is not that you haven't got . . . Ray's money, but that you know it's coming.'

'Like the prospect of eternal bliss,' Gideon said, 'it sours present pleasures without offering any certainty of future ones.'

'In this case, however, the odds do remain . . . favourable. Don't attribute any significance to what Ray did: he was a shrewd . . . assessor of a risk, but he was never very interested in character. What is a member of Lloyd's, after all, but a bookmaker with a reliable tailor? The only person I ever saw him take a deeply . . . personal attitude to was his driver, a chap called Jordan. He saw a lot of people killed, one way and another, through the desert and up into Italy, but he never seemed too . . . affected until Jordan got killed, right at the end, when we were up in . . . Piedmont. No conceivable blame attached to Ray for scrambling out of his tank when it was hit; Jordan would've come out of a different hole if he hadn't been cut in half by the bazooka that got him, but Ray kept asking whether he'd got out and we had to tell him he had because he would've gone straight back to find him otherwise. We said he was in the ditch on the other side of the track. By the time Ray found we were wrong, it was possible to walk on back without . . . losing movable parts from your anatomy. You have to remember that your father's best time was when you weren't there. Jordan died while you were safe in mummy's arms. He was glad you were, but there was also something you weren't, and could never be, that that . . . docile squaddy was. Dead, of course, being no small part of it. Won't your bank manager stake you in view of what can scarcely be denied you for ever? I'll gladly pen him an extremely dignified and persuasive letter.'

'She could live for another, Christ, twenty-five years,' Gideon said.

'What he liked about Jordan, I suspect, was that they ... had nothing in common. It was an impersonal relationship of the deepest possible ... intensity. You can only have those with total strangers, and probably only in a war, or a catastrophe. If you renounced your ... inheritance, completely, signed it away, do you think it might give you the energy to make the necessary money for yourself?'

'I work extremely hard,' Gideon said, 'sometimes for sixteen hours a day. I hardly think that I sit around waiting for a friendly word. For a *Luftmensch* I have an extremely heavy schedule.'

'Then I mustn't keep you ... from it,' Barry Woodward said. He lodged his whole hand in Gideon's, back to front, making their farewell an abstruse ritual. The gesture altered the position of the solicitor's eyes, so that his handsome head, flashes of distinction at the temples, took on the dated allure of an Edwardian portrait. The best men do not make the best of themselves, Gideon thought, in quite so conscious ... a manner.

He was due to meet Stephen Hellman, before their postponed Gold Cup match, at an Italian restaurant in Southampton Row, not far from Woodward's office in Lamb's Conduit Street. There was no sense in going into the West End; Gideon was becalmed, in that shallow tuck of time, without a purpose. He sat with a newspaper whose front page boasted of how much more interesting tomorrow's edition would be than today's, watching London faces as they trooped to the Underground or waited at corners where rendezvous were due. His mother's long refusal to sanction the release of his inheritance was maddening and it was also the warrant of his youth. He still had his life in front of him, however much his gut might say otherwise, because of the stagnation imposed by Eleanor's obstinacy. His most intense game was still with her. Hatred had become a vice he could not entirely hate.

He watched Stephen Hellman cross the road with a coldness that owed something to Mr Fagin, the righteous

115

spy, and something to Stephen's cousinship, professionally speaking, with Barry Woodward. The barrister and the solicitor were the banal beneficiaries of the injustice of life: what happy city would ever need either? Stephen stood on the white line, between the buses, his scuffed briefcase in his arms. There was something almost parental in the tenderness with which he carried it to the near pavement and then took its handle and let it fall the length of his black overcoated arm. He looked at the world, a dark-jowled, unyoung man these days, with the blown anonymity of those who have made a bit of a name for themselves. Stephen was not a celebrated celebrity, but his success at the bar and as a broadcaster conferred a modest notoriety: he never knew when he would be known. His smile came from keeping pace with those who were actually slower than he was, just as his courtesy at the door of the Trattoria Tuscana was that of a busy man who can afford to defer to those less in demand than himself.

'I know, I know,' he said, 'I swore I'd be here first for a change. I picked up the phone to tell my clerk no more calls and what did I get? You've guessed it! One more call.' He was hitching his good coat to an antlered hook before it was fully off one arm and ducked to be free of it, making the movement into a small bow to a pair of glossy young men, in blue shirts and grey suits, who had plastic-covered graphs on the table between them.

'Well, at least whoever it was, it wasn't me, was it?'

'Unless your name is Miki Constantinides, gent of this city,' Stephen said, 'not. How are you, Gidman?'

'Oop for t'coop,' Gideon said. 'Still in pawn to my mother.'

'No more trouble with Tom, I hope?'

'The family think I'm making an unnecessary fuss. Gideon Shand, the Wilderness Years. I hope they're right. In my *osso buco* I'm pretty sure they're not, but I don't want to see them proved so. Double-binds are my speciality, Steve, you know that.'

Stephen ordered brusquely, but the agility of his eyes behind his smart glasses seemed to win complicity from the waiter. 'Pamela O.K.?'

'She has a lover,' Gideon said, and admired the steadiness of Stephen's gaze, the unhesitating silence with which he waited for an explanation, or a joke. 'Platonic.'

'That can be nasty.'

'Seventy-three years old and said to be dying.'

'I hope it's not going to affect your bidding,' Stephen said. 'The Proctors, shingled or doubled, have never been easy pickings. And what does your well-placed mole tell you about Deakin and Butterworth? They sound rather like a classical concordance. I'm told they play for the Ministry of Defence.'

'A pair of nature's quarter-finalists,' Gideon said. 'You've got new glasses.'

'Yes, well, you can't get new eyes. Shall we discuss ticktacks or rely on native flair, as usual?'

'Kick and rush have got us where we are today. And where are we today? In contention at least. The twins are the real danger. Let's hope that the scurvy or whatever it was has done something to interfere with their communications system.'

'In the last analysis,' Stephen said, 'perhaps it's all my fault. Not Pamela and the Platonist, but the whole absurd complication over your father's will. I never realised how angry he was getting that time I came to stay with you. He really did think the British fought the war to save the Jews, didn't he?'

'And didn't we? Here you are, after all.'

'Some of us. You should've let him kick me out of the house and good riddance. You'd never have reviewed Neil Laidlaw's little opus and today you would have been Fellow and Tutor: man and superman, instead of man and boy.'

'I don't believe that the Laidlaw review was the only reason why they elected de Brandt. In any case, the book *was* a scandal and someone had to say so. I did the right thing and the college didn't want it done. So much the worse for the college.'

'I hardly dare to tell you this,' Stephen said, 'but – '

'They've made you an honorary Fellow.'

'Now I don't need to tell you. I helped them avoid a wodge of tax on the dockland property. What could they do that didn't involve paying me properly except render tribute to my altruistic sagacity by giving me the right to dine and put my feet up, *per Christum Jesum dominum vestrum*? Should I have refused? All my refusals take the form of acceptance, I'm afraid, Gidman. I'm only ashamed now I come to boast of it to you, in a hangdog sort of way, of course.'

'Miranda already calls you Sir Stephen.'

'Does she so? How is she? Still as beautiful as ever?'

'On the contrary: more so. She's involved with a clergyman.'

'Married?'

'No, but that's the good news. He's right-wing, very clever and bisexual.'

'Remind me of the bad news.'

'Piers Rougier, his name is, known to write for the *St James's Review*. He did a piece recently defending Socrates' accusers, if you saw it. He's got the most extraordinary confidence in himself, and I can't claim it's not well-founded.'

'When you say "involved", you don't simply mean they choose the hymns together for the harvest festival, I take it?'

'The modern priest doesn't seem to find sex incompatible with pastoral duties.'

'Why do we always eat here?' Stephen said. 'The food gets worse and worse. Fidelity is the strangest of human habits.'

'How's Miriam?'

'Almost certainly in the lotus position. She's heels over head in love with yoga. Apart from that, she's very well indeed. Does your mother take the same dim view of me that your father did, do you suppose? Because in that case you could always advise her that you and I have finally had a big bust-up – I passed your forcing bid, let's say, or something rupturous like that – and, who knows, your maturity might be established at a stroke?'

'I was thinking of hiring someone to do her in, but the wretched felon had a change of heart and he's decided to go into a Trappist monastery.'

'Sounds the ideal candidate: the very instance of a man

who can keep his mouth shut. Greed and morals do go together in the most miraculous manner, don't they? I'm sure your fond mama is quite convinced that she's honouring your father's wishes and furthering your spiritual education. If she smiled just once at the fact that she's living on the interest, she'd wither and die *sur le champ*. All the best jokes, so gentlemen used to maintain, belong to the straightest faces. Talking of *champs*, we should proceed to the one of *bataille*. The Proctor twins would like nothing better than to disqualify us for ducking under the ropes a second after the appointed hour.'

The brothers' flat was in a whited block near Great Portland Street underground station, but Stephen was quickly into a taxi, holding the door for Gideon with a hospitable arm and reinforcing foot. Tamara and Oleg Chernoff, their team-mates, had parked their Saab against a RESIDENTS ONLY sign. 'Can't leave it there, mate,' P.C. Hellman said to his friend's backside.

'What? What?' Oleg's furrowed face came up indignant with guilt. 'Oh blast you, Stephen, just because you never learnt to drive!'

The twins were in their sixties. They wore identical schoolboy glasses, woollen ties and grey-blue sports jackets. Since they shared a passion for bridge and for Venice, city of bridges, their apartment sported trophies from both: rose bowls and tortured glass. Polychromatic clowns clutched armfuls of cigarettes; age-glazed chocolates came in a gondola. Gideon and Stephen played against the twins in the dining room, while Oleg and Tamara squared up to Deakin and Butterworth in the lounge. The Proctors had been an established partnership even when Gideon and Stephen first played for Cambridge. If one had recently been ill, Geoffrey or Bernard, the disease seemed to have debilitated them equally: they were like one person who could sit in two places at the same time. The bridge world whispered that their singular understanding was supplemented by sharp practice, but though they often did well, they never excelled. If they drifted off course, they had no maps to consult but each other's, and they were identical: when one was lost, so always was the other. Gideon's steadiness and Stephen's flair combined well against them. On the eighth hand, Stephen made three spades, doubled and redoubled, despite a personal holding of only three trumps to the nine. Gideon held ace, queen, ten, eight over the doubler, which was not what he had expected.

At half-time, the teams joined their respective partners to compare results so far. Geoffrey or Bernard provided biscuits and coffee (in cups lionised with the Doge's insignia) and left their opponents in conclave. 'Not a brilliant session so far as we're concerned, I'm afraid,' Tamara said. She was wearing a black dress with a red sash, blackened hair turreted on top of her head, a black ribbon around her slim, stretched throat.

'How the hell did you manage to bid six clubs on board eleven?' Stephen said. 'Messrs Proctor and Proctor stopped in three.'

'He was very, very naughty,' Tamara said. 'You *were*, Oleg. I signed off three times. Once, twice, three times!'

'We're only five match points down, I make it,' Oleg said. 'My lord, in my estimation these biscuits offer *prima facie* evidence that Deakin and Butterworth have been stealing provisions from their place of employment over a considerable period of time. Exhibit A: a plate of 1972 civil service *petit beurre*. I rest my case.'

'And there goes the whistle for the second half,' Gideon said. 'And they've got it all to do!'

'For God's sake, Tamara,' Stephen said, 'either kick him harder from now on or put on a pointier pair of pumps.'

'Keep it up, you two,' Oleg said. 'Are we ready to resume?' He opened the door of the dining room. 'Gondola, gondola!'

During the second session, Gideon managed to conjure the crucial ninth trick from nowhere while making three no trumps vulnerable and was rewarded with that straightfaced smile, all from the eyes, with which Stephen celebrated without raising a glass. Three hands later, Stephen bluffed Bernard (or was it Geoffrey?) into stopping in a part-score when six hearts could have been made (game was easily available) and the two friends finished the evening with the flushed modesty of likely winners. The twins blew their noses at the same time and were not happy with the arithmetic which suggested that they had scored well below par. However, when the two teams rejoined their other halves for the final reckonings, Tamara's face warned that she had no happy news. Deakin had not only bluffed the Chernoffs out of that six-heart contract, he had actually played in four diamonds himself, while the Proctors were at least making three hearts with three over-tricks. All Stephen's ingenuity had not prevented their opponents from making a plus score in both rooms. In fact, like Stephen, 'the Deakin object', as Oleg called him, had opened one heart with queen and another. On the face of it, there could hardly be any complaints, since the same bluff had been perpetrated in both rooms, but Oleg was unappeased. 'I'm sorry to have to say it, and I will indeed keep my voice down, but your obedient servants are bloody cheats.'

'They only seem to have adopted the same tactics as ourselves,' Gideon said.

'They psyched three times in the match,' Oleg said, 'if I'm right – '

'Considerably less often than we did,' Stephen said.

'Granted, but did one of you, just before each flight of fancy, make a casual reference to Venice, throned on her hundred isles?'

'Darlingk, you're imaginingk things; he's imaginingk things!'

'I have no imagination,' Oleg said. 'I make no excuses. I played like the famous drain. *Cloaca maxima, ego sum,* and *mea culpa, mea maxima culpa,* no one's denying it, least of all my nearest and dearest. Nevertheless, we have been less than ethically hornswoggled.'

'I make it they win by four imps,' Gideon said. ''Tis pity, but 'tis equally true. Now let us gallantly say cheese, because here they come.'

Sheepish with victory, their opponents came into the dining room. As Deakin thrust his score-card in front of Gideon's eyes, to make sure that their figures tallied, he dislodged a lighter in the form of a candy-striped mooring post with a souvenir inscription on the base. 'What is it

121

that the Venetians call these things?' he asked, as he retrieved it.

'Another psych coming up?' Oleg said.

'Oleg, naughty!' Tamara was pulling hair from the nape of her neck and fixing it under the big comb at the back of her skull. 'He's so naughty!'

'Well, jolly bad luck,' Geoffrey or Bernard said.

'Good luck in the next round then,' Gideon said.

'We shall need it,' Butterworth said. 'We certainly needed it tonight.'

'Not really,' Oleg said.

The team-mates stood by the scratched Saab and Tamara offered apologetic kisses as Oleg massaged the newly wounded paintwork. 'He did say not to leave it there, darlingk.'

'Something ought to be done,' Oleg said. 'Fragrant cheating. *Fragrant*: I can still smell it from here.'

'Injustice is a terrible thing, Mr Chernoff, sir, but it's sometimes better than justice, what I've seen of it in various choice locations, all expanses paid. Tamara, you're looking juicier than ever, if I may say so. Imagine what Deakin and partner have waiting for them in suburbia, chum, and thank your lucky stars and accept your unlucky stripes. Taxi!'

'You're a lucky bugger, Hellman,' Gideon said, as they slammed themselves into the taxi and turned for a last wave at their team-mates. 'Everything comes along at just the right moment for you.'

'Or do I come along to accommodate the moment? Hugh is the dupe of Hume?' Stephen sat hunched forward, briefcase clenched in his lap, as if he were looking for someone in the drizzle-shiny streets. It had once been Gideon's habit to drive back to Chaworth after a match, no matter how late it ended, but one night he woke up in a ploughed field in Cambridgeshire, since when he always stayed with Stephen, first in King's Bench Walk and then in the new flat in the Barbican. From its terrace window, the gilded cross of St Paul's hung like a loud foreign order on the purple chest of the night sky. Stephen shucked his shoes and slid into the kitchen on his socks, touching prompt switches on the way.

122

'*Were* they cheating, do you suppose?' Gideon said. 'Funny that Deakin and friend should choose to talk about Venice, considering that it's Proctor and Proctor who're the Venetomaniacs.'

'Any text can furnish a code, can't it? Local colour, we all take it on, don't we? Bacon and eggs suit you, Rabbi? Perhaps Geoff and Bernie picked the others up on the Rialto. We shall get no redress, *ci sono convinto*, so it's over and out, Roger, if you ask mine. Sunny side up?'

'Never touch them any other way,' Gideon said. 'I have a funny feeling that one of my neighbours fancies little girls, and more than fancies them from time to time, but I haven't got any proof of that either.'

'Plates in the bottom cupboard, Mycroft,' Stephen said. 'By "more than fancies", you don't mean that he does them in, I presume?'

'I'm not even sure that he does them; he may merely press this week's free offer into their hot little hands and then handle them a little hotly. Should I do anything about it, do you think?'

'Are we talking about morals here,' Stephen said, 'or the law? Because I don't know any more than you do about the former and I'm much too expensive when it comes to the latter. Do you want to? You're not concealing evidence, are you?'

'I'm just like Oleg,' Gideon said. 'Strong suspicion, no proof.'

'You'll probably find that the cops are in the same situation. We all know infinitely more than we can ever act on, don't we? The truth will not out, and when it does it often stops being true.' Stephen tilted the eggs in the non-stick frying pan and they slid over the rim on to freckled grey stoneware plates. 'Are you trying to make more trouble for yourself perhaps, by – ?'

'I like the man,' Gideon said.

Stephen put the eggs in front of his friend and came back with Rosenthal knives and forks. 'You want to do *something*, don't you?'

Gideon knifed one of the yolks and lifted yellow on a piece of bacon. 'I just might go and kill my mother, I suppose.'

'You take things too well,' Stephen said. 'Behave too well. You used to lug my trunk to the station for me, didn't you, at the end of every bloody term? I didn't think I was taking advantage of you, but of course I was. You think you're weak, Gideon, don't you? I suspect you're really very strong and people keep wanting to weaken you because of it. You submit out of strength, not weakness.'

'That might have been true once; I doubt if it is now.'

'It's partly my fault,' Stephen said. 'Perhaps more than partly.'

'That's a kind of greed,' Gideon said.

'Good,' Stephen said. 'Good.'

'Listen, I knew what I was doing when I wrote that review. All the time I was exposing Laidlaw's dishonesty, his complete lack of moral sensibility, all the time I was doing what you pretty obviously wanted me to do, I was writing it against you, Stephen, as well as against him. If I'd been entirely on your side, if I'd actually been a Jew, I daresay I would've hesitated. All the time I was writing it, I guessed that I was dishing myself. Maybe I was doing it to punish you for being right, to punish . . . I'm not as different from my father as I might be. You took it as the proof of our friendship, that I wrecked my career for the sake of truth, *ruat coelum* and all that, but I'm not so sure. You made friendship into something I could hardly bear. You wanted it to involve so much, and yet not quite enough. And I . . . '

'I understand,' Stephen said.

'That's your damned speciality, isn't it?'

'We won tonight, didn't we, and yet we lost?'

'What's that got to do with it? Or – ?'

'I can make it have something,' Stephen said. 'I was thinking that we had no control over Oleg and Tamara. What they were doing and what we did were totally separate, and yet we choose to play with them and they nearly always drag us down. There's a kind of comedy in having done so well together and yet knowing that we can't leap higher than gravity allows. Not on this planet anyway. I liked you. As soon as we met, I wanted to have you as my friend. There was something marvellously

124

appropriate about becoming bridge partners, wasn't there, because it gave us an intimacy that wasn't – what? –'

'Sexual,' Gideon said.

'I never liked male flesh,' Stephen said. 'Did you?'

'It was a kind of suicide,' Gideon said, 'that article. Never. You thought it was murder; it was suicide. Vanity makes you think you did something to me, that the thing backfired and I was . . . but it's not like that at all. I wanted you to be responsible for it, even though you weren't. Because my wanting that to be the case is precisely what proves that it wasn't. I never meant to talk about any of this tonight.'

'I'm flattered,' Stephen Hellman said.

'I think it's to do with Miranda, Stephen, funnily enough. Is that thing supposed to be flashing?'

'Who the hell can that be?' Stephen said. 'What time is it in Lichtenstein?' When he picked up the flat telephone, the light no longer flashed. 'Hellman. Who? Oh! Rather. Just one moment.'

'Sorry to disturb you,' Pamela said, 'but it's Tom. He's in hospital with a broken arm, bruised ribs. I found him on Strang's Steps, more or less unconscious. Perhaps they were waiting for you to be out of the way, perhaps . . . '

'Is he in much pain?'

'They're keeping him in overnight. It's quite an ugly fracture. They also kicked him so much it hurts him to breathe.'

'I've left the car in the car park, I'm not sure if they lock them up at this hour, but I'll get over there right away. I should be home in, oh, three to four hours.'

'Mandy says please don't drive now. You ought to get some sleep. Nothing's going to change between now and tomorrow morning. Did you win?'

'Stephen and I won, but the others lost. We lost. I'll be there by, say, nine or ten in the morning. How are you?'

'Mandy's with me. We're all right. I'm sorry to do this.'

Stephen was pouring more Chassagne-Montrachet into Gideon's glass. 'Damn all this philosophy,' he said. 'As soon as Tom's fit to travel, you're coming down to Suffolk to stay. Miriam's got pals in the property market.

I've only to pass the word and she'll have a dozen places lined up for you to see.'

'Pamela said to say hello,' Gideon said, 'and she's sorry to – '

'I can always arrange money to tide you over.'

'It's not that simple. Pam's got her patients, I've got mine, in a manner of speaking; the kids're in school.'

'Don't be such a German Jew,' Stephen said. 'He who hesitates is up the spout. Miriam'd love to help. She's stuck down there with Hansel and Gretel, our tame krauts, it drives her to Tupperware parties, she's so happy with her lot.'

'Tame krauts?'

'Someone has to mow the lawn and the cocker spaniels. I take particular pleasure in being a model employer. You've connived at your own destruction for long enough, Gidman, it's time to give the world a twist *en contre-sens*.'

'This man who – who's in love with Pamela – he spent part of the war in Tourcoign. Do you remember Tourcoign?'

'Do I remember Tourcoign?' Stephen said. 'Do I *remember* Tourcoign? No, I don't remember Tourcoign. Should I?'

'Where the car broke down, the old cheese-grater. We spent the night in that unbelievable hotel.'

'*Le knocking shop du Nord!* Was that Tourcoign? Believe it nor not, that was the only time in my life that I ever saw anyone else actually fucking, apart from cinematographical representations which I have attended in the course of my duties as a part-time authority on copyright and other *louche* topics. Come on, Gids, grab a slurp of this and look on the bright side. We could always ditch Oleg and Tamara and form a new model army. Have some kitchen roll.'

'I'm terribly sorry,' Gideon said.

'Tears don't bother me,' Stephen said. 'I've seen strong accountants break down and sob uncontrollably when their Cayman Island tax shelters fail to keep the wolf from the whore.'

'I just don't know what's going to happen,' Gideon said.

'My crystal ball is in my other scrotum,' Stephen said, 'so don't look at me. But here's my prediction for the next little while; you're going to do some quick sleeping and I'm going to fix for my regular chappie to come and pick you up at six o'clock and take you to your car—'

'There's no need.'

'Of course there isn't, but allow me my petty ostentations. You're going to go to Chaworth General and see Tom and then, as soon as may be, and maybe sooner, we're going to arrange a swift evacuation.'

Gideon hit tears from his face and took the plates to the stainless steel sink.

'Mrs Idiot can take care of all that in the morning,' Stephen said. 'It'll be all right, Gidman, you have my word on it. I can't stretch to anything more substantial for the moment, but you're coming to stay for as long as you like. I may not be able to call you tomorrow, because I have to be in court all day, on account of some foolish virgin who didn't check the difference between residence and domicile.'

'What difference is there?'

'Well, there isn't any really, but that ain't what I shall be telling their lordships. Residence, I shall be claiming, is where you are and domicile is where you'd like to be. You have a residence, Gideon, but we have yet to find you a domicile.' Stephen put his arm across Gideon's shoulder. 'Gondola, gondola, my friend!'

8

Even at half-past six, there were hitch-hikers facing the Renault as Gideon drove up the ramp to the A1. He had passed the only girl before he could be sure of her sex; the wing mirror announced that he had missed a slim blonde with accordion creases behind her jeaned knees. A few yards further on was a young man, sub-titled 'Chaworth' on a cardboard strip. Gideon was looking at the blonde when he pulled up. The young man bent to the window and Gideon leaned to open the door. 'Your lucky day,' he said. 'I'm going to the very place.'

A nylon sausage, frankfurter-orange, was squeezed on to the back seat, next to books Gideon had already had a reminder about, and the young man, in a quilted jacket and green, brushed-cotton jeans, gave him a clean smile as he settled in. He had a Scorpio tattoo on his right wrist; the cipher underlined pollen-gold hairs. 'Salesman?'

'In this heap? I'm ... well, what am I? I'm a jack of several trades. I lecture, I write reviews, I do a bit of television ... You probably wish you hadn't asked. I probably do too.'

'Up early.'

'What do you do?'

'I've been working with this plumber.'

'In Chaworth?'

128

'Brent. I'm going to see someone. Up and down, I do quite a bit of it. Something wrong?'

'Oh yes,' Gideon said, 'absolutely. Very much so. But it doesn't matter.'

'I'm not . . . '

'I didn't sleep a lot and I . . . my kid's in hospital. My son. Got beaten up coming home from school.'

'Clever, is he?'

'His only known crime,' Gideon said.

'He wants to thump them.'

'*I* want to thump them, but where does thumping get us?'

'Provoke them, does he? You write songs at all?'

'One thing I haven't got round to,' Gideon said. 'That, and the hexameter epic. Give me time. Give me space.'

'I write songs.'

'And what about the music?'

'On my way to that, aren't I? I think I'll have a bit of a zzz, O.K.? I just do the words. That's why . . . ' He indicated the road ahead and then turned sideways, knees up, head against the corner between the seat and the window, and made himself tidy. Content to be impersonal, Gideon drove the boy rather than himself, vigilant while the other slept. Tiredness kept him uneasily alert as he headed for Chaworth. He could have sworn that he did not actually yawn once until the very moment when the young man woke and caught him doing so.

'Tired?'

'Not far now.'

A board by the roadside spelt out: TEA AND SAUSAGES, 100 YARDS. The young man touched chapped lips with the back of his anchored wrist. Gideon took his foot from the accelerator and drifted towards the lay-by where a drop-sided truck had been parked on old puddles. 'Fancy something?'

'If you do.'

The tea was yellow-brown and very hot. The sausage, mittened in a white bun, farted fat as Gideon bent to it. The young man leaned back on the Formica shelf, propped on high elbows, and drank a glass of milk. Gideon had the impression that his companion knew the bone-

129

headed man who served them, though they exchanged no spoken greeting. 'Nice sausage,' Gideon said. 'Sure you won't?'

'You enjoy it.' The hitch-hiker sucked blue air through an invisible straw and released it from flared nostrils. 'Country!'

Gideon relished the heat of the tea, another slow gradient between himself and what he would find at home. Wary of the receptive look the young man was giving him, he avoided being too direct in his thoughts. They had radios in hotels and hospitals which, even when turned right down, so that no sound was emitted, were still technically on. Gideon feared that his own consciousness sometimes gave off waves which a sensitive companion might pick up. It was not always a good idea to be too clear in one's mind. He looked at his watch and left some of his tea on the Formica shelf.

'Better?'

'Much,' Gideon said.

'Got a bird in London? Overnighting, were you?'

'Actually, I was playing bridge.'

'Where'd you sleep?'

'A friend's place. Careful . . . That's where I heard about my son.'

Rubbing his head in the corner of the car, the young man watched Gideon start the engine. 'Not in danger, is he?'

'No, my wife – '

'I've got this new song, it's called "It's over, Casanova". I'm going up to have this pal of mine put music to it. You can make a lot of money still with songs.'

'More than ever, I should imagine. How does it go?'

'"It's over/Casanova/you say you're a Rover/say you're a dog/and it's over/Casanova/over." I'll get myself a BMW, if it catches on.'

'I was in one this morning,' Gideon said, 'funnily enough. Chap gave me a lift to my car.'

'Slept badly?'

'Single beds . . . ' Gideon said. 'When you're not used to them.'

'You need a stretch. Know the abbey, do you, just up along here?'

'I've never seen it,' Gideon said. 'Often meant to.'

'It's only a mile or so off the road.'

'It won't take long, will it?'

There were reddish stone walls around the abbey and a Gothic lodge with glistening green gates. The drive went between dun bursts of rhododendrons before bending to the left towards the ruins, whose unglassed front was paned with sky. A grey lake was scuffed by the wind. There seemed to be a secret climate here; the sky wore a towering white hat, edged with black.

'Do you want to go in?'

'Do you?'

'I'm happy just to look,' Gideon said. 'I hate tours and guide books and those things, don't you?'

They walked through an archway leading to the abbey church. Soft grass pinched Gideon's heels. The young man tiptoed on tooled boots. Skirting the church, they came to steps leading down into a garden with a long terrace above a herbaceous border. A peacock, spoked with a sorry fan, stalked along the terrace and down brick steps which took it to the lawn.

'He had the right idea, didn't he?'

'Who was that?'

'The bloke lived here. He knew how to do it. Poet, wasn't he? I'm surprised you stopped. I didn't reckon you would. On the road. Why did you?'

'To give you a lift, didn't I?'

'Being in a hurry.'

'Company keeps me awake,' Gideon said.

'Always sends me to sleep.'

The ancient house was crowned with a cross that carried four equal arms. The peacock, for no remarkable reason, gave out a sudden scolding yell. Its little head lost dignity. The two men smiled at each other, more from embarrassment than shared humour; coincidence be-friended them. A gentleman gardener, in boots and a deerstalker, trundled through the arch above the brick steps with a wheelbarrow. Gideon turned away, but the young man stopped and gazed at the uncurtained win-

131

dows of the great hall. 'It's not open.' The gentleman gardener was doing his duty. 'How did you get in here?'

Gideon had reached the rose garden. In the centre, a dry fountain was stubbled with lichen. The roses had fattened to hips; frost-blackened leaves rattled in the breeze. The young man's dawdling provoked Gideon more than the gardener's reproach. A shiver stirred him to square his shoulders and make for the car, which he expected to see at any second, round the next corner. The world was a little bigger than he expected.

Two cars and a coach had arrived and were parked in the yard. Their foreign occupants were reading the sign at the closed door where tickets and souvenirs were supposed to be on sale. Gideon could have backed the Renault and turned to leave without coming into the eyeline of the waiting tourists, but he contrived a wide enough arc for them to get a clear sight of his passenger. By mistake, he stubbed the horn and made them look up.

The rhododendrons bushed high on both sides of the drive once more. As the cambered roadway veered to the right, a narrower track was visible, cutting north towards a stand of oak trees. 'Go up there a sec, why don't you?'

Gideon turned the wheel, as if this was the real purpose of their detour. Untrimmed bushes clapped the sides of the little car. Where the roadway was clear of shrubs, autumn leaves had felted the ditches. Gideon stopped and switched off the engine. (His key was bent; he had to be careful.)

'Sherwood Forest,' the young man said.

'More than likely.'

The young man leaned towards Gideon who, expecting him to point out some other feature of the landscape, turned his head to the window.

'Let's go over there,' the young man said. 'It's nicer. No one about here.'

'What for?'

The young man opened his door and hopped round to Gideon's side of the car to play the footman. Gideon looked at his watch, but the young man put his arm round his shoulders and directed him to the stand of trees. With a steadying push, he placed him against a thick trunk.

'Don't worry.' He drew Gideon's thickening penis from his pants and chafed it until it could stand on its own. Gideon's head was back against the bark, his eyes on curdling clouds. He felt the lips and the tongue and the gorgeous movement. The breeze grew cold on him when the chapped mouth was withdrawn. He turned his head towards the abbey, high-chinned, not to be grated by beard. The lips returned, and the tongue that knew its business. He said, 'No, no.'

It was cold again. 'You sure?'

Backing his flesh against the knotted harshness of the tree, nailed by the arrows of desire, Gideon was thoughtless as a target.

'Nice?'

'Yes.'

'Say please.'

It was cold again. The young man was standing beside him, against the fat tree.

Gideon braced himself not to look, but he felt the smile, heard the wink.

'Please.' Eyes closed against the ending of the dream, he cried out at the measured tenderness. 'We must go,' he said.

'Aren't you going to give me a kiss? *Please.*'

'No,' Gideon said.

The young man scanned the trees, the sky, the rusty fence that began and stopped for no clear reason. The ground swallowed semen in front of him. 'All right then,' he said, 'fair enough.'

Was every reprieve also a disappointment? They were soon on the main road again. 'There's Chaworth,' Gideon said. 'It's amazing how far away you can see it from. Must be a good twelve miles. It makes me think of the Roman legionnaires marching up here to the camp. They always built them to pretty well the same design. That way, I suppose, the soldiers felt they weren't all that far from home.'

'Did that make it worse, do you think, or better?'

'I imagine it had to make it more, well, unexceptional,

and unexceptionable. There must be an easier way of putting it than that, but I can't think of one for the moment. If everything is alike, why should one ever find a moment when anything in particular becomes unendurable?'

'Appreciate the lift,' the young man said.

'And I the company.' They had passed the turning to Blackley Cross. A factory was smoking behind heavy hedges. 'Where do you want exactly?'

The young man indicated ahead, where the Minster ruled the horizon with its long frown. 'You wouldn't have a spare ten, would you?'

Gideon drove with care. Lorries beat southwards, screening and releasing the wind in rectangular welts. 'To tell you the truth, I don't have a spare anything.'

'You said you did things for the telly.'

'Have you got a particular problem?' Gideon said.

'Just the usual one.'

Gideon made an awkward favour of reaching into his trouser pocket, eyes on the narrowing road. He came up with two pound notes and held them across to his passenger. 'If that's any use to you.'

The young man left the money in Gideon's fingers as they crossed the railway and then he ran his warm hand over Gideon's wrist and knuckles and palmed the cash. 'No obligation.'

It was just after half past nine when Gideon turned into Beacon Terrace. Pinching crumbs of sleep from the corners of his eyes, he checked his zip and went into the house, a stranger with a key. Pamela's glance from the front room made it familiar again. She was talking on the telephone and turned her body , as if shielding something delicate. It brought him to her, arms around bones and softness. 'I'll look in this afternoon,' she was saying, not for the first time. 'Without fail.' She made a burden of what had been her pleasure and sighed as she replaced the receiver. 'He almost seems to hope I'll let him down.'

'Cruel is kind sometimes, isn't it?' He kissed the orange lips, tongue seeking the little pinch between the front teeth.

'You seem to be home.'

'We're going to get out of this damned house,' Gideon said. 'We're going to get out of this damned *town*.'

'Do you want something to eat?'

'Have you had any sort of apology?'

'I did see Aileen in the street. She burst into tears as soon as she saw me and had to run into her house.'

'She's an old porcupine: she has only one trick. But in her case it's not a particularly good one, is it? I'm going to get the police on it this time, Pam. I don't care what anyone says, this time no one's going to get away with it.'

'Meaning I'm not?'

'Meaning it can't go on. *Can* it? Stephen wants us to go and see them at the weekend. You . . . Miriam's going to look out some cottages in their area. Frankly, this isn't something I'm prepared to refer back to my executive committee. Who needs Chaworth?'

She shrugged from his embrace. 'We can go and get Tom, if – '

'I'm not waiting for a death in the family,' he said. 'Stephen – '

'Oh all right,' she said, 'all right.'

Tom watched them coming down the ward, his plaster arm like a white weapon sheathed across his pyjamas. A blade of sunlight grazed new hairs on his lip and gingered his eyelashes.

'So they finally gotcha, did they, kid?'

'Hullo, dad.' The boy's eyes were on his mother.

'Lucky I wasn't there,' Gideon said, 'or someone important might have got hurt. I'm really sorry, Tomkins.'

'It's all right,' Tom said. Gideon might have been doing what the Monahans had failed to do; he became their excused apologist. 'Could you ask them to bring my clothes, mum?'

It was a day without reliable identity; Tom's presence in the house defeated the calendar. He did not have to go to bed, yet he was a patient. His breathing required Gideon at least to match its rhythm, to share the bruises. When Pamela went to keep her afternoon promise to Mr Fagin, Gideon watched his son painting his Spitfire as if he had been offered, and then denied, a share in the work. Tom's competence almost made his fracture into a fraud, he handled the model and the brushes with such dexterity. Gideon retreated to his little room, where everything was the same and everything had changed, and resumed the drudgery of rewriting the material for hello-it's-Jack. He did not stop to make tea (though he took care to ask Tom if he wanted anything) and typed with uninterruptible urgency when he heard Pamela shut the front door and the ting of the Raleigh's bell against the wall.

The telephone rang as they were sitting down to tuna spaghetti and cabbage. Stephen was laconic and practical: he and Miriam expected them for the weekend and she already had two or three properties for them to inspect. The financial side was not something they should worry about for a moment. What were friends for?

'So,' Miranda said, 'we shall meet the famous Stephen Hellman at last.'

'You've met him before,' Gideon said, 'only you don't remember.'

'So we shall *re*-meet the famous but forgotten Stephen Hellman at last.'

'I've never met him, have I?' Tom said. He was drawing a bi-plane on his plaster with a magic marker. It took a lot of breath through the nostrils.

'We shall have to hit the road *de bonne heure*,' Gideon said. 'I hope it won't clash with anyone's weekend plans.'

'Go ahead,' Miranda said, 'make a third London airport of my carefully structured programme.'

'You don't have to come,' Pamela said.

'If there's going to be champagne, count me in. What's true love when it comes to the high life? Unless, of course — '

'Was Sean Simmonds involved this time?' Gideon said.

'He's got this girl,' Tom said. 'He says she's a goer.'

'I should think he's boasting, wouldn't you?'

'Probably. What *is* a goer?'

'A fraudulent male term for a girl who is shameless enough to have the same sexual desires that the unfair sex has, and gives rein to them. Are you thinking of going back to school with that?'

'He's not going back before the weekend,' Pamela said, 'at the very earliest.'

Tom soon fell asleep under his stars, a child crusader with his arm entombed on his chest. The mauve Mini came noisily to collect Miranda. There was to be another little jazz session at the Minster. Gideon and Piers waved to each other through the night-dusty glass of the sitting room. Pamela had gone upstairs to have a bath. Joining the conventional calendar with a little jolt, like a shunted truck, Gideon went to the television set just as the heroine in the classic serial was being led to her death in the public square, under lopped plane trees. Was it stated in the novel that she was wearing the same dress she had unbuttoned when she let the notary sample her bosom? It was from the lawyer's balcony that the camera chose to watch the guillotine, the executioner's punctilious glance at the clock on the *préfecture* and the snap of the leashed blade. The director wished upon the notary a sigh of sexual release as the head fell, heavy fruit, into its creaking basket. A wet Maître Barottin buttoned his black coat and limped to his office.

Pamela was brushing her teeth when Gideon went into the bathroom. He stood behind her and put himself into the steamy picture in the mirror. She was wearing her green dressing gown. As she bent to spill white from her mouth, her flesh rose against him. Her face was furred by the mirror; he could not read it exactly. Hips slippery from her bath, and the powder, her dressing gown shifted easily up the polished warmth. He squared her against the basin before his thick bolt locked them together. He moved his hands and bracketed fresh flesh. His breath was loud, like pain, or anger, as she leaned her head back against him, eyes frowned shut. He might have been some rooted trunk that she could rely upon. Desire made him blind too. He closed his eyes and fucked and fucked until clean fingers, and nails, came and triggered him.

9

CONSTABLE'S WAS a lemon-yellow, double-gabled Suffolk farmhouse, with a steeply pitched roof of grey slate. The Hellmans had converted the thatched barn into a playroom, though both Ben and Emma were at a progressive boarding school by the time the work was finished and could use it only in the holidays. The white five-bar gates had been hooked open by the time the Renault nibbled the gravel. Two golden-brown spaniels ran, barked and crouched, with friendly tails, as Stephen, in check tweed trousers and a Saloman anorak, trotted to re-close the gates. Miriam, poppy-mouthed, came out of the house in purple leotards with a wide-collared white sweater over the top. Her hair was gloved in a tight black bandeau. 'Well,' she said, 'you finally made it!'

'And so have you,' Gideon said. 'Doubled and redoubled, by the look of it.'

'What a lovely place!' Pamela said.

'Come on in and have a drink. Miranda, oh dear, aren't you pretty? And Tom, so much bigger than I expected! How is it today, the arm? I hope I'm going to be allowed to sign it too!'

'How are you, *maître*?' Gideon said.

'Masterly,' Stephen said. 'Except that I never warned you to bring swimming things.'

'In *November*?'

138

'God help us,' Stephen said, 'we've built a little winter pool. Miriam likes the exercise and I like the expense. It's a perfect marriage. Of course, there's no need to wear anything at all, but people are funny.'

'Daddy, you have to come and see this kitchen,' Miranda was calling as the two men entered the house. The hall was stone-flagged and the flourish of staircase went up under a pair of Dendy Sadler paintings, the first of a lawyer consulting with his client and the other of two society women having tea in a panelled morning room, appropriate with knick-knacks and bibelots. The new kitchen was blond with Scandinavian fittings; its white brick walls carried a Steinberg poster in a steel frame and six Perspexed photographs of an ancient port in the Persian gulf, signed and numbered. The far wall was all glass above the double sink and looked out on a courtyard with a huge fig tree. The facing playroom was an inaccurate reflection of the house. 'Isn't it amazing?' Miranda said.

'This wood is lovely,' Pamela said, 'what is it?'

'Beech? Maple? I.C.I.? I shall have to consult my cheque stub. Meanwhile I propose to open some shampoo unless there are any militant vegetarians in this party, are there?'

'Vegetarians?' Tom said. 'Surely wine . . . oh, I get it!'

'You will if you stand too close to people who've got it already, Tom. It's all for Miranda really. You see, I've already put the flutes out in your honour. Flutes for the flautist? Subtlety is the badge of all our tribe, unless you've met some of the examples I have. Venetian these, Gideon, specially in case we ever have to make another psychic bid. Poor old Oleg, he's still seething.'

'Flutes?' Tom said.

'The glasses you drink champagne out of, Tom, are called flutes,' Gideon said. 'Or rather the glasses some people drink champagne out of.'

'Your father', Stephen said, 'always has his out of paper cups, but that's because he comes of classy stock. We *parvenus* have to try and do things properly. Here you are, Miranda; play me a little tune on that, if you can. So! Here we are then: chin-chin and welcome to suburban

Suffolk. Double-chins all round, in fact!'

'Speak for yourself, handsome.'

'And this is my wife Miriam, of whom you may hear more 'ere the day is done. I was telling Gideon, if anyone wants to swim before lunch, the puddle waits.'

'And if anyone wants lunch before swim,' Miriam said, 'they'd better move out of here and let me get on with it. Stephen, why don't you play the butler and show them their apartments?'

The guest flat was above the treble garage (the Mercedes 350SE, Miriam's VW Golf and a space for Hansel and Gretel's Mini estate). There was a separate staircase and front door, for which Stephen promised them a key, not that they would really need it. Hansel and Gretel were both honest and clean in their habits. Anyway, they lived in a cottage beyond the summer pool and would not tread on anybody's toes. After mastering a tap in the bathroom which mixed hot and cold water to any requisite temperature, Tom was of the view that they should look no further for their new home. Pamela stood between aubergine and yellow curtains and looked across dimpling lawns towards the hard tennis court, red and green in its half-skirt of windbreak. Gideon was interested in the books which Stephen had evidently selected for them; one was a study of divorce by an American journalist.

After mushroom soup, *filet de boeuf en croûte*, with peas and *pommes Lyonnaises*, during which they drank a couple of bottles of Château Cissac, Miriam produced apple amber and cream. Stephen came up from the bottom of the fridge with some Château Coutet he swore had to be finished, although it looked quite untouched. 'When it comes to clients,' he said, 'I favour those whose gratitude comes in liquid form, preferably by the dozen. You may think this golden syrup testifies to my palate, but no, it testifies only to my tongue and its profitable wagging.'

'No need to be modest, Stephen,' Miriam said, 'no one was thinking that it testified to anything else.'

Her hair was very black and she had put on more make-up for lunch. She had slim white arms and plump breasts whose size she emphasised with theatrical movements. When they had had coffee, under the brown Matthew Smith nude in the drawing room, she went to change her clothes and thickened her mascara. 'I do want you to see Quince Cottage,' she said, 'before it gets dark.' Grey-trousered, she drove the big Mercedes (ski-latches on its roof) with competent casualness. They crossed a bridge over the London road and were in cowpat country, with untrammelled hedges broken only where milk churns gleamed on wooden platforms. The stench of pigs twisted their noses.

Quince Cottage was at the intersection of three roads. A signpost promised villages 1½, 2¾ and 6 miles away, but the bent fields, heavy soil pleated from the plough, seemed large enough to demonstrate the curve of the earth as they drooped to a twigged horizon. The cottage, three up, two down, was of rosy brick. Dormer windows, under a scowl of thatch, looked over a seedy front garden. The gate was almost locked by black-stemmed nettles. 'Somehow I don't think the people are going to be in,' Miranda said.

'No one's lived here for almost a year,' Miriam said.

Gideon saw the look that passed between Stephen and Miranda and glanced to see if Pamela had spotted it too. She had walked away, along a cinder path, towards the overgrown orchard; the branches of the plum trees bent to the ground, weighing a crop they had long shed.

The cottage was deserted, but not quite empty. An oak table, with two narrow benches, went from the front to the back of the kitchen. There was a high stool, with a spade-shaped seat, scooped for the buttocks, next to the Aga. 'Complete with map of Australasia,' Miranda said, tracing a damp patch next to the stable door that gave on to the back garden.

'It does need a few things doing to it,' Miriam said. 'And the garden has gone rather.'

'Nothing that can't come back,' Miranda said.

Miriam managed a smile and went into the sitting room. Gideon left Miranda and Stephen by the Aga. Pamela was coming through the front door and looked at Gideon as though he was with a different party. The sitting room had oak pillars supporting the beams. 'A four-poster lounge!' Gideon said. Miriam was trying to open a cobweb-snagged window; she seemed to have too many clothes on to do it. Gideon took over the stiff job. 'Personally,' he said, 'I could live here very happily. Where are the nearest shops and things?'

'You do drive, don't you?' she said.

'Of course.'

'Stephen doesn't. He likes to be helpless. Five or six miles to Tesco's. It's very cheap, because it's an executor's sale, and I've got a very reliable little man – '

'None more so,' Stephen said, coming in with his parody of an important walk. 'How did the song go? You can rely on me . . . '

'Pam's making herself at home!' Gideon pointed up at her footsteps in the room above them.

'The heir lives in New Zealand,' Miriam said, 'so he's not in much of a position to drive a hard bargain.'

Pamela appeared in the doorway of the sitting room and then some haughty modesty took her away from them and out again into the darkening garden. Her image was at every window, quick or slow, as she passed the people in the sitting room, each of them seeing her differently. She was there with them, like a ghost, and not there at all. Miriam frowned and was rubbing at a stain above the soot-shaggy fireplace. When Pamela joined them again, she was carrying a dry posy of winter-shrivelled herbs. 'I love it,' she said.

'No need to sound so peevish, mama,' Miranda said. 'That is the verdict of us all, is it not?'

'It remains only to find the money,' Gideon said. 'Tom, you start digging in there and the rest of us'll – '

'Shouldn't you at least see one or two of the other places I've got lined up?' Miriam said.

'You all go ahead,' Miranda said, 'I'm buying this one with mama.'

The decision seemed a joke that Miriam was not quite able to enjoy. Either she thought that they were being polite (and would renounce their enthusiasm when they were free of obligation) or that it was frivolous to fall in love so lazily, with the first place on offer. Pamela herself appeared bemused by her own lack of hesitation. As they drove back to Constable's, she chewed at her forefinger and looked keenly at cottages whose lights were beginning to shine behind their gates. Tom sat in the back corner of the Mercedes, lumbered with his white arm.

Hansel and Gretel, whose names were Erik and Trudie, had returned. The Italian lamps had been lit, globes of opalescence, one each side of the Dutch-tiled fireplace, and tea was soon being wheeled into the drawing room. Stephen wanted to know whether Tom was interested in computers; Ben had this Texas Instruments set-up in the playroom. Tom showed new knowledge at once; Gideon had no idea that he was so well-informed, but apparently his friend Clarky was heavily into computerology. In proud surprise, Gideon watched Stephen walk away with his son. He had to get to his feet and go and look at books.

The seclusion of the study, with its partners' desk, Queen Mary chair, a brass lamp, long-necked, behind it, Victorian brackets between shelves learned with legal volumes, enclosed Gideon in a snug trap. He was glad to get away from the women; Miriam was showing Pamela the drawings their architect had done for Hansel and Gretel's cottage. Willie and his wife were coming to dinner, though they had not been told, Miriam promised, that the Shands might be moving into Quince Cottage. The lie was a cosmetic that brightened her bright eyes and lent vivacity to her tongue.

A section of Stephen's library, remote from the Law Reports which backed his handsome chair, was devoted to Jewish affairs. Good God, the very book which Gideon had so recklessly agreed to review, almost twenty years before, was pinched between Wasserstein and Gilbert, both of whom seconded the case which Gideon had been the first to argue. He sat with the foxed pages before him, in Stephen's winged chair, and was surprised to taste again the same nausea at the mandarin's nicely-spoken complacency. There was a lump at the back of the book, which at first he took to be the badly folded dust jacket. When he changed his position, to read more deeply, it slipped into his lap and he realised that it was the very article that he had written, three dense pages from a

143

defunct weekly. First he scanned the irrelevant back of the cutting, dated with eclipsed names and forgotten issues, its prose once perky with ironies now callow or incomprehensible, before he turned to his own peroration.

It is hard for those inexperienced in the practicalities of policy and the machinery of a great career to understand why a man like Lord Laidlaw should feel himself obliged to defend the indefensible or to deny the manifest. There is perhaps something heroic in loyalty to colleagues whose actions would seem nasty in small boys and contemptible in the pettiest functionaries of a corrupt republic. We can imagine with what scorn these men would have been treated had they belonged, say, to one of the city states whose aberrant policies and vacillating principles the young Dr Laidlaw so searchingly denounced in early work which is only just being superseded. The style, self-consciously in the tradition of Gibbon and Macaulay, has not changed, though like some exiled patriot who makes his sword available to a dubious cause, here he puts it in the service of cowards and time-servers, of hypocrites and place-men. Nothing, I am sure, is more inadvertent, so to say, than the link which Laidlaw so clearly demonstrates between the mentality of those Germans who, as their defenders argue, were only doing their jobs and our Foreign Office officials who, with neat pens and perfect grammar, minuted the callously logical documents which Laidlaw chooses to quote with such selective candour. In great matters as in small, *Consequences* treats us to a painful reminder that elegance of argument is no safeguard against smallness of mind. If the style is the man, then this use of Augustan prose must cast doubt not only on the value of the well-balanced period but also, in desperate times, on the value of the well-balanced man. The chilly clarity of the narrative raises questions not only about the nature of diplomacy but also about the notion of the civilisation which men like Neil Laidlaw supposed themselves to be serving. It seems typical of him that he can defend the secret actions of the powerful, while at the same time glorying in his own incapacity – as a temporary but important member of the Allied Control Commission – to have any impact on the decisions which he implemented with such zeal. Blaming the defects of democracy for whatever has now been exposed to the scrutiny of those whom this lifelong academic is pleased to call 'carping intellectuals who have never been called upon to execute a policy or to modify it when obliged by the impersonal forces of history', his lordship derides democracy for whatever is abhorrent to honour or justice on the grounds that the kind of 'retribution' (Laidlaw's inverted commas) for which 'some shrill and intemperate voices' called, and may still be calling, would never have been tolerated, at the time, by the electorate of the victorious powers. It is to be noted, though Laidlaw does not care to note it, that when the allied oligarchs decided to return two

144

million exiled Russians to their native country, so delivering the majority of them to death or concentration camps, no apprehension over the possible views of the populace was suffered to deter the prompt execution of furtive decisions. It is not the impersonal forces of history which determined that this promise should be honoured (since it was convenient) and another ignored (since it was unlikely to lead to powerful embarrassments); it was particular men in particular positions, making particular calculations. To argue that there can be no morality to international affairs requires sterner proof than a pious reference to Thucydides and the sneering dismissal of well-meaning naïveté, 'understandably, if misguidedly, getting in a lather about a few cases of ill-judged leniency or even fewer cases of covert partiality.' When we are speaking of unspeakable but thoroughly documented crimes, it is sheer mystification, where it is not systematically mischievous, to suggest that nothing could have been done to punish those who committed them, whose names and addresses were known to the all-powerful conquering authorities and whose behaviour, so far from being secretly endorsed by the crass electorate, whose verdict Laidlaw and his friends respected only when it suited their predilections, was universally condemned except by the best people.

Historians usually observe certain courtesies, and rightly, when engaged even in the most vigorous polemics. It is neither common nor desirable that we should ascribe personal iniquity to those with whose views we differ or whose interpretations affront or offend us. I do not wish to say that Neil Laidlaw is a villain, but how can he be absolved of moral vacuity if he can bring himself, for no clear principle of personal honour or professional thoroughness (his 'memoir' bristles with selective accuracy), to use all his powers of sympathy in order to obfuscate the brutalities of the Nazis and the flippancy of their conquerors, while deploying all his considerable sarcasm and condescending rhetoric in order to deprecate the 'wailing' of the victims and to deny the scandal of their treatment? At the heart of this superb style, there is, quite simply, no heart at all. It is a matter for individual consciences, if also of public interest, to consider whether such a man, whatever the diligence he has shown as an academic or as a seconded *apparatchik*, has any claim to be considered worthy to be the head of a great college, let alone the custodian of its honour. Let him be crowned with coronets and draped in ermine, but let him be absent from places where, amid carping intellectuals who must never be bent by prudence or influenced by tact, he could never, and should never, again feel at home.

Gideon folded the dated cutting along its yellow creases once more and closed it into the back of *Consequences* by Neil Laidlaw, until recently Master of the college to which Stephen had just been elected an Honorary Fellow.

10

WILLIE AND Jan Cashmore were nicely dressed and nicely spoken. It was hard to know what it was that made them appear quite so flushed. Willie soon proved that he did indeed know perfectly well that the Shands were thinking of moving to the district, but he refrained from advertising his professional availability while remaining genial with sound advice. Before dinner, Stephen mentioned that he had always wanted to have a cloister and wondered whether it was possible to turn the fig tree courtyard into a four-sided walkway where he could indulge in secular meditation. He did not, it was evident, want Willie to feel that he and Jan had been invited only to make up the numbers or to audition for work. Business was poor for architects and likely to get worse, so Stephen gave Willie a good appetite for the salmon trout (Trudie's speciality) by hinting at a new commission. Despite Cashmore's wry lamentations about the state of the economy – he had been obliged to cut his staff yet again – his wife was so keen a supporter of the government that she was holding a coffee party at 'Pincher's Mill', in honour of the local member, on the following Wednesday. She was terribly sorry that Gideon and Pamela would be gone by then. 'You could have met some nice people,' she said, rosy with her own certainty, 'but I'll get you another time.'

'I'm not sure that we're necessarily of your persuasion,' Gideon said.

'Then I shall have to persuade you,' she said. 'Stephen and Miriam weren't Blues when they first came to the district, were you?'

'Now then, Jan,' Stephen said, 'you mustn't boast of your missionary successes at table. Save them for the synagogue.'

Red, Jan said: 'This is delicious, Miriam. So juicy!'

After dinner, Tom wondered if it would be all right if he went back to hunting the Wumpus. Miranda was promoted from silence by her brother's exit and asked about local music. Luckily Willie Cashmore knew a member of the L.S.O. who lived on the estuary and who, he was sure, would be helpful in finding her a teacher. As for schools, Jan said that although personally they had chosen to have Julian and Vicky board, there was no shortage of places of which well-spoken people spoke well; she was sure that Tom – wasn't it? – would have few problems. Pamela smiled unconvinced agreement. Gideon too knew that they would never be able to afford the fees, but his wife's polite reticence struck him as supercilious. He tried to bring her into a conversation about the Open University, which Jan Cashmore suspected of being 'pinkoid', if not worse, but she raised a flat hand, like someone covering a glass when offered more wine, and refused to have an opinion about whether he should go on teaching. Stephen was agile with decanters and bottles; the evening carried all the marks of effortless civility, but something about his host's assiduousness seemed to Gideon almost demeaning. Why should a man used to abstruse argument, and the demands of a profession where learning was not ascribed merely as a courtesy, take so seriously the petty punctilio of provincial life? Presumably, the ritual of the law engaged Stephen more passionately than the enactment of domestic civilities. Here in his own house, amid the treasures he had earned and chosen, the proofs of skill and taste, he was whimsically vigilant in order to prove to a deferential and hungry architect, and his fat, small-eyed wife, that he was qualified to be their host. Simul-

taneously, his posture hinted that he was aware of the sly
sufférance to which he had consented. The aged cutting
about *Consequences* had reminded Gideon more keenly
of what Stephen was once like than of his own lost years.
The prose might have echoed the stuffiness of Laidlaw's
high English, but the zeal with which he had followed his
model, and his prey, had been borrowed from Stephen's
undergraduate zest for parody and derision. Gideon's use
of the grand manner was at once audition and resignation. In that challenging final sentence, where he had not
only doubted Laidlaw's credentials but also impugned his
worth, he saw how insolently he must have seemed to
serve notice to the College Council that he attached
scant importance to their corporate accolade. After that,
how could he seriously have hoped to be elected to a
fellowship? The scornful tropes (ah tropes!) of his article
said hail and farewell in the same hot breath. Whom had
he hoped to please by them, unless it was his present host
who now bent over forwards to make the right impression on nullities? The old Stephen, the young Stephen,
winked at him once across the space between the two
buttoned-leather Chesterfields, in disdain for all this
luxury, this camouflage, this apology, and Gideon took
his own broad smile in his hand and palmed it for later.

He could see Stephen, in his undergraduate rooms in
Third Court, wonderfully eloquent, though his precise
form of words, unlike his posture, was beyond recall, as
he asked tenderly whether there was any way that he
could assume the odium he forecast would fall on Gideon
when the Laidlaw review was printed. Could he not, for
instance, simply sign the article himself? There was no
way, Gideon had replied, that its true authorship would
not emerge; any moderately specialised intelligence
would recognise that the detailed passages of the review
had to be the work of a historian, not of a merely
eloquent amateur. By postponing discovery he would
succeed only in appearing furtive or craven. The assassin
must present himself in person and accept the responsibility for his just act. How strenuously sincere Stephen
then appeared as he argued for suppressing the review
altogether! He wished that he had never suggested to the

editor that he send the book to Gideon and he warned of the vindictiveness of academics and, what could be worse, the delight some of the dons would take in promoting their own mediocre fellowship candidates at the expense of an obvious choice who had announced himself deficient in soundness. Fellows had to live not with abstract principles but with each other; their comfortable seclusion was dependent, in part, on those in high places who would be only too glad to find unacknowledged reasons for dispensing their favours elsewhere. Gideon had chosen to ignore that there was no incautious or fearless academic realm where, as he had suggested so hopefully in his article, intellectual honour was the only thing that counted. However exactingly deferential he might have intended to be, his election would threaten to bring enthusiasm into a society where sleeping dogs were generally encouraged to lie. Gideon had many reasons for mollifying the forthrightness he showed in his article, but he had one reason not to, which overrode them all: his decided commitment to Stephen Hellman.

Over coffee, in summery German cups, Stephen urged Willie to tell the Shands a little about the facts of life in East Anglia. They should not think that they were quitting Chaworth for any promised land, should they? The local market town had been systematically, and profitably, uglified by a clique of architects and builders whose taste and standards Willie had been rash enough to question, when he and Jan first came down from London. He had done it properly, through the local Conservation Society, and then only after he had been appointed to its Fine Arts Committee on the recommendation of the R.I.B.A. Maurice Phipps, the head of the developers' syndicate which had the ear and, as Stephen asserted, other notable organs of the planning authority, went out of his way to say that he and his colleagues would greatly welcome William Cashmore's informed views and that he hoped that he would not pull his punches. 'And what happened then, Mr Cashmore, in your own words, asked counsel meaningly?'

'Let's not have the whole story again,' Jan said.

'It's not again for us,' Gideon said.

'Phipps came up to me after a meeting of the committee and said he'd like us to have lunch at Lampeter's Lodge, which is the big local expense-account place, and I must say we had half of a really slap-up meal.' Cashmore blushed under the rigid grin of his wife and Gideon recognised a tincture of malice in Stephen's prompting. 'Then, well, to put it briefly, he said that if I wanted to work in the district, it might be a good idea if I learnt that there was a time to speak and a time to keep silent.'

'Did he walk out or did you?' Gideon said.

'Willie did,' Stephen said. 'He walked out of there and into here, more or less, didn't you? Legally, there wasn't a damned thing I could suggest, but at least you've managed to survive without rattling your cup of coins in the hideous bloody shopping precinct that Maurice, of course, succeeded in foisting on the town, despite decent citizens' cries of oy and whoa and, in selected venues, Jesus Christ.'

'It's actually not all that bad,' Jan Cashmore said, 'is it, Willie, the development?'

'I hate it,' Cashmore said, as though he were expressing agreement.

'He went about it the wrong way,' Jan said. 'I don't blame him, but he did. He should have waited till he'd made his name.'

'I did make it,' Cashmore said, 'I made it mud, and most of it has stuck.'

Pamela said: 'I love the kitchen.'

Cashmore leant forward and squared the heavy volumes on the glass table between the Chesterfields. The blood gathered in his forehead, under the chaff of greying fair hair, and he nodded; a point might have been made against him.

'We wondered what the wood was,' Gideon said.

'Isn't it maple?' Jan Cashmore stood up. Her husband was still not satisfied with the position of the monograph on Sinaitic icons which topped the stack. He put his hands flat on it at last and pushed downwards. He should have risen with a smile, but the glass was suddenly ice: the thrust of his hands slid him forward. His head loomed at Pamela. Alarmed eyes were level with hers before he ducked forward and dived across the books and glasses, face down between Pamela and Stephen. Jan glared at the company and it was Miranda, in the spoon-shaped Victorian chair by the fire, who was the first to jump forward and put a hand on the lay figure of the architect. They had to ease him off the table, where wine was dabbling the edges of a limited edition of Verlaine's *Hombres/Femmes*, and through the narrow gully between it and the Chesterfield, before they could turn him on his back and loosen the naval tie and break open his top stud. He moaned, contentedly it seemed, and wanted to settle to a deeper sleep.

'Has this happened before?' Pamela said. 'Is he epileptic?'

'Certainly not,' Jan Cashmore said.

'What about some brandy?'

'Certainly not,' Pamela said. 'You'd better call the doctor, or an ambulance.'

'What do you make of it, Pam?' Gideon said.

'It may be a heart attack, it may be a stroke. Undo his shoes, would you, and get a cushion under his head? Keep him very still.'

'Could it be – could it be the dinner?' Miriam said. 'And the – ?'

'It doesn't have to be serious,' Pamela said, 'but we must get help.'

Stephen was already through the double doors to his study. White spittle gummed a silly smile on Cashmore's purple lips. He sighed deeply and seemed balder, as if his wig had slipped. The scalp was flecked with dandruff and had a woody whiteness.

'Tom's still in the playroom,' Gideon said. 'And look at the time!'

'He doesn't have to get up in the morning,' Pamela said.

'Seb Martindale's on his way over,' Stephen came back to say. 'He's ordering an ambulance. He says hospital has to be the only place to treat this kind of thing.'

'Epileptic!' Jan Cashmore said.

The doctor was cautiously doubtful whether it was a

heart attack, though one never knew; he agreed with Pamela that it was probably a stroke, which was not necessarily worse or better news. The ambulance men collected their patient without fuss and Jan Cashmore said that she would follow them in the Maxi. 'Why not let me drive you?' Gideon said. 'I don't think you should be on your own.'

'I shall manage very well,' she said. Her face was clear of its charge of blood; her eyes denied anyone the right to patronise. 'I shall only have to bring you back. It'll all get much too complicated. Thank you so much for the evening. It was nice to meet you.'

Stephen shook Sebastian Martindale's hand with professional camaraderie, as if some debt had been repaid, holding the other man's forearm and smiling intimately, without making light of the occasion. The whole remaining party was keen to open the gate and make sure that Jan Cashmore backed and turned without a scratch. When she and Martindale had both followed the ambulance out of the gates, Stephen shut and bolted them, quietly; there might still have been an invalid on the premises. They stood in the sharp air (the cobwebs on the roses had begun to shine with frost) and spent the warmth they had brought from the house, before they turned with a common shudder and loped for the front door.

'I thought it was a joke, you know,' Stephen said. 'I thought it was a party piece: man belly-flopping into waterless pool. Saturday night, I don't fancy his chances of finding a local consultant sober, if at all. I told Seb to pull whatever strings might still have bells attached to them. I don't reckon they'll have BUPA, will they?'

'With the boy where he's at school?' Miriam said. 'I should think that takes just about every penny.'

'I shall have to help them,' Stephen said. He walked through the hall, past the Dürer etching and the little Whistler dry-point of a waif standing, in a cheeky posture, at a table in a tenement, and into the drawing room, where the Rosenthal glasses had been left for Trudie in the morning.

'We should be thinking about bed, I suppose,' Gideon

said. 'I shouldn't be surprised if Tom was asleep over in your playroom.'

'I should be surprised if he weren't still on the Wumpus trail,' Stephen said, 'or if he'd not graduated to craftier prey. Have a little more Armagnac before you pull the plugs. It's so rarely that we see you.' The women had gone into the kitchen to make a cup of *tilleul*; their indistinct voices offered intimations of a harem.

'Are they close friends of yours?' Gideon said.

'He does good work, Willie, but there's something in him which seems to have prevented him from catching the tide, for all his nautical experience. Jan's rather a pill, didn't you find? He has excellent qualifications and if he had those entirely spurious attributes which lead on to fortune, I suppose he'd've been one of the leading men of his generation.'

'We can't all be Stephen Hellman,' Gideon said.

Stephen looked at his nails. He had long white hands, franked with clusters of dark hair which silvered in the light of the Italian lamps. The fingers should have belonged to a taller man. 'I had a very strange feeling when Willie had his attack,' he said, 'a strong desire to take charge of the case. One can very easily understand the impulse of the impostor. I was once flying to Salisbury, or Harare as we must now learn to call it, if we want to work for the forces of progress and unity, and they asked if there was a doctor on the plane. It was all I could do not to leap up with my overnight bag and pass myself off as a licensed saviour. My father always said I had surgeon's hands. He was particularly keen that I not merely talk with them.'

'But you did have an advocate's tongue,' Gideon said, 'or was it a surgeon's, considering how cutting it can be?'

'I don't understand why things come into one's head, do you? Or what importance one should lend them. At this moment, what are you thinking about Willie Cashmore? Do you hope he lives or dies?'

'I hope he lives,' Gideon said. 'Good heavens!'

'Oh so do I,' Stephen said, 'so do I. But out of a kind of frivolous indifference more than anything else: I want to be able to enjoy tomorrow.'

'You and the Duc de Guermantes,' Gideon said.

'I've never read it,' Stephen said, 'do you know that, Proust? I often have to bluff when it comes to specifics. Why do you think successful persons collect pictures and Meissen and Degas' sculpture and Picasso's ceramics, to which latter you are more than welcome? Because it's the easiest kind of culture to assimilate; it enables them to quote without having to remember anything and to play the anthologist without having to go into the garden and tend the flowers.'

'I'll make a note of it,' Gideon said.

'All success carries its share of bluff, and hence deserves to fail. Poor Willie, he's devoted all his ingenuity to concealing his origins. We went for a walk together once on the estuary; very beautiful down there, if you like miles and miles of mud and puddles. What I like about it is the faintly sinister air of desertion. The Navy used to have a training range on the foreshore and they did endurance training there too. Something about the atmosphere must have made for confidences – '

'Or something about his companion,' Gideon said.

' – and he started telling me about his childhood in Pinner, Middlesex. It was almost as if he were accusing me of something when he told me about himself. Perhaps I'm romancing; it's the poor man's only creative act – '

'Which poor man did you have in mind?'

'Poverty is not necessarily financial,' Stephen said.

'Not unless you've got no money.'

'You saw how frightfully nicely Willie talks, how keen he is to be tweedy and do the right thing? He sends his boy to one of our leading public schools and practically has to take in washing to pay for it and, of course, the reason is not far to seek; he was brought up in darkest suburbia and, what is more, what is *less*, he is not of wholly Aryan provenance.'

'Stephen, is there no category of being that really concerns you apart from this obsessive dichotomy of yours?'

'Obsessive dichotomy? How dare you employ that term in a room frequently used by my lady wife? I think that's precisely what your sharp consultant would diagnose that poor Willie was struck down by. Obsessive dichotomy, no less! I don't think he'll ever recover either. He had a grandfather called Isaacs and that's why he wears clean socks and subscribes, though he can't afford it, to every bloody appeal for the restoration of our historical church's copper-topped roof. Don't shake your unbalding head, sod you, because I haven't made this up and I'm not personally responsible for the life-histories of my casual acquaintances – '

'I am delegated,' Miranda said, 'by fond mama to tell you that the hour approaches one in the morning and that your son, my brother, cannot be expected to cross the valley of the shadow all by himself. Am I interrupting work of national importance?'

'Why don't you go and rescue him?' Gideon said.

'Ah, well, I have an answer to that, which is, mama is bloody tired herself and wouldn't mind your company in the land of nod. Hint, hint. She's had a lovely day, but. And. If.'

'We rise late on Sundays,' Stephen said, 'but I suppose Pam's right. After all, we may have to go and hold the widow Cashmore's hand.'

Once upstairs, Tom played for longer than his parents' patience easily endured with the variable tap in the bathroom of the flat. They were already in bed before he had had enough. Gideon wore clean pyjamas and sat beside Pamela on the American fitted sheets as if waiting for inspection on his first day at a new school. Tom came and kissed his mother and was kissed by his father and turned out the light for them as he left, the little housemaster.

'What do you make of it?' Gideon said.

Pamela had disappeared in the darkness but now came vaguely back as the moon thinned the curtains. 'That cottage is for me,' she said.

'I was thinking of that poor man.'

'He's in a very bad way, I'm afraid,' Pamela said. 'I can't see him ever being himself again.'

'It seems – I don't know – curiously pushy of him, doesn't it, doing something so immodest as having an attack like that the very first evening we meet him?'

'You've been talking to Stephen all right,' Pamela said, settling into her half of the guest bed, hip high against the moonlight, head down.

'What did you make of him after all this time?'

'He's fatter and balder and more conceited and he hasn't changed a bit,' she said.

'You've been listening to Stephen all right,' Gideon said.

They woke to sunshine and the peremptory coaxing of their host as George and Martha barked at the paper-boy, paws splashing the gravel. Stephen was wearing a brocaded dressing gown over a striped nightshirt that fell short of gilt-buckled pumps. His hair was ruffled on top of his head, as if he too had a master who had cuffed him, with rough affection, as he did the dogs after they had run back to the front door to be dosed with flattering forgiveness.

When Gideon and Miranda crossed to the house, they found Stephen, in the same costume, talking in careful syllables, on the telephone. The *Observer* was folded open at the leader page on the marble table before him and Gideon saw that the main article, 'Crime and Punishment', was by their host. He was looking into a printed mirror. 'There's no reason for you to feel the slightest necessity to do anything, Jan,' he was saying, 'apart from what is absolutely central, which is to be there when he wants you. Is there anything at all you need at home? And how about Jonathan? I see. No, it isn't; it's absolutely nothing. Miriam'll see you tomorrow.' He nodded, with two little jolts of the unshaven chin, before he clicked off the telephone and then replaced the receiver. 'They're still not too sure what it is, but let's hope it isn't catching: it obviously isn't doing him any good. They can't run the full set of checks on him until tomorrow, so he'll have to live till then, won't he?'

'You've written something in the paper,' Miranda said.

'I knew you were coming,' Stephen said, 'so I thought that I should puff myself up as big as possible. A frog he would! When it came to who should reply to the L.C.J., it was between me and Piers Rougier in the final.'

Gideon said: 'I told Stephen about Piers writing for the *St James's Review*.'

'By his works I know him,' Stephen said. 'A formidable fellow in his way. Not that I think he was ever too likely to be found houseroom by this particular publication.'

Miranda said: 'There's no need for anyone to apologise. Talk, talk, talk, is something I'm more than used to.'

'Sorry,' Stephen said.

'*Are* you?' Gideon said.

'He's in the public domain, isn't he? What I said was pretty well true actually.'

'You mean it was false?'

'Come on, Gidman, time for breakfast. Rougier was proposed as a plausible *advocatus diaboli*, but I was greedy for more space than could easily accommodate two nibs. Read the piece and you'll see that it's very much his territory: do we have to renounce the idea of retribution, of punishment, simply because we no longer have a metaphysical warrant to inflict it? Can there be a civilised rationale for imposing deliberately painful penalties on criminals rather than for trying to rehabilitate them, as the cant has it?'

'Do I have to answer right away, sir?'

'I didn't mean to upset her,' Stephen said.

The sunshine softened the ground sufficiently for Miriam, in leotards and another shawl-collared sweater, to take a fat net of bulbs to the lawn near the greengage tree and crouch down, knees on an old cushion, in order to bury them in holes she twisted in the sod with a patent tool. Every time she drove it down, her hips rose and she showed her tight behind to the house, each buttock holstered in a purple parcel. She rose and fell, with regular energy, while Gideon stood in the window of the drawing room, Stephen's article in his hand. Behind him, sitting next to the biscuit-stiff embers of the fire, its author wore half-glasses to look at the other papers.

'What do you think, Gidman? Have I made a fool of myself or do I bid fair to be the spokesman of a rational but never soft-hearted revisionist liberalism to which a sturdy answer will have to be given, if one is to be found at all?'

'I haven't finished reading it yet.'

'Alternatively, are you interested in pink-ponk by any chance? I find it an excellent way of being too busy to help with the lunch.'

'You write very plausibly,' Gideon said. 'Table tennis? I suspect that you'll humiliate me, but the lamb and the slaughter are ever destined to meet this side of infinity, are they not?'

'Hey,' Stephen said, 'don't catch my style too quickly, will you? Miriam won't appreciate polysyllables at table. You could write that sort of stuff on your head.'

'I'd have to shave it first,' Gideon said. 'I don't happen to be a Q.C. and bar, do I, and a frequent member of our panel here this evening?'

'I ought to get you to ghost them for me,' Stephen said, 'and we could go ski-ing on the proceeds.'

'Mandy thinks I've told you that she and Piers . . . You do like to say the generally unsaid, don't you?'

'Whereof one cannot speak *is* inclined to be my favourite topic.'

'I'm not sure how much anyone is supposed to know.' Gideon's gaze was once more on the November green of the lawn and the burrowing neatness of the woman bent before him. He enjoyed her rhythmic competence, under the switching tendrils of the gaunt trees, her busy humbling of herself, glassed away in the open.

'How much does she?' Stephen said.

'The only perfect punishments, or rewards, we devise are for ourselves, are they not, my capitain?'

'And the best are those where the two coincide exactly. That is what we call happiness, is it not?'

'This is a lovely place,' Gideon said. 'Miriam works very hard, doesn't she?'

'I have no complaints,' Stephen said. 'And if I do, there's always BUPA. Yes, she does. Come the spring, you can see me mounted upon my motorised mower, doing my bit in the *panzer-division*, and I also have at the roses when the moment is ripe, but most of it Miriam does and does very well. She and Mr Morley are very peasant help in times of trouble. I could scarcely have a better wife. What about that ping-pong?'

Stephen put on a pair of worn tennis shoes, with blue flanges. Gideon was ponderous in his shoes and slippery in his socks. Stephen's hurtling smashes and crashing retreats as he reverted to defence demanded an agility Gideon could not match. His opponent panted and grimaced and was so determined to win that, as he smiled his way to defeat, Gideon felt superior to the wide-nostrilled enthusiast whom he was obliged to congratulate. At the bridge table, Stephen adopted courtly dignity in the face of misfortune; it was an extension of his legal style to suffer unfavourable results with a wry eyebrow. Here, privileged by ownership, he reverted to the scowling adolescent whom Gideon taught squash in the college courts and who, although he had never played before, was enraged to lose even a single point to his tutor. Gideon had played for his school and, in those days, was faster and sharper than his friend. One evening, Stephen smashed his new racket, from Gray's, against the rubber-bruised wall and announced that the smell of the game was repulsive. Henceforth he would take his exercise playing snooker at the Union.

After lunch, Pamela said that they should really think about leaving; the drive was long and some people had school in the morning. When Tom was not eager to leave his Texas Instruments, Stephen took the boy's part with a keenness which made Gideon look at his watch and adjudge that four o'cock had better be the limit.

'Five,' Stephen said. 'You can't leave before tea. It wouldn't be British.'

Having defeated Gideon at table tennis, Stephen proposed that they try *pétanque*. The Hellmans had a *gîte*, Stephen would put it no more grandly than that, near Ramatuelle, and he had brought back authentic *boules*. They used one of the previous day's champagne corks for a *cochonnet*. Once more, Gideon was reminded of the commitment, even in a trivial cause, which could turn Stephen into someone for whom any inclination to thwart him was an infringement of the rules. He ran into the house in order to fetch a tape measure after the rough calibrations of a twig failed to convince him that Gideon's latest throw was closer to the mark than his own.

When the telephone rang as they were halfway through a vital phase of the competition, he hesitated and hesitated, but the women were somewhere in the far garden and he had to go. Stopping at the scheduled (Adam) door, he frowned at the position of the balls which had already been pitched; serving notice that he would know, should anything be shifted during his absence. And so Gideon was alone when he heard the farp of a horn at the front gate and an old six-cylinder Bristol drew up with a deer stalkered man at the heavy wheel. George and Martha skidded on the threshold of the door and raced down the gravel, ignoring the importance of the precise disposition of the *boules* in their path, and took up their barking stations, front paws on the second bar of the gate.

The driver of the Bristol, gauntleted right hand on his external brake, seemed to pride himself on his immobility as Gideon unlatched the white gate with a questioning politeness, while the other hand unbuttoned his throat. 'Comrade Shand, can it be?'

The voice came without any warm disguise. 'Can it really be?' Gideon said. 'The Michaeljohn *tout entier*?'

At the door of Constable's, Stephen made a long neck at the disturbed *boules* for a moment before he straightened and walked towards the fuss. 'Sorry, but that was the Home Secretary,' he said, 'waxing effusive about my thousand words. How are you, Peter?'

'You never told me this was coming,' Gideon said.

The dogs went wagging backwards as the gate was opened and the stiff Bristol came into the drive. Michaeljohn shucked his Raglan and stood in a tightening grey suit and college tie. Miriam appeared in a pink and black woollen outfit, with a white ruffled shirt and torero's scraggy tie. She had put on white legs and black patent pumps. Behind her, Pamela was unchanged, though something in her watchful humour seemed to imply, to Gideon at least, an apology for allowing Miriam to appear in so ridiculous a fashion. Treading carefully among the *boules*, showing her palms, Miriam was prepared to kiss Peter Michaeljohn. He creased his face for a smile, but kept his lips latched over his teeth. 'You've timed it perfectly, Pietro,' she said, her hand on his arm standing for a large embrace. 'The kettle is boiling. The crumpets are crumping!'

Miranda was coming down the stairs in a thick towelling robe which her hostess had lent her; MH was monogrammed on the left breast. 'I'm just on my way for a quickie before tea,' she said.

'I don't suppose you're swimming, are you, Peter?' Stephen said.

'No, this is known as walking,' Michaeljohn said. 'When I swim, I move my arms altogether more decisively and tend to proceed in a largely horizontal fashion, generally in an aqueous element.'

'Bloody hell!' Miranda said. Gideon winked at her; she could not remember when he had last done so and it made her sad. As Peter Michaeljohn walked on, smiling again with unparted lips, Miranda took Gideon's arm and held him to her. 'What thing of sea or land is *that*?'

'He is probably the next Master of my old college,' Gideon said. 'One Professor Peter Michaeljohn.'

'Must I hurry back?'

'Not for his sake.'

Miranda smiled without parting her lips and moved her haunches in an exaggerated way as she hustled for the pool. Alone in the hall, Gideon took a moment to look at the detail of the lower of the two Dendy Sadlers. On the short return wall between the bottom stair and the drawing room door was a little Matisse etching of a naked woman with a sprig of hair under her raised arm. A tsk, tsk of sardonic sympathy came to Gideon's ears like the symptom of some problem in the woodwork. When it was repeated, after Stephen had mentioned the Proctor twins, he realised that it was Peter Michaeljohn uttering a sound which must have become characteristic during the last twenty years.

'We do have an excuse,' Stephen was saying, as Gideon came in, followed by the tea trolley. 'Oleg Chernoff's convinced they were cheating.'

'Excuse? Even cheats can and should be mastered, or where would our masters come from? Only among equals does the cheat have an advantage. What are you doing these days, Gideon?'

'*Je bricole un peu partout*,' Gideon said. 'What about you, P.M.?'

Pamela and Miriam were nudging the trolley over the thick edge of the carpet by the new fire. Michaeljohn had stood up at the women's entrance; his unhelpful courtesy made him obtrusive. He was of an angular build, lean-faced, broad-shouldered and with a back end which stuck out so that his legs went to the ground a foot or more behind his chin. 'Pamela *what* was it?'

'Parsons?' she said.

'You acted, didn't you, for a while?'

'When the A.D.C. were a woman short.' Pamela was looking at Stephen.

'I wonder if you realise, Mrs Shand, that it was I who officiated at your husband's first marriage? With a certain Hellman S. If it hadn't been for my suave ministrations, never the twain would have met. The world would have been a different place.'

'Are you still picking the university bridge team single-handed, Peter, in your usual democratic manner?'

'I remain in a purely advisory capacity.'

'They also serve,' Gideon said, 'who only stand and sneer?'

'Why did you never come back to Cambridge?'

'Only one small reason; I was never invited.'

'I'm promised – or should it be warned? – that there are plans afoot, and perhaps even on wheels, such is progress, for putting the entire wisdom of the university on to cassettes so that all, not to mention sundry, may have us at their fingertips. You have electronic experience, Gideon, do you not? Might such a programme not be rather up your street or tree-lined boulevard?'

'Is this a college project?'

'No, no, no. But the Press has formed a subsidiary and I've been asked to serve on the board.'

'I know nothing about electronics as such,' Gideon said.

'But a lot about programming,' Pamela said. 'About scripts and – '

'Ah yes, of course,' Michaeljohn said. 'I must make further inquiries about what precisely they require.'

'I say,' Stephen said, 'I suppose Miranda can swim?'

'And life-save,' Gideon said.

'But one can never save one's own. We were warned never to let anyone swim by themselves. It's very warm in there. I think I'll just make sure that all is well.' He went like a parent with a humane excuse for abandoning children brought to school for the first time.

'It's not Cambridge the *place* that Gideon misses,' Pamela said.

'The people, is it?' Michaeljohn said.

Gideon looked into the fire and at the blue tiles that decked the surround. Each was different and some had had to be halved in order to suit the scheme. One such half showed a plump behind, of indefinite sex, bent over a table. A man was about to scourge it with a bundle of twigs. When at last, by way of bucolic scenes, Gideon brought his eyes up into the room once more, he saw that Miriam was holding the teapot towards him. The spout quivered slightly; she might have been posing for a photographer slow with his shutter.

'You mustn't think I'm teasing,' Peter Michaeljohn was saying, 'when I talk about your husband coming back to Cambridge.'

'I don't think you're teasing,' Pamela said. 'I think you're torturing; don't you?'

Gideon was a traveller suddenly aware of being in the wrong company. He stood up, clumsily apologetic, and went from the room. Michaeljohn smiled and had more room for his cup and his creased legs. He acknowledged Pamela's boldness with his toothless grin. 'I was never among those who agreed with the course the College took,' he said. The effort to be agreeable led him to open his mouth more widely. Pamela saw short teeth, sleeved in shining gums, their carious brown abbreviated by the pink. 'In those days, I was hardly a power, still less a glory. Not a few of us held the view that Gideon had had a raw deal – as those who go on lucrative sabbaticals still tend to come home saying – and I've always hoped that something approaching justice might still be done. Alas, his publications have hardly helped his case.'

'They've helped his family,' she said.

'Admirable, admirable, but scarcely relevant to restitution, if that is what's at stake.'

'He couldn't do it all by himself,' Pamela said. 'A friendly word might have made a difference, let alone a helping hand.'

Michaeljohn made a showman's gesture towards Pamela and smiled wetly at Miriam as if she were a crowd, Pamela his star, or stooge. 'You were good to him, when we were not, or *they* were not, as I should prefer to say. The College's – what? – pusillanimity gave you your chance, and you took it.'

'You people remember one thing about a person, don't you, and it lasts you all your lives?'

'To whom am I being assimilated, Mrs Shand?' Sharpness put Michaeljohn in an excellent humour; he smiled unguardedly once more as Miriam serviced his cup.

'Gideon should have been the leading young historian of his generation,' Pamela said.

'Doctor Johnson was denied his patron,' Michaeljohn said, 'but we still have his dictionary. Surely only the weakest need go to collegiate walls in order to fulfil their destinies.'

Miriam moved slightly on her seat, settling to something, her expression so lively that she might have been at the centre of the conversation; eager shifts of attention lent her silence the lineaments of garrulity.

'I think you're being kind in order to be cruel,' Pamela said.

Once again, Michaeljohn pointed at her with an appreciative sweep of the arm. Miriam put her hands together and clasped them, like someone who has almost clapped, in a concert, at the end of a movement and, at the last second, manages to disguise ineptitude as etiquette.

All this time, ready at any moment to amble towards the passage which led to the winter pool, Gideon was in the hall, beyond the half-open door at the end of the drawing room, hardly able to hear the precise words that were being spoken, stirring them into the strange soup of the afternoon, to which Stephen's paintings and other trophies lent a sumptuous, minty flavour. Gideon tasted something on his tongue that demanded a drink he could not name; he had an odd thirst, brought on perhaps by the Gentleman's Relish on Miriam's toast, perhaps by something in the hot, sweet atmosphere of Constable's itself. Above all, however, it was Pamela's low voice which held him there, the voice, it could have been, except that it was not, of quite another woman.

'If he had you,' Peter Michaeljohn said, 'I scarcely think he had any need of us.'

Pamela put her cup on the trolley and made sure that neither china nor cutlery would be displaced when it was moved. Her precision seemed part of an answer which was delivered in full simply by the way in which, when she was ready, she looked into Michaeljohn's thick-lidded green-grey eyes. Miriam moved this way and that and her poppy-red lips eased apart, with delicious reluctance, as Pamela considered the man who faced her. She seemed to take inventory of his qualities, or their lack, with a professional facility so unhurried that it took only a few long seconds. She was intensely interested and drew breath, in the middle, through the little cleft between her nice teeth. Like a glassed text, her eyes scanned him with appreciative accuracy. He made one great move, finally, and raised his arms and locked his hands behind his head, hauling the suit jacket up over his wide hips and giving himself great empty shoulders.

That silence pushed Gideon along the blanched corridor, bawdy with eighteenth-century cartoons, leading to the little pool. Stephen stood on the composition margin (which was falsely squared into regular slabs) looking down at Miranda on her back on the wobbling quilt of water. Her diluted flesh framed a scorch-black heart. Her head was in a yellow bathing cap and thus shorn of hair was singularly naked; she might have been punished, like the girls of whom Daniel had heard, in cruel and condign fashion, but the effect was of election. Her face liberated by the accidental severity, she seemed to be baptised, there in the shimmering water, into the possibility of a new life. Shuddering free of her fixed position, as Gideon came in, she went swimming away, a young girl enjoying a treat, feet feathering, white-soled, auditioning for her father.

11

NUMBER 17, Beacon Terrace found a buyer less than a month later. A supermarket executive, seconded to supervise and co-ordinate the building of the new complex which would eventually overlay the Roman camp, did not even care to quibble about the price, since he would be assisted in its payment, and Ken Bristow was sure that they could complete by Christmas. Gideon had been candid about the infertility of the garden and the need for a damp-course if the passage to his little room was ever to be fungus-free, but not even honesty failed to be the best policy. 'Miracle,' he said, when contracts were about to be exchanged. Nothing, it seemed, could now prevent what the whole family appeared to want.

Miriam telephoned more frequently than Stephen; Gideon answered more frequently than Pamela, who was giving more time than usual to her patients. Miriam kept after the people at her end (Gideon dreaded that they might lose Beacon Terrace without having a firm hold on Quince Cottage) and she was beating down the builders who were to make the cottage habitable. Cashmore's partner, a sensitive young man who had dropped out of 'the A.' just before his finals but who had all Willie's expertise, without the expensive qualifications, was being an angel. Willie himself was now home, in a wheelchair; his attack had been diagnosed as a stroke, but he had been promised that his mental powers would not be affected. Physically, however, he felt the effects, especially down his left side. If it were not for Aubrey Pitt, he would have had to close his practice.

Gideon did not advertise the family's departure from Beacon Terrace; it became a pleasure to act as though their dangling were to be endless and nothing had really changed. He had, of course, to notify Milton Keynes that he would be moving to Suffolk, but no one in Chaworth would have to hear of the new arrangements for students of Modern History until after Christmas. So comfortable was it to give the impression that they were staying that Gideon began almost to dread the day when his cover would be blown. He counselled Tom and Miranda to say nothing to their school-fellows and he was pleased when Pamela too clung to her routine. He had feared that her passion for Quince Cottage might dwindle away. In dark moments, he suspected that she was holding him to a decision she must know he was willing to renounce. Could her steadfastness be a kind of tease? However, when he did his sums, and failed to come up with happy answers, she maintained that they could manage. Stephen was ready to tide them over any expenses the bank refused to meet, so what was there to worry about?

'There's always repaying Stephen,' he said.

'You were the one who insisted on going.'

Her impatience reassured him. He wanted what he did not want. Early in December, he went with laggard punctuality to Fenn, Bristow to sign the final papers. When it was done, he saw that rain was falling heavily, bringing darkness on the early afternoon. He asked young Bristow to let him out the back way, so that he could take the short-cut home down Strang's Steps, to which the office garden, parallel to Mr Fagin's, gave access. He walked slowly; the donkey-jacket protected his top half, but if he hurried, his corduroy knees caught cold. He grinned at the unsteady plashing of the drops as they drooled from the big trees arching Strang's Steps. The castle sweated and its black face grew polished. He loitered like a prisoner who could not quite believe his luck and almost lacked the will to make good his escape, though the worst was over. Cramped, he stood with his hand on the iron gate on to Strang's Steps and its cold branded him. Pips of rainwater fell on his shoulders.

'So you're flying away, Mr Shand, are you?' Cora Simmonds had turned up to face him, all of a sudden. They might have been playing sardines, the way she assumed her right to seek him out. 'Is that the size of it?' She carried her polychromatic umbrella and wore the nylon-fur coat and brilliant scarf. 'And not a word!'

'A wing and a prayer, Cora, but the latter under my breath. Actually, I was going to come over – '

'You should be a happy man, Gideon, these days. Up, up and away! So why are you not? What is keeping you so gloomy? Not money? Money should never be a problem for you.'

'Man is born rich,' Gideon said, 'yet everywhere we see him talking to his bank manager.'

'Money will come to you,' she said. 'You must not be afraid; you must go through with things. Then everything will be all right for you. Never think I'm joking, will you? I never joke. I laugh; I don't joke. You'll see. Because you could be some man, Gideon, Gideon. Some man. You never did tell them, did you? You have a tongue but you know better than always to use it. You like the richness of things, the dark of them. You talk about reason, but you think about things it cannot touch.'

'The cur has his reasons,' Gideon said.

She smiled, but not falsely, as if she took the reference; it was a smile at the concealed insolence of the man, at something she could tell, but never say. 'You could be a devil, couldn't you?' she said. 'Why deny it?'

'I never said a word.'

Her face was huge now and ugly, those lips, the leering eyes, the bang of moist hair as she leaned the umbrella over him and grew older in his hard gaze. She laughed, but she was not joking. The laughter was loud, but only he could hear it. Under the nylon hood of the umbrella, she tolled like a private bell. The gate was between them, but they were together. His phallus was a thrust fist he need not show her. She was another gate, swollen and grotesque, beyond the one on which he leaned, and the key to it was there between his legs. She was hideous; he hated her nigger hole and the rebel desire that refused to own her hatefulness, or to find it hateful. He wanted to take this idiot lust and thrust it into her face, like a brick. Sanity rode him like a lie, forcing him to civil measures. How could he want what he did not want? He must get past this woman who knew him, though he did not want to know her, whom he desired though he could think only with horror of her acquiescence. (Submission and rape became one appalling thing as embarrassment dreamed her legs apart.) It was not very difficult, he found, to open the gate and supply a British face; the donkey-jacket made a skirt for the swollen key in his trousers. The two of them went side by side down Strang's Steps and she saw him, under her nylon, to his door while Sid Minches watched them through the windscreen of his taxi, dry wipers batting back and forth across the cloudiness.

Hello-it's-Jack Knightley telephoned to say that Hugo was jumping up and down at the way *The Meaning of War* had taken on a new dimension, *verb. sap.*, under the new constraints. As a response to Gideon's 'miracle efforts', they were going to arrange to have him chauffeured up and down from Quince Cottage; his ideas had turned the doubtingest Thomas on the main board into a true believer. Good news came in the guise of a disappointment; the prospect of petty fame in an area where he would no longer be living was salt in a wound for which he could hardly expect treatment. The money would help to repay what Stephen meant to lend them, but Cora's insinuations coiled themselves around his visions of the future. Her smile gloated in the centre of them, benign Medusa turning him to putty. Not to be rich, but to be richer, kept him on a treadmill with a fitted carpet. The move itself weighed more and more heavily on him: he packed his papers with officious care, making sure that all his correspondence was in dated order. Tom had resumed his schooling and came home each evening conspicuously good-natured. He even went to the Youth Club with Sean Simmonds and announced that he had *danced*.

All her childhood, Miranda had been careful not to disturb Gideon when he was working. As she grew up, her lessons with Peppino and, more recently, her affair with Piers Rougier occupied much of her free time, but ever since the trip to Constable's, and the certainty that the family's days in Chaworth were limited, she had behaved as if they were already packing up: old rules no longer applied. She ignored the closed door and how could Gideon pretend that he was working when she found him merely parcelling up old drafts of educational scripts or lecture notes? Yet he could not greet her bouncy entrances without a wince, as if she were bringing him something he feared, the nicest possible notice to quit. She offered to take the pictures from his walls, although there were still a couple of weeks before the men were due. 'No, no,' he said, 'I've still got work to do in here and the Muse'll stop reporting, if Muse she be, unless I'm careful. *Laisse-moi tout cela!*'

Miranda leaned across the desk and just managed to bracket him with her arms. 'You take so much trouble, dear popsicle, don't you? I'd love to know the real you one day.'

'I haven't time to make up anything quite so ambitious,' he said. 'Do I do it for you? I thought you did it for me.'

'I could be boring and say that's maybe why neither of us . . . but I won't, because if we want to be bored, there's always E.M.T.V. esquire, isn't there? I met Piers's friend the boxer.'

'I see,' Gideon said. 'And how did that go?'

'Not the full fifteen rounds,' she said. 'Who on earth is Glenys Harrington? A secret admirer?'

'Read it, gentlewoman of the jury, and decide for yourself.'

'Two hearts doubled with an overtrick? Hardly material for the blackmailer's despicable art, I must admit. Do you write back to her?'

'I write back to everybody.'

'You know, it's going to be really good at Quince

170

Cottage. It'll all have been worth it in the end.'

'In the end, nothing's worth anything, but let it pass, let it pass.'

'Nearer and nearer draws the time, the time that shall surely be, and who wants that a second sooner than necessary? Have you ever had a fight with anyone since you were grown up?'

'Since the day before yesterday? No. No, I don't believe so. Oh, once, if you can call it a fight and if you can call me a grown-up.'

'Over a woman?'

'I suppose it was really.'

'And who won?'

'The woman? I don't think anyone did. It ended in a sort of shame, or sham, dustings off and attempts to make a joke of the whole thing. I later perfected the technique, as you were about to point out, as a way of life.'

'I don't understand families,' she said.

'*Familles, je vous déteste.* Gide, André, the author's muted respect for. What's wrong with them?'

'Do they matter? Do they not? They're as solid as, oh, what's solid? And at the same time they're as fragile as, oh, do you remember that multicoloured clown you brought me from Venice, after you'd been to that Bridge Congress, or so you impudently claimed, and it suddenly exploded one day for no detectable reason whatsoever?'

'I always thought you dropped it and wouldn't admit same.'

'It was lovely to be suspected, but actually it just went orf. I think secret lines of force probably come together in my bedroom, don't you?'

'It's almost beyond dispute.'

'I did it with him,' she said.

'I'm sorry?'

'Or rather with them. For him. By, with or from, what's the difference?'

'Mandy, do you think you could possibly – ?'

'I don't know what I think about it, I only know that it happened. And that at the time it seemed, well, the only thing to do.'

'Should I know about it?'

'Do you love me?'

'Do you love him?'

'Ruggiero?'

'*Ruggiero?*'

'My latest name for Piers. Rougier segues into Ruggiero. Are you home? Are you dry? Are you with me at last?'

'Why?' Gideon said.

'It's tougher to tell than to do, popsicle, isn't it?'

'They didn't force you, did they?'

'I did it for Piero,' she said. 'I wanted to give him what he wanted because I wanted to see him change, I wanted to see him affected. He wants to embrace the whole world, to encompass it; it's not a matter of personal kicks for him, it goes beyond that. He wants to know the wholeness of things.'

'He's a very plausible rhetorician by the sound of it and I don't trust him one bit.'

'Trust doesn't come into it. Trust is to do with repayments, with investment, with expectations. Piers at his best is the present to the nth degree.'

'But you had to tell someone about it, which suggests that you're not made of quite the same stuff.'

'He blessed the occasion. Oh, I don't mean in the name of the Father and of the Son, but he made it significant, exciting, not sexually exciting, though it turned out to be that too, but dangerous, *brilliant*! I saw stars, I thought I was flying through the galaxies. It opened doors. You know what the latest theory is, don't you, about there being doors that lead into the next galaxy and if you can only beat the alarm system and burst through them, you're into literally another life? That's how I felt.'

'Then what's brought you back to earth, little daughter?'

'I expect my alarm went off, or theirs did. Piers was there, you do understand that, don't you? He was with us all the time; officiating, you might say.'

'Thanks for the *precision*,' Gideon said. 'I also might not.'

'Are you angry? Are you shocked?'

'I think I simply am,' Gideon said. 'I can't give you a breakdown. It would involve ... dismemberment, and I'm not into that, even if Piers ... '

'You think they made use of me, but that's male vanity. I felt wonderful, because so much was being asked, and given. I felt as if I was somehow above Christianity, beyond the things that puzzle Piers so much that he has to be absolutely certain about them, away in a galaxy – I said that, didn't I? – where none of the Commandments applied, where a whole new scheme was open to me. Isn't that quite a thing to feel for allowing Harold to have his way with me on the vestry floor? You think they were just taking advantage of a gullible young thing, don't you? I swear to you that I was way above them. I also liked it. I liked the choice, and being chosen.'

Gideon was dating some papers which had been piled in inverted sequence.

'The early Christians were always being accused of it,' she said, 'that sort of thing.'

'And they were always denying it, weren't they? Would Piers?'

'It's not a crime, is it?'

'It's not something that's likely to procure him preferment.'

'His game is with God,' Miranda said. 'He's shown me a different sort of world. Christianity lost its nerve, or the people who might've given it nerve lost theirs. Because what it's about, that sort of thing, can never be codified, can never be *said* to be right, it can only *be* right.'

'Why tell anyone about it?' Gideon said.

'Not anyone,' she said. 'Someone. I love you.'

'That belongs to a different logic,' he said. 'Sorry. Lecturer's jargon.'

'*And* I suppose I'm not sure that I haven't been had.'

'Every deliberately selected way of life has its element of that. Whatever man does, or woman does, there is always, *always*, the sense of having been wrong, of having been cheated. Jung's Shadow. A Jung man's fancy ... No one in the world regrets what he's done half so bitterly as he regrets what he hasn't. Hence the intolerance of all moralities, their determination to make *impossible* what they cannot merely deplore. All free speech depends on somebody's being silent. And, yes folks, thought for tonight has gone into extra time!'

'Oh don't,' she said, 'don't, don't, *don't*. Bring other people into this; apologise. I'm loving it so. You use that larky style, it's as if one of the awfuls had come into the room and you had to . . . entertain them.'

Gideon sat in the captain's chair, chin in his hands, Miranda on the desk above him, her feet in a drawer, and they might have been on a raft they were no longer able to direct, resigned to its drifting and facing different horizons without knowing to which pole the breeze, or the storm, might carry them. Separately, they were on the move together.

'It's going to be fun, isn't it?' She lifted her feet from the drawer as though she had found them at last. 'Living near Sir Stephen?'

'We shan't see much of him, I don't imagine.'

'*C'est un gros bonnet, n'est-ce pas?* I bet she really will be Lady Miriam one day. Was he always your best friend?'

Pamela was knocking on the door. Wearing her professional shoes, she had come so discreetly that they jumped at her arrival; they might have been naked. 'I'm sorry to come from Aix to Ghent with this kind of news,' she said, 'but Athol Simmonds wants a word. What could I . . . ?'

Gideon half forgave what he half welcomed and, with a nod that tucked one side of Miranda's mouth under her cheek, he straightened up and went to the door. Pamela stiffened to a sentry to let him by.

'Oxford!' Miranda said.

'I'm not selling anything, sir, so there's no call to get your cheque-book, or your shot-gun. I've got some good news, is all. Graham Noble's come up trumps, which is a damned sight better than coming up turnips: he's found us a publisher, man.'

'You and who else, Athol?'

'Didn't I promise you a split? Well, they're paying a thousand quid advance; sounds like peanuts to me, but two-fifty of it's yours, my friend, shells and all. Take it or I'll leave it, it's all the same to me.'

'I don't want your money,' Gideon said. 'Do you want to come in and – ?'

'And I don't want yours,' Athol said, 'which is why I've brought it over. No thanks. I've told the shareholders I'd take them to the wrestling in the Moot Hall. Cora loves a grunt and a groan. You'll find it comes in handy when you're tipping the fellows doing your move. The cash, the cash. Amazing how a few quid can stop accidents happening, isn't it? Which brings me to my next point: if you're really moving on, as rumour has it, you'll be needing some haulage people, won't you? Or are you planning a tactical fire to collect on the insurance without having to hump the stuff at all? A new life for Shand and Associates, is it, then?'

'Out of the frying pan probably.'

'I'm *into* frying pans, as a matter of fact. Toughened glass, non-stick, last a lifetime, or at least long enough for the salesman to get out of the country. I'm reckoning to clean up, which is exactly what these particular articles are good for. Just wipe a clean cloth around them and you've got a clean surface, and a dirty cloth. Am I thinking of marketing cloths? Am I thinking of anything else? Yes, I'm thinking of getting an eye full of liniment hot from Giant Haystack's pectoral development. Good luck on it, Shandy, and if your new place needs any furniture, give me a buzz and I'll give you a rate. We shall miss you.'

'You've been very kind,' Gideon said.

'Leave an address, won't you? Because if the book takes off, you'd better be ready to cup your hands. How about a telly adaptation? Play our cards right, I could yet look a bigger fool than I do already. It'll take talent, mind: yours. So keep in touch. I appreciate everything you've done, believe me, more than I can say.' Athol held out a brown hand and squeezed Gideon's with a warmth that should have ended a worthier conversation. The ghost of it stood with Gideon as he watched the silly man cross the street to where too much light seemed to be shining from the cerise doorway in which Cora and Sean waited, wearing more clothes than two people needed.

Gideon and Pamela were undressing when they heard fire engines on the Nottingham Road. The bells made a long tangent to the city, but finally carried their wrangling away from Chaworth. Another appliance, like a late spaniel, went on its urgent way a few minutes later, but this time Gideon merely smiled at his wife, to prove that he was relieved that the bells were not for Miranda.

'The sooner we get out of here the better,' he said.

Pamela rumpled her forehead and nodded, as if that was what she had been saying for ages. Her face cleared and she put cream on it for the night. Abruptly, she turned to Gideon, eyes widened, and he had to shake his head, as though he had begun to say something and then had thought better of it.

In the morning, Gideon borrowed Tom's tranny to listen to the local news over breakfast. There had been an eighty-five thousand pound fire at a novelty factory at Blackley Cross. The premises had been partly insured, but that was no compensation – so the owner, Mr Athol Simmonds, had told E.M. local radio – for the destruction of his business or, more important, the forty-two members of the work-force who were now, regretfully, certain to lose their jobs. Mr Simmonds had seen nothing untoward when he last visited the premises the previous afternoon. He had had to be fetched out of the Moot Hall to be told of the disaster. 'Nearly three years of hard work has gone up in smoke,' a shattered Mr Simmonds had told E.M. local radio's Gareth Jones.

12

WHEN THE HOUSE was empty, it was as small again as
when they first saw it. The Monahan boys, Brendan
and Darren, whose coughs excused truancy whenever it
suited them, watched the aproned men fit the pieces into
the lagged lorry. Pamela had gone for the last time to see
Mr Fagin; Gideon was alone with the boys and their
steady, blue-eyed attention. Their huskiness as they
asked obvious questions struck him as an involuntary
apology for driving him from Chaworth. Here were those
impersonal forces, brainless bullies, before whom Neil
Laidlaw had once abased himself. There was a grateful
link between these puzzled mechanicals, immune from
routine judgment thanks to the chronic ailments of the
untouchable, and the fastidiousness of those who loaded
them with the responsibility for everything sordid, brutal
and convenient.

'Won't we ever be seeing you again, Mr Shand?'

'I don't suppose so,' Gideon said, 'unless – '

'Have you got a new job then, have you?'

'That's right, Darren.'

They offered hands pulled warm from tight pockets. It
was as though they were passing him something disrepu-
table. He nodded and made a vague gesture of absolution
before going back to check that everything was out of the
house. Tom came past him, in the passage, carrying the

W.W.II Spitfire. Gideon made it awkward to get by, hoping that the Monahan boys would have started on their way home, but he heard Tom call out to them. Their husky goodbyes were as cautious as the pulling of a knife from its wound. Gideon was more severe through the uncurtained glass of the empty sitting room than he had cared to be in the street. The Monahan boys stayed to talk to Tom for a few moments and passed the Spitfire from hand to hand, impressed and unclumsy, so lightly that anything might happen, though nothing did. They returned it to Tom, who looked at its undamaged state with a sort of amazement, undercarriage upwards as the brothers backed away and, strangers even to each other for a moment, left the scene, accidentally together, like the last two members of a dispersing congregation, or mob.

Miranda walked up from the Nottingham Road as Tom was fitting himself into the Renault. The removals men called that they were off and, a minute later, the pantechnicon eased down from the kerb. Gideon walked through the nakedness of the house (a few paces took him from end to end), while Miranda sat in the back of the Renault with her brother and asked him questions.

Gideon was in the bathroom when he heard Pamela at the front door. A spent toothpaste tube lay in the lardy hollow beside the greening cold tap. The only personal relic left in the house was Tom's luminous universe on the slope of wall above where his bed had been. Pamela went down the passage to the kitchen, which she had already checked, and then to Gideon's little room, before he heard her shoes snap on uncarpeted stairs. Through the half-open door he caught sight of the young woman whom he had first brought to Beacon Terrace. There was a heat in her cheeks and green life in those slightly pop eyes; the Oxford hair was a flame she quenched briefly with both hands, before catching the boss of the stairhead and holding it there, drawing breath through that cleft between her front teeth.

He ran the tap and the coiled tube clinked on the enamel. Her mouth opened and she moved to meet him. 'Was I a long time?' He had not heard that voice from her

178

since the house was last empty. There was harshness in it and something uncompromising, neither anger nor threat, but alien. She might not have been his wife.

'How did he take it?' Gideon said.

'How did he take it?' she said. 'He took it.'

'Was he very upset?'

She leaned against the doorpost of Tom's room and was taller for it. 'He's dead, Gideon.'

'Dead?'

'He wanted to do it and he did it.'

'Yes? How?'

'He took poison.'

'Jesus! You didn't get it for him, did you?'

'He'd had it ever since the war. Ever since Tourcoign. They gave it to them before they went, in case they were caught and . . . '

'I know,' Gideon said. 'I saw the repeats. How are you?'

'Here, aren't I?'

'You knew he was planning to do it, didn't you?'

'Planning and doing aren't always the same thing.'

'Were you actually there? Actually . . . '

'I said I would be.'

'And you kept your word. You didn't actually . . . administer it, did you?'

'Cyanide doesn't have to be administered. They had to be able to take it on their own. You bite the capsule, that's it.'

'Have you called the police?'

'Not yet,' she said.

'Well, Jesus Christ – '

'Nor yet Him,' she said.

'What are you going to tell them?'

'More or less what happened. I shan't tell them that I knew he had the stuff. I don't see why I should, do you?'

'I see why you shouldn't. The kids are in the car. All set. What did you do exactly? Did you try to stop him?'

'I took his hand as he bit the thing, and, the exact truth is, I put it under my skirt and . . . like that. My answer to . . . them . . . is that I was in the other room, getting my things together and heard a crash and went in and there he was, already dead.'

179

'You still should've called an ambulance,' he said.

'Yes,' she said, 'of course. But I didn't. I sat with him until . . . until his hand was dead and then . . . I came home.'

'We'd better get through right away,' he said. 'Do you want me to do it?'

'I'd better, hadn't I?'

'Why didn't you tell me?'

'Would you have welcomed it?' She went down the noisy stairs, one-two, one-two, to the telephone.

Her professional voice sounded a deception. He was not sure what he was doing in Miranda's room, grimacing and clenching his face and fists, bumping against the walls as though they were unfamiliar furniture. *Why* he felt what he did and what he actually did feel were so confused that panic was an economical response. All the practical questions, of whether to go or stay, of whether he should contact Barry Woodward, or Stephen, jostled pettier and grander ones, whether he approved, disapproved, cared or didn't care, was touched or appalled, impressed or mortified. He was everything. Her action had divorced him and he reeled under its impersonal impact. She had not meant to do anything to him, that was the measure of her independence, and of what she had done. He burned with cold up there in the turned off room; the door was open, so how could he break it down? He bent his forehead against the pane of the window and saw the children in the steel and glass nursery below him. He was left, but he could not leave; he was alone and yet he was not by himself. She needed him, but what did he need, or want? The fields of force crossed in Miranda's bedroom where the broken clown had snapped, without a fall.

Inspector Telfer arrived in a badged Escort. He wore his scuffed mackintosh, but he had buttoned a plaid winter lining inside it; he looked rougher for it. As they waited for him in the front room, Pamela put on age like a disguise. She hung a cloak of patient distress around her shoulders and found it almost too heavy for her. Mr Fagin became one of a roster of patients whom she visited for hire; his personal life had never interested her as much as

180

his knees, on which she generally worked, though he also had an arthritic thumb. That he should have taken poison in her presence, well, *almost* in her presence, became an assault which it was her duty to bear but which had shocked her by its premeditation.

'And why did you run back here, Mrs Shand?'

'My wife . . . '

'Mrs Shand?' Telfer said.

'I'd only gone in to say goodbye to him, I'd told him the names of a couple of other physiotherapists who were willing to take him on. I suppose – well, I wasn't at my most professional.'

'It's only just round the corner,' Gideon said, 'no time was lost.'

'Your children, Mr Shand, aren't they still out there in the car? It's not getting any warmer, is it? Shouldn't you – ?'

'We were supposed to be leaving for Suffolk,' Gideon said. 'As you can see, we can't very easily stay here. Our furniture . . . '

'You'd better get them in,' Pamela said. She might have joined the police. 'Presumably the inspector's going to want to get the story straight.'

Gideon looked back into the sitting room, furnished only with its telephone, and Telfer and Pamela might have been debating the suitability of the property for the home they proposed to establish together. She nodded at his questions and then answered them so frowningly that she appeared to flatter their intelligence.

'Had you any idea,' Telfer was asking as Gideon returned, 'that he was contemplating suicide?'

'None at all.'

'How seriously ill was he?'

'You must ask the doctor. I went there to help him get about as much as possible. He was fighting a losing battle, but then who isn't?'

Miranda and Tom were so neatly packed in the back of the car that they had told Gideon that they preferred to sit tight. He stood in the cold hall and saw an envelope which had been crushed behind the door by the comings and goings of the removals men. It contained a scratchy letter from Cyril Lack, undated, in which he asked whether he could bring his 'book' for Gideon to see, at a mutually convenient date. He enclosed s.a.e. for the favour of a reply.

'There were other things wrong with him then, were there, apart from – ?'

'I can't specify, professionally, but yes, obviously.'

'Did you administer pain-killers?'

'They hardly need administering these days, inspector. The instructions are on the bottle. Even at the terminal stage – '

'You knew him to be at that point, did you?'

'It's not a point. He was past three-score and ten, wasn't he? And after that . . . he was a sick man, and an intelligent, sensitive one.'

'You liked him?'

'It was my business to like him, to some extent.'

'But you liked him personally, as well as, well, in the way of trade?'

'Yes,' Pamela said.

'And what were his feelings for you?'

'I hope he liked me,' she said.

'It's rather an extraordinary thing, isn't it, that he should do this on your last visit? What does it suggest to you?'

'He could hardly do it on my one but last, could he?' Pamela said. 'I suppose he was going to miss me.'

'Did he say as much?'

'Yes,' she said. 'But then he was very polite. He could hardly say less.'

'I think you had better come back there with me now, if you would. Do you have a key to the house?'

'No,' she said. 'I used to ring. He had a remote control system.'

'You had a special ring?'

'Oh, it was never . . . I'm a punctual sort of person.'

'I can imagine that you would be. We'll find a way to get in. You had some good talks, did you? What about?'

'Anything he liked. The war. It helps them relax, you know, when you're working. It's not easy to get them to do it, especially when they're in pain.'

'But you have the knack?'

'It depends on the patient. I'm sorry I . . . wasn't quick enough to guess that . . . of course, I never knew he had anything like that in the house.'

'How could you?'

'Shall I come along with you?' Gideon said.

Pamela looked at Telfer as they came into the narrowness of the hall. 'No need for that, sir,' he said.

'If my wife wants me to come . . . '

'I shall have the inspector,' Pamela said.

Gideon watched Telfer hold the badged door open for Pamela. Pamela gave the children a little wave and Gideon went to explain where she was going; with any luck, she wouldn't be long, but what did they feel like doing in the meanwhile? They could buzz down to Moffatt's for a Coke, if they felt like it.

'I think I'll go for a bit of a walk.' Tom got out of the car and walked up towards the Monahans' and beyond to Strang's Steps. On the way back, he stopped and stared at number seven, as if it was a quotation he was at pains to memorise.

'Do you think they'll let us go?' Miranda said.

Gideon was in the front of the car, in the passenger's seat. 'Why not?' he said. 'Mummy hasn't done anything wrong.'

'That's all right then,' Miranda said.

13

IT WAS NEARLY nine o'clock before they arrived at Constable's. A new lamp had been installed in the driveway, a 'double-header' as Stephen described it, which could be turned on from the house, greeting or warning as the occasion deserved: thieves and visitors were given the same welcome. Telfer had been efficient and understanding. Once Pamela had signed a brief statement and her story had been corroborated by what was found at Mr Fagin's house, she was free to go wherever she wanted, as long as she left an address. Meanwhile, Miriam soon told them, the pantechnicon had arrived at Quince Cottage and the terribly nice men had unloaded most of the stuff into the downstairs rooms, which Mr Garrod, Miriam's little local builder, had made habitable; the place was now so crammed with furniture that there was no question of moving in until he had tackled the upstairs. The Shands would be staying in the Hellmans' guest flat for a little while yet. (Tom licked his lips.)

Mr Fagin's death had not been mentioned during the drive. Nor was it discussed at dinner, except as the vaguest of 'accidents' preventing a prompt arrival; luckily, the roast guinea-fowl tasted no worse for the delay and Stephen himself had been late from London. He entertained them with an imitation of the dullest judge in the

High Court, culling gold from dust by his mordant mimicry. If Gideon guessed that it was an act that he had produced before when the company was not too lively, there was generosity in the self-mockery it involved. (Mr 'ah-*Hell*man' was a frequent butt for his semi-deaf lordship's pursed rebukes.) Gideon also wondered whether this self-deprecation might not be the prelude to the news of some further advance in Stephen's career or an apology for a new car perhaps, or a new work of art.

They went into the drawing room and there was indeed a new double icon on the bright wall above the Italian lamp to the left of the fireplace. 'You've found yourself another Greek ship-owner, Stephen!' Gideon said.

'My dear Sherlock, I can keep nothing from you. Macedonia 1750 roughly, if you hadn't already dated it. Lefteris pays his bills with singular reluctance, even for a native of the eastern Mediterranean, but his debts he meets with great speed. Do him any sort of favour and he can't move quickly enough to dispel the shame of it. Not that I intended my services to be a favour, in reality, unless he proposes, as he probably does, to contest my fee. Why does one always fall for scoundrels, I wonder?'

'They don't oblige you to behave well,' Pamela said, from the spoon-shaped chair where, legs aslant, she was holding a Rosenthal glass of Grand Marnier by its little foot.

Tom asked whether Wumpus-hunting was still in season and the casualness of the leading question made them all laugh, him last. 'You know where,' Stephen said, 'and you know how: go on over whenever you like. I'll invoice your father if anything goes wrong. Ben'll be home in – what? – three weeks and I shall get a wear-and-tear report from him. Meanwhile, consider yourself a season-ticket holder, Tom.'

Miriam said: 'I've arranged for us to meet Mr Garrod at the cottage at eight o'clock. I hope it's not too soon for you.'

'The sooner the better,' Pamela said.

'If you want to leave Tom here,' Miriam said, 'that's perfectly all right with me.'

'He can do his share like everyone else,' Pamela said.

'I agree,' Gideon said.

Pamela looked at him as though he had contradicted her. 'In which case, I don't think we should be too late now, do you? It's been . . . '

'We rarely stay up late on weekdays,' Miriam said, posting house rules.

'*We* rarely do,' Stephen said. 'I sometimes do. Beauty sleep no longer being a major investment of mine. But be off with you, fair ladies. Gideon and I will finish our poison and not a sound shall we make as we creep up the stairs.'

From the doorway, near the cabinet with the Meissen army, Miranda blew them a kiss. 'Nighty-night, fond sirs.'

'Only one?' Stephen said. 'Who's it for?'

'Daddy, of course.'

'Is that fair?'

'Is love? Is war?'

'What a girl!' Stephen said, when she had closed the door, leaving a Cheshire smile where she had been. 'What do you think, Gidman?'

'You remember Chekhov's gun on the wall, don't you?'

'My gun isn't on the wall. It's locked in the cupboard.'

'Along with the skeletons?'

'No conceivable reason why skeletons should always rattle or guns always go off. Not that mine isn't a nice one. Miriam gave it to me one Christmas. One inter-denominational festival. The half-pay colonel next door, i.e. the major, bred tame pigeons for a while. Rather too successfully, as it turned out, and eventually turn them out he did, among our peas and beans and similar tasty targets. The idea of the gun was that I should show them who was master. Two problems arose: one of which was the pigeons (*were* the pigeons? Difficult tongue English!) who did, literally, arise. Hitting them on the wing requires a childhood not spent in rural Mill Hill. You never catch up, do you? Overtake possibly, catch up never! On the other hand – problem number two on your hymn sheet – if you blitz pigeons on the ground, you shell your peas prematurely and almost certainly reap nothing but has-beens, which state is worse than the one you are seeking to improve, in addition to which, even with Mr Purdy's double-barrelled help, you can still miss the feathered fiends. Conclusion: however bad problems are, solutions are almost bound to be worse. *Or*, why I now vote Conservative even though Jan Cashmore makes the worst coffee, and conversation, in the county.'

'How is he?'

'Willie? He's at rest,' Stephen said. 'No, he's . . . quiescent, convalescent and not far off senescent. Previously, he couldn't do it and now he can't do it. He has this funny smile.'

'You should be an actor,' Gideon said.

'Sir, do you serve me notice that my time in the legal profession has reached its term? Pamela . . . you must be doing something right, because I've never seen her look so . . . well, I was going to say brilliant, which is the cant word these days among the progressively schooled, to judge from Emmy's letters, but, yes, brilliant.'

'A man killed himself for her today.'

'*For* her?'

'I wasn't going to mention it,' Gideon said.

'That's generally how one gets to hear things, isn't it?'

'She was there when he did it. One of her patients. He left a note, they discovered it when they went back, absolving her of all knowledge of his intentions, but naturally she was rather shaken. It was the man I told you about. The one . . . '

'I rather guessed it might have been.'

'You're not an easy man to surprise.'

'On a good day, I can be tolerably alert to the obvious. You said "for" her. That always suggests love, dedication, a kind of pointed – not to say Greek – gift. Today! Hence . . . Love *and* war, you might say. Of course it's entirely your business, to use a shamefully inappropriate image, but shall you never tell Miranda? It's probably vanity, especially now that I've seen her again, but I somehow thought that enlightened Grauniad readers such as yourselves would end up with bursts of liberating candour. Odd, isn't it, how one comes to use terminologies one loathes, cadged from schoolboy magazines one doesn't like to be seen reading, but reads? What's stopped you?'

'You know how it is, Steve: you make the biggest mistakes at trick one. After that you can do all the thinking you like, dream up all kinds of *coups* that might retrieve the situation, but it's still trick one where it went wrong, if it did, and that trick's been well and truly turned. Oh, one says it will matter less and less as time goes by, but . . . Cowardice? Prudence? Sloth? Good intentions? Some deadly sin like that. You've seen what she's like; you can imagine what she'd make of it.'

'Perhaps she *is* what she's made of it. I have a feeling that she's not an easy girl to surprise.'

'Knowing things and saying them aren't necessarily the same. Whereof, thereof, as Peter used to say.'

'It'll never come from me, Gideon, rest assured on that one.'

'Does Miriam know?'

Stephen stood up, with a showy little struggle, a twist of the face that enabled Gideon to see him a judge, not very pleased with counsel. 'If you like, that's my marker. Whereof, thereof. Miranda is nothing to do with me. She is not the Malvinas; I have no residual claim, no national myth to service, no flag to raise. I'm pleased, but secretly, and only secretly, I assure you; that's precisely my pleasure. If she knows, or guesses, or has intimations, she's maybe the stronger for them, for the same reason, so long as we never speak of it, any of us, except you and me, perhaps, because we . . . I wouldn't even want to discuss it with Pammy, with Pamela. I'm not even sure we should . . . Walls have ears, and other organs, sometimes.'

'I don't have documentary evidence, my lord, but my impression was that it was you who raised the matter.'

'I flirted, you're right, and I apologise.'

'I'm very grateful to you,' Gideon said, 'over the money. We couldn't have done anything without it. But I intend to repay it as soon as I can, as I hope . . . '

'I'm drumming my Semitic fingers,' Stephen said. 'Look at the rings on my sausagy paws! And, if I'm not mistaken, I may be slobbering a little from my thick lips.

188

Take your time, my dear, the interest is clocking up, *nu*?'

'Quite frankly, I hate it when you do that.'

'Don't encourage me now. Pay it back as and when; it's no big deal, ten fahsand pahnd, I promise you – out of vanity and self-esteem, of course. Don't please feel that you've somehow fallen under my power. I'm glad to see that damned flat being used and we'll soon have you out of here before the blot thickens or troubles bubble. Anything that has to do with money partakes of comedy, Gidman.'

'Pamela thinks Peter Michaeljohn's a virgin,' Gideon said. 'What do you think?'

'Peter? I've never cared to imagine him engaged on any type of congress apart from one devoted to our common pasteboard pursuit. Don Juan-les-Pins is about his mark, I daresay. A virgin? He could well be, but he's had quite a lot of people, I reckon, in the course of his celibacy, hasn't he? There's a fleshiness about his address that somehow disqualifies him from, well, innocence at least, isn't there? He has Biblical knowledge of a kind, when it comes to others; it's there in his eye, and in that feeling one has that he contrives his own deliberate obscenity, that mouth, the Etonian technique of oral groping. He's too deliciously repulsive not to be an operator of some kind. How are you for money right at the moment?'

'I can lend you a bob,' Gideon said. 'I had a small windfall just before we shook the dust.'

'By money being a comic matter, I meant that it can't furnish tragedy. *The Merchant of Venice* is undoubtedly something to be played for sobbing great laughs; Shylock's comedy arises precisely from the fact that he takes it seriously. He's the fox that refuses to enjoy hunting, an essentially unBritish reluctance! You remember Ruy Lopez on the scaffold, whining that he believed as keenly in Jesus Christ as the holiday audience that had turned up to enjoy his exemplary evisceration, Molly and the kids. He had the spoilsport illusion that being innocent was some sort of physic against having his privy member thrust in his mouth before he said goodbye to Christianity and its, on balance, undoubted benefits to mankind.'

'You should talk to Piers Rougier.' Gideon stood up

with the decisive tact of someone alert to a busy man.

'It's only a matter of time, I daresay, before our paths, not to say our swords, cross. Piers and I, I mean. Talkers tend to meet a lot sooner than parallel lines, especially when they can add spice, and *poids*, to an informed debate which, as usual, has to be calculated to end as a score-draw on the programme-controller's kewpong. Once you're in the cottage, Gidman, we can and will, I promise you, act as though we were as far apart as ever. We shall not live in each other's pockets or other crevices; our commerce shall be through the most diplomatic channels. You don't trust me, do you?'

'The boot is rather on the other extremity. I want to repay you so much, to prove that you can trust me, that in a way . . . I seem to specialise in mental contortions these days, Steve, I don't know why. I see everything in the most elaborate script – '

'I have a colleague who writes to me from Scotland,' Stephen said, 'and he has the most beautiful fist, as they used to say, I've ever seen. I imagine he's the most admired correspondent that anyone could have, but I also suspect that he often waits in vain for the postman. Who wants to prolong a relationship with someone who makes him look cack-handed from the outset?'

'Thou art the man!' Gideon was on his way to the door. 'I can visualise you collecting a lot of things, but why porcelain soldiers?'

'Napoleon, for and against,' Stephen said, 'and in my case neither; but both. He opened the gates, didn't he, the little whopper, and let us out of the ghetto and into the voild? He deserves his fragile shrine, my little Pagod. I'm in no hurry for repayment, for much the same reason, I dare say, as you're in a hurry to make it. Oh, somewhere I like the idea of honest Antonio sweating over his argosies, and somewhere else – though very adjacent, Richie – I like the idea of disclaiming a pound of anything, of not wearing that old gabardine and not worrying over-much who spits on it. What you don't trust are my motives and the funny thing is, you're right and you're wrong. I amuse myself with sly purposes, but *au fond*, I have none. There's probably a zest of atonement in the cocktail, but not enough to gag on. I wanted to get you out of that bloody Chaworth and if there's a certain piquancy in playing the lordly part, well, what would you from a *parvenu*? I like to think of us as old friends. I'm shy of saying that I love, or even loved you; despite all the gay improperganda, I still think of love as basically a matter between members of the opposite sex. *We* can do better than *that*! David and Jonathan? In death they were not divided, but that's as far as it went.'

'Oh stop it, Stephen, why – ?'

'It's strange, if the truth be told. Because I wanted you, in some sense of the word, some very clear and possessive sense, as soon as I saw you on old Maitland's staircase, the Head of the School in person, but I am quite certain I never desired you, or any other male. It's almost embarrassing, isn't it? Which is probably why it has to come up. Almost as uncomfortable as an old married couple remembering how he used to come on her skirt and tie terrible knots in her bra straps. They weren't the same people then and they talk about their old – correction, young – selves like the kids who give the doge a bad name.'

'I'm going to bed,' Gideon said, 'or I shall find Pamela asleep.'

'Oh, one thing while you're here, would you be good enough not to break into the house in the middle of the night? It'll set the bloody alarm off and we shall be surrounded with hoops of steel, if you believe the ads.'

'Say goodnight to Miriam for me,' Gideon said. 'I can't tell you how grateful we are for everything.'

He half-woke to the buzzing of the telephone beside the bed. It was an unfamiliar sound, created by a privatised firm. Seeking to mount a plausible dream, he could imagine only that someone was at the door, and then he was awake, and thinking the same, only to realise at last that the unobtrusive telephone was on Pamela's side. He arched himself across her. Miriam hoped that she hadn't woken them, but Aubrey was never late and Mr Garrod was always reproachful if you were later than he was. Breakfast was waiting and it was going to be a lovely morning.

Gideon's key broke in the Renault's lock just as they were about to follow the Golf out of the gate. Tom was not markedly vexed at being left behind in the playroom after all, while Erik went into Colchester to try and get a new key. The rest of the family played sardines with Miriam in the VW. Stephen had caught an early train and would not be back that night. The complicated details of domesticity gave Miriam the pleasure of command. Wearing a pair of pink corduroy dungarees, with a black roll-necked sweater and suede half-boots, she did hope they were going to like what had already been done. However, they were to feel absolutely free to say if there was anything they didn't like about Aubrey's ideas. She had tried to keep the costs down, but she feared that that didn't mean that they were not going to be higher than the numbers they had first thought of.

A Ford van, a Suzuki motor-bike, a Rover 2800 and a high-saddled bicycle with small-diameter wheels were already at Quince Cottage. Miriam edged between them to park the VW on the cinder patch inside the fence.

'They've done rather a lot.' Having feared that nothing would have been done, Gideon now saw, with apprehension, how much had been. Miriam's prattle had not been aimless: she must have suspected that he would be dismayed by the conspicuousness of the expenditure. She had been preparing him for something she knew had already happened. For instance, Simple Simon, the owner of the Suzuki, was busy on the lean-to shed next to the kitchen in order to turn it into a work-room. Aubrey Pitt, very tall and waxen-fleshed, with pink hands that seemed always to be coming moistly from his mouth, looked everywhere except at Gideon while explaining that the kitchen wall was so damp that it was actually an economy to renovate the shed. Frowning, Gideon was exhilarated to find the work too far advanced to be cancelled. The shed's floor had been levelled and Simple Simon was about to unpack bundles of parquet. The walls were of beaverboard; a big work-surface was of the same material. There were shelves wide enough for box-files as well as for books. 'Where exactly would you like to have the electric points?' Aubrey said.

'Look, this is all very well, but what sort of budget are you working to here? I mean – '

'Miriam – '

'My name is not Miriam, Aubrey. My name is Gideon Shand and I shall be paying for all of this, down to the last pfennig, hence my legitimate concern that we should not run riot. I gave absolutely no warrant for anything on this scale – '

'We've deliberately kept it basic, down to the minimum.'

'Less is more expensive, isn't that the slogan? I really think that we ought to have an absolute ceiling – oh, I know, absolute ceilings are never included in what architects are taught, but seriously – '

'Sorry to short-circuit the command structure, fond papa – '

'Aubrey and I are having a bit of a chat,' Gideon said, 'if you could possibly leave us to it, Mandy.'

'Ah, long words of one syllable! I demand pardon, Herr Oberst, but there's a move to get the furniture out of the front room and into the garden where it belongs so that we can hang curtains, lay carpets and do other nice things like that, and – if I may be permitted another brief word before sentence is pronounced, or as it would certainly be on East Midlands T.V. (pause for breath at the wrong moment) *mis*pronounced – it would be a big help if big masculine hands were available for such *déménagement*. Roger and out. Miranda and out. See you there, huh?'

'The kitchen wall – '

'You mentioned that,' Gideon said. 'And I don't want you to think that I don't appreciate your initiative, but what you really must begin to understand is that this is my place – our place – and that the Hellmans, Miriam, Stephen, may have been invaluable in helping us and so on, *invaluable*, but that they are only friends, not the owners. I'm not sure exactly how the professional side of all this is being worked out, by the way. I mean, are you merely advising us personally or is this being done through Willie, William Cashmore's, um, practice or what? Are you approving all the bills and so on? And, forgive me, are you actually qualified to handle all that sort of, of technical stuff?'

Aubrey Pitt paled in the light that burned through the morning mist and flared into the half-finished room. A hand on the wide work-surface seemed to be involved in some arcane sport which involved leaning all his weight on it. 'We were given a budget.'

'I say, are you all right?'

'And I think we're keeping to it. And if we don't, or can't, Miriam – '

'Look, I know you mean well, and I like what you're doing, but Miriam can't be a permanent point of reference here – '

'We're doing something rather more ambitious for them at Constable's,' Aubrey managed to say. 'I don't think as of yet . . . '

'Well, think! Because the two things have to be kept entirely separate. I'm sorry to launch straight in, but it's vital to recognise that from the very beginning or we shall have savage disaster on our hands.'

'Where's the crash, Gideon? Where's the wreckage?' Miriam imported a scent of Rive Droite into the sawdust. 'Oh, isn't this heavenly? It's coming on so well, Aubs!'

'I wanted to know about the electric points,' Aubrey said. 'As soon as we get those in – '

'I took it on myself, Gideon, to give the O.K. on the little office, because you can't really type in the drawing room, can you? And I know that if you're anything like Stephen you'll be insufferable unless you've got your sanctum sanctorum – '

'My sanctum sanatorium, I think you mean.' Gideon looked to Aubrey Pitt for complicity and did not find it. 'It all looks lovely, but that's not the main issue.'

'The main issue!' Miriam said. 'That takes us back to the electric points.'

'Oh, one thing: do you use an electric typewriter at all?' Aubrey said.

'You should, Gideon. Stephen even uses his for thank you letters.'

'I don't think we need have electricity in here at all,

frankly,' Gideon said. 'I'd sooner work in lamp-light and it'll save – '

'It'll only save some cable, actually, and plugs and switches.' Aubrey had pushed himself away from the work-surface and seemed now to appreciate the joke he had failed to register earlier. 'And the insurance if you use oil-lamps – '

'You'll want an electric machine sooner or later, Gideon, and then you'll be in a fix.'

'I must go and help move this furniture.' Gideon went through the cosmetic smell of Miriam as if it were part of her body and had to be fended aside with a polite hand.

She came after him, bow-legged on the half-boots, crunching cinders in her haste. 'Gideon, Gideon, before . . . He's very easily, you know, *thrown*, Aubrey, very easily discouraged – '

'I'm relieved to hear that.'

'He has to be handled with kid gloves.'

'I was being as delicate as I could, but kid gloves are rather beyond my wardrobe.'

'Stephen told you not to worry. About the money.'

'Yes, well; yes, I know, but even Stephen doesn't dispose of total control over my anxiety mechanism – '

'Are we going to plant this furniture in the garden or aren't we, popsicle?'

Tweedy Mr Garrod was giving instructions to Simple Simon in the kitchen. He either finished just as Gideon came in to get the sofa or thought it prudent to pause. The builder wore a check cap and gave the impression that he was on the way to a social event which might involve old soldiers. (There was an indecipherable pin in his button-hole; his clubby tie implied something Gideon could not read.) His leathered face and shifty, unfrightened eyes announced that they had seen more unnerving sights than a client who was not sure where the money was coming from. Before he went off in the Rover, Garrod walked Miriam several yards down the lane and appeared emphatically satisfied with what he was told. Gideon planted the last armchair among the stumps of the nettles Pamela had already cleared and watched Miriam as she put a leg over the sagging fence and headed for Simple Simon. On her way into the hammering, she offered a newly-painted red grin and waved brightly. 'All right if I have a few more bulbs in my new dressing room, Gideon, is it? Because that's all we were discussing, Mr Suspicious.'

Having put him down without a bump, she showed no signs of malice when she came out of the cottage a few minutes later to report that two of the bedrooms would be habitable by the end of the week. '*Some* news is good news, you see!' She was off to a charity coffee morning she had promised to look in on, but she would be back before lunch. Gideon performed a lot of hand-signals to guide her back into the lane, even though the disappearance of the Rover had made it an easy manoeuvre. 'I say, I'm sorry if – ' He bent to her window. 'It's simply – '

'All forgotten and forgiven,' she said.

'I'll remember that,' he said.

She kissed the space between them before accelerating into a neat turn that pelted his shins with gravel from the verge. Miranda was hanging curtains in the sitting room. Gideon was deputed to spread the rugs. 'Mama is down the garden, discovering the sources of the White Nile according to first enthusiastic accounts. Not only a well, it seems, but a spring as well as a well, making well, well, well in all. Have you been having words with madam?'

'I haven't been having music, *disons*. People with money can never really believe that there's anyone who's without it.'

'You're going to be a celeb any minute now though, incha, dad? And that will bring in the lucre at a rare rate.'

'I don't know that it'll even happen, and I shall hardly turn into a gold-mine if it does. I'm not sure I can really buzz up and down to see Hello-it's-Jack as often as – '

'We'll keep a light in the window,' Miranda said. 'Or at least an oil-lamp.'

'Big ears you've got,' Gideon said.

Miranda sat down on the boards and was biting cotton from a reel out of the luxury biscuit tin where Pamela kept her sewing things. The hem of one of the rumpled curtains must have snagged on something in the move. When Miranda bent to the work, the back of her neck was naked and white where she had lifted the hair. 'You're not to say no,' she told him. 'No, you're not.'

'It's all going to get a bit complicated unless I'm careful.'

'Then don't be,' she said. 'I'll come with you now and again, if you like. You'll get no marks for keeping it simple, you know. God is not mocked.'

'*Verb. sap.?* Piers promises?'

'You're right; I am thinking of seeing him maybe when you're doing take two, or three, or however many it takes. This can't be love, because I feel very peculiar about it, but it seems to be *something*, because ditto. I'm not sorry to be away, but I do rather want to go back.'

'You've been very good,' Gideon said. 'I know it means something to you and you've not cudgelled us with it.'

'I want you to be happy,' she said.

'Don't get greedy now!' Gideon looked out of the diamonded window at the furniture in the garden. 'What a sorry collection! It makes you wonder why we bothered to bring it at all.'

'What're you going to do with your desk?' she said. 'Aubrey Thing hasn't exactly allowed space for it in your office place, has he?'

'Are you after it?'

'What would I do at a desk? Tom might find it useful is all.'

'I only thought as you're taking "A" levels in the summer . . . '

'I like our furniture. Are you ashamed of it? You're not bothered what our learned friend will think, are you? Or his lady wife?'

'I'll tell you exactly what I think: for the same price, or rather for less, in view of the move, we could have nothing at all.'

'Sometimes you're wonderful,' she said. 'Wonderful! Oh, look, we've got a caller!'

The old man was wearing a coat cut from a tartan blanket. Gidéon was on his way to the gate, but Pamela was there first and hurried the visitor past the cottage and down towards the well which she had cleared of the ivy that cumbered it.

'You'd think he was expected,' Gideon said.

Pamela had found a bucket in the shed and was hauling new water from the darkness. The tramp reached for it with mittened claws and scanned his face in the yielding mirror. The gleaming surface rocked the sky between his and Pamela's lowered heads. When he said something to her, she nodded, like a learner, and took the bucket between her gloves while the tramp found an old water-bottle under the tartan and held it for her to fill. She looked into the other's crusty face until water reared from the neck of the bottle before splashing between them. Standing the bucket against the well-head, she clamped it there with her foot. After a second's frown, she put the flat of her hands against the man's forehead and closed her eyes.

'You'd better tell Pamela to watch out,' Miriam said, 'or you'll have them all here, all the time. The word goes round with incredible speed.' She was holding a basket filled with greaseproof packets, a thermos down one side. 'I hope you don't mind me coming back in your car. I thought you might be pleased to see it.' The Renault was on the cinders. 'How's it going with Aubs?'

'I've arranged a cooling off period,' he said, 'in accordance with government policy. What I really do need to know, minister, is the full amount of the projected damage.'

'We did discuss it on the phone, several times, but . . .'

The tramp bowed to Pamela and then he sidled past Gideon and Miriam, with quite another face, rattily bearded and scowling, his water-bottle like contraband, and went out of the gate as if he had dodged payment. He loped along the lane until the hedge tucked him from their sight. Gideon had the feeling that he had not so much gone away as found somewhere to hide; he and Pamela might have been playing some kind of unannounced game.

'I'm not too sure what has to be added to what,' Gideon said, 'and what includes what.'

'I'll get Aubs to set it all out, shall I?'

'That would be a solution of stupefying comfort to fuss-budgets and budget-fussers of a nervous disposition.'

'There's no need to be sarcastic about it.' Miriam seemed more offended by gratitude than she had been annoyed at his sharpness. 'I've brought some lunch, but don't worry, I shan't make a habit of it. I just thought, the first day – '

'Miriam, please believe me – '

'Why do men always say that when they want you to swallow a whopper? Please believe me! Please believe me! I wish I had a pound for every time I've heard that one.'

'Surely you do have, don't you?'

'I don't need them,' she said. 'Be perfectly clear about that, please.' The make-up that had smoothed the creases at the corners of her eyes and mouth now accentuated them abruptly. Was that grey at the roots of her expensive hair? Away from the lee of the house, Pamela was spared the cloud that put age on Miriam. Her forehead was silvered as she looked down into the shifting mirror in the round zinc frame at her feet. 'And a lot more besides,' Miriam added. 'Pounds.'

'I don't doubt it for a second.'

'You smile when you're worried, don't you? Did you learn that from Stephen or did he learn it from you?'

'What's he got to worry about?'

'He still does the hurdles, doesn't he?' Miriam said. 'And in wig and gown . . . '

Miranda had drawn the curtains in the sitting room and came out of the front door. 'Tara! Now we can sit in the garden without anyone spying on us from the leownge. Hello! Do I detect an atmosphere that is not merely that of gravity in the lawful execution of its inevitable functions?'

'Miriam's brought us the most wonderful picnic,' Gideon said. '*Pam!*'

'I'm coming.' She walked away towards the shed at the edge of the paddock as if to honour what she had just said.

'Shall I give Aubrey a shout?' Gideon said.

'It's not that wonderful,' Miriam said. 'He'll wander out in a minute.' She went across the cinders and into Gideon's proposed office.

'Words have been issued with new meanings this morning, it seems, papa.'

'New every morning is the love/Our wakening and uprising pruv,' Gideon said. 'I say, your chap doesn't write pop songs by any chance, does he?'

'My chap?'

'*The* chap. Piers's chap. Harold. Does he write lyrics by any chance?'

Aubrey followed Miriam to the table as if he had been given a last chance. They all sat down under a thickening sky; the legs of the chairs took odd angles from the earth and tilted them out of alignment as the picnic was handed round.

'Did you tell me he had tattoos?' Gideon said.

'Bound to have,' Miranda said.

'Who did?' Pamela said.

'I knew a girl at school,' Miriam said, 'who had a red rose tattooed on her behind.'

'What about Simple Simon?' Miranda said. 'Doesn't he get any crumbs from the rich person's table?'

'He brings his own,' Aubrey said. 'He prefers it that way. He goes down into the wood and has them there. He's a vegetarian, you know.'

'I'm surprised you're not,' Miranda said. 'You've got the complexion for it.'

'I was for a while. Then the doctor told me to go back. Simple Simon has another secret, by the by. His brother is the murderer.'

'*The* murderer? What murderer?'

'Raymond Thicknesse.'

'It can't be true,' she chortled. 'His name is really *Thicknesse*? Who did he murder?'

'An old woman,' Miriam said. 'He got away with eighty-something pounds, but not very far. They'd told him she kept her life savings under the bed. He tried to choke it out of her where the other hundred thousand were and she died of fright, isn't that the story, Aubs?'

'And he told you who he was?' Miranda said. 'Or rather who he wasn't?'

'He told – he told my – he told William.'

'Does he drive the van?' Gideon said. 'As well as – '

'He's got a licence. Is there any reason why he shouldn't?'

'Tell me about the man who used to live here,' Pamela said.

14

THE EVENING before the Shands were to move into Quince Cottage, Miriam insisted on a proper dinner party. Pamela did not know what she was supposed to wear and was sure that, whatever it was, she did not have it. Miranda could not decide between her War On Want number or the silver sheath which Yolande Bairstow had given her as a leaving present when they quit Chaworth. She offered to lend Pamela whichever one she liked, but she liked neither.

'It's not a formal occasion, Pammy,' Gideon said. 'She doesn't mean it to be anything but a pleasure.'

'A pleasure for whom?'

'She's been cooking more or less ever since yesterday,' Gideon said. 'I assume she means us to enjoy it. The smells are quite promising.'

'She takes too much trouble. It's a kind of ostentation, if one's honest.'

'If one's honest,' Gideon said, 'I'm not sure it's the best policy.'

'You could wear my grey trousers with your purple top,' Miranda said.

'I should like to get dressed by myself, I think,' Pamela said, 'if the spectators could bear that for once.'

Gideon put on his seminar suit, with a college tie, and deferred to Pamela's annoyance by going over to the main house. Only for a few more hours might he enjoy the amenities of Constable's without specific invitation. Stephen, not unusually, was going to be later home than he had said: Gideon was brief master of the library, where the murmur of kitchen voices scarcely reached. Diffident usurper in his host's Queen Anne chair, he lifted the single-piece telephone and pressed the numbers for his mother.

'When we're straight,' he said, 'you must come and see the cottage. It's not Graveley quite, but it has a certain modest rusticity.'

'I was wondering how it was all going,' Mrs Shand said. 'I'm *so* glad it's such a success.'

'You've got people there,' Gideon said.

'I'm sorry, dear?'

'People,' he said. 'Company. Are you giving a dinner party?'

'Oh, no, no, nothing like that. I never do any more.'

'You can afford it,' he said.

She laughed, away from the telephone, and came back to say, 'I've got Lady Chapman here and Mrs Rhodes, they're collecting.'

'That's quite an achievement in the circumstances,' Gideon said. 'For what?'

'It's nearly Christmas,' Mrs Shand said.

'I've never heard of that one,' Gideon said. 'What're you going to be doing?'

'For Christmas?'

'If you like,' Gideon said.

'I shall spend it here, I suppose. I shall have to see what invitations I get, shan't I?'

'I'll try and get down, but the cottage isn't finished yet and there are so many things to do.'

'Don't worry about me, dear,' she said.

'I worry about little else,' Gideon said.

'Your father used to say that,' Mrs Shand said. 'How did it go?'

'And little Else worries about me,' Gideon said. 'It's an old music-hall number, isn't it? You could come down and put up at an hotel. There's quite a nice one not far away.'

'It's too far for me to drive,' Mrs Shand said. 'And they're so expensive. How did the children like the new place?'

'The children are delighted with it,' Gideon said, 'and since we're all children, we're all delighted.'

'And Pamela?'

'I said: "We're all delighted," mother. It's a big burden, of course, but it had to be done. What's happening?'

'The ladies,' Mrs Shand said, 'they have to be going. They've got other calls to make and it's getting late.'

'Is it not?' Gideon said. 'I'll speak to you again soon. We haven't got a phone at the cottage yet, but we'll get one eventually.'

'You went to see Mr Woodward,' Mrs Shand said.

'Have they gone now, mother? Yes, I saw Barry.'

'He said how well you were looking.'

'Be as generous as I know you will, won't you, to the ladies? I'm sure they need the money.'

He tried the drawers of the partners' desk. Could there be a revolver in one of them? He found gold and silver pens and pencils, stationery in various styles of print, hotel envelopes (no writing paper) which testified to the cosmopolitan nature of Stephen's clients, a pair of new gloves, still yoked together like soft handcuffs, a box of pins with china heads, catalogues from auction houses and (in an old spectacle case) a packet of contraceptives, with one missing. He weighed one of the neatly rolled things in the palm of his hand and squeezed it between thumb and forefinger before returning it to the sprung case from Levy and Levy of Mill Hill. He remembered the heavy shell frames of the glasses Stephen wore when they first met. Why had there been something enviable in them? His friend's focussed glare made perfect sight seem a flaw.

The telephone trilled. After a few seconds, it stopped: Miriam must have picked it up. Gideon smiled at the silent grey thing, an unmusical box with the lid closed on its available tune. When it was raised from the blotter, next to the tortoise-shell pen-and-pencil sheaths, voices were liberated.

'I hoped to be on the six-forty,' Stephen was saying,

'but I shall have to make it the seven-thirty. Can you entertain them till then?'

'I'll tell Erik to be at the station in good time.'

'Unfortunately someone sent something over I had to give an opinion on at the last minute.'

'Don't miss the seven-thirty, will you?'

'I've been thinking about you this afternoon,' Stephen said.

'Yes?' she said.

'Oh yes,' he said. 'Are you alone?'

'Trudie's here helping me.'

'Then I'll see you later.' The telephone gushed silence in Gideon's ear. Then Stephen said, 'Only one more night of them.'

Miriam was wearing her latest tunic of many colours, subtle wool weaving from plummy purples through to peachy rose, with ribbed hoops of some stiffish material to which tiny mirrors, no more than winks of light, had been attached over the shoulders and below the strict neck. She was agile in black velvet trousers and silver half-boots and somehow her hair was thicker than before, in braided loops, as black now as the velvet.

Pamela had decided on her green woollen suit, with the ruffled silk shirt and black court shoes. Her face was almost without make-up, defiance in the nakedness of it. She looked at once modest and immodest, as if she had scarcely bothered to dress at all. Miranda was in Yolande's silver sheath, cold-shouldered, shampooed hair scalloped above her nice ears. Tom was ready for speech day, in grey flannels and school blazer.

'Rightly or rightly,' Stephen said, when the guests came into the drawing room, 'we decided against dressing the set with a selection of local dignitaries and other antique furniture. Much nicer just to be ourselves, if that can be managed, don't you think so?' In black coat and striped trousers, his professional voice declared that he had had a successful day, about which he would say nothing more. 'I hope you'll take it as read that we've assembled the best company available to celebrate whatever it is that we're celebrating.'

'Moving in day,' Miriam said.

'And moving out day,' Gideon said.

'Systole and diastole,' Stephen said, 'where would we be without them? Were the young people not here with us tonight, one might be tempted to say that we shouldn't really be at all. Now let's declare this impressive congress in plenary session and get under way with the first bottle.'

'But first,' Gideon said, 'a shmall presentation from the temporary tenantry.'

'What's this? A Christmas cracker?' Stephen said. 'You should have, you should have!'

'Come to think of it, Miriam, I'm not sure that this is your sort of present at all. I hope you won't feel – now I wish I hadn't said anything.'

'Now we all do,' Miranda said. 'Personally, I think Miriam'll find it really useful.'

'Good God!' Stephen said. 'In the name of the law! Wherever did you find it?'

'First shop on the left going up North Hill,' Gideon said, 'no problem at all. He promised me that it was the genuine article, as used by the Bow Street Runners.'

'Yes,' Miranda said, 'they used to run up to people with it and hammer them vigorously about the head in justifiable self-defence, thus setting a useful precedent for drilling the wrong man full of holes and claiming that he might well have been someone else, which would have entirely justified the whole procedure and, come to think of it, might well justify almost anything a boy in blue could ever feel like doing.'

'School going well, Miranda?' Stephen said. 'This is truly a remarkable object.'

'If you look carefully', Gideon said, 'you'll see that it's inscribed, in invisible writing to avoid embarrassment or damaging resale values, with our very fervent thanks to a couple of extraordinary people who've saved us single-handed from a very nasty pickle indeed.'

'Single-handed is a slight lapse from your usual high standards, papa, isn't it, in view of the fact that there are two of them – and four hands?'

'Nice of you to blow the whistle, Mandy. I was watching for your linesman's flag as soon as the ineptitude was out of my mouth.'

'I shall dangle this richly embellished example of the cudgel-maker's art on a hook by the front door,' Stephen said, 'and it shall serve henceforth to repel boarders, or at least repellent ones, into which class the present company will never fall. And now it's Perrier Jouet time, my friends, the bubble-makers with the initials Uncle Adolf loved to see!'

While they were eating Miriam's *quenelles* (she had put out sauce spoons, because after all the trouble she had taken, she didn't want anything wasted!), Stephen noticed Tom's silence. 'How are things going at the new school, now that you've had time to . . . ?'

'Only one problem,' Tom said, 'no computer studies for "O" levels. They can't get a teacher, they say.'

'They'll say anything,' Stephen said.

'Your hair looks marvellous, Miriam,' Miranda said.

'They'll even say that,' Stephen said. 'This sounds like a serious problem. And they may occasionally be right, which adds to the rich tapestry of things. Mind you, I imagine that by now you'd probably have more to teach him than he'd have to teach you.'

'Oh no,' Tom said. 'I've only got through the Basic book and now, of course – '

'Now, of course not,' Stephen said. 'I was wondering why you were wearing Banquo's sorry countenance, and now the penny has dropped. Come back to radiant life, poor ghostly Tom! Have you got a bicycle?'

'Not really.'

'When I'm a judge, if I'm a judge, *any* judge, you're the sort of witness at whom I shall gnash my teeth, not to mention other fanged portions of my anatomy, young Thomas, because either you have a bicycle or you don't.'

'*We* have a bicycle, my lord,' Gideon said, 'but it's basically Pam's. The rest of us are just along for the ride.'

'Who'll finish this for me?' Miriam said. 'Pamela?'

'I couldn't,' Pamela said.

'And I shouldn't,' Gideon said, 'but I bloody well will, because when will I get the chance to eat at a three-star restaurant again?'

'And Mr Tactful rides again,' Miranda said, 'but not necessarily in this direction.'

'Come on, Pam, you can recognise one of Gideon's hyperboles when he unleashes it, can't you?'

'Gideon's absolutely right,' Pamela said. 'Miriam's not the kind of cook you come across every day of the week. This is the best thing I've ever tasted.'

'Bicycles,' Stephen said, 'you can have too few of a good thing, you know, and having wished you into a cottage quite a few miles from the beaten track and other reliable forms of transport – '

'A track surely can't *be* a form of – '

'Nice of you to point out the slight loss of metaphorical style in there, Miranda, but not *very* nice; having, as I was saying before I was so politely interrupted (*don't do it again*), secluded you from communal wheels, it seems only fair that we should address ourselves to your mobility problem.'

'We have no problem,' Pamela said.

'But you do have an address. I really do feel responsible for having introduced Tom to the horrible fascinations of the Wumpus and his back-up system. It's a guilt I cannot lightly dismiss. At the least, you must feel absolutely free to come on over here whenever you feel like it, or even more often than that.'

'It's very nice of you.' Tom left a little space after he had spoken, in which Gideon could see uncertainty whether to say 'Stephen' or 'Mr Hellman'. Their host's smile recognised the difficulty too. 'But won't – ? I mean – '

'Ben's always trying to get me to understand what he's up to on the thing,' Stephen said. 'I should be delighted and honoured if you'd agree to be my proxy henceforth and for evermore, world with end. Mim, whatever happened to that low-slung thing that Ben used to ride?'

Miriam was hot with a silver dish of quails she was bringing to the table and managed only a watchful shudder of ignorance. Trudie followed with *pommes de terre soufflées*, each one almost as big as the birds they accompanied. The *pièce de resistance*, however, was a large flat dish of mixed vegetables which had been composed into a mosaic with the unmistakable image of Quince Cottage in the centre of its garden, greenly hedged with spinach. They had to clap.

'Only one question remains,' Gideon said, 'and that is, what are we going to eat for vegetables? Because one really can't put a work of art like that in one's mouth.'

'If only they were all edible, I sometimes think, Gidman. Imagine what one would give for *suprême de Venus de Milo*, with a white wine sauce and garnished with a few asparagus spears in tender phallic tribute. I think it's in the barn somewhere, Thomas, and I vote we go and have a look for it by torchlight after dinner. Ben's got a ten thousand c.c. Honda at this point and he never rides the damned thing.'

'We're not having anything else given to us by you, Stephen,' Pamela said.

Miriam bent into the steam to lift quails on to the plates in front of her. Stephen decided to work on a new bottle of Léoville-Lascases 1961, but his eyes had time for Pamela as the screw-pull worked its silent extraction. A blush of effort stained the sides of Stephen's nose and his lips were tight against the ready eloquence of his tongue. Miranda looked fixedly at Gideon. Tom simply gazed at the vegetable picture of Quince Cottage, eating it whole with admiration before it should be destroyed, piecemeal, by the serving spoon.

Miriam's pains seemed suddenly to embarrass her, as if some carping intelligence had suggested a sour motive for creating something so imaginative and – since she must now demolish it, before its owners – so ambiguous. Tears balanced on those silvered lids. Her red talons trembled before beginning the hospitable destruction of what she had been so nice to make. Cheeky breasts pouting above the line of the sheath that vased her, Miranda bolted from her seat and went to put an arm around her hostess and kissed her matt cheek. Miriam's confusion brought Stephen's swollen gaze from Pamela to Gideon, from whom it seemed to solicit some betrayal of his wife. Feverish with all the visions that crowded on him, Gideon addressed himself to the brace of little birds now set before him.

'The hardest thing in the world,' Stephen said, 'is to persuade people that you really don't want something that you really don't want. Sincerity is the most unconvincing of human modes, don't you think so? It has no place in art or in life, so one wonders where it does belong.'

'There can be sincere art, can't there, Stephen?' Miranda said. 'Music?'

'But even there, correct me if I'm right, there is no way in which a performance can be *justified* by its sincerity. To be sincere can never be of aesthetic interest, can it? One shouldn't confuse naïveté with sincerity, any more than one should confuse scepticism with tolerance, eh, Gideon?'

'Sincerity has real meaning only in the domain of love, surely,' Gideon said. 'Not that I know whether your lordship would allow that that has any place in what you would call life.'

'Sincerity and love,' Stephen said, 'would you care to speak to us on that one, Pamela?'

'I don't speak,' Pamela said.

'Accurate recollection is at the heart of all art and all malice,' Stephen said. 'Hence . . . hence what? The impossibility of an art of happiness. When Orpheus looks back, he kills Eurydice. How shall we analyse that one? Easily: when we see the reality of what lies behind us, we destroy it and, in due season, ourselves.'

'I don't understand it all either,' Miriam said.

'Oh I wasn't . . . ' Tom said.

'Of course you do, darling,' Stephen said. 'Women understand everything, except what is said.'

'Tom isn't a woman, Stephen,' Miranda said.

'Orpheus betrayed his art in needing to check that Eurydice was really there. He should have known that what he could not see, what his imagination alone could conjure, was the real Eurydice, *his* Eurydice. We look back in order to destroy what was there, not to preserve it. Verification falsifies. Hence, if I may make a quantum leap, all this talk about certain events in recent history which we all deplore, some of us. The word killeth. Hence talk, talk, talk.'

'You must meet our old friend Lack,' Gideon said. 'You know what I think he'd say? Sincerity has a place in love when that love belongs to God. God would be the one person with Whom it would be ridiculous to be insincere. Indeed with Whom the very idea of an insincere relationship is impossible.'

'Was that you talking or your friend Lack, papa? How about a spot of station identification?'

'It was logic, I think, basically. And logic has no author. Talleyrand was about the only person I can think of who actually tried to outsmart God. By confessing and claiming absolution on his death-bed, when he had nothing to look forward to except, alas, the infinite, he achieved the spiritual equivalent, you might say, of scoring the winning goal on the very verge of full time, or at least an equaliser. I wonder how well God regarded that particular piece of cheeky wizardry. No one, I suspect, ever made a better point against Pascal, by taking Pascal to his own limit. After all, the old moralist had claimed that we might as well embrace the true faith, because if we held it to be false and it wasn't, we should pay for our error with hell fire, while if we bet on its being true, we should at best find ourselves in eternal bliss or, if we were after all mistaken, we should be no worse off than anyone else, since death would indeed prove to involve universal extinction. Talleyrand got his money on at the very last minute, but didn't Jesus himself say that it was never too late? God is a croupier of souls who promises never to call *rien ne va plus* until the last breath is out of the runner's body. What were we talking about?'

'Bicycles,' Stephen said.

'Please could we not?'

'Dammit, Pammy,' Stephen said, 'I remember you – I remember you in a red rage because some government or other wasn't going to do anything about people having two houses. It was seriously suggested at some point in this island's vaporised past that two abodes were a lot worse than one and that it shouldn't ought to be allowed. And Pamela was in the lobby with the Jacobins, deny it if you dare.'

'That was a long time ago,' Pamela said.

'In other words, guilty as charged. And now here am I simply trying to wish a disused concatenation of scrap metal on a worthy young cause and you take umbrage. Take the bloody grid rather and do everyone a good turn.'

'I did ask you,' Pamela said.

'Sincerity,' Stephen said. 'You see where it gets you? It's all right with God, but risky with other ranks.'

'Is this *serious*?'

'This, Thomas, is indeed what passes for serious among dissenting adults. Hard to credit, is it not? Between ourselves, let me offer you a piece of free advice. (Invoice follows.) When faced with gift horse, saddle up and go to town, whatever helpful bystanders have to say.'

Pamela said: 'You haven't changed, have you?'

'Was I always in this pair of trousers?' Stephen said. 'That's not my recollection, or my tailor's.'

'You're going to have the last one, aren't you, Gideon?' Miriam had a quail on the big spoon for him. 'I'm relying on you.'

'I've changed out of all recognition,' Stephen said. 'That's why it's so easy for everyone to know who I am.' He tilted wine into his glass and sat looking at it, thick-shouldered, a droop of hair on his three-creased forehead.

'I say,' Tom said, 'if there isn't anything else – '

Everyone laughed, except for Stephen, who smiled, but not at the same thing.

'I think there probably is something,' Gideon said, 'or what's all this weaponry for?'

'I went to a banquet in the City last week,' Stephen said, 'and there was so much silver on the table that I asked my fancy-dressed neighbour which of the selection was for eating with and which for stealing. I had the feeling that he counted all my spoons into my mouth and counted them all out again. I left with nothing more silver than my tongue in my cheek. If you want to go and rehearse the end of the world instead of having pud, young Tom, no one will count it against you at the last trump.'

'Are you sure?'

'A question asked only of the uncertain,' Stephen said.
' "I'm quite sure," said the sceptic. Go, and the grace of
God go with you, if you can stand that sort of company.'

'Do you not like sorbets, as a matter of interest?
Because that's what's coming next. A pear one.'

'I don't even know what it is.'

'We'll leave it in the fridge for you, Tom,' Stephen said,
'and you can have it whenever you want it, or don't want
it, to cover all the possibilities, unless your mother
doesn't approve.'

Pamela's head went forward. She might have been
bending to some silent grace. Gideon's desire was as
demanding as his resentment, but he knew neither what
he wanted exactly nor exactly what he resented. Meanwhile, Trudie had brought frosted wine glasses from the
freezer. They contained testicle-shaped scoops of an
almost colourless sorbet. Tom cleared his throat before
not saying anything and went from the room. Leaning
across the table, with public deliberation, Stephen put a
hand on Pamela's shoulder and squeezed her until she
came upright and looked at him. Spoons chimed against
cold glasses.

Miranda said, 'I know you're not supposed to ask, but
that's not the only reason I'm doing it: what's this at the
bottom, Miriam, that makes all the delicious difference?'

'It's a mixture of Kirsch and Sauternes, Miranda. It
takes the curse off the pear essence, even though it's the
essence of our own pears.'

'I made some *eau de vie* last year, we had so much
fruit,' Stephen said.

Pamela looked away: a puckered comma of uncertainty aged her right cheek.

There was still a Rosenthal fork in front of Gideon and
he tested its prongs against the back of his hand, nagging
pale flesh till it admitted blood. 'I phoned my mother this
evening, Steve,' he said. 'Which reminds me, I owe you
for quite a few calls since we checked in and before we
check out.'

'I'll put them down to consultations with overseas
clients. How was she?'

'Exceptionally genial. That's how I knew she must have people with her, preferably titled, and one was. It's funny how some people have taken Bishop Berkeley so literally they exist only when other people have them under observation.'

'It's true of everyone who's failed to be what he should have been,' Stephen said. 'Freedom alone needs no witnesses. We have done those things which we ought not to have done and there is no health in us. This is the most superb dinner, Mim.'

'Oh, that's all right,' Miriam said.

The last course consisted of a chocolate *soufflé* sparkling with icing sugar. There was a sigh from those at the table; appreciation was tinged with shame that, no longer hungry, they were required to puncture something so pretty. Miriam broke the cuffed surface with a vigour that made big portions for everyone, the least they could do for her. Gideon managed enthusiasm he could not blame his wife for lacking, though he did. When at last it was seemly to say goodnight (everyone had a busy day ahead), he kissed Miriam on both cheeks and held her against him.

Stephen sat with the neck of an Armagnac bottle in his hand and watched his wife taking her congratulations. He moved his chair and it stood, that scraping sound, for the speech he might have made. The lights flickered, as if some invisible proprietor was suggesting closing time, and they heard the mumble of thunder. 'I'll go and tell Tom he'd better drink up,' Gideon said.

George and Martha were running about the dark lawn in front of the house when at last he followed the slow Tom towards the flat above the garage. The dogs scuttled towards the front door, but Miriam waved them away. 'You've had all you're going to get,' she said, 'you greedy things. Go and do your doings.'

As Gideon and Tom came through the brick archway from the barn, the dogs swerved to yap at them like strangers. Gideon put flat hands down to quieten them and sidled into what light there was in order to declare himself. 'We ought to think about an animal, I suppose,

214

at the cottage,' he said. 'I shouldn't like Pam to be by herself.'

'She'll have you, won't she?'

'My bark isn't as loud as my bite,' Gideon said.

'Oh you and Stephen!' Miriam said. She had removed her silvery half-boots and he saw bright red socks. 'You never say anything straight, do you? You're both exactly the same.'

'But that's as far as the similarity goes,' Gideon said. 'I was actually thinking if I was away for any reason. You gave us the most marvellous evening. I can't thank you enough.'

She stepped her socks into the cold gravel and steadied herself on Gideon's arm. 'He's got a woman, hasn't he?' she said.

'He certainly seems to have,' Gideon said. 'And he appears remarkably happy with her.'

'See what a stranger you turn into as soon as I really want to talk to you? You didn't even like the dinner really, did you?'

'You took so much trouble – '

'I have to do something,' she said.

'I don't think I've ever known anyone quite so active in quite so many directions.'

'Balls,' she said, 'and you know it. *I* certainly know it. Who is this Tamara?'

'Tamara?'

'There's someone in his life called Tamara. Don't deny it.'

'*Tamara!* She's the wife of our partners in the Gold Cup. Tamara and Oleg, the latter of whom is a highly uxorious husband, not to say possessive. I don't deny it; I affirm it.'

'He married me for my money,' Miriam said. 'Or rather daddy's money. Rich little rich girl, that was me. He's got a woman somewhere, I don't care what you say.'

'It's nothing to do with me, Miriam. I don't know what you – '

'Why are you all such cowards? Why do you always hang on to what you don't really want to keep and . . . ?'

'What do men really want? Frau Freud never put that one squarely to the boss, did she?'

'Nearly twenty years,' Miriam said, 'and I've hardly understood a word. I wonder if that occurs to you. I know what's going on, but I haven't really understood a word.'

'As Stephen was saying – '

'Oh, you're so loyal!' she said. 'Why are you?'

'It's not loyalty. I like him.'

'Well, what's behind it?'

'He's an extraordinary man. *Is*n't he?'

'You know why he works so hard? Why he always takes on one more thing, no matter what it is? He's on the telephone now. Because he can't stand the reason that he wanted me in the first place. I had money. He didn't. Or not enough of it. Now he wants to have enough not to need me any more. For that not to have been the reason in the first place.'

'If that were true,' Gideon said, 'surely he'd have enough by now, *has* enough by now.'

'Must you . . . ?'

'I'm only trying to show you how absurd you're being.'

'No, you're trying to make me absurd.'

'It may be to your credit,' Gideon said, 'but I don't think you quite appreciate what an attractive woman you are. I remember when Stephen first met you and came back and talked about you till well after three in the morning. *I* wanted to talk about bridge hands. I can assure you that your financial prospects were by no means paramount among the assets discussed.'

'He wanted me all right,' she said, 'in the hands up department. But that was just something that comes with the equipment. It wasn't *him*. Or *me*. Oh, he still likes to stuff. But what . . . well, it's too late now, I suppose. I was the fool. Or was it the villain? If I'd really loved him, I wouldn't have married him, would I?'

'He was scared stiff you'd turn him down, I know that.'

'He was certainly stiff, but scared? I couldn't believe it, I was such a nice girl. The way he . . . He had no shame at all, not with me. Kept showing it to me. Is everyone like that?'

'Absolutely,' Gideon said.

'I'm embarrassing you.'

'You're certainly having a good stab at it, aren't you?'

'I don't *care* if he's got a woman, if that's what you think, but I want to know.'

'How many unhappy people have said precisely that? And then . . . '

'There is someone, isn't there?'

'You know him much better than I do.'

'But he's not the same person with me.'

'Then we can't really talk about him, can we?'

'How you wish I'd go away!'

'You know how awkward it is when couples – '

'Yes, I do,' she said. 'And I like seeing you feeling awkward about it. Because you don't ever begin to realise how awkward *we* feel, women, when you're being clever and when you're being condescending and nice. I say, it's not your wife, by any chance, is it?'

The spaniels were looking up at them, eyes marbled by the vague light. Thunder shifted on the horizon; sparks of lightning flashed now and again. They could hear the first drops of rain. Miriam, a girl in her socks, pressed both hands on the bar of Gideon's forearm and raised her face to his. He kissed the reddened mouth and felt its stickiness and the stab of quick, hot tongue. 'Take it up to her,' she said. 'Take it up to her, go on.'

'You're a very naughty woman,' he said.

'Come and see me,' she said.

'Miriam – '

'Alternatively,' she said, 'don't.'

15

GIDEON'S FIRST fears about Quince Cottage appeared groundless: the Hellmans were tactful enough not to call too frequently, nor yet to stop calling at all. Constable's might have been thirty rather than three miles away. The postman proved that the Shands were not forgotten; if Jack Knightley had to say hello by letter, he did not fail to do so. (Everything was 'on track'.) Miranda received thick envelopes with a Chaworth postmark, but though she pounced on them, she did not fret when a week or more went by without another. The cottage had seemed remote when first they visited it, but the familiar grew around it and seemed to encroach, like the trees in the ghost story, without their menace. Simple Simon always had one more little job to do, but Aubrey verified that the work had been well done and the Christmassy weather was almost welcome, so snugly did the family relish the warmth of the cottage. In the evenings, they would clear the sanded table in the kitchen and Tom and Miranda did their homework in front of the Aga, while Gideon flagged library books for a possible new series on forms of warfare. Jack Knightley expected to start taping *The Meaning Of War* early in the new year, perhaps during week six.

Pamela seemed to be too busy in the house, and the garden, to prospect for new patients, but Gideon sometimes heard visitors at the creaking gate when he was at work in his insulated shed. An oil heater made it quite hot in there. At lunchtime, he would affect a little start of surprise when he found food waiting on the kitchen table and Pamela there. One day, when he had heard the gate more often than usual, he said, 'You seem to be becoming very popular.'

'It's not me, it's the garden. Or rather Casey's garden.'

'Not much in at the moment, is there?'

'There have been things,' she said, 'and that's really what they come for.'

'Who are they, for Christ's sake?'

'People with various kinds of problems. Simple people. He used to look after them.'

'And what do you do to them?'

'I suppose I try to do the same.'

'I hope you know what you're doing.'

'Why?'

'If you're treating people who have serious complaints, I mean.'

'You never worried about it before.'

'You did what you were trained to do before. It can be rather risky, can't it, dishing out – well, I don't know what you're doing, of course, in reality.'

'No,' she said.

'So what are you?'

'What are you?' she said.

'This is very good ham, very good indeed. Do you give them medicine or what?'

'I give them or what.'

'Oh Pammy!'

'Why have you started calling me that? You didn't ever call me that till we came down here. They're herbal remedies. Things anyone can make for themselves, if they know how.'

'Did he charge them for them?'

'They sometimes gave him something if they wanted to.'

'What about the water?' he said. 'The well.'

'Oh it's supposed to have certain powers. Simple people say that waters can have completely different tastes,

219

one kind and another, if you attune yourself to them.'

'Who are these simple people in present-day England? I thought national insurance had abolished simplicity.'

'They come in the gate,' Pamela said. 'Look for yourself. Vagrants, gypsies, farm workers, their wives, people who don't believe in doctors – all sorts.'

'And you are just finishing up Casey's left-overs, Pam – Pam? Or are you also proposing to restock?'

'I've made a few kinds of basic tea, that's all. They seem to go down quite well.'

'What about your other patients? The normal kind. When are you planning to find some of those in the neighbourhood?'

'Am I planning to?'

'You're not afraid that some of these callers of yours might be a bit strange in the head at all, are you?'

'They are,' she said, 'some of them. But they seem to respond to me. That's why they come back. They say I've got something of Casey about me. Probably it's the place. I felt it as soon as we came here. I wanted not to like it. I'd *decided* not to like it. But then it decided that I would, and I did, and I do.'

'Even though what?'

'It tires me sometimes,' she said. 'It's as if there was something here that made me work and work. It's like a kind of exercise, Gideon, seeing some of these people. I feel tired, as if I'd been struggling with something in my mind and it came out in my body. I suppose I love them in a way, even though they disgust me.'

'You're an odd woman sometimes, aren't you?'

'I should like to be one more often, I think. How's the telly going?'

'It's really going to happen, it seems. I'm afraid it may be rather disruptive, having to go up there every so often. Can you bear it, do you think? I was considering buying a dog, a nice mongrel you could have for company if – '

'I should prefer not,' she said. 'I'm protected as it is.'

'Tom might like it,' he said.

'If they give him a bicycle for Christmas,' she said, 'I want you to give it back.'

'Why have I been elected?'

'They must be kept away from here,' she said.

'Steve and Miriam? They don't seem markedly obtrusive to me.'

'They're not a good thing.'

'They're not a thing at all,' he said. 'They're a couple of people who've been remarkably kind to us.'

'I've been dreaming about them,' she said. 'Especially about him.'

'Well, I suppose it's understandable. You and he . . . and you've not seen him all these years.'

'You may find this difficult,' she said, 'but he comes to see me. I don't invite it. He comes.'

'He comes? Let me try and get this clear. Do you mean that he literally pays you visits? No, you don't. You don't mean that he comes in person at all. He comes in your dreams. You dream about him.'

'I hate you sometimes.'

'I know.'

'I don't dream about him,' she said. 'He comes into my dreams.'

'You seriously feel that he forces himself on you?'

'You allowed yourself to be bought,' she said.

'Ah,' Gideon said.

'It's unforgivable, isn't it?'

'And is it forgivable to go along with it? Is it forgivable to be so strong that you make no resistance? You wanted this cottage.'

'It's unforgivable unless something changes. Unless you realise that everything you're so confident about is not really reliable in the least. Nothing is reliable, except God and the devil. And Stephen is the devil.'

'You still love him,' Gideon said. 'I do realise that. I suppose you think I don't know what you've been doing to yourself all these years.'

'You're afraid I'm going to say he's a Jew,' she said. 'He is a Jew.'

'I had heard,' Gideon said.

'You're trembling. You want to be ill. You want to be helpless just as you were when I first came to you. He possessed me too. That's how I know what he is and what he did to you.'

221

'Believe it or not, I've thought about – about the incident you're talking about, thinking about – over and over again. And you may be disappointed to hear that – '

'I'm listening,' she said.

'I wasn't cheated,' he said. 'I did it because I wanted to, because I had to, perhaps. You don't have any real idea of what I was like before, or even of what I actually did.'

'It doesn't really matter, does it,' she said, 'now?' She moved to the sink with the hammy plates and left him with the cheese. Without appetite, he cut himself a sliver of double Gloucester and took it in pieces from the knife.

'He doesn't mean to do anything but good, you know. He wishes us nothing but well.'

'*Us!*'

'All of us. You're altogether too touchy about that bicycle. O.K., we won't have it, we won't have it, even if it's offered again, but he could see how much Tom was going to miss the computer, and . . . '

'He *is* something,' she said.

'Pam, you're a bright woman. You know what you're saying and you must know why you're saying it.'

'You mean that you do and you think I don't.'

'Surely you can see that coming here, seeing Steve again, seeing Miriam, seeing Miranda with him, with them, seeing everything, it's opened your eyes wider than they'll really go. It's made you feel that our whole life is dependent on Stephen somehow and that leads you to bless, or curse, him with powers you can't honestly believe him to possess. What you miss out is how really decent and generous he is.'

'You don't know much about the devil, do you?'

'I don't know anything about him. He falls into the category of what Peter Michaeljohn used to call "thereof, whereof", things it's better not to talk about, because nothing useful can be said about them. You don't seriously believe any of this, do you? The devil!'

'I always wanted to be a doctor, you know,' she said, 'but daddy couldn't afford it, all the years of supporting me, and then I found I couldn't stand the blood. You might say that I let him off. I suppose I let him off all sorts of things, not least his not believing in what he was doing. You know what they say: parsons are paid to preach, not to practise. He was certainly one of those. I let him off because I loved him, and I didn't love him because he agreed to be let off.'

'He was your father. Daughters are allowed to love their fathers, and also – '

'We shouldn't love anybody, probably,' she said, 'when what we love is the weakness.'

'It's not too late,' he said. 'You could study medicine now, if you really wanted to. Miranda'll soon – '

'Yes?'

'Have her own life.'

'I'm going to tell her, Gideon,' she said, 'so that she does. I must have been dreaming all these years.'

'It's your right,' he said. 'But have you thought of how she's likely to take it?'

'What matters is that she should,' Pamela said, 'take it. I've had it for long enough.'

'I hope you'll be able to forgive yourself.'

'We can't forgive ourselves.'

'I also hope this is something that will pass, Pam. If it's this place that's brought it about, I'll happily think about moving again, if that'll – '

'I love this place. It's given me the strength I should have had all these years.'

A car had come down the lane and stopped at the gate. They heard the snarl of the hinge and the footsteps. 'One of yours?' Gideon said.

'No,' she said, as the knocker snapped on the front door.

'You're not on the telephone,' Inspector Telfer said. 'I hope I haven't come at a bad moment.'

'Not a man I expected to see,' Gideon said. 'Come in. Do you want some coffee?'

'I had a beer and a bun at the Shepherd and Dog,' Telfer said.

'What can we do for you?' Gideon said. 'And what's the latest from Chaworth? We haven't been here that long, but – '

'It feels like home,' Telfer said. 'How are you, Mrs Shand?'

'Exceptionally well,' Pamela said.

'You've heard about the fire, I suppose?'

'The fire?'

'Mr Simmonds. He's been charged with arson. You're not surprised, I don't suppose.'

'I never liked him,' Pamela said.

'We hardly knew him, did we? Should you really be talking about it?'

'It's not my case,' Telfer said. 'This is a very unusual kitchen these days. Homely. This kind of cottage, you don't find it in our neck of the woods. The beams. I can see why you went for it. Of course, he hasn't been found guilty yet. We shall have to see what the jury says.'

'He's been committed for trial though, has he, poor old Athol?'

'You're a man who knows the niceties of the law, Mr Shand.'

'I do watch the telly from time to time, inspector.'

'Are you planning to get the telephone at all? Because I'm sorry not to have made contact.'

'They actually say he burned the factory down? I can't believe it. Why would he?'

'Upwards of two hundred thousand pounds might seem quite a good reason to some people.'

'I can't believe it,' Gideon said.

'You can't believe anything, can you?' Pamela said.

Telfer looked at the corners of the room and seemed to find it necessary to swallow the last crumbs of his bun, or the last drops of his beer, with renewed care. 'I don't know', he said, 'if anyone has been in touch with you from Chaworth at all recently.'

'We hear from people,' Gideon said.

'Mrs Shand?'

'No, I don't think so,' Pamela said. 'Why?'

'The will,' he said.

'Will?' Gideon said. 'What will?'

'No, they haven't,' Pamela said. 'I'd forgotten there even was one.'

'Fagin?' Gideon said.

'You've forgotten?' Telfer said. 'Meaning that you knew at one point?'

Pamela said, 'Gideon, why don't you . . . ?'

'Is this an official visit, inspector? Because if it is, should you not announce it as such?'

'There's no secret,' Telfer said. 'No concealment. Mrs Shand was told that there were bound to be further developments. A man dies of cyanide poisoning, there has to be an inquest. And if and when further elements come to light, we're bound to investigate the whole thing in view of them. The will was lodged in a rather unusual place and it's only recently come to be found. Strange man, Mr Fagin.'

'Gideon, I'd like to talk to Inspector Telfer alone. I know you've got a lot of work to do. My husband is about to do a T.V. series for East Midlands.'

'I shall look forward to it.'

'I think somebody ought to be with you,' Gideon said. 'And I also think that you should make clear exactly what kind of an interview this is, inspector.'

'I'm a policeman,' Telfer said, 'and I'm making a routine inquiry. I happened to be in this district – '

'You drive pretty well a hundred miles – '

'My driver does the driving.'

'Shouldn't he be here? I thought inspectors were like royalty, they always had to have an attendant, someone to hold the train, or at least the notebook.'

'Where was it?' Pamela said. 'The will?'

'Guess.'

'I couldn't.'

'My wife was particularly fond of old Mr Fagin,' Gideon said.

'He had a devious side to him,' Pamela said. 'Mischievous, but very straight-faced. He'd been a sort of spy, as you probably know.'

'It was attached to the bottom of his lift, Mrs Shand, with adhesive plaster. It wasn't discovered until a surveyor came in to check the house for valuation.'

Pamela was leaning against the sink, both hands under her behind, rocking on the small seat they made. Her feet flexed and relaxed and her chin was raised to the lowering sun so that it seemed to clock a white bruise there. The rocking tightened the grey skirt across her hips;

Gideon could see the little package in her pants. Telfer was rearranging his gloves on the table in front of him; he made a complicated manoeuvre of it, as though there were several of them.

'Well, aren't you going to tell me?' she said.

'Of course,' Telfer said, 'this is entirely unofficial. They probably had difficulty tracing you. It appears that he left you ten thousand pounds.'

'Should we admire your timing, inspector?' Gideon said.

Telfer looked at his gloves as if he had reason to think that one of them was missing and then he raised unsmiling eyes at Gideon. His beard glinted from the same slanting light that lay on Pamela. 'It's something the court will be certain to take into account,' he said, 'and which will almost certainly mean that the inquest will have to be re-opened. I thought as I was in your district – your new district – I could save some time, yours and mine, by calling in. There's nothing more to it than that.'

'And nothing less,' Gideon said.

'If Mrs Shand feels that she'd prefer to say nothing until a formal inquiry gets under way, that's her privilege.'

'Ten thousand pounds,' Pamela said.

'Useful sum,' Telfer said, 'even today. He never mentioned it?'

Gideon said, 'I strongly feel, darling, that – '

'I don't mind talking about it,' Pamela said. 'And I don't care who knows, or when, that I had no idea whatever that this was coming or that I absolutely can't accept the money. I wish you'd go and finish that script, Gideon dear.'

Telfer and Pamela waited for him to leave. Pamela had spoken with a tenderness which Telfer seemed to find most considerate, to judge from the ramping of his moustache, which stood for a smile. The rage which slapped Gideon's cheeks scarlet apparently did not come from her at all. He stumbled on his way to the door, as he passed between the inspector and his wife, and frowned at Simple Simon's level floorboards. 'None of this can conceivably have any value as evidence,' he said. 'I'm sure you realise that, inspector.'

'My sergeant's up at your village church,' Telfer said. 'I'm told there are some very unusual brasses. He's by way of being quite a buff. This is a courtesy call, nothing more, and if you'd prefer me to wait by the gate, I'll happily do so. It's a nice afternoon.'

'I don't want the money,' Pamela said, 'for reasons I'm sure you understand.'

'I'd like to be sure,' Telfer said. 'I think I can guess, but I'd much sooner you told me. I'm not *asking* you to tell me, mind.'

The voices spoke to Gideon through the common wall as he sat in his shed. He was wearing brown corduroy trousers, bought at the surplus stores now erased at Chaworth's Regency roundabout development. As he sat down to his papers, listening to the two of them, he saw that his flies were undone. He put his hand to the throb of his sex; it moved like a bagged pet.

'I was properly paid for what I did,' Pamela said, 'and I never expected anything to come from – from what he felt for me. You know what I'm trying to say.'

'I do indeed, Mrs Shand, but it won't make any difference, I'm afraid.'

'It makes a difference to me,' she said. 'It ought to make a difference to you.'

'Do I follow you, Mrs Shand?'

'It isn't that the money wouldn't be useful; it's just that I couldn't trust myself if I took it. I should always think that perhaps I'd had it in mind all along. My husband – '

'Yes?'

'Money – his father was a rich man and when he died – he should have left him a lot of money and he didn't – '

'Should have? In what way?'

'He was an only child. He had a brother, an older brother, but he died before my husband was even born – '

Gideon was drawing on a half sheet of paper on which he had made a false start when trying to analyse the 'big wing' strategy that could well have lost the Battle of

Britain. 'The history of why certain plans were not adopted', he had written, 'is the history of an alternative world.' There he had pulled the paper out of the machine and torn it. Now a woman with big breasts and a black vee stretched out under the abandoned sentence. He had meant to say, he now realised, something not quite the same: 'The history of a different world would involve little more than one or two different decisions, which need have nothing to do with morals or ideology. Wars are not won or lost because people are right, but because they are not wrong. A right decision is one which turns out not to be wrong; a wrong decision is one which turns out not to be right. The way that one writes history is only one such decision. What is believed by the reader is merely what is not disbelieved by him.' The programme into which this might have fitted had already been printed up and approved by Jack Knightley. The truth (or falsehood) of Gideon's *aperçu* was superfluous to requirements.

'Perhaps I'm exceeding my place, Mrs Shand, but if I may offer a piece of totally unofficial advice, I suggest most strongly that you think again. I'm not saying you should keep the money, but you can always give it away, can't you? I strongly suggest that you don't make any announcement about it before we've put the inquest totally behind us. Do you see the sense in what I'm saying?'

'If I give the money away, it has to go through my hands,' Pamela said, 'and in that case, I might as well keep it. I don't want the will to – to even touch me, that's the point. I don't want to have to think about all the times I was with Mr Fagin, and see them differently.'

'And what about the last time?' Telfer said.

Gideon buttoned and stood up and stretched his arms as wide as they would go across the shed, from the common wall to the shelves on the far side. He could not quite bridge the width and, aware of the futility of it, he moved his feet further apart as though that might lengthen the stride of his arms.

'The last time was no different from the others, except that it was the last. Not until the moment when I turned

228

my back and – it happened. You want me to have done something, don't you, inspector? Why? And what?'

'You told me previously he loved you. Did he write you any letters?'

'Certainly not,' she said. 'You're right: I would say that, wouldn't I? Well, I've said it, and it's true. People don't write to people they see two or three times a week.'

'Everything's been known,' Telfer said. 'People write to people they see every day. I've seen that. I believe you, of course.'

'Of course you don't,' she said. 'Or rather, of course you do *and* you don't. In the same sort of way, if you like, I felt something for him and I didn't feel anything for him at all. I felt the strength of his feelings, and that – does something to you, doesn't it? Too much perhaps. You're not a woman.'

'You've penetrated my disguise, Mrs Shand.'

'Old joke?'

'Old joke. You see, he's wished something on you and you can't do anything about it now. I'm sorry but he's made you what you are, which is someone who stood to gain by his death. It doesn't matter if there are letters or if there aren't, though it's probably a lot simpler if there aren't.'

'The factory got burnt down because it was insured, is that what you're hinting at, inspector?'

'I believe you, Mrs Shand, when you say you never wanted the money – '

'Oh, I wanted it. It would have been very useful. (Still would.) It's not the money I don't want, it's the idea of wanting it. Of *ever* having wanted it. I never thought about him . . . giving me any *more*. I'll tell you the truth: he used to overpay me. You could call it tips. I never felt bad about it because it happened at the time. You think I ought to lie to the inquest, is that what you're saying?'

'That's what I'm *not* saying,' Telfer said.

'In the sense that . . . I get it.'

'I do wish you'd called for an ambulance right away.'

'I explained to you – '

'There again,' Telfer said, 'there can't really be an explanation, can there? Nothing can really explain why a professional person, finding someone in a dying condition, wouldn't do what they'd presumably been trained to do.'

Gideon's arms came down to his sides. He jumped one foot up to the other. The small window was almost cancelled by a shutter of dark cloud. When he went to the door, the voices were lost to him. He had to decide to go back, if he was to hear more. He crumpled the crude woman in his fist and thrust her into his pocket before stepping into the afternoon. Dark cloud franked the western part of the sky; the rest of it was still blue, though paling beyond the orchard across the lane. Standing by the Renault, on the cinder patch, Gideon could see but not hear the couple whose conversation he had been hearing without being able to see them. Pamela came close to Telfer, as Gideon leaned there on the cold metal, and held something up between them, tiny evidence that turned into a cup. She had made some coffee and the two heads dropped now, hair alone visible, as she and the inspector sat down to it. His wife's face was lost to Gideon, and all her body, except for the crest of that Oxford hair. He had never realised how much the very top of a head could move, how eloquent it could be. Telfer was less mobile, but then he too moved the inch or two of what was visible to Gideon and the sense of his earnestness, however cunning, and his attention to Pamela carried into the afternoon. He turned Pamela into a stranger to whom he had better rights, or to whom he could talk more closely, than Gideon himself. Seclusion domesticated them. He was trapping her perhaps, perhaps unofficially, without practical outcome, acting a better policeman than his profession allowed. He knew that Pamela had lied and that, unless she confessed it, no one but he would ever know that she had. The trick had been turned and it needed a slip by her to allow it to be inspected again. No one could ever prove anything about the lie of the cards. For all that, they had lain in a particular pattern. Teased by the modesty that made her deny him something, Telfer was acting out of passion, a longing respect for Pamela's dark motive. The inspector's face rose in the window and his hands were chatting. He moved around the table, paused, sipped and was bending, arms braced, as he asked or promised or confessed something that made Pamela's head come right back, so that a shine of forehead gleamed for a moment. The inspector did not, surely, believe that she had poisoned Fagin. Could she really have forced the lozenge between his teeth and obliged him to bite on it? There was no sign, surely, of a struggle, nothing suspicious enough to warrant an accusation. Had there been, would Pamela have been allowed to leave Chaworth at all? The discovery of the will could not change any of that. The question remained whether she had been more of an influence on Fagin than she had ever admitted. Could she have worked on him, threatening him with her disappearance from his life, until he could escape from his dread of losing her only by the decision to leave before she did? It required nothing of her except her existence, except her candour, except that stored resentment, of which Gideon had only just had proof. He had known it and he had not known it (after all, they were married) from the very beginning, when kindness was an element both admitted, gladly, in their relationship. She had been Stephen's girl when Gideon first began to realise what kind of step he had taken in writing the Laidlaw review. The faces of Stephen and Pamela, a couple to him, at that moment, whose unity he took naively for granted, carried the first announcement of how badly his article was likely to be taken by the college council. In later days, he almost believed that he might have survived as a fellowship candidate, had he not been awakened so unmistakably, by that ominous pity of theirs, to the seriousness of his case. At the time, he found himself comforting them, assuring them that Stephen in particular was making too much of it, not being sufficiently British about the whole thing. True, he had been startled by Peter Michaeljohn's warning that it might be advisable to give an imminent scholars' feast a miss, so as not to provoke a polarisation of sentiment among the dons. On the other hand, of course, his absence might look guilty. Having done the right thing, he was pitched into a situation where whatever he did would be wrong.

It did occur to him that Stephen showed a certain greed in claiming the greater guilt for himself. Had Pamela been aware of that when she came alone to Gideon's rooms in Portugal Place? She swore that Stephen (in London auditioning for Frank Jarman's chambers) had particularly asked her to visit him. She must have been pregnant then and it was possible, when he thought about it, that some breach had already taken place between the lovers. Despite the warning signs, Gideon had been dazed by the violent reactions to his review. There was particular outrage at his demand that Laidlaw be disqualified from the mastership to which, a few weeks later, he was elected, *nem. con.*

Gideon could not really believe that Pamela had impelled Fagin to kill himself. It was understandable that she be horrified by the consequences of an exit which seemed gallant, even prudent, until her patient was actually suffering his quick torment in front of her. After all, the old man was probably escaping from a crueller inquisition; alien doctors and nurses would never suffer him to die with the speed only the illicit could afford. The little tablet, supplied by the practical authorities as he boarded the Lysander for Tourcoign, or Dijon, was something he had never been *instructed*, still less encouraged, to use. Supplying it was a concession to the courage of the individual who undertook more than could fairly be expected of him. The poison allowed life to be a dream for him. Cornered by overwhelming force, and unable to bluff his way out, he was allowed to pinch himself into death. Although he was not commanded, not even advised, to read life for the sort of nightmare from which such an escape was advisable, the unspoken hint was there. He was trained to survive, but it would be understood if he elected to call life a day. Fagin's decision to die was beyond any printed code; such a solitary journey could have no brochure. Having elected to be his witness, Pamela too had bitten on something she could never spit out.

Gideon was still strong in Portugal Place that day when Pamela came to see him. He resented the implication that he had broken down or was in a state. He had

232

been working (on Napoleonic economy) when she arrived and was more polite than gratified when she sat down by the cold cones of the gas fire and announced that she felt Stephen had done something, whether he realised it or not, which made it impossible for her to marry him. Gideon had no regular woman (his thesis made such demands on his time) and he and Pamela and Stephen had seen a good deal of each other, without ever being a self-conscious trio. Pamela's confidence, if it was that, was almost impertinent. She apologised by asking his advice. 'You mean you've already made up your mind?' he said, and she liked his wit, then. Stephen was 'mad to marry her' (her very words), but it appeared to amuse her, without a tooth in her smile, to refuse someone so resolute, so desirable (she admitted that with a down-ward look) and so ambitious.

'I'm ambitious too,' Gideon said. The silence that followed was so busy with unspoken speeches that they both laughed at the end of it, like children holding their breaths more because it was something physical than because either had hiccups. There was nothing practical in their thoughts, merely the growing pleasure of having them in common, if they did.

'I'm pregnant, you see,' he remembered her saying then.

'Not really,' he said.

'No doubt about it.'

'What will you do?'

'I don't know,' she said. It was the first sign she showed him of her vanity: the decision to marry Stephen, she was telling him, was quite apart from what she should do about the baby. The hardness of the long look from those slightly bulging green eyes, the suggestion of nakedness which seemed to deride whatever long approach to her he might have in mind, gave him a new breathlessness. He actually had to go and fight for air with the damned window on to the little garden. A broken sash cord could make a guillotine of it: you had to bend your knees and crook your wrists and force it up and then slant it in the loose frame so that it stubbed its own leading edge and came to a sideways stop.

233

'It'd be rather absurd, wouldn't it,' he said, 'to have the baby and not have Stephen?'

'Probably.'

'You're not R.C., are you?'

'My father's a parson,' she said. 'I couldn't be C.er of E. than that, could I?'

'You're medical in a way, so – '

'No problems at all, except that I don't want to. If I did that, I'd probably marry him; he'd probably marry me.'

'Forgive me,' Gideon said, 'but don't you love him?'

'Oh that,' she said. 'Yes.'

'He loves you.'

'Yes again.'

'I don't understand this, I don't think,' Gideon said. 'Should I make some tea?'

'No possible way you shouldn't,' she said. 'He doesn't know it, but loving me isn't what he really wanted. I turned out to be something he wasn't bargaining for.'

'Bargaining . . . '

'Oh yes, it does,' she said. 'It's always a kind of bargaining, having to do with other people. You get into things. You get them into things. He thought he'd picked up a nurse, you know, that day he cut himself on the ravioli.'

'Shall I tell you something terrible?'

'X certificate?' she said. 'Do!'

'That day he cut himself opening the tin, he bled into it, quite a lot. It was a nasty gash and I went into the scullery and there he was, a bit dazed, and dripping into the tin. Then he got himself together, went off to the hospital, and I was left with the lunch. Sunday morning, the only tin we had of the beastly stuff. Ravioli in tomato sauce! I heated it and that's what we all ate when the two of you came back from the hospital.'

'The blood of the lamb!' she said. 'How did you stomach it? I couldn't stand the blood, you know, or I was going to be a medic myself.'

'I think it was you being there,' Gideon said. 'You'll think me a ghoul, but it really rather amused me. If I was an ancient Greek, I'd have the Furies after me by now.'

'Perhaps you do have,' she said.

234

'I'm not going to give up,' he said. 'Over the fellowship. Someone suggested that I withdraw, not even submit my thesis, shop elsewhere, but I've had it damned well typed and I'm bloody well not going to waste it.'

'You know what Stephen says? The worst thing for you would be if Laidlaw wasn't elected Master now.'

'Remind me of why, if you can remember.'

'Oh I can,' she said, 'easily. Suppose they don't elect him, because your review would make them look foolish – or even wicked – if they did, then by voting against him they'll have done so much of the right thing as they can ever be expected to do. After which, one thing they certainly *won't* do – I hope this isn't – is give you a fellowship.'

'So I must now hope they elect Laidlaw, if I'm to have any chance of being a fellow.'

'Poor Gideon,' she said. 'The swine.'

He nodded at the cold fire and when he looked up he saw the woman he wanted to marry.

16

'STRANGER!'

'I wouldn't quite put it like that. Only too familiar might be more to the point. I hesitated about coming over, but – '

'He who hesitates is lost!'

'Then I can't have hesitated properly, can I?'

'A lost *soul* perhaps!'

'Nice of you to say so.'

'He's not at home, I'm afraid, if that's who you've come for.'

'Nothing important,' Gideon said. 'I was just off-chancing really – '

'He's never at home this early. You should know that by now. Is there anything I can do? Did that electrician ever show up?'

'With his tail between his legs.'

'There's no better place for it! Do you feel like a glass of sherry while you're here?'

'Rather early for that, isn't it?'

'That's why I thought it'd be a good idea. He's got this big pow-wow in guess where, Cambridge. Big, big decision time. Should they or should they not invest the college's millions in something unbelievably copper-bottomed, or is it tin? Grown men must decide.'

'I mustn't be too long,' Gideon said.

'And you'll never be too short and speaking of someone

who undoubtedly is, let me tell you how lucky you are.'

'You're in very good form,' Gideon said.

'I've been in the kitchen all day, *all* day. Emmy comes home tomorrow, Ben the day after. Do you understand about charitable status?'

'I know we've enjoyed it for quite a while. Why?'

'Because that's what it's all about apparently. Whether the college'll be endangering it by investing in this property. Or perhaps it *isn't* a property. I do know one thing it is and that's b,o,r,i,n,g.'

'If you're an honorary fellow I suppose you have to accept your ration of tedium.'

'Oh, it doesn't bore *him*. Of course, he may not really be in Cambridge at all. I can't exactly call and find out, can I? They hate women, don't they, those people?'

'They are nevertheless slowly being obliged to concede that they are likely to have to continue sharing the globe with them in ever greater proximity. The bullet has been bitten on, as a matter of fact, even in the great college to which I once had the honour . . . '

'Oh Gideon, what a lot of trouble you take over the things you say! Do you take as much over everything?'

' "No," he retorted briefly. "No, I don't. Only trivialities." '

'You've caught me in my working clothes, I'm afraid.'

'They're a credit to your trade,' he said. 'Is that new?'

'It was at the framer's. Stephen kept meaning to collect it, but you know what he's like. It's a Rembrandt.'

'Yes, I . . . Shot in black and white, I see.'

'You can't have coloured etchings, can you?'

'I suppose you could always colour them.'

'Are you flirting with me or are you being rude?'

'Must I choose?'

'Framed money, Stephen calls it.'

'But not in front of the neighbours, I imagine.'

'He's capable of it. Oloroso or Tio Pepe? I'm afraid that's about it at the moment. Unless you want something else.'

'Uncle Joe will suit me fine. What's the news of Willie Cashmore? I keep meaning to go over, but I've been so busy, and not having the telephone . . . '

'Do you want to see upstairs?'

'I'm sorry?'

'What he's done to our bedroom? Aubs has been supervising, but it's Willie's design and inspiration. I *hope* it's inspiration. Bring your glass. I'll bring the bottle.'

'So he's back on the job, is he?'

'I don't know about that,' Miriam said. 'You'll have to ask Jan, won't you?'

There was a long vanitory unit under a hoop of theatrical dressing room lights. The octagonal basins had mixer taps, of course, and there were marble shelves between them, rising to the apex of the arch, jewelled with Venetian jars and pots. The thick grey carpet went up two steps to the sunken green tub with its choice taps. Behind it, more marble shelves had pretty things on them. Stainless-steel Venetian blinds made for brilliant privacy.

'And here we are in California!' Gideon said.

'You sit this end for the bath and that end for the Jacuzzi.'

'And swim up and down if you can't make up your mind?'

'Have you ever tried one?'

'I promised my mother,' he said.

'How is your mother?'

'In rude good health, I fear. Does it require skill?'

'Enormous. You have to sit still and let it do its stuff. Do you think you're up to that? It's only the most refreshing thing in the world.'

'Is that all? I must give it a whirl some time. Oh no, of course, it must give me one.'

'Why not now?'

'I never explained to Pamela where I was going.'

'All you have to do is take off your clothes and relax. I'll run it for you.'

'It is tempting.'

'You know what Stephen would say: don't be so English.'

'But I am,' he said.

'So am I,' she said. 'Would you sooner I waited outside?'

It'll tone you up. I can see you need it.'

'Nice of you to say so. Well, why not?'

'Good for you!'

She was practical with the necessary taps and then pushed on the mirrored doors that faced the vanitory unit. They sprang apart to reveal folded towels, maroon, white, brown and pink. She shook out a monogrammed robe and laid it on the velvet-seated loo. A grandfather clock faced the low-pedestal fitment.

'I feel like the grand Turk,' Gideon said.

'You'd better not look like him,' she said. 'Powder, toning lotion, what else can I offer you? I spend hours in here. It's marvellous for the blues.'

'I shall attempt not to imagine Jan Cashmore *dans ses oeuvres*,' he said.

'I don't think I follow you. Enjoy yourself!'

'Is it supposed to be doing that?'

'Is it supposed to be doing that! If it didn't, I'd call the people.'

He sat in the seething froth, snubbed on a little rubber mat that prevented him from slithering into the wide centre of the tub. As the bubbling heat worked its soft massage, the grandfather clock slowly lost its hands in the steam. He lay there in the easy cage of water, the metal blinds chinking slightly behind him, like small change in a comfortable pocket. He stood up at last, a fool to make the decision to get out now rather than later, and sleeved himself in the warm linen, Stephen's initials on his breast.

Miriam was standing at the end of the canopied bed, drawing a black stocking up one crooked leg. She wore a silk shirt over elaborate *eau-de-nil* underclothes. The whites of her thighs showed above the stockings and below the lace of her short slip. When she turned to him, he could see how fine the material was. She took a stocking to its suspender and pinched it in place. 'You've gone and got dressed again,' she said.

'It is December.'

'Not in here,' she said.

'I think your hospitality has probably gone far enough, don't you?'

239

'He does have someone, you know,' she said. 'And he almost certainly has tarts when he goes on these trips of his. I mean, why else would there be tarts? People must have them. Anyone who likes making money as much as Stephen does must have some secret reason for wanting it, don't you agree?'

'I've never regarded Stephen as particularly . . . '

'Come! He can't get enough of it. I don't mean that he's – what's the word? – avaricious, I mean that he can't stop. *Can* he?'

'He'll have to, when they make him a judge.'

'If they do.'

'One of the most brilliant men at the bar?'

'You know the English,' she said. 'They love . . . disappointing people. Look at you!'

'I've had enough of doing that in the bathroom. It's all right if you're a beautiful woman, but . . . '

'He goes to Hong Kong, he goes to Singapore. You know what they get up to in Singapore. They do absolutely everything. In packs.'

'I've never been entirely sure what everything is. I mean, people do everything in Buxted, don't they? They do it everywhere. And I rather suspect that most of the time it isn't all that much.'

'It's a sight more than talking about it. You've never had money, have you? You never have to wait for anything, or anyone. Look at you!'

'Again, so soon?' he said.

'You think I'm one too, don't you?' she said, with a gesture. 'I'm not.'

'If I could think what you meant,' he said, 'I might well.'

'He thought so too, at first,' she said. 'Perhaps he still does. First impressions do tend to stick, don't they?'

'Are they ever wrong?'

'I should have come in with you,' she said. 'That would've settled it. It always does when I get in with him. He likes me to get out first and dry and powder. He likes to see me doing myself up.'

'Miriam . . . '

'My father was rich and his name was Lyons. Sounded likely, didn't it? And I seemed like a good girl. Hands off!

240

I slapped him once. Was he embarrassed! Well, you can't blame him. He'd already had Pamela, hadn't he? And here was I . . . Not that I knew. I never thought about where he'd been before. Did you have anyone before you had her? You don't have to tell me. It's all so interesting, though, isn't it? Why ever don't we talk about it all, all the time, instead of politics and money?'

'They call it indirection, don't they?'

'Don't be so bloody patronising,' she said. 'Why aren't you a bit closer? If you don't come a bit closer soon, I shall have to put the rest of my clothes on, won't I? You were for ever in there.'

'I thought I was quickly in and out,' he said.

'You could be, couldn't you? And no one would be any the wiser. You looked at me enough, didn't you, when you were here? Did you ever think of stealing something?'

'From you? Certainly not.'

'It'd be funny, wouldn't it? Pay him back with his own things. Snuff boxes are quite a good market, I believe. Have you seen these? Regency, and v., v. naughty, if you look closely. They've had quite a rise in recent months.'

'I don't think I've ever stolen anything. I'm not clever enough to get away with it. A friend of ours – well, of mine – he's just been accused of burning down his own factory. I can't really believe he did, and then again . . . '

'Is that why you wanted to see Stephen?'

'About Athol?' Gideon said. 'No.'

'Why are you like you are?'

'If I knew, I wouldn't be, would I?'

'Have I got snakes in my hair?'

'If you have, rest assured they're only little ones, Medusa. Nothing visible.'

'You don't trust me.'

'It's never a nice thing to do to people, is it, if you can help it?'

'I suppose I could always pay you,' she said. 'There's a thought! I won't bite. *He* bites. He *bites*. I think he's always secretly waiting for me to say no to him. I think if I said no to him I'd see him as he really is. And that's probably why I never do. I like not doing it. He thinks I like what he does, but what I like is not stopping him. I sometimes think there isn't anything I wouldn't let him do, just for the pleasure of not doing what he still sort of expects me to do: say no. He puts his hands round my neck sometimes as if he's rehearsing the big squeeze. They say it increases the pleasure, don't they, strangulation?'

'I've heard it mooted,' he said, 'but I rarely go to the parish council any more.'

'You mustn't think he hasn't made me happy. He's sort of got me wrong, from the start, but perhaps that's the only way I could bear to be taken. I'm not much, if you want the truth.'

'Who is? Name, name!'

'He thinks I am really, still, but my family denied it because they were ashamed. J,e,w,i,s,h. You couldn't believe I meant that because you thought the same as he did. I'm not though. Now what do you say?'

'I don't know why you think it's so important.'

'He fascinated you, didn't he, when you first met him? And wasn't that why? Be honest.'

'At my age? What fascinated me, as you put it, was what was unusual about him, personally, his brains, his . . . not what he had in common . . . '

'You don't have to tell lies to me,' she said, 'because it doesn't matter to me, one way or the other. Tell me you really hate them, tell me you really don't: I agree with you either way. Seriously! Sincerely! He's made me see double, you see: clean and dirty, straight and bent, I see the world both ways. Hate and love aren't very far apart either, are they?'

'We have to hope not,' Gideon said.

'She doesn't like me, does she? That's something else altogether. Your wife. Do you like this?' She was offering her wrist to his nose. 'Duty frees!'

'Delectable.'

'Oh come on,' she said, 'you can't really be such a wimp.'

'Just back from the States, Mrs Hellman?'

'We went to Aspen last year. He likes to ski. He likes to dice with death in the afternoon and dice with dice in the evening.'

'And what do you do?'

'I swim, I play tennis. Indoors. I took lessons from a girl who played in the Wightman Cup. Of course she was really wasting her time, but we were wasting our money, so it came out even. Shall I take my lipstick off?'

'Take everything off,' he said.

'He's a bloody Jew and you know it. That's what helps me survive, knowing that he is and I'm not. Nice, aren't they?'

'They're lovely.'

'They used to be pinker, but you can't have everything. You can have *nearly* everything, which is more in a way, isn't it? What about you? Get 'em off! You can't go back on it now. He's streets ahead of me all down the line and yet I've got it over him. I also did aerobics. I still try to keep it up. No battle like a losing battle, is there?'

'Miriam – '

'No questions; no answers. It's better that way. This never happened, so we may as well get on with it. Three hundred and twenty pounds these were, hand-sewn, that's why I'm being careful.'

Gideon heard a little cough before the tap sounded hollow on the bedroom door. 'Madame?'

'Yes, Trudie? Blast the silly . . . What is it?'

'Ze reverend, madame.'

'Christ!' Miriam said. 'I'd forgotten all about him.'

Gideon smiled at the cornice and admired the brass rails above the pleated apricot curtains. Waiting for himself to subside, he patronised her haste to be dressed and the casualness with which she passed a few words for the parson ('There in a minute, Trudie, tell him!') through the heavy door. The dark head went to one side, an eyebrow fluttered, as she mimed frustration and apology. 'Doesn't matter,' he said.

'Bloody little man,' she said, 'and his bloody roof. I wish they'd *both* blow away. Will you come and see me again? I hate the afternoon. By which I mean, *normally* I hate it. Is she very possessive?'

'I'm very possessed,' he said.

'Sounds interesting. Will you tell me more? Some time soon?' She was perfuming wrists and neck as if she had something to hide. 'I could always try to get rid of him. The vicar, I mean. If you feel like hanging on.'

'I must go,' he said. 'I'll – what did we use to say? – make myself scarce. I'll make myself scarce.'

She went out, to amuse him perhaps, on a wing; she must have had dancing lessons, once. Gideon stared at the empty place on the crocheted coverlet where her weight had been; his desire stiffened in the dream of her; the ghost of her scent piqued his nostrils. Desire and dislike had been matched in her presence; desire and something else – not quite disgust, not quite affection – glossed her absence. The sound of her voice proposing sherry to the vicar came back up the stairs like a backhanded caress, offered amid civilities. The French knob of the door was still warm from her hand and rose fleshily to his touch. The house was the woman.

How should he escape? Below the window, the vicar's bicycle was propped against a pilaster of the scheduled doorway. As Gideon looked down, the front wheel rode sideways and spilled black metal into the gravel. He saw it as a skimpy skeleton, dressed with meagre flesh: flat little feet, starved arms, a single tartan buttock. The man must have seen the Renault and would surely guess that Miriam had a visitor. The report to God was as good as made: damnation was assured. Gideon went into the commissioned bathroom for his boots and socks. The low pedestal, green jade toilet solicited him, hairless porcelain invitation. He undid his buttons and measured himself in the long glass. The mitred flesh would not soften. Dunce, capped with desire, all thought contributed to its hard heat. Accusing himself of age, he was shamelessly young; claiming youth, he stared at a greying hack.

The telephone cawed in the bedroom. He heard Miriam answering in the hall. 'Hell-o-o!', while the young vicar stood at the Meissen cabinet, chaplain to Napoleon's china army. Gideon was still for the pleasure of listening to Miriam's gaiety as she almost interrupted, waited and tried again. How much were the snuff boxes worth? And where could he take them, straight-faced, if he actually did make off with a couple? The elegance of their improprieties made the gleaming enamel bulge towards him, tricked him with a coiffed woman, un-skirted to her waist, closely admired by a nankeened man, with plenty of the ready, who was lending a hand to another woman, no less handsome, plumped on the bed beside the other couple. It was an advertisement not only for pleasure but also for cash: *pecunia vincit omnia*.

Gideon went along the balustraded landing, above the prattling Miriam, who had a hand to her breast, and passed white doors before coming to the back stairs, steep as a ladder set in a well. One hand on the banisters, he vaulted down to the Portland floor of the back entrance and fled to the Renault, empty-handed thief. He cursed its noise, though Miriam would enjoy the lie she would have to tell the vicar.

He saw but made no sense of it, could not for the moment even give a name to the running girl. Was she running from an enemy she had so easily outdistanced that she was alone with her terror? Was she merely exercising? And if so, why in such improbably indoor clothes? Her hair jolted and flew, all dark and liquid about the charging head, a wild cap that might at any moment fly off, it seemed, and leave her bald with panic. She ran straight at him. He braked and the Renault squatted in the tarmac like a tailless puppy wanting to play. Miranda bumped against the metal and drooped, gape-mouthed, chin almost on the hood, barking painful words: 'Where – have – you – been? Where – have – you – been?' How could it be so difficult to produce such a commonplace? It cost her such hurt that she gasped and let her eyes yell through the windscreen. Gideon watch-ed the stranger become his daughter. Personality caught up with her like stragglers who reach the finishing post and group themselves in bowed apology around a winner. 'Where the hell have you been?'

'Get in the car,' he said.

'You *bastard*,' she said.

'What's happened, Mandy?'

'Mum,' she said.

'Is she hurt?'

'Hurt? Is she hurt? What were you *doing*?'

'What's he done to her?' Gideon said. 'Has he taken her away?'

'How could you leave her?'

'I can't be there all the – what's happened, Mandy, could you tell me that now, do you think, please?'

'She's been . . . I came home . . . Tom's there . . . '

'Is he still there?' Gideon said. 'Telfer?'

'Is he still there? How do you know his name?'

'The policeman.'

'*Policeman?*'

Gideon wanted to be at the cottage and he also wanted the journey to be longer. He wanted to stop and have the truth from the girl, and tell it to her. He wanted to be crossing a continent on that mile down the lane. Miranda looked at him with disgust, schoolgirl face blanched of make-up, a furious child who imagined that he should know everything she had to tell him by the mere contagion of her horrified self. He did and did not understand and she knew that his hesitations were cover for a conclusion he had already reached. Until it was confirmed, it was a cruel hope. She knew that too. Gideon wished for the catastrophe he dreaded; his dread was part of its creation, the girl's rage insisted. And what of her own absence and her own exultation, he wanted to know, what place did they have in the crass event neither of them had planned or wanted?

'Is she hurt, Mandy? I want you to tell me,' he said, the patient father.

'You brought him here,' she said, 'you bloody fool!'

'Don't talk to me like that, please.'

'Don't put it off,' she said. 'Because that's what you're doing. Get there!'

He backed the car into its cindered place. Light from the cottage windows squared the darkness. Tom was sitting with Pamela at the kitchen table. Scabs of fat thickened into pale shadows under the sausages in front of him. Pamela's hair was a silly wig. She rippled her brows at Gideon, a question. Her lips were skin, cut and bloodless. Below the torn hair, the side of her face was pimpled with tiny scabs; she might have had a bad shave. A flannel blushed in a pudding basin on the Aga. Tom forked a sausage from its fat slot and took it to his lips. Miranda stood in the doorway, one ankle cute across the other, and made strict lips, the sergeant.

'Tom,' Gideon said, 'would you be good enough to take that in the other room?'

Miranda unlatched her feet to let her brother pass, touching his hair with her palm, as if to make up some quarrel.

'Mandy, will you go with him now, please?'

'I'm – ' She caught Pamela's nod and, making obedience contempt, followed Tom into the other room.

'Now what the hell has been happening?'

'Hell has been happening.' Pamela's hands, those nice hands, found things to tidy on the tidy table.

'Did he *hit* you?'

'To some extent,' she said. Her chin was frail with humour. She looked at him when she had finished speaking and dared his reading.

'Telfer hit you?'

'Telfer? Telfer? What's Telfer got to do with it?'

'I went out – I went out because I thought you might need help. I went to see if I could get hold of . . . If it wasn't Telfer, who was it? What exactly happened? I didn't mean to . . . abandon you. On the contrary . . . '

'You had a caller,' she said.

'I . . . ?'

'You were gone for quite a while, you know. Your friend. Not mine.'

'*Stephen!*'

'Oh God,' she said. 'Stephen! Not Stephen. You've got two more guesses. Not Stephen. He came to see you, he saw me. Was there anything I could do? There was something he could, and did.'

'What?'

'You know what.' Her nostrils flared and he smelt burning material in the Aga. She had changed her clothes. 'I was lucky he didn't kill me, I suppose.'

'I still don't know who you're talking about. I daresay I should, but I don't. I don't even know what exactly . . . I'm sorry if I'm being dim, but . . . '

'He'd had your letter. You gave him the address.'

'You write to people, you always . . . Cyril Lack.'

'He said he had some work he wanted you to see. He showed me what he could do as well.'

'Have you called the police? When did this happen?'

'Are you home?' she said. 'Are you dry? I don't want to call the police.'

'How soon after Telfer did he come? And was that all right?'

'He's very strong, your friend.'

'I used to go and see him in Chaworth clink, that's all.'

'You were very, very nice to him. Lame dogs are very much your style, aren't they?'

'And yours, aren't they?' he said. 'We ought to get the police.'

'I offered him a cup of tea and he sat over there, nice and quiet, quiet and nice, and I was pouring it out when he said that I frightened him. I believe I did. He started sweating. It came out of him like . . . like pus, from a wound. His face . . . yellow . . . ' She jailed her face in her fingers. He waited and she turned again towards him, an actress ready to go on now, and sorry about that. 'I sometimes wondered how . . . how they began. They begin like everyone else. He told me about himself. Rapes. Nicely. And all the time he was being nice, I knew what was coming. Just like life! His words were mice all over me; I crawled with the things. They were damp, and alive, like sperm. I burned my dress. And my . . . '

'I know,' Gideon said. 'I'll kill the bastard.'

'All the time I was praying you'd come home. And I knew you wouldn't. It had as good as happened already before it happened at all. But not quite as good.'

'Oh my God, I love you, Pammy.' He saw the Kitchen Devil by the bread board, its fangs and blades. 'I'll kill him.'

'He drank his tea and wanted to wash the mug. I tried to take it from him. He's very strong. You'll have to grow a bit, son! He used the mug – it sounds silly – to stay close to me. He wanted to talk to me about his case, he said, and he was annoyed when I said I didn't know anything about it. He said he'd told you all about it. I said I wasn't you and he was quite peeved, as if I should have been. "You're supposed to be married," he said. He wanted you and there I was. And there I was.'

'Did he hurt you?'

She lifted her skirt and showed him the blue marks on her thighs. She pulled down her pants and showed him everything. There was nothing to be seen, but he nodded at the wound she wanted him to recognise. She made a doctor of him. There was the sound of petty speech from the next room. He touched her bruises and tried to take her pain for his own. 'He grabbed the knife,' she said, 'and threatened me with it. I remembered that old Confucius-he-say thing, but it didn't really work. I never thought it would. I tried to pretend that he was someone else, but there wasn't really anyone I wanted him to be. It might as well be him really. He pulled out before he came, if you're interested. Tactful, wasn't it? That's why I burnt everything.'

'What about seeing a doctor? Do you think – ?'

'He wanted me to see it coming out maybe. Never trust a man when he's being considerate, eh?'

'I really am most frightfully sorry. I don't know what else to say. What happened afterwards? I mean, how did he . . . come to leave?'

'He came and he left,' Pamela said. 'Tom arrived home. He heard him, went outside, said "Good evening" and Tom said the same and then he nipped on the bike and pedalled away.'

'He took the bike?'

'It'll probably be found,' she said. 'If you're worried about the heirloom. The only thing around here that's mine. Funny! There is one thing to be said, I suppose: he probably won't come back, whereas Telfer – oh Telfer – undoubtedly will.'

'He likes you,' Gideon said.

'My troubles will never end,' Pamela said. 'Did you see Stephen?'

'I saw Miriam. He's in Cambridge.'

'How was Twinkle-toes?'

'She twinkles all over,' Gideon said. 'Our friend should have gone there.'

'You went there,' Pamela said.

'Do you think you should go to bed?'

'I think I should go to China,' she said. 'You must be hungry. Or did she give you something?'

'We had a sherry,' he said.

'Did you indeed? Two straws?'

'How long was he actually here, Cyril?'

'For ever,' she said. 'For ever. He's still here, isn't he?'

'No,' Gideon said. 'And if he ever comes back, I'll kill him. If I ever see him, I'll kill him.'

'Don't make promises,' she said, 'unless you mean to break them.'

'I can't believe this has happened.'

'It hasn't,' she said, 'to you.'

'Oh yes, it has,' he said, 'and you know it. Shall I run a bath?'

'And fill it with the blood of the lamb that washeth away all sins? You want me to be clean before you touch me again, is that it?'

'That doesn't begin to be it,' he said.

'On the contrary?'

'I beg your pardon?'

'Is what you usually say, but you decided not to, I gather.'

'Did he . . . ?'

'What?'

'I was wondering all kinds of . . . Did he really suppose that he wouldn't be found out, that we wouldn't . . . ?'

'We won't,' she said. 'Perhaps most of them know that. Men know what women will do, don't they, long before they do? Men know what we'll agree to even when we're still convinced that we never will. They get away with it all the time.'

'Don't put me in the same club as Cyril Lack, Pamela, whatever . . . '

'We shall never be honest. We shall never never never be honest. No matter what happens, no matter what has happened or will happen, we shall never be truly what we truly are.'

'The economy couldn't support it,' Gideon said. 'There aren't words enough. Because you're right: "on the contrary" is the heart of the matter. To be true we should

250

have to accept that the false and the true are endlessly and necessarily confused. We should have to accept that plus is a form of minus, that everything that is also is not and everything that is not most certainly is, and that everything we say to each other depends on what we don't say and that what we don't say is present in our acts and what we dare not act is present in our speech, or in its silences or in its pacing, and that all the world's a stage, and what has been said before needs to be said again.'

'I suppose I enjoyed it,' she said.

He was a yard from her, but it was too far for him to reach. Disarmed, his hands hurt at his sides. Tom came in with his plate and took it to the tap. 'You did well, I hear,' Gideon said.

Tom was deaf with the drumming of the water. He had come to do one thing and to leave again. He blushed with that determination. He turned and saw his father and could not avoid him this time, empty-handed. 'He left his scarf,' he said. 'I found it by the front gate.'

'Let's hope he catches cold,' Gideon said.

'I should've bricked him,' Tom said. 'That's what the Monahans would've done, Darren and co.'

'I wonder if – no,' Gideon said. 'Tracy was a different sort of thing entirely. I half-suspected that Athol might have . . . There was something strange about him that morning he asked me over to the house. And she knew something she wasn't going to come out with, Cora.'

'Everybody does,' Pamela said.

'Her father leathered her,' Gideon said. 'That might've made her inclined to go to someone else. Athol . . . I think perhaps they loved each other, Tracy and him.'

'I think I will have that bath,' Pamela said. 'I feel . . . '

'It's now or never for the police,' Gideon said. 'I'm sorry to insist, but . . . You remember what Telfer was like about . . . '

'I'm going to take the money,' Pamela said. 'Did I tell you?'

'I shall try not to capitalise on it.'

She trailed a hand against him, like a child casually scuffing a fence, as she went out of the kitchen. He heard the water being run upstairs; the cottage gurgled with it. Tom had physics in the morning and took his book to bed. Miranda waited for Gideon in the sitting room where the furniture from Beacon Terrace looked dowdy against white walls and ebony-dark beams. She was snug in the bucket chair, stockinged heels under her. The braiding drooped from the rusty nails along the bottom of the upholstery.

'Let's be clear about one thing,' Gideon said, 'I won't be blamed.'

'You mustn't be greedy,' Miranda said, 'must you?'

'The man never told me he was coming; I never invited him. He's a somewhat retarded psychopath object, who – who – '

' – stole your life away?'

'Examine your own feelings, Mandy. Be as honest about them as you're – inventive about other people's.'

'I may not be here much longer,' Miranda said. 'If you want to know the results of the examination. I'm thinking of going back to Chaworth. It's got nothing to do with this evening.'

'These divorces aren't possible, and you know it: this evening now has to do with everything that happens from this moment on.'

'You're inspired with titles for songs tonight,' Miranda said. 'What a shame they've all been sung before!'

'I love you with all my heart,' Gideon said, 'and how odious you can be sometimes, do you know that?'

'Most of it,' she said.

'I thought you liked it here.'

'You're talking to mama, I think, aren't you? She's the one upstairs in the bath. I think it's a very nice cottage and I don't so much want to leave as be elsewhere. I thought it would all be hunkydory, and in a way it is, or was. Oh dad, if only we weren't related, you'd understand without any difficulty whatsoever! The young should live passionately and in the face of all the odds, didn't someone say that once? They must have; you should have. I can't tell you any more than I'm sure you know, because I should lose it in the telling. How patient you'd be with me if I'd been in gaol! Well, childhood is a gaol.'

'Wait till you endure the punishment adults have to accept with cheerful resignation.'

'I have a rather intimate acquaintance with them,' she said. 'And I'm sorry for you. I wish I wasn't: you deserve better than that.'

'Piers,' he said.

'Piers plus,' she said. 'All that and Harold too.'

'I need you here,' he said.

'You're afraid she'll hate you? You *hope* she'll hate you? Why do we crave the terrible things, all the time, always, even when everything is as we want it to be? Think of Stephen!'

'He made quite an impression on you, didn't he?'

'You make him sound like something in the past. Well, I suppose that's where he is really. All he can take to heart is what never happened to him. Perhaps that's not so different from you and fond mama. He's got every damned book practically that was ever written on the subject, hasn't he? Hitler and . . . That's why he can't take anything that happens in the present really seriously: even when he's being serious about it, there's something sarcastic – something remote – about him. He's waiting for something to go wrong so that he can join his ancestors, really be one of them. The world's a joke to him, but essentially a Jewish joke: when you laugh, it's because it hurts, and especially because it hurts him. It's a vanity in him and all his acquisitiveness comes from it, don't you think so?'

'There's something great in him,' Gideon said.

'His pettiness? Oh I am clever, I'm clever sort of like him, I think, because it won't do me any good, because it'll almost certainly be my ruin, just as it's his, isn't it?'

'I hardly associate Stephen with ruin. He's done just about everything that I always dreamed of doing, and he's got everything . . . '

'And everyone? Why ever did he marry her?'

'Don't grace him with too much fineness, will you? Part of the pleasure of being clever is the realisation of how stupid it can make you: carnal appetite is the comedy that makes the tragic condition impossible to sustain, unless you choose to die.'

'He's very generous, isn't he?'

'What did he offer you?' Gideon said.

'He makes himself low for her, so that she won't feel too diminutive.'

'The son of man,' Gideon said. 'It's in the family.'

'What?' she said. 'You were going to say something.'

'I was going to say everything. Not, of course, that there's all that much of it.'

'I shall never find anyone like you,' she said.

'Not by going away, you won't. You don't want anyone like me. And then, of course, it's because of that impossibility that you find me what I am, not that . . .'

'At least I'm not on drugs, am I? Things could be worse.'

'You've got your whole life in front of you,' Gideon said.

'Yes, folks, and a great big gaping black hole it looks from over here.'

'At least take your "A" levels. Give yourself a chance not to do things that you could do, not things that you couldn't.'

'My new history man is value for money, I must admit.'

'Why didn't she – why didn't you – call the police?'

'They can't put the clock back, can they? Stolen property like that . . . What was done was done. You know how they treat women in those sort of cases. All that understanding and sympathy and let's have a closer look at the scene of the crime, shall we?'

'It leaves it all . . . here, among us. I don't know how to get rid of it. I don't think . . . I *do* think she doesn't want to lose it. It's – *hers*, like the money. Oh she's welcome to both; I want her to have them. It's her baby. That's not very worthy, I know. It's probably mad in a way, but there it is.'

'Oh dad. Oh dad.'

'I want to kill him, if it's him I want to kill. I can't endure it.' His sobs barked against her breast. She pressed his head to her as he jolted, sicking up words like stones. 'I thought I could, I meant to, I can't.'

After a moment he looked curiously at her, as if he had

254

given birth to something long clenched inside him and was curious to know if it was alive.

'Poor dad,' she said.

'My poverty', he said, 'is a temporary condition, but as for dad . . . '

'Say it,' she said. 'I know, don't I?'

'Probably. The genes carry their nagging messages from generation to generation. It's not uncommon and it's not very dishonourable. Nobody did anything they need be ashamed of, which is presumably why we've never talked about it. It's hidden out in the open, isn't it? Did he drop any hints at all?'

'You knew from the beginning, did you?'

'Of course. Otherwise . . . '

'Things would've been completely different? *Would* they?' She tried on a smile; it did not fit too well. 'We're not related then?'

'In law . . . '

'You've been joking all along,' she said. 'That's what he did to you. He made you . . . straight-faced, as if the joke was yours, not on you.'

'On the contrary . . . '

'Where else indeed?'

'It was our idea. Your mother's and mine. She wanted it – '

'And here it is! *Eccomi!* And you?'

'I wanted to marry her. I never consciously considered whether she would have had me under any other circumstances, if everything had been equal. Equality is a state not to be found in nature, isn't it? I'd like to think that she'd have had me anyway, but her . . . condition . . . Oh, not that she ran for cover. I loved that about her, her defiance, the refusal to be any man's property. I wanted what couldn't be possessed, I suppose. I was possessed by what I could never have. And there's something . . . '

'Go on,' Miranda said, 'damn you.'

He woke to her, almost surprised. 'I don't owe you this,' he said. 'I was the only person, I thought, who could see how remarkable she was. We were young, but I realised that she'd already . . . missed something: she was extraordinary, but she could never be anything in this world but ordinary. He brought her back to Portugal Place as a pick-up. He'd used his power, perhaps the suggestion of money – he drove a car, after all, and we very few of us did in those days – and the promise of a meal that wasn't baked beans on toast and she came with him, just like that. It was sordid and impressive, his ability to shop for women. Even those who . . . He had no imagination there, your father. I served the ravioli that Stephen had cut himself on, the tin . . . you remember.'

'You wanted to tell me all this then, didn't you?'

'Yes, but why? And why now? The answer is pure invention, Mandy, in my opinion. Whatever we say about motives is pure invention. Not false, invented. Speech doesn't come from deep sources, doesn't reveal hidden things way down in our psyches; the more eloquent we are the more recondite our motives, not because we're more capable of perceiving what is really happening but because we're more incapable of denying the possibilities of horror and cruelty.'

'Should I take notes?' she said. 'I *should* take notes.'

'I married them with that tin of ravioli,' he said. 'It had Stephen's blood in it. It . . . what I forgot is that myths never forgive accidents, the little twists that make the cook part of his meal. Because, of course, I ate the same beastly stuff; his blood became part of me, just as it did of her. Oh, a drop or two – I exaggerate, of course – but enough for the myth to be furnished. It's amazing how sacramental a tin of ravioli can be, don't you think so?'

'You had a fight with him once. What about?'

'I can hardly remember now.'

'In other words, you have total recall?'

'My basic quarrel with him was that he was going to be a success and I quite clearly was not.'

'But you were cleverer than he was. He told me that himself. You were heads and he was tails.'

'And tails it was! It was a historian: he left me the past and helped himself to the future. This fight – shall I tell you my . . . ? Why not? He laughed when I said that I'd asked Pam to marry me. He laughed, not out of derision, more out of relief. He didn't mean to take it lightly, but . . . perhaps he was celebrating, perhaps he was embarrassed, since I'd agreed to be the father of his child. Perhaps he was flattered, perhaps he was relieved. Every perhaps fathers a world. But he laughed. We were walking along the Backs. The marquees were going up for the May Balls. I can still remember rolling on the grass with him and the utter pleasure of it, Miranda! Fighting. The smell of the damp cuttings from the croquet lawn, the sky breaking into tumbling blue slabs, like broken ice in a tinted bowl, and what I remember as we fought, as I tried to squeeze the life out of him, was that I wanted to force the child out of his body, that's what I was gripping him so tightly for, to deprive him of . . . you. Fatherhood. Not that I knew it was you, of course. I wanted to squeeze it out of him, his title to you. He's a strong chap, Stephen, thick and . . . I always thought of him as more adult than I, hairier, of course, more manly. I suddenly hated all that in him, just as I hated the laughter that kept coming out of him. Even when I was half-strangling him, he seemed to choke like a clown. I wanted it to be a serious fight and he wouldn't have it. He refused to hate me. That was the one thing he couldn't manage to be generous about.'

'He *daren't* be generous about,' Miranda said. 'Have you noticed at all, dad, that something funny is happening to my nose? The genes are getting to it, intrepid little parties that they are! That's what . . . *sorry*, there you are rolling about on the grass and here I am talking about my facial features! For shame! Who won?'

'We had to stop. No one stopped us, except that people came strolling past and some of them gathered round and finally, well, finally, what stopped us was that we didn't really know what we were fighting about. There were so many reasons that there was no sense in going on with it. The audience killed the show. Perhaps . . . we didn't dislike the world enough to go on with it. Or one of us didn't. I'm not sure which. We acted together, without either of us being decisive. And it was an act that . . . wasn't private enough, didn't have enough in it, to go on to the bitter, brutal end. We stood up and I smiled, because I was still angry.'

'And you still are?'

'We were fighting over a logical impossibility, I think, defying the sky and the God – old man logic – that won't allow two men to occupy the same space. We fought to get into each other and out of each other, all at the same time. The bad fight, you might say.'

'You might say anything.'

'I loved him without wanting him in any physical way. Oh, I don't deny anything – *anything* – that anyone might care to say about it: you could claim that Stephen and I were two heterosexuals who happened to want each other passionately but for whom . . . you could say that. We came together by sheer accident: Peter Michaeljohn paired us when we both turned up at the C.U. Bridge Club. Did the old sod know what he was doing? He might well have done. You *can* be married by other means than ravioli, after all.'

'He took your space, didn't he? He wanted it and he took it and you let him have it. And then you took his, but it wasn't quite the prize you thought it was. Because another person can't be a prize. I have that on the highest authority.'

'They're the only prizes worth having. The devil proves that. Think about it. And so does propaganda from the Other Place. If propaganda can ever be proof.'

'The trouble with all these doomy conversations,' Miranda said, 'is that they're the most thrilling things in the world. My heart leaps up when I behold a thunder-cloud in the sky.' She jumped from her chair and was crashing to the floor in the same moment, branded across the hair-line with the red of her own energy, head driven against the beam. 'Oh ow! Ow ow ow.'

'I'll get you a cold cloth,' Gideon said.

'We really ought to have got a bigger cottage,' she said. 'I'll tell you something funny though – Buggin's turn – I knew I was going to do it. Knock me down with a feather next time, father dear, would you please? I'm going to have a yuge bump, but *yuge*. I think death must be a bit like this: a big wallop, nothing like as bad as you thought and then, oblivion. Or livion perhaps. Another one of those words that ought to mean something, like love.'

'The best thing you can do is go and lie down quietly with an ice-pack.'

'Don't try to marry me off, papa. You know why spy stories are so popular? Because everyone is waiting to betray someone or to be betrayed. Only the unbelievable turns out to be everybody's story. You can't reasonably expect women to be happy with the present arrangements, Prime Minister. God, it hurts.'

'What's happened?' Pamela said.

'The Cottage Strikes Back,' Miranda said. 'Papa and I were having a nice little *tour d'horizon* when suddenly it beamed me down, Scottie.'

Pamela took charge of Miranda's head, parted damp hair and saw the thick place. 'You'll live.'

'Oh matron!' Miranda said. '*When?*'

'Come on,' Gideon said, 'let's get you upstairs to bed.'

Miranda reached on tip-toe to kiss the beam. 'Sorry if I hurt you,' she said. 'All my life I've relied on the cruelty of strangers.'

Pamela had been washing her hair. She was turbaned in a white towel and wore a striped bathrobe. Her smaller face was steamed young, though it still bore the brand of her assault. Gideon followed her to the bedroom where she started to gun her hair with the dryer. Her head moved back and forth, as though she were reading the wall behind the bed. Gideon was damned if he wouldn't look at a book review in a grant-aided magazine. He chose to read and re-read a piece about *langue* and *parole* (again) rather than go so far as to turn a page. He might have been waiting for his appointment. When Pamela killed the gun and stood there, holding her hurt hair, he pushed the magazine away and looked up for his call.

'I think I shall cut it all off,' she said.

'Please don't do that, Oxford. Does it still hurt? Why did he hit you in the face?'

'I scratched him. He banged me. He banged me all right. Never mind: it's only my face.'

'I can understand you not calling the police,' he said.

'You could understand anything, couldn't you?' she said. 'Your prize pupil! *I* can understand . . .'

'Could I conceivably have foreseen . . . ? Perhaps I could have. Perhaps I should have.'

'God's impotence comes from His ability to foresee absolutely everything, doesn't it? Imagination and futility go hand in hand when you come to think about it, don't they?'

'I thought my presence wasn't helping, with Telfer, I mean. I was being too protective; I imagined you'd handle it better without me. What you really needed was someone more professional, or so I thought. Hence . . . '

'You don't have to make excuses,' Pamela said. 'I shall have to learn to be on my own some day, shan't I?'

'Or I shall,' he said. 'I never thought he'd actually come here, Lack. I put the address on the letter, but I assumed he'd write.'

'He loves you,' Pamela said. 'Oh yes. He wanted you; unfortunately, he found me. Unfortunately for him. I knew what was going to happen before he did. I saw it so clearly that there was nothing I could do to prevent it. Are you going to tell me that means I really wanted it to happen? I didn't.'

'I'm not going to tell you anything except that I'm sorry. Very, very sorry.'

'That's all you're going to tell me, I daresay, but that's not all there is, is it?'

'Love, love, love,' Gideon said.

'Don't you hate it sometimes?' Pamela said.

17

H<small>E LEANED</small> against the bedroom wall, his head cold against the plaster, eyes on her huddled body; he might have been the killer, alone with his victim. Her breathing was an insult; its regularity denied him. He made a small noise, feet to the ground, and wanted it to stand for some savage drumming. Staring at her shut face from the place where her clothes were ready for the morning, he could not make a single person of her or of himself: the focus was gone. Was someone moving downstairs? He craved an intruder, someone to meet, and crush. Moonlight spangled small change on the curved boards. Perhaps there was someone in the garden, her garden.

The lock of the back door snapped as he turned the key, like a metal twig. The Kitchen Devil in his warm hand, he stepped into the soundless garden; his slippered feet kicked the night as he crept towards the paddock. The bucket by the well had a moon in it. Flints made wet fruit in the concrete cake of the well-head. When he lifted the slatted lid, the silvered bottom of the shaft was milled with dust. He lowered the bucket, wary of a clash, until it dangled just above the narrow surface. Then he hitched the rope and jerked the bucket so that its stiff lip bit the water. The Kitchen Devil was on the ground between his legs. He hauled the bucket into the world, the rope first hair, then snake, and set it on the rim of the well. He took two handfuls of the new water and broke it against his face, cloven chill. Gasping, he looked up at the bedroom window where a cheating moon hung unbroken on the glass. What sound did a wild man make? He took the knife from the ground and flung it into the well. It drowned in its own bloodless wound.

He could not stand the cold stare of the moon. Bending under the quince tree, he stalked to the darker side of the cottage. Pamela had edged her herb garden with old tiles set on end, pygmy tombstones. The crust of the thatched roof cast a loaf of heavy shadow halfway across the lane and darkened all that lay between. Cinders munched under Gideon's feet. Darkness was mounted on darkness here and grew light in perverse consequence. How else did he see that the door of his work-shed was ajar? Suddenly, it sparked and went black again, as if a long eye had winked at him. A rumple of plastic lay over stacked wood against the side of the shed, a legacy from Casey. He took a brick from the gleaming sheet (there were several to keep it from flapping) and was armed. Uncertain whether he was playing Diomedes or Dolon, he leaned on the easy door. A cigarette breathed like a small animal alone in the shelved warmth.

'Try anything,' Gideon said, 'and I'll fucking well kill you.'

'You'll wake the kid,' the hoarseness said. 'There's going to be a frost. I saw it was open . . . '

'What kid?'

'The kid.'

'Stay where you are,' Gideon said, 'and keep smoking. I want to see that light stay right where you are. Where is this kid?' He had to put down his brick to light the oil-lamp. Before he capped it with the glass, the wick flared on a clutch of manuscript pages under one foot of the typewriter, work for sir, it might have been, delivered late. When he looked up for a face among the lightening shadows, there was none to meet him.

'She said to come back.' The comic frown, the thick brows, the waxed moustache should have belonged to a man on his knees. The dwarf could never add up to Cyril

Lack; the disguise was the thing itself. Smoke plumed pitted nostrils and hung about the pierced ears. Short arms held a heavy bundle against a prowed chest, the kid. Gideon left his brick by the alien manuscript. The words had been driven into the paper like nails. He made out their familiar slant, toppling towards rage: ' . . . there must be blood and a place for blood. They say that blood is wrong, but blood is right. Blood is inevitable: women know it, though they deny it. They demand it even as they refuse it. They want what they do not want and they don't want what they say they want. Blood is their life too. They have the truth in their hearts and lies on their lips. They are not made for talking: we will have to silence them or have them neuter us with lies. They *do* want what we have and they can get it only by saying that they don't. Equality stifles everything and leads to *vegetarianism*.'

The dwarf found fingers to take the wet cigarette from spit-red lips and sketch a question mark with it. Gideon moved the brick along the desk, for an ash-tray. 'Where do you come from and what do you want?'

'He was crying. I hoped I'd find her, but it was all locked up down there.'

'The shed,' Gideon said.

'You'll be the husband,' the dwarf said, in agreement. 'He's fallen asleep now, so I came in here.'

'It's the middle of the bloody night. Did you really suppose she'd be in the shed? If the child's sick, it should see a proper doctor.'

'Don't trust them,' the dwarf said.

'That's ridiculous,' Gideon said.

'Look at me; I'm not laughing.'

'Who sent you here?'

'The word goes round. Casey died, people were wondering who'd take over.'

'You met someone, didn't you, today, who told you to come here?'

'I've been with the kid all day. I heard nothing. Going to brick me, were you?' He was fastidious with the ash, one leg thrust forward to support the bundle against his chest. 'I only wanted her to take a look at him. She said to

263

come back; I came back. It needs some mixture.'

'I'm not waking her,' Gideon said. 'She's had . . . an accident. She needs to sleep. Anyway . . . '

'You can't do anything, I suppose?' the dwarf said.

'It seems to be very sound asleep.'

The dwarf strained to be taller with the weight in his pin-striped arms. Such red effort demanded privacy: Gideon had to look away as a fart browned the room. 'I'm parked down the road. Gallows Corner. The old main road. Dead now.'

Outside, the bundle seemed heavier: the dwarf tottered on the cinders and his weight-lifter's teeth grinned painfully under the waxed moustache.

'Would the wheelbarrow help?' Gideon said.

The dwarf laid the bundle between the wooden brackets of the barrow and left Gideon to wheel it. Centring the striped tie under his old throat, he pulled down the brass-buttoned waistcoat which was now revealed and crouched to make good a bow on his brogues, with a big-eyed glance at Gideon. 'Casey used to keep his wood in there,' he said.

'What was he like, Casey? Was he a good man?'

'He wanted paying.' That might have been a joke, the way the dwarf delivered it. 'Shall I tell you something that may astound you?'

The lane went straight between the winter hedges, but the dwarf made a meander of it as he walked, pivoted, turned and picked up the step, patient it seemed with Gideon's perambulating pace. 'I may have had my fill of astonishment for a while,' Gideon said, 'but you can try.'

'You've found your voice,' the dwarf said. 'I'm a baronet. My correct style is Sir Yeo Framlingham, Bart. What you have there is the future Sir Timothy of that ilk.'

'I hope it'll be a long time before he comes into the title,' Gideon said.

'We don't live long,' the dwarf said from where he was disapproving of something in the hedge. 'There's no one so ruthless as an aristocrat, I don't have to tell you that, do I?'

'In what respect?'

'One day I shall take it to the courts. The press will side with me, don't you agree, when the time comes? Not for any honourable motive, of course, but because . . . '

'What exactly will you be taking to court, when you decide to take it?'

'If it'd been a question of a peerage, I should never have hesitated so long. A lord has peers: there's the question of the whip. They like to make up the numbers. A baronet, on the other hand, always stands alone. He is not even a knight; he has no established moves to make.'

'I've always been rather impressed with baronets myself.' Gideon said. 'And I'd certainly say that it was a style superior to that of a life peer.'

'Look here,' the dwarf said, putting a brake on Gideon by pulling at his sleeve. 'Why shouldn't I be a baronet?'

'I can't conceive of any reason why you shouldn't.'

The moon frosted the macadam where they were standing. 'Look here.' Ringed fingers worked at his baby trousers. 'One penis. Two testicles. Count them for yourself. Who's got more? Have you? This is the authentic Framlingham tool and I defy you to deny it.'

'What's wrong with it exactly?' Gideon said. 'It seems to be sleeping very soundly. Have you given it anything?'

'I challenge you to say that it's not normal size. I'm as much an aristocrat as anyone of my degree. Look at this. I'm thinking of your wife. Look at this.'

'That'll do,' Gideon said.

'Watch me, watch me! That's who I'm thinking of. What's going through your mind? I'm sick? I'm deformed? I'm filth? I'm an impostor? I'm a baronet and I'm thinking of the lady of the house. Look at what's happening . . . '

'Stop that,' Gideon said, 'you – '

'Little bastard? I'm not a bastard. I'm in the direct line. This is the real stuff coming: the Framlingham mixture. Unobtainable anywhere else in the world. Watch, watch! Accept no substitutes: if the world had a cunt I'd make it all Framlingham, the future. I shouldn't have done that, should I?'

'Yeo,' Gideon said.

265

'You'll remember, won't you? Next time you see her.'

'You're running one hell of a risk, aren't you?'

'Aren't Yeo?'

'You'd better not come by again. Forget Casey. Casey's dead, his line is dead too. My wife . . . '

'You'll remember all right.'

' . . . hasn't inherited anything, if there was anything, that he could do. So I'm warning you . . . '

'I'm strong,' the dwarf said, 'and I fight dirty. You wouldn't believe how dirty, so don't come at me without thinking about it. If you want to mix it, you'd better mix a strong one. I've been beaten up by experts, but not by anyone else. The car's just up there, by the grit. I'm all below the belt. Remember.'

'You'd better go to the police in the morning,' Gideon said, 'and report this child's death. I believe it's dead.'

'You should have let me see her, shouldn't you?'

'Why did you bring a dead child to my house?'

The dwarf sat down on the cambered road with a bump, feet to chin. 'Give him to me,' he said.

Again, Gideon was the killer, returning the body. He set the knobbed bundle on the rumpled thighs above the toecaps of the dwarf's brogues. The baronet's face fell open and a long noise came from the hollow place; the eyes rolled white. Gideon found time in the blindness to snatch the handles of the barrow and turn for home. He denied the dwarf life by refusing to turn to see if he was still there. When he reached his cinders, he lowered the barrow, went into the shed and made himself busy with Cyril Lack's arguments. The last sheet was headed APPEAL: it called for a Solemn Pact of Speechlessness between all men and all women for at least one year (renewable).

Silence Alone can *heal* the world and allow God His chance to COME AGAIN. This silence must *include* an embargo on all printing and BROADCASTING. The Trades Unions *must* put their considerable weight behind us. Words are to be banned in ALL THEIR FORMS. No doctrine is to be preached during the *period of preparation*. Man must be free to will God and since He is indescribable, SILENCE ALONE can turn the key and admit him to our hearts. In that silence, mankind will wrestle itself back to a state of Purity and Balance, which is quite different from the politicians' equality. (*A chimera.*) All Will Be Permitted during this period, except speech or records OF ANY KIND. The Horrors will be Frightful, but they are a necessary prelude. Man must be denied the *deadly drug* – language. Only thus can we hope to be cured. Only thus can the latter days come to pass. God Must Be Moved.

On another line, like a clue in a crossword, was written: '*The Garden Will Be Open To All.*'

Gideon was sure that he had left the kitchen door unlocked, with the key in it, but he could not get back into the cottage. Afraid of waking Pamela, he went again into his work-shed. It was a quarter to three in the morning. Everything stormed his head that was comic and cruel, a silent rage that showed itself only in the inflections of his face, the twitches of a sleeping dog. Cyril Lack's manifesto and the taint of the baronet's fart made the little office a foreign place. *C'était comme l'Occupation pour lui (L'Inconnu).* He went into the cold again, bent for some crumbs of frosted earth and nagged the bedroom window with them until a light bloomed.

'You locked me out,' he said.

'I woke up. You weren't there. I came down. You weren't there either. So . . . I thought I'd hear you when you decided to come back. What were you doing?'

'Conversation with a baronet.' Gideon was cold now that he was in the warm again. 'A dwarf baronet. I heard something in the garden or somewhere and that's what I found.'

'Yeo,' Pamela said. She was wearing her quilted house-coat. The raw hair haloed her sleepsoft face. 'Did he tell you about his son?'

'I think it was dead, Pam. He had it with him but it wasn't breathing, I don't think. You know him, do you? He said – '

'He's been by,' she said. 'He's quite harmless. Do you want me to light the fire?'

'Aren't we going back to bed? No one's harmless, are they, after today?'

'Yesterday,' she said. 'I thought you might be staying down or something.'

'I'm full of emotions,' he said.

'I don't have any shortage of them myself.'

'Black things,' he said, 'without faces or identities. Belonging to ancient Egypt or somewhere like that.'

'Very distinguished,' she said. 'Mine don't come from anywhere particularly identifiable. Westgate-on-Sea probably. Most of one's demons were there at the cradle side, wouldn't you say so, professor?'

'He's done a terrible thing to us, hasn't he? Professor!'

'Everything passes,' she said, 'except what doesn't. Who has?'

'I was thinking of Cyril Lack of course.'

'But on mature reflection . . . ?'

'I don't want to be drawn into this,' Gideon said.

'Then why did you get up?'

'I heard someone, I told you. This dwarf.'

'You left me before, with Telfer. This person who's done a terrible thing, are you sure it isn't you?'

'Are you accusing me?'

'I leave that sort of thing to you. You're the public prosecutor around here.'

'If you hate me you must leave me,' he said. 'If you're indifferent to me you must still leave perhaps. Perhaps indifference is worse than hate.'

'But better than love?'

'I don't think that means anything.'

'Demanding more tenderness, more invention, more thought.'

'You still love him.'

'Oh Gideon! I'm so tired and . . . so *sore*.'

'I wish I could brick the bastard. Brick him, with a brick.'

'And have me visit you in gaol? When I was a little girl, I always thought it was goal that people went to.'

'As in "The Ballad of Reading"? One up at half-time. Well, there are those . . . but we won't worry about them at this hour.'

'I don't think I ever loved him,' Pamela said, 'necessarily. I thought what was happening to me *was* love. I thought it was something you caught, whether you particularly liked it or not, like flu.'

'I don't believe that for a moment,' Gideon said. 'I don't

mean you're lying, I just mean that personally I don't regard that as how things were at all.'

'You're mistaken,' she said.

'We can never know, can we?' he said.

'I can, and I do. You think you know everything.'

'Everyone was being kind, and a little − what? − devious, weren't they? All three of us were doing each other little favours and ourselves perhaps big ones at the same time. We were all lifting each other a little higher, believing, or not, that no one was left at the bottom, with his or her feet on the ground, or in the shit.'

'You told Miranda,' she said.

'She knew really, didn't she?'

'But you *told* her. Another sort of rape?'

'You've been deceiving these people, haven't you, into thinking that you can be another Casey, whatever Casey was, a sort of white witch, who can by-pass the N.H.S. and provide a more reliable service with fewer questions asked? Are you going to be doing abortions soon? She certainly took it as if it was no great shock to her. I was more shaken than she was.'

'I may have told her at one point,' Pamela said.

'And now you tell me? Christ, I find you incredible sometimes.'

'I probably am. Aren't most people? You find it difficult to believe in God; I find it difficult to believe in people. They seem much more unlikely to me.' Pushing her hair from her brow with the heel of her thumb, she gave Gideon look after look.

'Surely you *know* whether you told her.'

'Oh, I'm not interested in facts in the same way you are. I never cleared my throat like you do and . . . It simply emerged, I think, on one occasion when we were talking about things.'

'When did it? And did you tell her who her father was?'

'Oh, you're her father, you know that perfectly well, whoever else is. It came out, a question I didn't bother to answer and she . . . It wasn't *intentional*.'

'When you came to my rooms, what did you intend then? Anything? In Portugal Place.'

'Stephen asked me . . . '

'I thought so.'

'Intentions didn't come into it. He thought you were rather desperate, and you were, weren't you? He felt guilty. Perhaps he wanted you to have your revenge.'

'And did I? Did *you*?'

'I was afraid of him, I think, and – oddly enough – he was afraid of me. He gave me credit for something I probably never had: passion, intensity. It was more likely nervousness.'

'Have my revenge by having you. By depriving him of something he wasn't sure he really wanted. That doesn't sound like revenge to me exactly.'

'You must think very little of me,' she said. 'He thought rather more. He was afraid that I'd make him suffer. I probably would have. He needed to be in command, so that he could have enough time for his damned work, without having to worry about anyone else's. She's been very good for him in that respect, I imagine, don't you? No waves; only permanents!'

'No one thinks very little of you.'

'You left me to it,' she said, 'didn't you, with Telfer? With . . . '

'God help me, I thought I was being tactful.'

'But what were you?'

'If we never leave it alone,' he said, 'it'll never leave us alone. Perhaps we should leave here. Mandy wouldn't object: she wants to go back to Chaworth. Did she mention it to you?'

'I'm staying right here,' Pamela said.

She soon seemed to be asleep; her breathing matched itself to a rhythm that denied him. She belonged to a time independent of his. He chucked his clothes into the corner by the door and lay down next to his wife, shifty in his sweat. He was already at morning, charged with tiredness and yet unable to cash even the rest available to him. Deep in a dream he could not share, Pamela moved and was talking, a raucous language he could not fathom. She fought something beside him, kicking the bedclothes from his feet, pitching in a rough sea of feelings in which he could not even moisten his own. The violence of her cries filled him with envy and anger and frustration. She might have been joking; she might have been in torment. She thrashed in the hot bed and a flung arm fell across his chest. He caught her hand and that made him her gaoler: she shook herself free and yelped and switched on the light and glared at him. 'What time is it?'

'After four,' he said. 'Do you want something? You were having a nightmare.'

'Don't do that again,' she said, 'will you?'

'What was who doing? You were dreaming.'

'You can't help me,' she said. 'You can't protect me. If he wants me, he can always get to me.'

'What the hell are you talking about?'

'The devil has two,' she said. 'Did you know that?'

'Two what?'

'That's what he has over everyone else. You can have him both ways; he can have you. Or me. Or both, I suppose.'

'What were you dreaming?'

'And he never has to stop,' she said. 'He can't stop. He's never finished. We have to stop, if we can, get away from him if we can, knowing all the time that he's still there, waiting for us. One day he won't want us any more, we know that too. We don't know what we're supposed to do. Or rather, we know what we're *supposed* to do, but we don't know that it will do us any good, because we don't know, finally, if anything is any good or not, do we? I thought you were good.'

'What've I done wrong?' Gideon said.

'I know now what your goodness was. I don't blame you. It was mixed with so many things, wasn't it? I think you were good to do what you did about that book. I never really understood what was so terrible about the review you wrote. To tell you the truth, I'm not sure that I ever read it right through to the end. Of course, it wasn't tactful, if that man was important in the college, I could see that, Neil Laidlaw, but I never saw why Stephen felt so bad about getting you to do it. No one ever accused you of being spiteful or mistaken or anything like that, did they?'

'Intemperate,' Gideon said. 'That's worse.'

'It was Stephen's motives that were corrupt, weren't they?'

'Why corrupt? He felt an anguish that I . . . I don't know that I dare to tell you the truth, Pammy, after all these years. Knowing someone . . . you're afraid after a while that they already know everything there is to know about you. It's a kind of death that, isn't it? Another person too close makes one feel superfluous; treachery becomes the same thing as self-preservation. One must have a secret. I never liked Stephen in the same way that I liked, oh, people at school. He frightened me in a way. He had something – I even thought it was money at one point, opportunities – something dark and terrible about him. O.K., he was a Jew. I didn't want that to mean anything; nor did he, perhaps, but it did. He had this great charge of rage, of purpose, about him; this need to vindicate himself, to make the world pay attention – '

'Or just simply to pay,' she said.

'You really don't like them, do you?' he said.

'I'm not a politician,' she said. 'I don't have to have a programme. I'm not going to *do* anything to anyone. I don't have to declare my opinions at the Customs. I go through the Green Channel; I don't have anything anyone could ever want to discover.'

'You're a clever woman and don't deny it.'

'If I were, you wouldn't have to say it, would you?'

'Have I failed to teach you?'

'Have I failed to learn? It doesn't matter. You wanted to be Stephen somehow, is that it? And marrying me enabled you to work the switch. Or so you hoped. Having his daughter . . . Believe it or not, Gideon, I never thought about you like this until we came to Quince Cottage.'

'I shouldn't bother to blame the place, if I were you.'

'I don't blame the place. I'm grateful to it. I'm even grateful to the devil for fucking some sense into me.'

'The devil doesn't exist, Pammy. If the scales must drop from your eyes, don't bother to replace rose-tinted spectacles with shades, I shouldn't.'

'How alive we come when we hate people!'

'You're right, in a way, but only in a way, and there are

so many ways, if we're honest, endless ways, aren't there? I wanted to take his cross. I envied him the ... God help me ... the glamour. And taking it voluntarily, the weight of that rage and humiliation – don't forget the humiliation, because that's what's behind all their vanity and their energy and their will to impose themselves, shame, not at having survived but at having been able to do nothing. Stephen looks at the English and he passes himself off as one of them, sits in judgment, or soon will, and he knows that they don't care. He knows that he has only one set of alternatives: he can accept their terms or he can go down fighting, fighting himself, no one else, because no one else will give him a contest on the terms he wants. You think he's the devil? You wish he was; we all do somewhere along the line, because then he'd deserve the darkness, own the darkness, belong to the darkness, that we belong to ourselves, because we've inherited the unforgivable.'

'Tom?' she said. 'Mandy? *Mandy . . .?*'

'You are so reckless,' he said. 'You've been so ... so decent, so reliable, so patient and somewhere you're totally reckless.'

'Any woman is,' she said, 'who gives birth. You were there: you saw what happens to us. They turn us inside out. Envelopes with red linings ... Have you bought me a Christmas present yet? I haven't you.'

'There's still a day or two,' he said. 'This will all go by. One day ...'

'I don't know that I want it to, Gideon. I don't know that I can bear it to.'

'The ordinary always imposes itself in the end. It wouldn't be ordinary otherwise, would it?'

'They wear Wittgenstein T-shirts now,' she said. 'I suppose I did kill him really. We killed him. No, why should I share the credit? *I* did. I was the only one who knew what his feelings really were, how deep, how ... Telfer knows it too.'

'Did he ever actually say he'd kill himself if you left Chaworth?'

'Whereof, thereof! Oh, you two! The most important things are the things that aren't said because they can't

273

be said, ever. They become lies as soon as they get spoken. They get advertised on T-shirts.'

'Somewhere you're greedy, aren't you, Pamela? You want everything but you don't want to admit you want it.'

'Not everything,' she said.

'Oh yes,' he said. 'Even the rape, even that. You didn't want it to *happen*, I don't mean that – '

'Thank you,' she said. 'A lot of things have been said, but be careful all the same: there are still things . . . '

'Your kindness – generosity, heart – has always frightened me,' he said. 'No, intimidated me. Not quite the same thing, there's a nuance, there.'

'Damn your bloody French,' she said. 'By the way.'

'If you'd been less – accommodating, I might even have been able to be what you wanted, instead of wanting to be. What is it that's forced us all, all three of us, I mean, to be what we, someone else, not any one of us necessarily, seemed to expect us to be? You're not the only pure one, you know, Pam, and somewhere along the line, the long line, that's what you've wanted us to believe: that there was nothing you wanted, nothing you contributed to or contributed to you. You may see it with Fagin, what you contributed, but even that's a kind of vanity, not a true perception, a sort of . . . appropriation.'

'Do you know what he said to me tonight? He said, "The world isn't true, it's a change from the truth." '

'Cyril Lack said that?'

'The devil.'

'In your dream?'

'When he came to me.'

'When he was fucking sense . . . '

'Don't ever laugh at me again, Gideon.'

'Don't ever call me Gids again. Do we have a deal?'

'Do you think it's true?'

'Because he said it? Or because it's true? There's the crux. Does the devil always tell the truth or does he always tell lies or . . . does he leave it to us to decide? That would be the really devilish trick, wouldn't it? Well, if what's true is what is eternal, immutable, perhaps he was right. You know who really thought that one up, of course, don't you, Pammy? You did. You think I don't think you're clever. That's where you're wrong. There's been something deliberately concealed in you all these years and I've . . . I've loved it in a way.'

'Because it's what's made you unhappy,' she said. 'I made a Jew out of you, didn't I?'

'I lack certain essential characteristics in that regard,' he said. 'Or rather, to be accurate, I have a certain essential characteristic that they lack. I've sometimes wondered . . . '

'When have you ever done anything else?'

'You want to be punished for what happened to Fagin, is that what this is all about?'

'Not all of it,' she said. 'I don't want to be *punished* particularly.'

'You want something to happen, don't you?' he said. 'Lack wasn't enough for you.'

'The children aren't here for a change, and you can say all the things you ever wanted to say.'

'I'm tired, Pammy, is the truth.'

'I remember your face over Tom.'

'You take pleasure in this.'

'The terrible thing, the one completely terrible thing, is that there's pleasure in everything, in absolutely everything. We think we can deny it; we may swear it's not true, but there is. Everything that happens contains its little purse of pleasure for someone, somewhere. There's nothing we can't think of without some sort of appetite. Try.'

'I can, very easily,' he said, 'and so can you.'

'Nothing.'

'Perhaps they're right,' he said, 'to come to you, Casey's cases. You think it's the cottage, I think it's you. You felt what you felt when you came in here because it was your size: you fitted. They come to see you because you've come into the place, the rightful heir. Was there really a child, Sir Yeo's, or was he romancing or . . . ?'

'He brought me a child,' Pamela said. 'But whether he had it with him when you saw him . . . '

'You imagine that I've . . . had another life somewhere, that I haven't really given you myself?'

275

'I imagine nothing,' she said.

'You don't want me, you don't want him, what do you want?'

'Must I want something? Could you bear me to want not to want at all?'

'I thought it was love,' he said.

'So did I,' she said.

'Which of us wants forgiving?'

18

Erik sat in the car while Stephen came towards the cottage. Wearing a slightly waisted sheepskin coat with alpaca lapels and a Politburo hat, he made a positive journey of the walk across the cinders to the kitchen door. His pointed feet seemed small on the frozen ground and only the front half of his weight bruised the white. He might have been on invisible high heels.

'Forgive me,' he said, 'coming unannounced, but I am the announcement, as it were.'

'Do you want some coffee?'

'If you've got some going,' he said. 'Is Gideon here?'

'No, he's there.' Pamela pointed through the kitchen wall to Gideon's shed.

'Only I'm afraid I've got some news for him.'

'He can almost certainly hear what you're saying,' Pamela said. 'Can't you, darling?'

Gideon had been wishing her dead and she was dead.

'I'm sorry to be so abrupt,' Stephen said, 'but Barry Woodward telephoned and that was his message.'

'He didn't have anyone else he could contact directly, did he?' Gideon said.

'In the old days, he would've sent a telegram, but . . . '

'He's sent you instead,' Pamela said.

'I don't quite know what to say,' Stephen said. 'Alas or hurrah.'

'Both. It'll save us worrying about her over Christmas at least. Do you know what happened exactly?'

'It all sounded a trifle mysterious, to tell you the truth. Apparently there was some kind of a fire. I don't want to give you the wrong information, but she seems to have died of – I'm sorry if . . . – burns. Do you want to come to Constable's and call Master Woodward from there? I've got to go back for some of the straw I drop bricks with, so . . .'

'I shall have to go down to Graveley,' Gideon said, 'obviously.'

'I don't think the house burned down or anything.'

'Just my mother?'

'It may have been something electrical.'

'I'm debating whether or not to drive,' Gideon said.

'We didn't get much sleep last night,' Pamela said. 'I shouldn't.'

'I probably ought to leave you the car.'

'Will you do any good, do you think, really, going?'

'Good doesn't come into it.'

'After all, there's nothing you can do.'

'That's what takes the time,' Gideon said. 'Boom-boom.'

'I'll leave the stage,' Stephen said.

Excluded from their humour, Pamela poured more coffee. 'Do you want to take a case? You might have to stay overnight.'

'At least buzz back to Constable's with me and have a word with Barry,' Stephen said, 'I think you'll be gratified at his change of tone. I'm going on to town; we can entrain to London together and my chap'll take you to Victoria, or wherever.'

'The miscarriage waits,' Gideon said.

'In the presence of an old friend,' Stephen said, 'I remove my hat. *And* a lady.'

'If I'm not out of my depth,' Pamela said, 'why am I drowning?'

'It can be done in the shallows,' Stephen said, 'but only by the dedicated. Could it have been lightning, I wonder? Woodward will have it all at his leather fingertips.'

'You are terrible, Stephen, sometimes.'

'Famous for it, the ong-fong,' Stephen said. 'I say, Pam, while I'm here, could I possibly prevail on you to rescind your ban on secondhand bicycles? Christmas comes but once a year and the damned thing is no conceivable further use to us. If I told you that you'd be doing us a favour, couldn't you suffer me to have Erik wheel the damned thing round?'

'I'll go up and stow some pyjamas in a bag, just in case.'

'Nice one,' Stephen said.

'You can hear everything in this house,' Pamela said.

'Even what hasn't been said? *Especially* . . . ? You look – what? – this morning. Unsurprised will do. But *radiantly* unsurprised. Did you have a pre-monition?'

'I'm good at being unsurprised,' she said. 'Surprisingly.'

'I wasn't sure how Gideon would take it,' Stephen said. 'Good news and bad news, as they say.'

'You handled it with care,' Pamela said, 'despite your attempts to be clumsy.'

'Please don't be touchy about the bicycle.'

'I wouldn't put it among the first of my worries just now,' she said.

'It must be just about the last day of term.'

'Just about,' she said. 'Please don't.'

'I'm not,' he said.

'I did warn you. This cottage . . . '

'I'm quite unable to . . . analyse what I feel. I only know that I feel it. For no reason at all, you might say. Why did you get so little sleep last night? If that's not . . . '

'It is,' she said.

'I'm beyond knowing why I want you so much,' he said.

'You should . . . '

'What? What should I?'

'I can't tell you,' she said.

'He can't hear us. You know he can't hear us.'

'If I told you, it wouldn't be true any longer, would it?'

'We have done that which we ought not to have done and there is no health in us,' Stephen said. 'God dammit all.'

'I may be accused of . . . I don't know, murdering someone, I suppose.'

'Anyone I know? Not *me*? *Him*?'

'I haven't murdered you,' she said. 'Either of you, and you know it. I might have wanted to, but that's not a crime, is it?'

'I'll take Gideon to the station and – '

'No, you won't,' she said.

'Then I'll come back tonight,' he said.

'Miranda'll be here,' she said, 'and Tom.'

'Late,' he said.

'Well, here we are then,' Gideon said. 'Ready for prep school with my bag and my mac and my freshly scraped face.'

'You *shaved* for prep school?' Stephen said.

'I suppose I can always get a message to you via Stephen, can't I, or Miriam? Unless you want to call Graveley this afternoon.'

'I can never get the coins in,' Pamela said. 'Don't worry about me, I'll see you when I see you.'

'I'm really sorry about this,' Gideon said, 'but I don't know what else I can do. Will you come for the funeral?'

'If you want us to.'

'I don't think I've really reacted yet,' Gideon said.

'I think you have,' Pamela said.

The mid-morning train was not full; they had a first class compartment to themselves, Stephen by the window, Gideon across from him in the far corner, so that they had room for their black feet. 'What do you think you'll do now,' Stephen said as the greening fields, frosted now only under the bracket of the hedges, began to flit past the hot windows, 'leave?'

'Leave?'

'Quince Cottage. I don't mean you have to decide or anything. But if you're going to have money, why would you want to stay in a cottage in the middle of nowhere?'

'One doesn't want to keep upsetting everyone,' Gideon said. 'Pamela particularly likes it, you know.'

'She seems very tense to me. Unless that's me rather than the cottage?'

'She's discovered that she's inherited something from

the previous owner, Casey. A set of dependants, you might say, people who come there for remedies. She doses them with herbal tea. He's left her various recipes.'

'What's this about murdering someone? Was she joking?'

'I was on my way to see you yesterday – well, I thought you might be home – because this inspector suddenly turned up, from Chaworth. You remember that nonsense about the man who killed himself, one of her patients? It seems he left her ten thousand quid and that . . . '

'You saw Mim.'

'Yes, and . . . I went back to the cottage and – I'm sorry about this – but I found . . . '

'Gideon, what is this?'

'I thought I was laughing,' Gideon said. 'And I'm crying.'

'Take your time,' Stephen said. 'Is it your mother?'

'I mustn't show how relieved I am about that,' Gideon said. 'How schoolboyish! She might come back and cancel . . . You really don't know what happened? I'm a killer too, Stephen. I wished her dead so often . . . I can't believe I'm going to get away with it. Pamela was raped, while I was out of the cottage, that's why I didn't . . . try again.'

'Jesu! By this policeman?'

'Ah no. That would've been . . . well, we should've had something to make a stink about, shouldn't we? A friend of mine, a nutter called Cyril Lack I knew when he was in gaol in Chaworth. He turned up with some crackpot philosophical treatise he wanted me to comment on. He has this idea that all speech ought to be suspended for a year, at least, and that mankind should relearn . . . a sort of Nietzschean hot-pot he's picked up, or thought up, and he's pursuing me with. He caught up with Pam and . . . '

'Literally . . . ?'

'Do you think I ought to kill him?'

'Do you want to?'

'I did,' Gideon said, 'but I seem to have lost it this morning. She won't have the police, which is understandable . . . '

'Did he hurt her? I mean . . . ?'

'She was rather badly bruised and he pulled her hair very violently for some reason. I'll tell you the truth, Stephen, I think our marriage is more or less at an end. That's the last thing I ever wanted to tell you, literally. But . . .'

'Winter journeys in the sunshine, especially on trains, give rise to unreliable confidences,' Stephen said. 'Are you saying all this because you know I'm still in love with Pam myself or because you don't? You do, don't you?'

'Unfinished business and unfinished pleasure, they're very close together, aren't they? I don't have the least idea why I'm saying anything at all. I'm not intending to say it; it all comes out despite my fervent belief that I'd serve my own interests best by remaining silent. I've made that mistake before, you may remember.'

'I wish you blamed me,' Stephen said. 'You never did and hence I've always blamed myself.'

'Vanity,' Gideon said. 'It's always been your vice.'

'My virtue,' Stephen said. 'It's the one thing the impostor has to hold on to. It keeps him together, the actor's only adhesive. Faith unfaithful. You don't believe anything will actually come of this Fagin affair, do you? Fagin!'

'She may have done it,' Gideon said. 'I can believe everything of her, you might say. Not because I don't want her; because I fear that I can never have her.'

'Nobody can ever have anybody,' Stephen said.

'You come to her in the night,' Gideon said.

'Do I just? And what do I do when I do that?'

'She says you've got two pricks: you have her both ways at the same time. She likes it and she hates you for it.'

'What are you trying to do, Gideon?'

'Tell you the truth. She thinks you're a diabolical Jew. Why are you smiling?'

'What you think to be unspeakable is something I say to myself morning, noon and night. Not, of course, that I necessarily relish your reiteration of it. It keeps me going, Gideon. It arms my tongue and gilds my irony; it's my sword and my buckler and my certificate of honour and warrant for . . . malice. Its edge makes me courteous and its poison is my cordial. Think nothing of it; oh, think it, if you will, but not with any luscious sense of scandal or outrage, I shouldn't, because I know all about it. What you're thinking is only the pale shadow of what I think myself.'

The arrival of the ticket collector made commuters of them: they smiled at him and at each other and when at last Stephen found the tickets he thanked them, gentlemen. After he had closed the door, they preserved the geniality he had imposed. A broken bridge that had once had a purpose twitched past them, a high brick platform now, unattainable from both ends. The silence was as luxurious as a cigar; they drew on it, deep breaths that shallowed into nervousness only when exhaled.

'The vanity has really been mine,' Gideon said.

'You're a decent, honourable man,' Stephen said. 'Do whatever you feel you want to do or have to do, but don't bother to brand yourself with sins you haven't committed. Somewhere along the line you've got the idea that there should have been some great and pure passion between you and Pammy and that you've deceived her, or yourself, or someone, because . . . Well, I don't think marriage has got too much to do with great and pure passions. Consider, Gidman, the petty possibility that Pam just might be thrilled to bits to have a few bob for a change. Don't credit her with too much fineness. Assume her to be flesh and blood and don't oblige her to display qualities she won't thank you for wishing on her.'

'Oh damn Pamela,' Gideon said.

'*Passons outre*,' Stephen said. 'You know what puzzles me, thinking about Deakin and Butterworth – puzzles me, intrigues me – and that is, who made the first overture to whom? How did they *start* being cheats, if cheats they be, as Oleg continues to affirm *magna cum voce*? What kind of foreplay, do you suppose, preceded the frank suggestion that they cook up a code? What a huge step it must have been! Or was it a mere shuffle of the worst foot forward? Connivance, that's all it required, the certainty that the other man wouldn't blow the whistle, pull the communication cord, whatever. It must've been almost indistinguishable from love, Gideon, don't you think so? A moment of exhilaration, purity, transcendence. The same thing you must've got with spies and the seduction of spies, the Cambridge speciality! What's so strange, so delicious, if you like, is that the understanding that exists between, oh, the Proctor twins, for easy instance, the understanding that seems uncanny and beats the odds time and again, when it comes to a lead or guessing at a void or whatever, that understanding is *almost* the same thing, but what makes it clean, what makes it acceptable at least, is that *nothing has ever been said*. We know achingly what we crave of each other but if we come out with it, something is lost for ever. And yet, and yet, there remains that enviable bond between thieves, though you can't call it honour. Collusion replaces collision; you becomes I, that's all it takes! We should've shared her, shouldn't we? We shouldn't have said anything, but that's what we should have done. It's what she wanted and couldn't say and what we wanted and couldn't say, and yet it wasn't really all that difficult. There's a game to be played which combines fair and foul and we had the chance to play it.'

'It can't be played,' Gideon said, 'it can only be imagined. It's the excluded middle, the place where decisions can be postponed, not yet inhabited. It doesn't belong this side of Lethe; it's a game for souls. You can't cheat and not cheat; you can only dream of a place where such commerce might be entertained; heaven or hell, I'm not sure which.'

'Miriam has lovers, you know,' Stephen said. 'She fucks.'

'She thinks you do.'

'She likes young men. The Aubrey character is one of them. Generous! She doesn't want me to worry about her; and I don't. Worry is the one thing that doesn't enter our relationship. Cheats have that compensation above all, don't they? They're never in doubt. I do wish he didn't suck his fingers though.'

'Have you been having an affair with Tamara Chernoff?'

'Were you coming to me for legal advice?'

'I could imagine Pammy suddenly being in water rather hotter than she would've chosen to run for herself. I mean, this Fagin business hasn't been altogether unpleasing for her, so far; it's all unquestionably hers and that's the kind of entitlement people like to have. It's nothing to do with me at all, except that by trying to save the family, I seem to have destroyed it, and incidentally pulled the plug on poor, rich Mr Fagin, even though it was the last thing on my mind. She had the power to save him and she quite deliberately, I suspect, enjoyed it to the full. Of course, she was in an impossible situation: how could she have stayed in Chaworth, after what happened to her own son, merely in order to keep an old poop alive and kissing? Powerlessness and power were in perfect harmony, or counterpoint, and that was what entertained her, I suppose. Because she could do nothing, she had the gift of life and death.'

'Imagine a woman's world,' Stephen said.

London built around them; the stations matched neat titles to sprawl and disorder.

'The most difficult thing', Gideon said, 'is to see why they're so modest, so ungreedy. Is it the price of pleasure that makes them cautious? Or the fear that it won't be all that pleasant? They see everything in one, don't they, the best of them? Their eyes are so disconcertingly open.'

'And yet they're so easily deceived,' Stephen said. 'And bought.'

'Are they? *Are* they?'

'You've got money now,' Stephen said. 'What are you going to do – get back to Quince Cottage tonight or not?'

'I haven't the faintest,' Gideon said. 'I don't really know what there is to do. They always talk about putting things in order, settling people's affairs, but what does that involve on the ground exactly? I do rather advise you against . . . no, I don't.'

'I know what she's been saying to you about me, but that hasn't stopped me in other domains. What's the matter, Gideon? Are you waiting for me to tell you what you really want, or to make you want it?'

'Don't push me too far, Stephen.'

'Which of us is the bully, Gidman? Have you touched

her since last night, since your friend's visit? Have you wanted to?'

'I don't have to answer your questions. I won't answer them. I'm not answerable to you.'

'Pamela loves me,' Stephen said. 'What she thinks is her dream of me is really yours, isn't it, misaddressed? You've always credited me with powers I didn't possess. You thought I could get you that fellowship, didn't you? I was Mephisto and if you paid the price, I'd set you on the pinnacle of the college chapel and invite you to choose your stall.'

'Everything is true, isn't it,' Gideon said, 'so long as nothing happens? You pretended to search for an non-existent ticket when the man came in, just to kindle the hope in his boring little heart – the hope, the fear – that he was going to catch us out. You wanted the thrill of being the felon, knowing all the time that you were fully covered and that no charges could possibly stick.'

'You're a careful reader, Gideon, but you haven't answered the obligatory question. You thought I was the king of darkness and your whole life, so far, since the day we met on the stairs, has been lived in the expectation that somehow I'd honour our Faustian bargain and see you right. You bless and you curse me in the same gesture of credulity. You'll accept anything about me except my squareness with you: you insist that I have a plan and a purpose and the recipe of the month from the Kabbala. The one thing you refuse to hear is the possibility that I can misplay the hand through sheer incompetence or lack of technique, that I'm not a prince and that I'm in the dark just as you are, when I am. It's only recently, I must confess, that I've come to the conclusion that I shall never come into my diabolical title; if I fooled you, I also fooled myself. Shall we shake on it?'

'What do you damned well want of me?'

'Could anyone ever stand to know that the answer to that is absolutely nothing? The joke, my dear Gidman, is that I want neither your mind nor your body; my satisfaction, a malicious observer might conclude, is that I always thought that you were the powerful one, the one I had to fear, and favour for that reason. When I'm in your company, I'm in a minority; I know that I can never prevail by leaving it to nature. Jews are the most profoundly and systematically unnatural people in the world. It doesn't matter why, whether God or anyone else wished it so; it's the case.'

'She was right, I suppose: I never did come of age. Does anyone?'

'Only those who don't depend on the decisions of others. Old children, we see them starving on the box and we really feel we ought to do something about it, if only we could make the time.'

'Do you give a lot to charity, Stephen?'

'Uncountable sums.'

'I shall be able to repay you now, of course.'

'I'd sooner have the flesh,' Stephen said. 'I know this sounds silly, but do you want us to enter for the Gold Cup again next year? Only I've had the forms. Soon as you're knocked out, you're knocking in again.'

'You've never asked me before,' Gideon said. 'You've always . . . '

'How do you read that?'

'You bastard,' Gideon said, 'aren't you basically?'

'Thank you, partner,' Stephen said.

They were already on their feet as the train came into Liverpool Street. Its sudden lurch sent them dancing together. They toppled into the corridor, wrestling not with each other but with a force too impersonal to score against. They slumped gravely into each other, in their winter coats, snowmen spilling into the same space. Stephen's weight leaned for a moment on Gideon, like a victor, elbow knifing his ribs on the messy floor. He fought Stephen off, admittedly smiling, but hating being down there with the squashed cigarette packet, the beastly plastic cup and plastic stirrer, hating the oaf who had guttered him. Each might have been all right without the other; both were bruised by the dirt. They were up in a moment, furtive with humiliation, wincing at prudent souls standing, undamaged, by the double-jointed doors.

'You've been kind to me for long enough,' Gideon said. 'Blast you.'

'It's time to stop, Gideon, isn't it? Now that you're

going to be rich, there's no reason for you to deceive yourself any longer. Our partnership was of equals, but equality is something you couldn't endure, unless it was I who couldn't. The whole humour of it has come from the courtesies it demanded, our amiable falseness, and now that that seems to be over, so do other things, don't they? Unless you disagree . . . ?'

'I don't know where I shall be,' Gideon said, 'is the main thing.'

'I divorce thee, I divorce thee, I divorce thee,' Stephen said.

19

SHE HAD BEEN sitting in a wing-chair by the fireplace in the blue drawing room on the first floor of Graveley (the ground floor had been turned into a flatlet where Pritchett, her maid, lived with her humped sister, a retired cook who could not raise her head without using her hand). When Pritchett came in with the supper tray she saw that Mrs Shand was lapped in flames. There was no sound at first. It was like looking at a hot photograph: there seemed to be no movement either. Mrs Shand was making no attempt to escape her fate; she looked royally enthroned in it. Pritchett was a subscriber to the *Watchtower* and responded to the flames with wonder, and pride, imagining some kind of pentecostal election. She put down the boiled fish on the spinnet and made a quick inventory of expendable things – never the Persian carpet – she could not be reproached for using to swaddle the flames. Running from the room, she snatched the coverlet – spilling cushions – from Mrs Shand's bed, returned to the now raucous fire and tried to parcel it in pink. The hairless body fell into crackling and bones. A cooked smell broke from it.

The firemen could give no explanation. The electric points were neither overloaded nor scorched. Mrs Shand was not a smoker; she had not been playing with matches. Had the electric burner spat a spark on to the boards and so kindled the blaze? Something in the mystery was close to a joke: Mrs Shand had made even her death a sort of tax on her son, something so unlikely that Gideon would have to continue to pay amused, appalled attention to her for longer than any routine exit could have required. He almost loved her for it, the bitch, standing by the blackened place in the regular room. She had certainly made it difficult for him to speak casually, let alone malevolently, of her: whenever she was discussed, it would be in terms of that newsworthy departure.

'"All survivors are killers of the dead,"' Gideon said. 'Who was it said that? "And pay in death for the dying." '

'You could always afford to have someone check,' Barry Woodward said.

'I trust there won't be too many delays,' Gideon said. 'I shan't look kindly on them. My mother's will was presumably correctly drawn and even the oddness of the circumstances of her death can't cast much doubt on her sanity or its propriety, I assume – '

'The mantle of Elijah,' Woodward said. '*Mutatis mutandis.*'

'I shall be making all appropriate checks, however. You may imagine that since the trust is now broken and I can't be prevented from coming into my father's money at least, I shall be magnanimous about Graveley and its contents. I shall not; I shall be correct, but not in the least indulgent. Were you her lover?'

'He was bent, of course,' Woodward said.

'Bent?'

'Your father. He was in love with his driver and he never got over it. I did give you some indication. You are an only child, after all.'

'The world isn't short of those,' Gideon said. 'Have you any evidence?'

'Life isn't a court of law, Gideon, and a court of law certainly isn't life. When I say he was bent, I don't mean that he wasn't the soul of honour. He was *because* he was, I daresay. Brave and good and, as I say, bent. Did it never occur to you?'

'What?'

'Of course, in those days it was all very shameful,

something to mark one for life, or against it. I think he thought that Jordan was killed to punish him for loving him. It seems rather perverse, as an idea, on the face of it, don't you think? But then, of course, if someone had removed his flaw, there's no knowing what kind of a shit he might not have been.'

'I shall be getting my accountants to look very thoroughly into the administration of the funds during the period when you've been in charge of them,' Gideon said.

'That's a comfort,' Woodward said.

'And I shan't hesitate to go to law, or any other appropriate extreme, if there's been the slightest irregularity. And by the way, I leave it to you to make the funeral arrangements. You are, after all, the next of kin, aren't you, in a way?'

Glenys Harrington said that, by chance, there was a partnership at her club in Kilburn that evening, if he felt like it. Her flat was in a Victorian house with a paved yard in front of it. A plastic-domed man was tuning a propped Honda without a front wheel.

'Surprise,' she said.

'Your voice sounds white,' he said, 'on the telephone.'

'I've been around for a day or two.'

'Is the man with the motorbike anything to do with you?'

'I thought you'd be older,' she said.

'Tomorrow I will be. I thought you'd be – a lot of things you aren't.'

'Why suddenly after all these months?'

'My mother died last night. My wife was raped. Everyday reasons like that. I'm rich and I'm free, at least I believe I am. You live alone?'

'With a friend called Alice. She isn't here.'

'I didn't think I could see her. I mean to change my life.'

'My name doesn't begin with A,' Glenys said. 'Why did you start with me? Perhaps you didn't start with me.'

'Why did you write to me?'

'I'm a bridge junkie. I liked your style. You're not tight with a hand. Gideon Shand, I can't believe it!'

'Nor I. What stakes do you play, at your place?'

'Very low. Nobody has too much money around here. You thought I'd really be a typical librarian, I suppose.'

'Your cards intrigued me,' he said. 'One on its own wouldn't have, but the way they came so regularly. You have a sharp mind. You could do with some furniture.'

'You haven't been drinking, have you?'

'I don't need to,' he said, 'I'm drunk already. I've just been born. I've got my legs and – there's a funny thing, I've also got my inheritance which, in French, you could translate as legs. Do you speak French?'

'I can read it,' she said.

'*Je veux faire l'amour avec toi*. Can you read that?'

'You don't waste much time, do *vous*?'

'I haven't much to waste.'

'Are you serious?'

'Why else do you think that I rang you?'

'You didn't have the least idea what I even looked like. I might have been – '

'But you weren't, were you? I'll never forget something my father said to me the evening before I got married. He was homosexual, but I didn't know it. I was telling him – perhaps I was telling myself – how extraordinary this girl was I intended to spend the rest of my life with, how right I was to be marrying her, and he looked up with a sly little look and he said, "It doesn't really matter who you marry, you know, or do anything else with." I was . . . embarrassed. It was the only time I was ever naked with him, him with me. Two men. Probably it doesn't matter who your father is either. He was in love with his driver in the army, a chap called Jordan, who got killed.'

'You're the same man wrote all those articles?'

'My daughter thought you were my mistress. She likes to romance . . . Well?'

'You've got the nerve of the devil, haven't you?' Glenys Harrington said.

'I came here for compliments, and, by George, I'm getting them. Do you really want a partnership this evening?'

'And then I'll fuck you,' she said.

'Glenys Harrington. Do you want money? I'll give you

ten times everything we win tonight. A hundred times, if you like. The more we win, the more I'll lose. That'll give us a game unlike anything that anyone in the room is likely to be playing.'

'You're rough,' she said.

'Then why are you laughing?'

'A librarian?' she said.

'You and Alice . . . '

'It's been known,' she said.

'What does she do, Alice?'

'She does a little selling,' Glenys said. 'You come here to murder me?'

'I'm not that ambitious. Unless it's murder finding out what people are like.'

'We win, I'll fuck you. We don't, you can fuck yourself, O.K.? And I'll take that hundred times. We play five pee a hundred. Lose, it won't cost you more than pennies. Win, and you're in big trouble.'

The folding tables had awkward legs: only one pair of partners could be comfortable. Gideon might have been playing a game he had never played before: the intonations and motives of the Kilburn players were so alien to him. Glenys wore glasses; she scarcely looked at him during the first three rubbers. They lost them all. Then an Australian Chinaman called André went down fourteen hundred against them, a blessing that changed their luck. He made them look up at each other: why had he done such a thing, although no fool? Their losses were soon annulled and they began to win. Glenys looked at him; he looked at her. He saw the blood swell in her lips and the teeth taste the succulence.

Gritty snow was falling when they left the club. They walked in silence to Franklin Road. The wheel was back on the Honda. On the doorstep, she said, 'You don't have to, you know.'

'You do,' he said.

She moved her chin in the faint light, as if her eyes had lost their mobility and she had to tilt her whole face to scan him. 'I don't know what Alice is going to say.'

'I don't care what she says, as long as it's nothing.'

'And I thought you were *nice*.'

'This is nice.'

Her bed was a mattress on a plywood rostrum, a few inches from the floor. He told her to undress while he watched her. She wanted to turn out the fringed light; he stopped her. She sighed and smiled and sighed again and shook her head and unzipped her skirt. She was wearing red pants. Her legs were shining as if she had taken exercise. The black did not quite cover her body: in places she went rosy.

'You're taking advantage,' she said.

'We didn't have to win,' he said.

'You play a real good game.'

Her flat-mate arrived home a few minutes later. He heard the door slam and the call of 'Hello' and he had his hand on Glenys's mouth. Alice's heels sounded on the boards as she went to the little kitchen and then the bathroom. He kissed Glenys's salt lips and hurried the pants down her legs until they hobbled her ankles. Fear made her superior, but nothing she thought, even though he knew what it was, was going to make any difference to him. He was there to be callous. It was a wonderful thing to use her without apology. He told her what he wanted: mouth first, then other places. It was up to her to contrive what he intended to have. She was not apparently surprised. The first two times were quick. Then there was a pause. Snow was salting the dark window and she shivered. He took the fraying quilt and draped it over her shoulders. She did not take it as a kindness. Sweat gleamed on her small, separate breasts. He lay on his back, enjoying the chill. Her body was a question mark with the blush of her soles exposed. He took her feet in his hands and worked them for a while. Then he stood up and went naked out of the bedroom door. She straightened into an exclamation mark and glared at him. He shook his head, in agreement, and was on the splintery boards of the hall. There were holes in the wall of the flat where he could see lath and plaster. Cold bit him like an invisible beast. The lavatory had no seat. Clothes were hung over the bath, hers and hers. He had to wrench the handle two or three times before water jerked into the pan. He had hardly done anything. He looked into the

294

scabby mirror. A screw was missing. He touched the rusted socket. He could not recognise himself: the face that was there might have been a poster, the unwanted man. He pulled faces as if to make his expression match something he saw pinned there. He looked ill; his flesh was too many colours.

'Wake up,' he said. 'You're not going to sleep yet.'

'You're too old for three times,' she said.

'Don't talk,' he said. 'You'll wake Alice.'

'Unless she is awake.'

'You could get her in here,' he said.

'What do you want me to do now?'

'You know what I want.'

'Afraid to say?'

'It's up to you to find a way,' he said. 'I warned you.'

'Are you sick? Are you possibly sick, mister man?'

'Put some of this there,' he said.

'Where you find that?'

'In the bathroom cupboard.'

'That's Alice's,' she said.

'I'll get her another pot.'

'You scare me, mister man.'

'We agreed,' he said.

'I just might have brothers,' she said, 'or sisters. You ever consider that?'

'I'll take my chances,' he said.

'Man, you're in a dream here.'

'Where better?'

'I know who you are,' she said. 'You just remember that.'

'You haven't any idea.'

'And you know who I am. You're not going to work this thing for yourself, you know that, don't you?'

'Murder is a domestic crime,' Gideon said. 'Just you remember that.'

'When do I get my money by the way?'

'I'll write you a cheque in the morning.'

'You say you're loaded; how do I know that?'

'I'll leave you a cheque and I can assure you that it'll be honoured.'

'You don't know who you are, so how can you be so

sure you're this rich man? You don't want my ass, so why have it? I don't want you to do it, you don't want you to do it, so where's the percentile?'

'Go and get your friend,' he said.

'No, sir,' she said. 'That's out.'

'Then I will,' he said.

'You're in trouble, mister man. You're in deep, deep trouble.'

'Never mind the nigger talk.'

'Oh boy, oh boy! Save the best for last, isn't that the truth?'

'Librarian!' he said.

'How old are you?'

'You're right,' he said. 'But it's too late now.'

'Jesus! I mean *Jesus*.'

'No hope,' he said, 'no hope at all, none.'

'What's the living matter with you?'

'I rather think,' he said, 'that I may have laid down my life for my friend. My father died of shame that he didn't; I, on the other hand . . .'

'You should go home to your wife,' she said.

'Put your face down in the pillow,' he said.

'Bridge correspondent!' she said.

'I survived and Jordan didn't. Nothing is understandable and everything is clear. Everything matters; nothing matters. Get your head down in there; you know what I want you to be, be it.' He nudged her knees apart with one of his own and kneeled in the space, the pink pout of her up to him. He put his thumbs on her plumped buttocks and was in chapel, her flesh his *prie-dieu*. 'Dear God in heaven.'

20

Breakfast was a courteous, frosty thing. The sink was awash; frozen pipes had stopped it. The thaw would bring trouble. Alice scooped cups of dirty stuff and went to the lavatory with it. Gideon was angry to be helpful. Domesticity was forging its quick bars. He had to get away. Glenys was bruised with exhaustion; the night had put grey with her black, red in the whites of her eyes. She did not take a paper: she could read what she wanted at the library. Alice was half-Siamese, with an educated accent; she worked at the Institute for Oriental Languages, a captive to others' ambitions, not teaching but conversing with them, by the hour.

'I'm going now,' Glenys said, having difficulty with her watch strap. Little things seemed not to fit her any more: her hooped enamel earrings would scarcely go in either. She had left her sensuality in the bed, it seemed, refusing the obvious uniform. It teased his desire, which was never for her but against her, a prowling appetite. He wore his new character like borrowed clothes, wanting to be at home in them.

'Look,' Glenys said, when Alice was again at the table, 'don't be here tonight, O.K.? Because I've got to go out and there's no point.'

He sniffed. The smell of them was in the place. He alluded to it with his nose and she gloved hands round her coffee, like a posy. Steam glazed her cheeks and moistened her lashes. He took his pen from his pocket and wrote that cheque. 'We should do it again,' he said.

'Don't count on it.'

'A winning combination? Don't knock it.'

Alice might have been rehearsed: she made ready to go, but she was not going until they had. Gideon welcomed an enemy. How many days was it till Christmas? The calendar served notice on him; amnesia was beyond his wit. He had to go to the shops.

'If we simply played the usual stakes – the same as everyone else,' he said, at the corner, 'would that appeal to you?'

Light on her ankle-warmed feet, she was more attractive as she went to her careful bus (the driver had had to rub a rough visor in the frost-ribbed windscreen). The muscled buttocks flounced her coat-tails. As her path to the bus took her in a slight curve, she had the elated walk of a high-jumper, not in the least hurry yet, preparing to break a record, or to flop.

He went to a remodelled hotel in Bloomsbury, with a coffee shop and a polyglot foyer panelled with milky light. A tower of matching luggage, offal-red and light blue mostly, was stacked by the rotating door. The clerk took him for a foreigner and asked for his passport. He left his case in the room, went down Southampton Row to find Tom the present he had in mind (delivery was a problem solved by money) and returned for a bath. The trolley had just come with clean towels and tissues and foiled soap. The Spanish maid asked him if there was anything else he wanted. 'Of course,' he said.

In the hot water, he noticed where damp had acned the ventilation duct. People were talking in the next room, Americans. Each spoke with the simplified formality of someone thrown into the company of a fool. When they shut their door and were gone, Gideon began to cry. He cried not as a child, who hopes to be comforted, nor as someone bereaved, who denies consolation; he wept.

He went about London under the greedy decorations, armed with money, the futile bomb. Denied a plot, terror and sentiment played badminton with him: he was feathered into gentleness by impersonal strokes. Made for treason, there was nothing more he could find to betray, God or man. He was a translator without a text.

One morning, however much later it was, he saw in the newspaper that an intruder had been killed by a 'prominent Q.C.' during the course of a country house break-in near Colchester. Stephen Hellman had surprised a man in his drawing room late at night and, according to the report, had chased him into the cloister which was in the course of construction. There the burglar turned on him and Hellman defended himself with an antique truncheon. The blow must have been more violent than intended, or the victim had a thinner skull than Bow Street Runners had been used to cudgelling. He was in a coma for several hours and then died.

Gideon read the report carefully again, as if he might be expected to translate it into a language he did not know very well. The burglar was said to be a native of Chaworth, Lincs, though he had worked in London, a plumber's mate named Harold Pargiter, twenty-four. 'It's ova/ Casanova,' Gideon said.

He was crossing a road near King's Cross when a car came round the corner, without slowing for the studs, and he had to do a veronica to avoid it. In frivolous rage he slapped the haunch of the Fiat with his furled paper. The driver squealed in to the side of the arched street, jumped out and ran back towards him. He was curly-haired, short, swarthy, muscular. Gideon had gone on across the road and was walking towards an illuminated clock when the man reached him.

'You fucking bastard.'

'Learn to drive.'

'You know what you are? You're a fucking cunt.'

'And you are a bad driver,' Gideon said.

'Dirty, fucking bastard, you know that?'

'Go and get in your car and drive away, carefully.'

'I'm going to punch you right in the face. In the mouth. In the nose. On the jaw.'

'Come and do it in front of a policeman.'

'I'm going to fucking teach you a fucking lesson, you cunt.'

'I shall see you in prison,' Gideon said.

'You're a fucking coward. You're a fucking coward. You're a cunt bastard.'

'Get back to your car,' Gideon said.

'I'm going to hammer you, I'm going to hammer you very hard, my friend.'

'You're a dangerous driver,' Gideon said, 'and you're probably a dangerous man. You may be strong, you may not. Because you nearly killed me on the crossing –'

'That was not a crossing. That was not a crossing.'

'Have you learnt this from the Linguaphone by any chance?'

'Cunt. Cunt.'

'It's the first time I've ever seen a pimp in a J registration Fiat 127,' Gideon said.

The man had turned away. There were people between them before Gideon had the last word. Hair curling like a cheap disguise around his ears, the man walked on. Gideon took a side street where articulated lorries were backing, drivers leaning from the cabs to square their trailers under arched garages. He reached a place where several bridges carried the railway over the road. It seemed already to be night there. He had no cause to be walking that way, though he supposed that it would take him north. Taxis came out of a garage where they had queued to re-fuel. The Fiat appeared from a converging street. The pavement was blocked by lorries and Gideon was in the roadway as it came towards him. He jumped in behind a yellow trailer to dodge the metal. The Fiat stopped, reversed and stopped again, a door thrown open. The man was coming at him once again, his shoulders like a writ-server's, officially expecting trouble.

'You fucking bastard,' he said. 'I'm going to teach you a lesson.'

'Look,' Gideon said, 'you're a rotten driver. No amount of abuse will change that.'

'You're shit, your sort of fucking bastard, shit, you hear me?'

'You've got your damned nerve, quite honestly, I must say, haven't you?'

'Don't you swear at me, all right? Because I'm going to

teach you a lesson you won't damned well forget. You're a damned bloody coward, all right?'

'I should very much like to see your passport,' Gideon said.

'You take some risks, my friend.'

'My name is Gideon Shand. What's yours?'

'I don't have to tell you a thing. In my book you are nothing but a fucking shit.'

'Fine,' Gideon said.

'Yid bastard. I can say anything I like to you, you won't do anything about it. Nothing.'

'Whatever is the matter with you?' Gideon said.

'I'm bloody well going to flatten you into a pulp.'

'It's not often', Gideon said to a lorry driver, 'that one hears people talking in sub-titles, is it?'

'I'm going to punch you right in the face.'

'This man', Gideon said, 'is threatening me. He's not English and he's threatening me. If he attacks me, which he may, I shall defend myself, but I'd be grateful if you'd bear witness to the fact that his aggression is completely unprovoked.'

'Cunt bastard.'

Gideon waved to the yellow of a taxi and it veered to him from the lights. He touched it and was safe. 'I have your number,' he said, 'and if that vehicle is stolen, I suggest that you dispose of it as quickly as may be.'

'Sodding Jew bastard.'

'I want to go to Kilburn,' Gideon said. 'Do you know Franklin Road?'

The motor-bike was gone. There was black on the concrete. He had bought an evening paper, but there was no further mention of the death at Constable's. At the corner of the street, he looked at his watch, like someone who had made an appointment, and smiled with the tolerance of a man faced with familiar foibles. He might have been doing his duty.

'Not you again,' she said, with her shopping.

'I hope this isn't a bad moment.'

'No partnership tonight,' she said.

'I have to see you,' he said.

'Look,' she said, 'enough is enough.'

'Bound to be,' he said, 'but I haven't had enough.'

'Go away,' she said, 'because I have.'

'I want to fuck you once more,' he said. 'It's rather important to me.'

'I should call the police.'

'I'll give you two hundred pounds and I promise you I'll never come again.'

'What do you think I am?'

'It's nothing personal.'

'You truly total bastard,' she said.

'Cash.'

'You've got it with you?'

'I've got more,' Gideon said.

'I don't want you upstairs.'

'Then come to a hotel.'

'I've got things to do.'

'You know you're coming,' he said.

'Have you been in London all this time?'

'Yes, I have.'

'Are you going home for Christmas?'

'I don't want to talk about it,' he said.

'I'm not staying all night.'

He waited while she put the groceries inside. She sat silently with him in the taxi they were lucky to find. He had thought of the name of a hotel where he was not staying. He told the reception clerk that he had left his luggage in his office and some fool had gone off with the key. Meanwhile, he produced money.

'If you were going to kill me,' she said, 'you wouldn't bring me here and talk all that time at the desk, would you now?'

'You're a well-read girl, Glenys.'

The room was warm, as if someone had just left it. Double-glazing showed them a silent square with an elaborate lane system. Evening cars heading north paraded their cheap red jewellery.

'To think when you called me the first time, I was excited like a schoolgirl!'

'But you're not one, are you? Don't undress.'

'Oh Christ, man.'

'Do what I say and this can all be done quite quickly.'

'Then say and I will.'

'Kneel by the bed. Kneel down by the bed.'

'Do you want me to pray?'

'Yes, pray. Pray hard.'

'I'm doing that.'

'Oh, before I forget. This one is for Alice.'

'Is you a man of your word! Oh not again!'

'I'm giving you two hundred pounds,' he said.

'Do you have any idea why I'm doing this?' she said.

'I hope you're frightened,' he said.

'The money.'

She was wearing the same red pants. Perhaps she had several pairs.

'Something wrong?'

'Look at me, if you want to, but don't talk.'

He drew the curtains, awkward with the pulleys.

'Christ,' she said. 'Couldn't you have some sort of decency?'

'A friend of mine killed someone last night. With something I gave him. You want the money, you'll get the money. In under half an hour you'll have two hundred quid and you'll never see me again. Unless you come looking for me.'

'What do I mean to you? I wouldn't mind knowing.'

'You're my wife,' he said.

'Terrific.'

'All the way this time.'

'Oh God,' she said. 'Oh Christ.'

'Keep your face down. And I don't want you to do that.'

'I was only . . .'

'Maybe. But don't.'

He took her by the hair on her head and pulled her round to face him. Her top lip was swollen; he might have hit her, but it was her own anger that swelled there.

'Go on,' he said. 'Go on.'

'You better damned well have that money,' she said.

'I'll give you another hundred,' he said. 'You don't do it, I'll kill somebody.'

She looked at him and then she did it: she leaned on him with her hurt lips and did the work. When he threw her aside, he took his jacket and ran into the bathroom.

'I'll tell you something funny.'

'I could use a laugh.'

'I stole something this afternoon.'

'I thought you were a rich man.'

'From a shop in Oxford Street.'

'They have a lot of security in those shops.'

'Do you want it? Have it.'

'This is what you stole?'

'I can't give it to anybody else.'

'I'll take the three hundred,' she said.

'I shall only throw it away.'

'Give it to your wife for Christmas.'

'I think you'd better get out of here.'

'You bought it; you paid for it, didn't you?'

'I took it from a counter and went out the emergency exit.'

'You are one crazy man. One crazy man.'

'Glenys. . . '

'You had what you wanted, O.K.?'

'What about the occasional partnership?'

'I do have friends, in case you're wondering.'

'I hope you do,' he said.

'You made your contract,' she said. 'Don't bother with the overtricks, I shouldn't.'

'In pairs they count,' he said. 'You should know that.'

'And don't get clever. You wasn't clever before; don't get clever now.'

'What if I asked you to stay with me?'

'This little black girl is on her travels.'

'I'll take you to Turkey. Don't you want to go to Turkey?'

'This particular item is withdrawn from sale. Thanks for the wad.'

She ducked from the net of words and he honoured her agility, with a scowl. She had her things and she was on her way. He sat for a while, preparing an elaborate speech to explain leaving the hotel so soon, but downstairs no one challenged him: men with plastic names on their lapels swarmed in the lobby, touching each other and holding hands.

It was a wet evening and there were no cabs. He started

to walk towards the hotel where he had left his parcels. He was not sure of the way; something in him made him hope that he would never find it. He smiled at Jack Knightley and how anxious he must be to get in touch. The idea of leaving people in the lurch was sublime to him, a kind of conversion; its sharp gentleness fell on his face like the needling rain. He could taste the promise of death in it, and resurrection.

Since he too was lost, he imagined that the three men were coming to him for directions. The night had a dark humour and he fashioned a grin to acknowledge it. Two of them were black: the third was not. They seemed uncertain how to start, but when he broke away from them, briefly, they were more confident. They kicked him until he hurt enough to be still, clear-headed in a cage of pain. While they helped themselves to him, he did not cry out or expect anyone in the medical mews to come to his aid. He had time to think that he would not be pleased to be obliged to gratitude.

He lay, far from help, buckled and alone. They had kicked his face; his speechless tongue fitted his mouth like a fruit its rind. He waited for pain to ripen in him again. Impatient, he huddled under his numbness, a soul coffined in flesh. His ribs were saws: breathing was butchery. Red leaked from that fruity mouth. Plots seethed in his brain, the worms of reason. Language tracked him, a pace behind, to the borders of consciousness. He would have to die before he could escape its officiousness. 'One more river . . . '

Footsteps sounded the pavement, clicks and slurs, and were gone along the stiff hull of the city. Huddled against the stone, he was hardly more than lichen. The rain sharpened to sleet and stitched him with its casual cold. Down there, he could believe in God, as in a triviality. Bells were ringing.

'I didn't recognise you,' the girl's voice was saying, 'I thought it was an administrative goof. When hoity comes, can toity be far behind? Oh dad, you undeservingly poor old thing, what did they do to you?'

'How long have you been here?'

'Eighteen years,' she said, 'and many, many months. I

never thought I'd get the cue to say it before my birthday. You're going to be all right, you know.'

'And what's the good news?'

'You had us bloody worried. Whatever was the big idea?'

'I didn't commission this, you know.'

'Going off into the blue. The black and blue, as it turned out. You shouldn't have resisted them. You should've given them what they wanted and *really*, dad!'

'What's happened to Stephen?' he said.

'You saw.'

'I saw, he conquered. The story of my life, and yours.'

'No one blames him for what happened.'

'But he'll never be a judge now, will he?'

'I suppose I ought to feel guilty. You know who it was, don't you, he killed?'

'He should have died hereafter.'

' "O" level quotations can be a mighty comfort in time of trouble, can they not?'

'Presumably, you . . . '

'The necessary murder? Presumably. I wrote a letter to Ruggiero and told him a few things. I suppose I showed off rather – not the sort of thing you'd expect of me, is it? – and mentioned, well, pretty much everything there was to mention: Constable's and its constabulary, its many treasures and pleasures. It never occurred to me that there would be a head over Piers's's shoulder, watching with greedy eyes, though I suppose it should have. Did I or didn't I put him up to it? All I know is, Piers won't forgive me for it. In my father's house . . .'

'Your mother . . . ?'

'Pamela had to go to Chaworth.'

'What's Tom . . . ?'

'You do at least seem to remember everybody's names,' she said. 'A Good Sign!'

'I don't know what happened to me.'

'He went with her. He rather fancied the trip. Fagin's lawyer wanted to see her about the will, and the mackin-toshed wonder thought that if she went to see the people at the coroner's office, they might be able to avoid a broo or a haha. I always thought he was laying it on her, didn't you, Telfer?'

'She knows . . . ?'

'She does. She's very relieved to hear that you're all right.'

So what are you hiding, miss?'

'I was going to go with them myself, but . . . mission aborted. Do I look like a grieving widow? Poor Harold! It's Miranda I mourn for. Piers isn't being vindictive exactly, I suppose, but you could've fooled me and I think he probably did.'

'I always thought he was rather a fraud.'

'Rather a Freud, did you really? I don't think you're right in the least, not that I want to excite you. Piers never lied to me, you know.'

'That sounds freudulent in itself.'

'You're better,' she said. 'Fooling people doesn't necessarily involve deceiving them.'

'What're you trying to tell me, Mandy?'

'Nothing that isn't impossible to say. I suppose I want to say that my childhood is over and that I intend to dedicate myself with selfless intensity to the fluter's trade, thus procuring deathless fame and absolutely nothing else whatsoever.'

'Am I threatened?' Gideon said.

'I think you should know: Mummy's been seeing somebody. They came to the cottage.'

'Ah! He, she or it?'

'How shall I put it to sustain the suspense necessary to the multi-part dimensions of a major new series? A sacerdotal personage, with a head and other parts swathed in the cloth. Irish, not parsonical, a very present help in time of trouble, it seemed.'

'Are you supposed to be telling me this?'

'I'm not commissioned to do so, but I'm not *forbidden*, which lessens the charm. Are you in a lot of pain?'

'I'm a snail with a sore shell,' he said. 'The slug beneath the skin.'

'Were you never going to come back?'

'What did this personage do when . . . ?'

'Talked,' she said, 'and talked, cream on the back of

life's spoon, diffusing its smoothness on the face of the waters.'

'I'm rich now, you know,' Gideon said, 'but you can't tell, can you? He just talked?'

'He?'

'This priest – '

'I'm thinking of going to Germany,' she said. 'We could set up house.'

'Sentenced to life,' he said. 'While they were kicking me – and *were* they kicking me, they might have been old friends! – that expression kept going through my mind. My head was otherwise engaged.'

'I suppose it was as if her father had come back: you'd gone, her father Witchart had come back and she was feeling commensurately guilty, or innocent. Tom's been having dreams requiring parental guidance and clean sheets, if you want to know the latest. He thought it was V.D.'

'And what did you say?'

'I lied: I told him it wasn't. This priest bothered me. No, I don't mean molested, but they ain't half vultures for souls, the hounds of heaven, eh? Vegetarians also have their meat. Mama spent all her time reading these books she'd been given. She wouldn't even see her so-called patients any more. Cottage teas no longer a speciality! The old Oirish persuaded her that she'd been serving the devil, only a spoonful at a time, but serving him none the less. *Bref, cher parent*, she decided to go with the big battalions and join the Church, rhymes with lurch, which is what you'd left her in. *Così fan tutte*. That's what all the fans have been up to.'

'You're hiding something.'

'Patience!' Miranda said. 'It's here up my sleeve. This merchant of the mellifluous delivery failed to show up for the final examination. Mama had been up all night with the catechism like a sick child. I had to hear her.'

'Pamela?'

'The name has not escaped you.'

'Our shadows cast a heavy body,' Gideon said.

'Father Reardon, as I was rudely saying before you interrupted, manqued his rendezvous. I came home from the hill, where I'd been tooting my flute, and found fond mama in a dreadful pickle. (I shan't name the brand.) What could have happened to Father R.? She and I had to rush around all the local stations of the cross and guess what: none of the local Romans had heard of Father Reardon. *No esisteva*. And then, of course, when we attempted a description, the truth outed, and the lie.'

'Am I with you?'

'This priest who'd walked mama to the pearly gates and then failed to come up with the key had not – as one of my fathers might say – been licensed by the Beth Din. He was, to boot, and to spur, not even a he but a she, hence the lack of shadow when five of the clock did sound. Not that it matters, so we are promised, since they all count, Brian, and Mother Church isn't fussy about who sticks you in the back of the ecclesiastical net. Nice one? We'll be back right after the break.'

'She wasn't . . . ?'

'Embarrassed? Affronted? Disillusioned? A tiny bit pissed? Well, I was personally embarrassing to her, my presence. That's the main reason why I have to go away. I fancy Germany; there's nothing I can't do there. I can't stay in England.'

'Do you know why?'

'There's nothing wrong with it,' she said. 'You won't come with me?'

'If I did,' he said, 'you wouldn't have left, would you?'

'Does everything have to be an attack on you?'

'It seems to be the only language I speak.'

'You're right: he won't ever be a judge now, will he? He'll just have to go on getting richer and richer and richer.'

'To your eventual profit?'

'I'd thought of that,' Miranda said, 'dammit.'

'*Nous ne sortirons jamais de ce bordel.*'

'*Ne vous gênez pas, papa!* And what will you do?'

'I suppose that I shall have to think of others,' he said.

'Oh dad, oh dad, oh dad, and don't deny it, I sometimes think that you and I understand each other more thoroughly than any two other people in the world, so of course we shall have to imitate the best of friends. If they hadn't bashed you unrecognisable, would you have made a run for it, do you think?'

'What else can you do for it?'

'You could always try again.'

'*Germany*,' he said. 'It doesn't even call itself that, is that the attraction?'

'I shall never be under the illusion that I understand. *That*'s the attraction. Are you afraid of her still?'

'I have that comfort, I suppose.'

'I'm sure she'll forgive you,' Miranda said.

'You never know,' Gideon said, 'she might spare me that.'

FOR THE BEST IN PAPERBACKS, LOOK FOR THE

In every corner of the world, on every subject under the sun, Penguin represents quality and variety – the very best in publishing today.

For complete information about books available from Penguin – including Pelicans, Puffins, Peregrines and Penguin Classics – and how to order them, write to us at the appropriate address below. Please note that for copyright reasons the selection of books varies from country to country.

In the United Kingdom: Please write to *Dept E.P., Penguin Books Ltd, Harmondsworth, Middlesex, UB7 0DA*

If you have any difficulty in obtaining a title, please send your order with the correct money, plus ten per cent for postage and packaging, to *PO Box No 11, West Drayton, Middlesex*

In the United States: Please write to *Dept BA, Penguin, 299 Murray Hill Parkway, East Rutherford, New Jersey 07073*

In Canada: Please write to *Penguin Books Canada Ltd, 2801 John Street, Markham, Ontario L3R 1B4*

In Australia: Please write to the *Marketing Department, Penguin Books Australia Ltd, P.O. Box 257, Ringwood, Victoria 3134*

In New Zealand: Please write to the *Marketing Department, Penguin Books (NZ) Ltd, Private Bag, Takapuna, Auckland 9*

In India: Please write to *Penguin Overseas Ltd, 706 Eros Apartments, 56 Nehru Place, New Delhi, 110019*

In Holland: Please write to *Penguin Books Nederland B.V., Postbus 195, NL–1380AD Weesp, Netherlands*

In Germany: Please write to *Penguin Books Ltd, Friedrichstrasse 10–12, D–6000 Frankfurt Main 1, Federal Republic of Germany*

In Spain: Please write to *Longman Penguin España, Calle San Nicolas 15, E–28013 Madrid, Spain*

In France: Please write to *Penguin Books Ltd, 39 Rue de Montmorency, F-75003, Paris, France*

In Japan: Please write to *Longman Penguin Japan Co Ltd, Yamaguchi Building, 2–12–9 Kanda Jimbocho, Chiyoda-Ku, Tokyo 101, Japan*

The Glittering Prizes

The changing attitudes and styles of a generation that went to Cambridge in the fifties.

Adam Morris, Alan Parks, Mike Clode, Anna Cunningham, Barbara Ransome and others leave the university to discover varying degrees of satisfaction, success and material comfort. But over all of them lies the common memory of these heady, golden days spent in unravelling the knots of friendship, in exploratory sex and in *badinage*, that none of them will ever quite forget.

'Raphael's achievement is rare indeed' – *Sunday Times*

'Subtle, sinewy and immensely skilful' – *Hibernia*

Oxbridge Blues

For most of them the glittering prizes have tarnished . . .

Stylish, erotic and cruel, Frederic Raphael's sparkling collection of stories slices to the heart of a certain milieu, exposing those who cling to its affluent surfaces but who have lost the art of loving.

Uneasy and restless, the world they inhabit depends on treachery for survival and on infidelity to sharpen the appetite – a world where social, sexual and financial jealousies can snap the brittle bonds of affection and where the past seems a foreign country.

Frederic Raphael's watchful and witty pen shocks and provokes – but always tells the truth.

A CHOICE OF PENGUIN FICTION

The Dearest and the Best   Leslie Thomas

In the spring of 1940 the spectre of war turned into grim reality – and for all the inhabitants of the historic villages of the New Forest it was the beginning of the most bizarre, funny and tragic episode of their lives. 'Excellent' – *Sunday Times*

Only Children   Alison Lurie

When the Hubbards and the Zimmerns go to visit Anna on her idyllic farm, it becomes increasingly difficult to tell which are the adults, and which the children. 'It demands to be read' – *Financial Times* 'There quite simply is no better living writer' – John Braine

My Family and Other Animals   Gerald Durrell

Gerald Durrell's wonderfully comic account of his childhood years on Corfu and his development as a naturalist and zoologist is a true delight. Soaked in Greek sunshine, it is a 'bewitching book' – *Sunday Times*

Getting it Right   Elizabeth Jane Howard

A hairdresser in the West End, Gavin is sensitive, shy, into the arts, prone to spots and, at thirty-one, a virgin. He's a classic late developer – and maybe it's getting too late to develop at all? 'Crammed with incidental pleasures . . . sometimes sad but more frequently hilarious . . . *Getting it Right* gets it, comically, right' – Paul Bailey in the *London Standard*

The Vivisector   Patrick White

In this prodigious novel about the life and death of a great painter, Patrick White, winner of the Nobel Prize for Literature, illuminates creative experience with unique truthfulness. 'One of the most interesting and absorbing novelists writing English today' – Angus Wilson in the *Observer*

The Echoing Grove   Rosamund Lehmann

'No English writer has told of the pains of women in love more truly or more movingly than Rosamund Lehmann' – Marghanita Laski. 'She uses words with the enjoyment and mastery with which Renoir used paint' – Rebecca West in the *Sunday Times* 'A magnificent achievement' – John Connell in the *Evening News*

A CHOICE OF PENGUIN FICTION

Maia Richard Adams

The heroic romance of love and war in an ancient empire from one of our greatest storytellers. 'Enormous and powerful' – *Financial Times*

The Warning Bell Lynne Reid Banks

A wonderfully involving, truthful novel about the choices a woman must make in her life – and the price she must pay for ignoring the counsel of her own heart. 'Lynne Reid Banks knows how to get to her reader: this novel grips like Super Glue' – *Observer*

Doctor Slaughter Paul Theroux

Provocative and menacing – a brilliant dissection of lust, ambition and betrayal in 'civilized' London. 'Witty, chilly, exuberant, graphic' – *The Times Literary Supplement*

Wise Virgin A. N. Wilson

Giles Fox's work on the Pottle manuscript, a little-known thirteenth-century tract on virginity, leads him to some innovative research on the subject that takes even his breath away. 'A most elegant and chilling comedy' – *Observer* Books of the Year

Gone to Soldiers Marge Piercy

Until now, the passions, brutality and devastation of the Second World War have only been written about by men. Here for the first time, one of America's major writers brings a woman's depth and intensity to the panorama of world war. 'A victory' – *Newsweek*

Trade Wind M. M. Kaye

An enthralling blend of history, adventure and romance from the author of the bestselling *The Far Pavilions*

A CHOICE OF PENGUIN FICTION

Stanley and the Women   Kingsley Amis

Just when Stanley Duke thinks it safe to sink into middle age, his son goes insane – and Stanley finds himself beset on all sides by women, each of whom seems to have an intimate acquaintance with madness. 'Very good, very powerful . . . beautifully written' – Anthony Burgess in the *Observer*

The Girls of Slender Means   Muriel Spark

A world and a war are winding up with a bang, and in what is left of London, all the nice people are poor – and about to discover how different the new world will be. 'Britain's finest post-war novelist' – *The Times*

Him with His Foot in His Mouth   Saul Bellow

A collection of first-class short stories. 'If there is a better living writer of fiction, I'd very much like to know who he or she is' – *The Times*

Mother's Helper   Maureen Freely

A superbly biting and breathtakingly fluent attack on certain libertarian views, blending laughter, delight, rage and amazement, this is a novel you won't forget. 'A winner' – *The Times Literary Supplement*

Decline and Fall   Evelyn Waugh

A comic yet curiously touching account of an innocent plunged into the sham, brittle world of high society. Evelyn Waugh's first novel brought him immediate public acclaim and is still a classic of its kind.

Stars and Bars   William Boyd

Well-dressed, quite handsome, unfailingly polite and charming, who would guess that Henderson Dores, the innocent Englishman abroad in wicked America, has a guilty secret? 'Without doubt his best book so far . . made me laugh out loud' – *The Times*

A CHOICE OF PENGUIN FICTION

The Ghost Writer   Philip Roth

Philip Roth's celebrated novel about a young writer who meets and falls in love with Anne Frank in New England – or so he thinks. 'Brilliant, witty and extremely elegant' – *Guardian*

Small World   David Lodge

Shortlisted for the 1984 Booker Prize, *Small World* brings back Philip Swallow and Maurice Zapp for a jet-propelled journey into hilarity. 'The most brilliant and also the funniest novel that he has written' – *London Review of Books*

Moon Tiger   Penelope Lively

Winner of the 1987 Booker Prize, *Moon Tiger* is Penelope Lively's 'most ambitious book to date' – *The Times* 'A complex tapestry of great subtlety . . . Penelope Lively writes so well, savouring the words as she goes' – *Daily Telegraph* 'A very clever book: it is evocative, thought-provoking and hangs curiously on the edges of the mind long after it is finished' – *Literary Review*

Absolute Beginners   Colin MacInnes

The first 'teenage' novel, the classic of youth and disenchantment, *Absolute Beginners* is part of MacInnes's famous London trilogy – and now a brilliant film. 'MacInnes caught it first – and best' – *Harpers and Queen*

July's People   Nadine Gordimer

Set in South Africa, this novel gives us an unforgettable look at the terrifying, tacit understandings and misunderstandings between blacks and whites. 'This is the best novel that Miss Gordimer has ever written' – Alan Paton in the *Saturday Review*

The Ice Age   Margaret Drabble

'A continuously readable, continuously surprising book . . . here is a novelist who is not only popular and successful but formidably growing towards real stature' – *Observer*

A CHOICE OF PENGUIN FICTION

Money Martin Amis

Savage, audacious and demonically witty – a story of urban excess. 'Terribly, terminally funny: laughter in the dark, if ever I heard it' – *Guardian*

Lolita Vladimir Nabokov

Shot through with Nabokov's mercurial wit, quicksilver prose and intoxicating sensuality, *Lolita* is one of the world's greatest love stories. 'A great book' – Dorothy Parker

Dinner at the Homesick Restaurant Anne Tyler

Through every family run memories that bind them together – in spite of everything. 'She is a witch. Witty, civilized, curious, with her radar ears and her quill pen dipped on one page in acid and on the next in orange liqueur . . . a wonderful writer' – John Leonard in *The New York Times*

Glitz Elmore Leonard

Underneath the Boardwalk, a lot of insects creep. But the creepiest of all was Teddy. 'After finishing *Glitz*, I went out to the bookstore and bought everything else of Elmore Leonard's I could find' – Stephen King

Trust Mary Flanagan

Charles was a worthy man – a trustworthy man – a thing rare and old-fashioned in Eleanor's experience. 'A vivid, passionate roller-coaster of a book, which is also expertly crafted and beautifully written' – *Punch* 'A rare and sensitive début novel . . . there is something much more powerful than a moral in this novel – there is acute observation. It stands up to scrutiny. It rings true' – *Fiction Magazine*

The Levels Peter Benson

Winner of the Guardian Fiction Prize

Set in the secret landscape of the Somerset Levels, this remarkable first novel is the story of a young boy whose first encounter with love both bruises and enlarges his vision of the world. 'It discovers things about life that we recognise with a gasp' – *The Times*

A CHOICE OF PENGUIN FICTION

The Power and the Glory Graham Greene

During an anti-clerical purge in one of the southern states of Mexico, the last priest is hunted like a hare. Too humble for martyrdom, too human for heroism, he is nevertheless impelled towards his squalid Calvary. 'There is no better story-teller in English today' – V. S. Pritchett

The Enigma of Arrival V. S. Naipaul

'For sheer abundance of talent, there can hardly be a writer alive who surpasses V. S. Naipaul. Whatever we may want in a novelist is to be found in his books . . .' – Irving Howe in *The New York Times Book Review*. 'Naipaul is always brilliant' – Anthony Burgess in the *Observer*

Earthly Powers Anthony Burgess

Anthony Burgess's magnificent masterpiece, an enthralling, epic narrative spanning six decades and spotlighting some of the most vivid events and characters of our times. 'Enormous imagination and vitality . . . a huge book in every way' – Bernard Levin in the *Sunday Times*

The Penitent Isaac Bashevis Singer

From the Nobel Prize-winning author comes a powerful story of a man who has material wealth but feels spiritually impoverished. 'Singer . . . restates with dignity the spiritual aspirations and the cultural complexities of a lifetime, and it must be said that in doing so he gives the Evil One no quarter and precious little advantage' – Anita Brookner in the *Sunday Times*

Paradise Postponed John Mortimer

'Hats off to John Mortimer. He's done it again' – *Spectator*. A rumbustious, hilarious novel from the creator of Rumpole, *Paradise Postponed* examines British life since the war to discover why Paradise has always been postponed.

The Balkan Trilogy and Levant Trilogy Olivia Manning

'The finest fictional record of the war produced by a British writer. Her gallery of personages is huge, her scene painting superb, her pathos controlled, her humour quiet and civilized' – *Sunday Times*

A CHOICE OF PENGUIN FICTION

Other Women   Lisa Alther

From the bestselling author of *Kinflicks* comes this compelling novel of today's woman – and a heroine with whom millions of women will identify.

Your Lover Just Called   John Updike

Stories of Joan and Richard Maple – a couple multiplied by love and divided by lovers. Here is the portrait of a modern American marriage in all its mundane moments and highs and lows of love as only John Updike could draw it.

Mr Love and Justice   Colin MacInnes

Frankie Love took up his career as a ponce at about the same time as Edward Justice became vice-squad detective. Except that neither man was particularly suited for his job, all they had in common was an interest in crime. Provocative and honest and acidly funny, *Mr Love and Justice* is the final volume of Colin MacInnes's famous London trilogy.

An Ice-Cream War   William Boyd

As millions are slaughtered on the Western Front, a ridiculous and little-reported campaign is being waged in East Africa – a war they continued after the Armistice because no one told them to stop. 'A towering achievement' – John Carey, Chairman of the Judges of the 1982 Booker Prize, for which this novel was shortlisted.

Fool's Sanctuary   Jennifer Johnston

Set in Ireland in the 1920s, Jennifer Johnston's beautiful novel tells of Miranda's growing up into political awareness. Loyalty, romance and friendship are fractured by betrayal and the gunman's flight for freedom, honour and pride. 'Her novels . . . are near perfect literary jewels' – *Cosmopolitan*

The Big Sleep   Raymond Chandler

'I was neat, clean, shaved and sober, and I didn't care who knew it. I was everything the well-dressed private detective ought to be. I was calling on four million dollars'. 'A book to be read at a sitting' – *Sunday Times*